SALTY COWBOY

A COOPER FAMILY NOVEL, SWEET WATER FALLS
FARM ROMANCE BOOK 4

ELANA JOHNSON

ISBN-13: 978-1-63876-110-5

SALTY COWBOY

1

Cherry Cooper put on her blinker to turn right about five miles before the driveway that led to her family farm. She'd lost her mind, that was all. She could schedule a few sessions with her therapist and drive Jed Forrester out of her head again.

She'd done it before with Charlie, then with a man named Tyler, then Dr. Freeman. Then Jed.

And yet, she turned right onto the paved road that led to the corn maze at Forrester Farms, something she didn't even want to do. She hadn't been to a corn maze in years, and he hadn't invited her to stop by and get lost with him among nine-foot stalks and plenty of straw bales and scarecrows.

Why was she here?

The salty cowboy had told her he didn't want to date

long-distance. *I don't have time to drive to Casper every week, Cherry.*

The words stung at her brain as much now as when he'd texted them back in September. *After* he'd kissed her, of course. The man had likely gotten what he'd wanted, and he didn't want her anymore.

Cherry hated the self-defeating talk inside her mind, but she couldn't come up with another explanation as to why Jed had been so keen on texting and calling and getting together...and then gone cold.

After he'd said that, Cherry had been so glad she hadn't told Lee or Will about Jed. She didn't want to have to defend him, because he didn't deserve a defense.

"Then why are you here?" she asked, panic starting to set in. If Jed was working the corn maze, he'd see her car. He'd know she'd come by to see him, and that would only fuel his already huge ego.

The parking lot for the maze wasn't big by any means, and a single cowboy stood at the entrance of it. He didn't seem tall enough to be Jed, and Cherry couldn't turn around on the road anyway. She had to go into the lot to then go back the way she'd come, and she watched the man wave her to the right. She went that way, desperate now to get away from this place.

Why in the world had she come here?

Why not? her feisty mind fired back at her. She had every right to visit this public venue. She'd pay the fee, and she'd wander through the dry and dying stalks, and then she might have the strength and courage to continue to her family's farm. Her sister was due with her first baby tomorrow, and while Cherry had already been home more this year than she had in the five preceding it, she wouldn't miss being there for Rissa when she came home from the hospital with her first child.

She parked and got out of her car, tugging her hooded jacket tighter around her and zipping it up. She wore a pair of jeans that hugged every curve and had a thick seam going down the front of them and a pair of trail running shoes that had extra thick soles with a hiking boot grip on the bottom of them. She'd practically dressed for this corn maze, and she hadn't even known it.

She paid the fee to a woman in a make-shift ticket booth with a large American flag flying far above it and moved toward the entrance of the maze. Now that Halloween had passed, the place wasn't terribly busy, but a family had gone in ahead of her, and she walked slowly until she couldn't hear their voices. At every junction she came to, she turned right. Right, right, right, until she couldn't go right anymore.

Then she started turning left, and eventually, she had no clue where she was. The maze had big bridges built into it, so she could go up a dozen or so steps and stand on the bridge and look out over the corn stalks to try to find the way out. She didn't do that, because this corn maze had become a representation of her life.

Always making the wrong turn instead of the right

one. And if she did turn right, she found out later that she should've taken a left. She walked alone in the maze, just as she did in life. Sure, she had friends at work, and friends who lived in her neighborhood, but she knew it wasn't the same as having someone really close to her whom she could count on for anything.

Her mind needled at her, telling her things like, *It's probably time to come home, Cherry*, and *You won't have to see Charlie. You'll be okay.*

She definitely needed more therapy to let go of the broken pieces of her past, to knock out all of the bad tile and replace it with granite countertops or hardwood flooring. All of her siblings were now happily married or would be soon enough. Lee had just proposed to his girlfriend, Rosalie Reynolds, and Cherry had gotten a text last night about their celebratory dinner this upcoming weekend.

She'd taken the whole week off from her academic advising job in San Antonio, and she didn't have to be back for nine more days. So much could happen in a single hour, and Cherry didn't like making plans too far into the future.

Lee and Rosalie had set a date to be married in April, which was an idyllic month in Texas, with plenty of flowers and sunshine, all of which suited Rosalie so well.

At Cherry's wedding, there'd probably be black napkins and zero lace, because she didn't ever think she'd get married. She had, once, but that dream had died a slow, painful death that sometimes still haunted her.

Now, Cherry didn't dream at all. Life was just life, and she didn't want to get too bogged down in thinking about whether it was fair or not—it wasn't—or good or not. Such a thing was so subjective anyway, and she just wanted to do a good job, go home and eat something delicious for dinner, and try to find a way to ease her loneliness.

Once again, she turned left when she came to a crossroads, and she thought she should probably consider returning to the farm where she'd grown up. There was room for her there—or there would be once Travis's new house got built. She could live right next door to her sister and be the best auntie in the whole state of Texas.

As she walked over the hard-packed dirt ground, a voice came over the loudspeaker. "The corn maze is closing. Please make your way to the nearest exit."

If she could do that, she would, but Cherry honestly had no idea where she was. She could be in the middle of the maze or along an outside wall of it. She glanced around and didn't see any bridges in the vicinity, and she wondered what the cowboys here at Forrester Farms did to make sure all of their guests got out of the maze. Did they have cameras that would show her wandering around, panicked and scared?

Humiliation streamed through her, and she picked up

her pace as she approached the end of the aisle. Left or right?

She went left, practically jogging as another announcement to find an exit filled the air. "I'm trying," she muttered to herself. She'd given up praying for help long ago, but now she found herself with a plea in her heart for the Lord to guide her and help her get out of this maze.

Rissa and Spencer were expecting her, and she couldn't *believe* she'd turned off the highway too early.

A bridge came into view, and Cherry hurried toward it. She sprinted up the steps and looked out across the maze. The huge American flag flew above the ticket booth, and it was behind her. Away from the she'd been walking.

Helplessness crowded into her throat, and she swallowed against it. Perhaps the farm had a helicopter that could come pluck her from this bridge, saving her the energy and time of trying to go back the way she'd come. Perhaps she could just start crashing through the dry stalks as she forged her own path and made her own exit.

Footsteps crunched through the dry foliage on the ground below, and then they started up the steps to the bridge where she stood. Her heart hammered in her chest as she watched a cowboy arrive not ten feet from her.

Not just any cowboy.

"Cherry Cooper," Jed Forrester drawled. He didn't smile. He didn't approach. He wore a windbreaker that wasn't big enough to go across his broad shoulders, a pair of sexy dark denim jeans, and his gorgeous dark brown cowboy hat. He heaved a great big sigh and said, "I'll help you out."

Cherry wanted to argue with him and claim she knew the precise path that would lead her to safety. She couldn't say that, because it was the furthest thing from the truth.

"Well, come on then," he drawled in that deep bass voice that followed her into the depths of her slumber at night. He turned and went down the steps without waiting for her to say anything, and she didn't see any other choice.

He'd once saved her from Charlie at Travis's wedding. Over the months since then, his texts and calls had saved her from her dreary, quiet, lonely nights. And right now, he was literally saving her from wandering through this maze for the rest of the evening.

She followed him, reaching the ground just as he went back into the maze. She ran to catch him, saying, "Can you slow down?"

"Nope," he said over his shoulder. "We're closed already, and I've got more work to do before I'm actually done for the night."

Cherry panted as she reached his side. She didn't know what else to say. As they approached a corner, he indicated they should go left, and he led the way. He was taller than her, with much longer legs, and she figured as long as she could see which way he went, she didn't have to walk right beside him.

He didn't want her there anyway. Foolishness filled her, especially when she followed him to the right and then dang near plowed straight into him. She yelped and flung up her hands, her eyes slamming shut for some reason.

He caught her deftly, because Jed was sure and strong about everything. He didn't hem and haw over a long-distance relationship. He just said *no. Not for me. Thanks for the past few months.*

"Don't touch me," she said, swatting his hands away from her waist now that she had her feet under her.

"Why are you here?" he asked, not giving her an inch in this small corner of the maze. She'd turned right, and then it immediately jogged left again, but Jed hadn't taken the turn.

"I needed a few more minutes before I went home," she said, not giving herself enough time to censor herself.

"So you came here?"

"It's a public place," she said.

Jed searched her face, and Cherry had no idea what he was looking for or if he'd ever find it. He said nothing, sighed, dusted his hands, and took the right turn to go around the small corner.

"Jed," Cherry said, but she didn't know what else to say. She shouldn't have to say anything. *He* was the one who'd dumped *her.* He kept walking, and she followed, and only a few minutes later, they emerged into the parking lot. It wasn't the same entrance she'd used to get into the maze, but she spotted her car off to her left, across the whole dirt lot. Every other car and truck had gone, and another dose of foolishness hit her in the face like a bucket of icy water.

"Thank you," she said as diplomatically as she could, and she started toward her car. If she could make it there, she could get off this farm and bask in her own embarrassment without an audience. She held her head high as she walked, and because she was so focused on her goal, she didn't realize Jed had started walking too.

She finally heard his footsteps and turned to see him only a couple of paces behind her. "I'm fine now," she said.

"Do you want to go to dinner tonight?" he asked.

Surprise tripped through her, actually tripping up her feet too. She stumbled, and blast him, Jed reached out and steadied her. Everything in her life had been more stable since he'd whisked her away from Charlie at the wedding.

Everything.

"No," she said, not quite sure what question she was answering. Or even what she was saying.

His eyebrows went up. "You have dinner plans with your family?"

"No," she said again.

"Then why can't we go to dinner?"

"Because you don't want to," she said, frowning at him. "I asked you if you could do the long-distance thing, and you said no."

Jed's dark blue eyes blazed with fire. "Maybe I made a mistake."

"I haven't moved," she said. "I still have my job in San Antonio."

"I'm aware."

She was aware of how close to her he stood, and how she didn't want him to back up. She hadn't told Rissa or Spence what time she'd arrive, and honestly, her sister was used to her showing up whenever it suited her. She absolutely could go to dinner with Jed.

Not here, her mind screamed at her, and Cherry balked once more at the idea. "Where would we go?"

He folded his arms, one hip cocking out. "I suppose you don't want to go anywhere in town."

"Somewhere else would be ideal," she said.

He looked up into the darkening sky. "I can't believe I'm doing this."

"Then don't do it," she snapped. She spun around and marched away from him again. "You're no prince, Jed. I don't need to be rescued."

"You're no princess either, Cherry," he called after her.

He was so right, but she didn't stick around to tell him so. She reached her car and yanked open the door to get behind the wheel. She started the ignition and threw the car in reverse. Her car beeped and the seat beneath her vibrated as she started to back up.

She slammed on the brakes, her eyes finally catching

up to what the car already knew. Someone stood behind her.

Jed.

Fuming, she unclasped the seatbelt and threw open the door again. "Move," she demanded as she got out of the car. "Right now."

2

_____

Jed Forrester watched the gorgeous Cherry Cooper's fingers curl into fists. For whatever reason, that action made every cell in his body hot, and he wanted to get burned by this woman. Badly.

She wore a form-fitting jacket with jeans, cute hiking shoes-slash-runners on her feet, and her hair down. It flowed over her shoulders like liquid fire, the kind that burned low at midnight and didn't come from a bottle. She possessed deep, dark brown eyes with a hint of green if they caught the light just right. Jed had only seen that once, and he ached to try to find the ember of emerald in her eyes again.

"We can go to that pho hut in Beeville," he said, not quite sure why he couldn't let her drive out of his life again. In fact, he'd been the one to drive her away last time. It was only several weeks ago, actually, and Jed had regretted his text for weeks now. "I know you like that kind of stuff."

Cherry softened right in front of him, but she kept her chin high and her eyes slitted as she studied him. He supposed he couldn't blame her for not trusting him, though he'd always said things just how they were. He'd never tried to hide anything from her, but that was because he didn't have ultimate control over what came out of his mouth, not because he was so upright and honest.

"Come on," he said, trying on a small smile. "You can leave your car here and everything." He extended his hand toward her. "Come tell me why you're back in town."

Slowly, Cherry approached him, but she didn't put her hand in his. They didn't exist in fists anymore either, and she tucked them into her jacket pockets instead of touching him. "Rissa's having her baby tomorrow."

"Ah, of course," he said. He'd known Clarissa Rust was pregnant, and he should've known Cherry wouldn't miss being there to meet her new niece or nephew. "Boy or girl?" Lee might have told him at one point in the past, but Jed didn't carry details in his brain that didn't matter to him.

"Boy," Cherry said quietly, moving with him as he walked away from her car. "Wait, my car is still running."

She jogged back to turn it off, and she returned to his side with her purse in her hand too. "Okay, ready."

He smiled at her, but she barely returned it. He was used to that, as he was definitely the loud, jovial one out of the pair of them. Cherry preferred letting him take the lead, and while she'd smiled and laughed with him over the past several months, he definitely had to work hard to draw those things out of her.

Heck, he'd had to work hard for everything he'd gotten from Cherry. Even getting her phone number had been like pulling teeth.

His chest vibrated in a strange way as he stepped up to his midnight black truck and opened the passenger door for Cherry. She boosted herself up and into the seat in a single movement, which made Jed's mouth turn a little drier than it already was. She looked at him, and Jed could get lost in her gaze for a good, long while.

Move, he told himself, and he managed to step back and out of the way. He closed the door as his phone chimed at him, and he looked down at the notification. His brother had texted, and Jed's heart dropped to his knees.

Corn maze clear? You're feeding the horses at six tonight, right?

Jed couldn't believe he'd invited Cherry to dinner. He'd known he had more chores to do after clearing the corn maze. Had he known the lost customer in the maze had been her, he probably would've sent Chris to go in and get them out.

He tapped to call his brother, and the line only rang once before Chris picked up. "Hey, so I have a slight problem," he said, glancing over to Cherry and quickly moving away from the window. She wouldn't like being called a problem, and he'd already yelled at her that she wasn't a princess.

In reality, Jed hadn't stopped thinking about Cherry since he'd run into her at Travis's wedding. He'd only seen her once a month, and yeah, he'd wanted more. She'd offered him Casper, and he'd thrown it back in her face.

He looked up into the sky as Chris said, "What kind of problem? The kind where I have to find someone else to go feed the horses?"

"Yeah," Jed said with a sigh. "That kind of problem."

Chris let out a long exhaling breath. "The corn maze is clear, right?"

"Yes," Jed said, glad he didn't have to disappoint his younger brother again. He, Chris, and Easton ran their family farm together, and Chris managed all of the logistics of things, like a project manager, while Easton handled more of the big-picture items. He paid bills and made sure they had the men and women they needed to work the fields and handle the animals and bring in the harvest.

Jed excelled at details, and he pitched in and helped

wherever needed—fields, corn mazes, animals, agriculture. He spent a lot of time with a hammer or a saw in his hand, fixing whatever had started to break around the farm. Too bad he couldn't fix himself enough to keep a woman for longer than a few months.

Jed shook all of that away as he rounded the back of his truck. He and Cherry had been sort of dating for months now, and he should've said he'd meet her in Casper anytime she wanted. Breakfast, lunch, or dinner.

"What are you doing right now?" Chris asked.

"Can I tell you later?" Jed asked, reaching for the door handle.

"This has Cherry Cooper written all over it," his brother said.

"No," Jed said too quickly. "Why would it? She doesn't even live here."

"Her sister is having a baby any minute now," Chris said in a deadpan. "You must think I'm so stupid."

"No," Jed said again. He turned away from the truck and ducked his head. "Am I that obvious?" He spoke in a low voice, hoping Chris would say no.

"Totally," Chris said. "She probably doesn't think so, but I've seen you freak out about nothing for the past couple of months, and that was about the time you stopped talking to her. Or she stopped talking to you. I don't know, because you won't talk about her."

"Yeah, well, we can't all have amazing wives," Jed said.

"I'll tell Deb you said that," Chris said. "She's feeling less than amazing right now, so she'll probably bring you brownies later."

"*Mint* brownies," Jed clarified.

Chris laughed and said, "Have fun with Cherry." He hung up before Jed could protest that his "little problem" had nothing to do with Cherry Cooper. He faced the truck again, shoved his phone in his back pocket, and pulled open the driver's door.

"Sorry," he said. "Chris called."

Cherry trained her big eyes on him, her smile slow and absolutely gorgeous on her face. "How's Chris and Deb?"

"They're great," Jed said. "Pregnant again. Deb's really praying for a girl." He smiled and flipped his truck into drive. "I'm honestly surprised they're having another baby after the twins." He chuckled, and Cherry laughed with him. "They're a handful, let me tell you."

"You've talked about them before," Cherry said, looking out her window.

Jed quieted, because Cherry had, and he didn't know how to talk to her when she receded inside herself. He cleared his throat, uncomfortable in the silence with her. "How's work?"

"I'm thinking of getting a new job," she said.

He whipped his attention toward her. "You are? Where?"

"I have no idea."

"I'm sure there's something for you here," he said.

Cherry turned toward him, her arms folding across her midsection as she did. "Is that so? Here? In Sweet Water Falls, where there is no college for an academic advisor?"

Jed swallowed, not sure where to go with this. Perhaps he should just lay everything on the line. "You could work at your family farm," he said. "Or do something for a college online. Or take a completely new career path." He glanced over at her and turned out of the parking lot. "Didn't you tell me that once? That you wanted a new career path?"

"I can't remember," she said. "I probably did."

"Not anymore?"

"I don't know, Jed."

He frowned at the road in front of him, because if she didn't know, he certainly didn't. He felt too old to be having this conversation. He knew what his life held, and he'd always known. The family farm. Horses and hay fields and hard work. He didn't really have the luxury Cherry seemed to enjoy of picking and choosing the path she wanted to be on.

Although, he did have ideas which swirled through his head from time to time. As the middle son, he'd often thought of finding his own piece of land, and he pictured the farm south of his family plot. Then he quickly shoved those images out, because tonight was about Cherry, and he couldn't have his attention divided.

He drove the two of them to Beeville without much more conversation, questioning every minute of the way what he was doing. He honestly had no idea—and he was far too old to be doing things he didn't understand.

There was simply something about Cherry Cooper he liked and wanted to know more about. He wanted to help her in any way he could, and he didn't understand that either. His father had always told him he had a too-big heart to run the farm, but Jed had embraced that instead of trying to change it.

If there was an animal in pain or in need of something, he wanted to provide for it. When he was fourteen, he'd set alarms for a foal who'd been born too early and gone out to the stables every two hours to nurse it along until it was strong enough to survive without his help. In some ways, Cherry reminded him of that foal. In other ways, she was powerful and strong in a way that struck Jed as pure royalty. He could picture her entering a room and having everyone bow to her as their queen. She certainly brought him to his knees in such a way, especially after their first kiss a couple of months ago.

He pulled into the pho restaurant parking lot and came to a stop. "This is okay?"

"Yes," she said softly. She stayed put while Jed jumped from the truck and jogged around the front of it to get her door. He opened it for her and stepped into the space. She'd unbuckled, but Jed didn't want her to get out.

The words he needed to say had been building beneath his tongue during the drive, and he had to say them before he lost her again.

"Cherry." He reached up and smoothed her hair back. "I'm sorry about saying I didn't have time to drive to see you." He looked at her earnestly, hoping she could feel how genuine he was trying to be. "I've regretted that text every day since I sent it. Every minute."

She studied his face. "You didn't mean it?"

"I was frustrated," he said. "So I probably meant it in the moment, but no, overall, of course I didn't mean it. I think about you all the time, and I just don't know how to sweeten up and ask you to forgive me."

She smiled at him, and the heavens opened to him. Light shone on her, and all Jed could think about was kissing her. He wasn't going to do that today, because he didn't want her to think that was all he wanted from her.

"You are a bit salty," she said. "Maybe my sister-in-law could send you some of her truffles. They're as sweet as the day is long."

He smiled back at her. "Can we try again?"

Cherry hesitated for a moment, then she reached out and ran her hand down the side of his face. "I've missed you, Jed."

"I've missed you too," he whispered.

She leaned forward, pushing her hand up and

removing his cowboy hat. Normally, Jed didn't like it when anyone touched his hat, but Cherry had a way of doing things that he just went with.

Her eyes drifted closed, and Jed's heartbeat fluttered in the large vein in his neck. She pressed his hat to his shoulder blades, bringing him closer to her, and Jed touched his lips to hers in a soft, sweet kiss that he didn't try to accelerate or take to the next level.

The first time he'd kissed her had been explosive, and he hadn't been able to control the way things had spiraled and taken off. This time, he bowed to his queen and let her lead him in the kiss. She only kissed him for a moment before she pulled away.

"What's wrong?" she asked.

He opened his eyes and met hers. "Nothing."

"You're not kissing me back."

"Yes, I am."

She cocked her head to the side, and said, "Give me some of your attitude, Jed."

He grinned at her, semi-embarrassed at his limp kissing. "If you don't like it, don't kiss me," he said.

"I don't want to kiss you," she said. "I want *you* to kiss *me*."

Jed ran his hand up the outside of her thigh and along her waist. "We're going to pick up where we left off, is that it?"

"I'd like to," she said, and he liked that she didn't play games with him. She was a couple of years older than him, and perhaps she didn't have time for a relationship that wasn't going anywhere either. "So?" she asked. "Are you going to kiss me or not?"

Jed looked at her, trying to decide if he should tell her what truly ran through his mind or if he should kiss her the way she wanted him to.

3

Cherry didn't like the calculating look in Jed's eye. The man had never been to college, but that didn't mean he was stupid. "Just say it," she said, the fingers of her left hand still gripping his collar, and those of her right hand drifting up into his hair. If he didn't kiss her soon, she didn't know what would combust inside her.

"I don't want this to just be kissing," he said, clearing his throat in a gruff way. "I mean, I like that. I do. I just..." He tried to pull back, but Cherry maintained her grip. She knew what he'd do. Back up. Sigh. Run his hands through his hair. Then those dreamy, stormcloud-gray-blue eyes would find hers again, with a hint of worry and a bit of vulnerability and plenty of desire.

His expression changed as she predicted, but since she

wouldn't release him, he didn't back up or sigh, and she kept running her fingers through his hair.

"You want to be my boyfriend," Cherry said. "Like, a legit boyfriend, who doesn't have to leave the room to call me, and who I don't hide from my family."

His jaw jumped, and attraction sparked in those eyes. "Yes," he said plainly. "That's what I want."

Cherry did the sighing, and she looked past his face and over his shoulder. "I'd like that too."

"Yeah?" Before she could confirm, Jed kissed her. This time, it wasn't the type of kiss that had her leading the way, but he took control and decided how fast he moved, and how firm he stroked, and Cherry sank into his arms, the very muscles in her body unable to hold her up.

"Jed," she giggled as he slid his mouth across her jaw. "I was going to say something else."

"Say it," he said, his voice husky and hoarse.

"Can we wait to make things public and...official until after Rissa has her baby?"

Jed brought his head up, his eyes searching Cherry's again.

"I don't want to overshadow her," Cherry said, hoping he'd understand. "I do sometimes, even when I don't mean to, and I really don't want to in this regard."

"You showing up out on your family farm with a real boyfriend is going to blow your momma's mind." He grinned at her, and while Cherry returned it, she couldn't help thinking that the fact that she had a boyfriend blew her mind too.

"Me showing up on the family farm is mind-blowing enough," she said.

Jed did back up then, and Cherry slid down from the front seat of his truck. He laced his fingers through hers, closed her door, and they faced the restaurant together.

"No, it isn't," he said. "You've been back several times this year."

"Yeah," she said, her train of thought automatically switching over to what she could do here, in Sweet Water Falls—or close to it—for a job. "Maybe Beeville has something I could do."

"To do?" Jed asked, glancing at her.

"For a job," she said. "I was a secretary and an administrative assistant before I got my master's degree. I could maybe do something like that."

"City offices," he said.

"No one ever gives up those jobs," Cherry said, her mind still moving. "A company or something. Small business. Someone like Shay or Gretchen." She thought of her brothers' wives. "Or even Rosalie. I could run their office, all their financial stuff, everything, while they do...whatever they do."

She knew what they did, but she didn't know how much any of them needed an administrative assistant. Shay designed all of her own clothes, but she employed several people at Sweetspot, Cherry knew that. Gretchen had help in her candy kitchen. Rosalie... Cherry wasn't sure about Rosalie.

She could ask, she knew that.

She enjoyed dinner with Jed, the conversation lighter and easier now that she wasn't trying to hide from him, and he wasn't as salty as he'd been a couple of hours ago. He tossed some money on the table when the waitress brought their check, and he'd just gotten to his feet when Cherry's phone rang.

"It's Lee," she said, looking up at Jed.

"Answer him," Jed said with a kind smile. "I won't make a peep."

Cherry believed him too. She stood and swiped on the call from her oldest brother. He was only a couple of years younger than her, and they'd always confided in one another. She'd helped him a lot with Rosalie over the past several months, and she suspected if she sat down with Lee, she could open her heart and tell him everything she felt for Jed. He'd separate it all, examine it, and help her without teasing her.

She'd spent so long doing everything herself, thinking that was the way she wanted things, that she didn't know how to open those doors. Not even to Lee. Not yet, anyway.

"Lee," she said, just as someone dropped a stack of plates. A terrible clattering and shattering sound filled her world, and she winced away from it. If Lee had spoken, she didn't hear what he'd said.

"What was that?" she did hear, and Lee had to know she wasn't in her car, about to arrive on the farm he now ran for their father.

"Someone dropped something," she said, glancing over to the source of the noise. "I'm just finishing dinner. I should be to the farm in..." She looked at Jed, who shrugged one shoulder and held up a single finger. "An hour."

"Don't come to the farm," Lee said, his voice breathless now. "Rissa went into labor earlier today, and they're at the hospital."

"What?" Cherry started striding toward the exit now. "Why didn't you call me sooner?"

"Spence just called Trav," Lee shot back. "We all just found out too."

"Rissa." Cherry shook her head, gained the doorway, and flew down the steps. She turned in a circle, trying to remember where she'd parked her car. "She always does this. She says she doesn't want to be dramatic, and then she's dramatic."

"I just think she doesn't want everyone in the room for the birth," Lee said. "But Spence made it sound like she'd have him soon. Said we could come tonight. I'm headed to Mama's to help her and Daddy."

Cherry turned as Jed touched her arm. He nodded down the row, and she remembered she hadn't driven her car to this restaurant in Beeville. She hurried toward his truck, with him at her side. "I wish I was close enough to help. She wasn't due until tomorrow, and even then I expected her to be late."

"It's fine," Lee said. "See you there." He ended the call even as he said, "No, Ford, real shoes. We're goin'—"

Cherry broke into a jog which Jed didn't have to match. His long legs kept him at her side. "What's goin' on?" he asked.

"She's already at the hospital," she said. "Can you take me there?"

"Of course." He didn't come around to her side to open her door, and she swung into the passenger seat as he fired up the engine. He backed out and asked, "Do you want me to take you back to my place first? Then you can get your car." He flicked a look in her direction, but Cherry didn't hold his gaze.

Indecision raged through her. She could cover her dinner with Jed tonight easily. She hadn't told Lee where she'd been eating, only that she had. But if she told Jed to take her back to his farm first, she'd be even later getting to the hospital.

Something told her she didn't have that time to spare. "No," she said. "If you're okay with coming, let's just get to the hospital. Then you can take me out there after." She looked at him, trying to decipher his feelings on the matter from half of his face. "Okay?"

"Okay," he said, shifting in his seat. "Am I sittin' in the truck while you go in for an undetermined amount of time?" He still wouldn't look at her, and Cherry switched her attention out the windshield.

"No," she said. "That would be ridiculous. You'll come in with me."

"This won't be a secret then," he said.

"No," she murmured. "It won't." She hugged herself and gathered her courage. She looked at Jed again, and this time, he did meet her gaze and hold it. "It doesn't need to be a secret." She reached over and took his hand in hers. "I'm not embarrassed of you. I *want* to tell my family about us."

"It might overshadow Rissa," he said, squeezing. "I'm fine to sit in the truck, Cherry. Honestly."

She fell for him a little bit more then, her foot slipping down the mountain she so desperately wanted to cling to. She wasn't even sure why. She'd wanted to fall head-over-heels in love with someone who loved her back for so long, and Jed sure did seem to like her.

She just didn't want to fall first.

She was *tired* of falling first.

"I'll decide when we get there," she said. "Let's just get there."

"Yes, ma'am," he said, and he pushed on the gas pedal to do just that.

————

FORTY-FIVE AGONIZING MINUTES LATER, JED FINALLY PUT the truck in park, and Cherry released her seatbelt. "Come on," she said. "It makes no sense for you to sit out here."

She'd have to explain why Jed was with her, but Cherry was forty-six years old. She could do it. If she acted like she'd driven her car, and someone wanted to leave for some reason, she'd have to say why she couldn't drive. Or...something.

She knew that *something* would come up that would force her to explain to her family that she didn't have her car and hadn't driven herself. Then they'd find out that she'd made Jed sit out here and wait, and she couldn't even imagine the looks she'd get then.

No one understood her the way she wished they would, but she also couldn't fault them for that. She hadn't told them much over the years, and she'd been the one to put up and maintain the walls between her and everyone else.

Knocking them down would be hard, but Jed caught up to her and slipped his hand into hers. Suddenly, Cherry wasn't so alone, and she sure did like that. In truth, she liked that the man at her side was specifically Jed, but she didn't know how to deal with that right now, so she filed it away for later.

Inside the hospital, Jed knew right where to take her. "Deb's had two kids," he said. "I know where maternity is."

Sure enough, he took them right to the maternity ward, and only then did Cherry's footsteps slow. Down the hall and around a corner, she found a small waiting room outside a thick, heavy wooden door.

Travis sat on the couch, his wife Shayla at his side. She was pregnant too, and she rested one hand on her baby bump. Lee paced, and his son, Ford sat in a chair, his phone in front of him. Will and Gretchen sat side-by-side in a pair of chairs, their heads bent together, whispering.

She couldn't see Mama or Daddy, and Cherry said, "Lee," drawing everyone's attention to her and Jed. All six pairs of eyes landed on her, then slid to where she held Jed Forrester's hand.

Lee turned, stared, and blinked, his eyes back on Cherry's in that next moment. "Hey," he said, jogging toward her. "You made it."

She embraced him, really feeling the love her brother held for her sink through her, and asked, "Where's Mama and Daddy?"

"They went back to see the baby," Lee said. He held her for another moment and then stepped back. "Howdy, Jed."

He shook the other man's hand, and Jed said, "Hey, Lee."

Lee cocked one eyebrow at Cherry, but before he could say anything, her siblings arrived, and Cherry got separated from both Jed and Lee. Before she could get back to him—the man didn't need to be introduced to her brothers and their wives, but it would probably be nice for him—her daddy came out and said, "Oh, good. Cherry's here. Rissa's asking for you, baby."

He put his arm across her shoulders and squeezed, his smile wide and bright. "That baby is so adorable."

Mama sniffled and wept, and Cherry stepped in to hug her too. Her mama was frail and bony, but she could still give a good hug, and she said, "She'll be thrilled you're here."

Cherry swallowed her emotions, which had started to teem beneath her tongue. "How many people can go back?"

"Just two," Mama said. "Lee? She said she wanted you to come too. We'll watch Ford."

"Thanks, Ma." Lee stepped toward the big door that led back to the patient rooms, opened it, and gestured for Cherry to go first.

She cast a look at Jed, who stood next to Will. He smiled at her and said, "Go on, sweetheart. I'll be right here." He looked like he was really enjoying himself, but Cherry didn't know how that was possible.

She almost rolled her eyes but refrained at the last moment. She nodded, turned and met her brother's eyes, and then stepped past him. She would not cause more drama than she already had, and since only two people could come back at a time, perhaps Rissa wouldn't have to know she'd shown up with her new...boyfriend.

"Sweetheart?" Lee murmured from behind her. "So you're dating him?"

"Yes," Cherry said, feeling her defenses fire back into position. "And it would be great if you just kept it to yourself right now. This is about Rissa."

"Fine," Lee said, a hint of happiness in his voice. He glanced over to Cherry. "But it's a good thing, Cher. Why do you look like you're going to stab something if you have to admit Jed's your boyfriend?"

She wasn't sure why she needed to defend who she dated. Or that she dated at all. Nothing much made sense, and she needed some time alone to sort it all out. But right now, she couldn't wait to see her new nephew, and she lasered her focus on him...and her sister.

4

Jed laughed at something Will said, though he wasn't entirely sure the man had meant to be funny. Will scared him a little, though they were close to the same age. But with Lee gone, Jed had little choice but to settle down on the couch and wait for Cherry to come back.

Her daddy looked at him, a smile on his face, and Jed returned it. "How's the farm, Wayne?" he asked.

"Doin' real good," Wayne Cooper said. "How's things goin' for you lot next door?"

"Real good," Jed drawled back to him. "Chris and Deb are gonna have another baby next year." He looked over to Travis Cooper, who sat with his wife. At least they'd all resumed their seats after Cherry and Lee had left. Jed hated awkwardness, and standing over something was never good. "When is your baby due?"

"Beginning of April," Shay said with a smile. "We don't know if it's a boy or a girl yet."

"Are you hopin' for one or the other?" he asked, his gaze moving to Travis. While Easton wasn't married, Jed had been around Deb and Chris enough to know how polite conversation went regarding pregnancies and babies.

"Not really," Shay said, looking at Travis. Travis shrugged and kept his mouth closed, and that meant one thing: He wanted a boy.

Jed said nothing about that. He just kept his smile in place. "Well, congratulations. Deb's hopin' for a girl. She's got those two twin boys, and wow." He chuckled and shook his head. "They're terrible."

"How old are they?" Shay asked.

"Almost three," Jed said. "I can almost understand what they say when they talk, and Deb's a master at deciphering things."

"Cherry was like that," Chrissy Cooper said, her eyes opening slowly. She gave Jed a warm smile, but anyone could see she wasn't real healthy. He'd known about her cancer for years, of course. She'd been in the hospital this year too, and Jed had helped put together a couple of meals for the Coopers during that time.

"That girl couldn't speak sentences others could understand until she was almost four years old." She slipped her hand into her husband's. "Remember that, Wayne?"

"I sure do." He lifted her hand to his lips and kissed the back of it, the gesture so sweet and so real to Jed. He felt how much they loved each other—and Cherry.

"How long have you two been seeing each other?" Chrissy asked, and every Cooper ear turned toward Jed.

"Uh." He chuckled, not sure how to answer that. "Officially? I'd say we just started dating today," he said. "Tonight."

"Tonight?" Will asked. "Really?"

"Yeah," Jed said. "We saw each other a little bit after Travis's wedding, but..." He didn't know how to say he'd ended things with her when she insisted they meet in out-of-the-way locations. "It's hard to date long-distance."

Every eyebrow shot toward the ceiling, and Jed realized just how badly he'd messed up.

"Is Cherry moving back?" Will asked.

"I thought she was happy in San Antonio," Wayne said, looking from Jed to his wife.

"She is," Chrissy said, frowning. "I don't know what she's doing."

"Surely she'd have said if she was quitting her job," Travis said, his words sharp and tossed into the conversation almost angrily. Jed wasn't sure what that was about, as he didn't know all the complexities of Cherry's relationship with her siblings.

One by one, they looked back to him for the answers, and foolishness wound through Jed. "I don't know," he said. "Nothing's been done."

"So she still has her job at the college in San Antonio," Wayne said.

"Yeah," Jed said. "I guess we're just gonna give it another go." He got to his feet. "I'm gonna go get a soda. Anyone want anything?"

No one did, and Jed made his escape as quickly as he could without looking like he was running from the Coopers. "Idiot," he muttered to himself the moment he rounded the corner and the weight of their gazes left his back.

He paused, pressed his back into the bricks, and pulled out his phone. *I messed up*, he sent to Cherry. *I mentioned something about us dating over the past several months and how it didn't work out because long-distance is hard, and then everyone in your family had questions about you moving back here.*

He sent the message, the panic clear in the words. *I'm sorry*, he sent next, exhaling like he'd just made a terrible, terrible mistake. The thing was, with Cherry, he might have. He knew she didn't want to stay at her farm, and now that Clarissa had had her baby early, she wouldn't want to stay with her sister either.

Do you want to stay in cabin four again? he sent next. *Free of charge.* Before, he'd made her pay twenty bucks for a couple of nights, because Cherry hated charity.

She didn't answer, and Jed didn't know if she'd read his messages. If she was mad, she'd tell him she could get a ride back to the farm with Lee or Will or Travis. If she wasn't, she'd say *it's fine, Jed. Cabin four sounds great. Will you make me breakfast?*

A man could dream, and Jed sighed as he pushed away from the wall and headed down the hall. After he'd gotten his carbonated, caffeinated soda and chugged half the can, he tapped to call Chris.

"Hey," his brother said. "I handled the horses."

"Thank you," Jed said. "I'll take the morning shift for you, so you can stay in bed."

Chris said nothing, and Jed liked stunning him into silence every now and then.

"Listen, I'm at the hospital," he said, and Chris sucked in a breath.

"Why?"

Jed weighed his words carefully. "So Cherry did stop by the corn maze tonight."

"I know," Chris said, glee in his voice. "Her car is still in the parking lot."

"Yeah." Jed let out his breath. "We went to dinner. Her sister had her baby, and now we're here for that."

"Ah, I see."

Jed wasn't sure why he'd called Chris. Maybe he just wanted someone to tell him he wasn't crazy for feeling so strongly about Cherry. Chris had teased him, sure, but he'd also leant a listening ear and given great advice when Jed had asked him to.

"So are you seeing her again?" Chris asked, his voice

low. "I'm not gonna wake them up." The last bit was clearly for his wife.

Jed listened to his brother's breath, then the squeal of his screen door, and he knew Chris had just gone out to his front porch. Since he had a wife and family, Chris had built a home on a parcel of land just beyond the corn maze, with easy access to the highway that no one used but him and Deb.

"I don't know," Jed said, though he did. "I mean, yes. Yes, I want to see her again. She still lives in San Antonio, and honestly, Chris, that's the reason I broke up with her last time."

"I figured," Chris said. "It's not an easy drive up there."

Jed didn't agree or disagree. It wasn't the easiness of things. It was the time they took. He'd rather have Cherry living right next door than two hours up the Interstate. "It just means I can't see her every day."

"Well, you're an every day type of man, Jed," Chris said. "That's why you didn't like the situation last time."

"Yeah." He couldn't argue with that. "I just—maybe she doesn't want to see me every day, Chris. I think that's where I'm stalling. Because I *do* want to see her every day. Talk to her. Touch her. *See* her. And not on a video. And she was happy getting together for lunch for a couple of hours once a week."

"She liked talking to you on the phone," Chris said in Cherry's defense.

"Is that enough?" Jed asked.

"I don't know, brother." Chris exhaled mightily. "The distance definitely complicates things for you."

"Her family's here," he said, looking back the way he'd come. "They know now."

"That's a good step," Chris said brightly.

Jed ran his hand up the back of his neck, pushing his cowboy hat further forward than he liked. "Yeah." He fixed his hat and drained the rest of his soda. "I'll handle the chores in the stables tomorrow."

"I appreciate it," Chris said wearily. "We had an epic battle with the twins and spaghetti-with-*no*-meatballs tonight." He gave a chuckle, but it wasn't entirely happy. "I have no idea how we're going to handle things once we're outnumbered."

Jed laughed just to cheer up his brother. "You wrangle dozens of cattle at a time," he said. "Kids are just like that."

Chris laughed too, but Jed could hear the exhaustion in the sound. It pulled through him too. To think, a few hours ago, all he'd wanted was to clear the corn maze, feed the horses, and fall asleep on the couch with Fish keeping his feet warm. The dog refused to lay on the floor if Jed didn't have to.

The night had turned out radically different than he'd envisioned, and he was still trying to decide if the change had been good or not.

He hung up with his brother, and while his phone still sat in his hand, it chimed. Cherry's name popped up at the top, and part of her message read, *It's fine, Jed. I'm not sure—*

He tapped, his heartbeat doing the same thing, to see her whole message. It had started the way he'd hoped, and his fantasies roared to life again.

Her full message read: *It's fine, Jed. I'm not sure how long I'm going to be here tonight, and I hate making you wait for me. I know you have work to do still, with an early morning. I can get a ride with someone back out to the farm.*

He read it once, then again, and then a third time. It was a combination of how he thought she'd respond if she was mad and if she wasn't, so now he didn't know what to think. Cherry Cooper perplexed him, he knew that. He could feel the wounds inside her, and he wanted so badly to mend them.

"You can't mend a person," he told himself. He'd been working on himself recently, with a pair of earbuds and a purchased set of mental therapy lessons. Mindfulness, it was called. Making better choices. Coming at situations from a better mental place. Taking care of himself before others.

But with Cherry, he didn't want to do that. He'd stay at the hospital all night if he had to, just so she could sit and hold her sister's baby. Then he could drive her home and see her soften as she fell asleep in his truck. He'd carry her inside cabin four and put her to bed, kiss her forehead, and whisper that he'd be back in the morning to make her an omelet.

For Cherry, he could go without sleep for days.

He shook his head, because his soft thoughts for the woman drove him mad. He wasn't sure why they existed, other than to torment him, and he didn't want her to know how much he liked her right now.

I don't mind staying, he said.

I'm headed out.

With that promise, Jed walked back to the waiting room outside the maternity ward, arriving about the same time Lee opened the door and Cherry moved past him. Their eyes met, and she looked like a brand new person. She shone with glory and light, and Jed couldn't keep his smile off his face.

"She said anyone else who'd like to go back can," Lee said.

Jed stood outside the circle of Cooper family members while Travis got to his feet and said, "I want to see him. Will?"

"Yeah, me too."

The two brothers left, and Cherry came closer to Jed, her hands tucking into her front pockets as she approached. Jed wanted to reach out and slide his hand along her hip and bring her closer to him. Instead, he asked, "What did they name him?"

"Bronson," she said. "He's the cutest little thing you've ever seen."

"Yeah?" Jed looked up to her gorgeous auburn hair. "Is he a redhead like all you Coopers?"

Cherry smiled, and the radiance of it almost blinded Jed. Now that he'd seen her like this, he knew what true joy looked like on her. "Yeah," she said. "A little, I think. He doesn't have much hair."

Jed put his hand out and hooked her fingers with his. He focused on their hands instead of looking at her. "Where are you going to stay tonight?"

"I think I'm gonna stay with Mama and Daddy," she said.

Jed nodded, his eyes going back to lock onto hers. "And that's okay?" She hated staying at her family farm, and to his knowledge, she hadn't stayed there for even a single night since leaving town years ago.

"Yeah." She exhaled and stepped into his arms. Jed wrapped her up easily and held her close, not caring that Lee's laser gaze drilled into his forehead. "I think it'll be okay, and it's time."

"All right," he whispered. "I'm ten minutes away, and I'll come anytime. No questions. Cabin four is empty and ready for you."

Cherry's arms around his reminded him of everything Jed wanted that he hadn't known he wanted until he'd run into her at Travis's wedding. "Thank you." She stepped back and smiled. "You really don't have to stay."

"You're not mad about me sayin' stupid stuff about you maybe leaving your job, are you?"

"Of course I am," she said, her smile telling a different story. "Do you know how many explanations I'm going to have to give now?" She swatted at his chest, and Jed chuckled as he dodged backward.

"I lose my mind in small-talk situations," he said.

She shook her head, that gorgeous smile making him so, so happy. "You've got to learn to control what comes out of your mouth."

"Like you're so good at it," he shot back, still grinning.

"I am," she said. "About a lot of things, including my job."

She was better than him, and he knew it. He'd hoped she wouldn't realize it until much later in their relationship, but Cherry wasn't a dumb woman. He couldn't leave without a time and place he'd see her again.

"Breakfast?" he asked. "My place? Seven-thirty?" He'd have been at work for a couple of hours by then, but he could swing that. Scrambled eggs cooked fast, and he probably had some ham he could chop up and put in the eggs.

"Make it eight-thirty, and I'll bring it," she said, giving him a sexy smile that accelerated his pulse once more.

"Deal," he said. He wanted to kiss her, but Cherry nodded, tucked her hair behind her ear, and turned to return to her family.

"See you tomorrow, Jed," she said over her shoulder, and that was clearly princess-speak for, *Go, cowboy. I'll talk to you later.*

So Jed waved to the rest of the Coopers and then went. On the way home, he couldn't think about anything or anyone except Cherry. He really didn't want to mess up with her, and he found himself praying that this time would be the time that he could make a relationship stick. That he could control what came out of his mouth. That he could get a woman to fall in love with him, so he didn't have to be alone forever.

He wanted to be Cherry's safe place. The one person she trusted explicitly. The man she could share anything and everything with, and he wouldn't judge her. "Probably shouldn't call her princess, then," he muttered, and he decided right then and there not to use that term for her anymore.

The idea of being her prince though...Jed did like that, and as he turned into the dirt driveway in front of his cabin, his lips quirked up. "Help me help her," he prayed, finally finding the right words. If Cherry needed rescuing, Jed wanted to be the knight in shining armor to do it.

She just couldn't know she was the princess in the tower until she was all the way in love with him.

"So listen," he coached himself. "Learn. Be patient. She'll come around." After reassuring himself, and praying for the right thing, Jed was finally able to stop obsessing about Cherry. Well, for five minutes at least.

5

C herry didn't see Jed in the parking lot at the corn maze. "Thanks, Will."

"Yep." Her brother watched her get out. Watched her unlock her car. Watched and waited until Cherry buckled, adjusted the air, set the music, and finally pulled out of the lot ahead of him. Annoyance sang through her, but she couldn't fault him.

Showing up at the hospital with Jed Forrester's hand locked in hers was a big deal. Her siblings knew she dated, and her parents knew she wanted to. If only Cherry could unknot the multitude of issues boiling inside her, she'd know better what the next step should be.

As it was, she made it back to the family farm where she'd grown up. She looked right at the first fork, and taking it would lead her past the cowboy cabins, past another road that led to Lee's, and then past Will's and out to Rissa's and Travis's. They'd taken up all the available family housing here at Sweet Water Falls Farm, and Cherry hadn't minded.

Until now.

Lee had told her that Mama and Daddy would be moving into his house once he and Rosalie got married, and then he'd have the picturesque farmhouse where they'd all grown up. She made the left turn toward the white structure that usually made her smile on a dark night like this one.

Hardly any lights shone in the windows though, and that kept her smile at bay. Mama and Daddy should've beaten her here, but she reminded herself that they were both older now—a lot older—and didn't have to wait up for her. Mama had looked one breath away from passing out, and Lee had left first to bring them back.

Her brother's truck didn't sit out front, which meant he wasn't there. He had a son to take care of, and a fiancée to call, and Cherry couldn't help the slight depressive feeling that overcame her as she brought her sedan to a stop. She retrieved her bag from the backseat and went inside the farmhouse.

A candle burned on the front table, and Cherry went over to it, catching sight of the note that had been tucked under the edge of the jar. Peace touched her soul, and something inside her that had been ragged and torn healed. She reached out and ran her fingertips along the bottom edge of the paper, remembering all the times Mama had left a note for her exactly like this.

Late nights after her rehearsals and plays, when her parents and younger siblings had come home ahead of her. Mama would always write her a note and list all of her favorite parts of the show. She made the other kids do the same, and Cherry looked up and down the dark hall to the right, wondering if her parents had kept that box of her memories after she'd left the farm, the town, and them behind.

All of them.

She exhaled, the truths she needed to tell them buried so deep, she could barely bring them to the surface anymore. Tears pricked her eyes, and she couldn't imagine saying the things she'd kept bottled and dormant for so long.

"You must," she whispered to herself. "It's time."

She slid the note out from underneath the jar and held it closer to the flame so she could read it. *Lovely to see you, dear. I love you with my whole soul. See you in the morning. Mama*

Cherry pressed the note to her heartbeat, wishing she'd done things differently. Twelve years ago, if she'd acted out of faith instead of fear, what would her life had been like?

She knew she wouldn't be standing here, like this, filled with regret and wondering how to rid herself of it.

PS. Any bedroom is ready for you. Take your pick.

Cherry took the note with her and went down the hall. Mama and Daddy's bedroom sat at the very end of the hallway, as Daddy had remodeled the farmhouse to make the master suite bigger, with a walk-in closet and en suite bathroom about fifteen years ago.

Cherry's old bedroom sat two doors down, but she didn't go to that one. She'd shared with Rissa, and neither of them had lived there in a long time. Instead, she went in the first door she came to, which had been Lee's room. He hadn't wanted to share with the other boys, and Will and Travis had a bedroom on the opposite side of the hall that Cherry remembered smelling like old cheese and wet shoes most of the time.

The memory made her smile, though it didn't bring happiness to her nose. In Lee's old room, she flipped on the light. Most traces of her brother had been removed, save for one. His FFA trophies, which he'd earned with perfection. Daddy had always been so proud of Lee, and he'd made a display case for the gold and silver it still housed.

A family photo of the seven of them sat below the case, the bottom of the canvas almost touching the top of the dresser.

Cherry hefted her bag onto the queen-sized bed and clicked on the lamp on the nightstand. Then she turned off the overhead light—she didn't like them shining down into her eyes—and closed the door softly behind her.

Only then did she feel like she could relax, and she quickly changed into her pajamas and climbed under the thick quilt that Mama had made herself. She and Granny used to sew, crochet, and quilt every Monday, and Cherry could still see the two of them in her mind as plain as day. They'd be in the huge sun porch off the back of the house when Cherry and the other children got off the bus after school.

Granny would have something delicious to feed everyone for dinner, and the farmhouse vibrated with laughter and joy, fun and familial fighting, and most of all, love.

Cherry hadn't felt those things in such a long time— well, besides the arguing she did with her siblings. She heard about that plenty, and she certainly wasn't blame-less for some of the fights that had happened over the years.

She leaned her head back against the puffy pillows, wondering who else Mama and Daddy had hosted in this room. Surely not very many people, and yet the room waited as if Mama had known Cherry would need it one day.

She sucked back the tears threatening to overflow and reached for her phone. She went to the conversation with Jed, their interactions from that afternoon and evening flowing through her mind. They had a unique relation-ship, that was for sure, and Cherry's chest caved in on itself when she thought about telling him about her past indiscretions.

Do you have any secrets? she asked him, wondering if it was too late for him to be awake. The clock hadn't quite ticked to ten yet, but he was a farmer and would be up by five, most likely.

She texted her fellow counselor in San Antonio, Willie, and told her about her new nephew. Willie gave all the right answers, with the appropriate number of exclamation points, and Cherry smiled at her phone.

She messaged Lee, as she hadn't had much time with him alone, and she wanted to know what he thought of her and Jed. She asked him, once again thinking it might be too late to get an answer.

With her phone resting—silently—on the nightstand, she got out her toiletries and went across the hall to brush her teeth. Everything felt too old and too small in this farmhouse, and she told herself it was just because she hadn't been here in a while. Eating a few meals at the huge family dining table didn't count, and she knew it. She hadn't stayed here and slept here and let her spirit feel the inner breathings of this house, this life, where she'd thrived for a long time.

She felt those things now as the very walls whispered things to her she'd long forgotten. She didn't have to elbow Lee or Rissa out of the way to answer the rotary phone, because she knew the caller would be Sabrina. She didn't have to stretch the cord as far as she could to get into the second bedroom, where she'd close the door right over the cord just to talk in private.

Lee had disconnected the cord at the base once, and boy, had she been mad. He didn't care, because he had a call coming in from someone about some experiment they were doing with cow's milk, and the moment he'd snapped the cord back into the phone, it had rung and he'd answered it.

She brushed her teeth, thinking of when she'd challenged Travis to a race down to the pond, and they'd both come back bloody. Mama had been so mad—first about the mud, and then about the blood. She'd taken care of them while lecturing up a storm, Texas-mama style that Cherry didn't soon forget.

Daddy worked long hours, and while he was stern and didn't put up with whiny children, he'd always hugged her tight—so tight, Cherry thought her spindly ribs might crack—and told her he loved her each and every night before she went to bed.

She'd never once thought her parents didn't love her, and that only made what she'd done so much harder for her to swallow. By the time she finished brushing her teeth, tears streamed down her face. She tried to stem them, but one couldn't stop the tide simply because they wanted to.

In between sobs, she darted back across the hall and closed the door, hoping she wouldn't wake her parents. A forty-six-year-old sobbing past their bedtime was the last thing they needed tonight.

Thankfully, Cherry had plenty of experience stuffing unpleasant things onto shelves and hiding them behind easier things to think about. She controlled her emotions and stopped the tears. Sitting on the edge of the bed, she picked up her phone and found messages from both Lee and Jed.

Lee had said, *I think if he makes you happy, Cherry, you should do what you can to be with him. Isn't that what you told me?*

Yes, she thumbed out. *Thanks, Lee.*

She wasn't sure if Jed made her happy or not. Honestly, with him, it was either hot or cold. She sure did like talking to him, and she liked having him at her side. She didn't feel so alone, and she didn't feel like life wasn't worth living when she knew she could text or call him, and he'd be so glad to hear from her.

At the same time, she knew she'd deliberately *not* called or texted him in the past to keep him from getting too close.

"Gotta decide what you want," she murmured to herself as she navigated over to his text.

Sure, he'd said. *Who doesn't have secrets?*

Are they big or small? she sent him next, sure it would drive him crazy. He'd told her once that he'd rather call than text, because texting took both hands and too much time. She'd laughed and told him he couldn't call her during work hours. So he'd called at night, almost every night, and Cherry had missed that so much in the past couple of months.

Some of both, he said. *What about you?*

I've got some of both too, she said. Her heart pounded as she typed, *One really big one I'm scared to tell anyone.*

You can tell me, he said. *Anything. Anytime.*

Maybe one day, she said, sure she was lying to him right there in writing. *Night, Jed.*

Breakfast tomorrow, he said. *I can't wait to see you again.*

Cherry sighed as she plugged in her phone, and with those happy words—*I can't wait to see you again*—revolving in her mind instead of all the things she'd done wrong in her life, she managed to fall asleep pretty quickly.

————

"Thanks, Daddy." She smiled up at her father as he finished pouring her coffee. She lifted it to her lips as it was, black and rich and deep. He made the best coffee in the world, and this smelled like the blend she'd gotten him for Father's Day.

"Sure," he said. "What are you going to do today?"

Cherry lowered her cup and looked over her shoulder. Mama hadn't come into the kitchen yet, and it was half-past seven. "I have a breakfast date with Jed," she said.

"Then I thought I'd come back here and see if there's anything you guys need from me."

Daddy reset the coffee pot on the burner and glanced up at her. "The back porch needs to be swept and covered."

"I can do it," Cherry said.

Daddy nodded, something sharp in his expression. "So you don't want breakfast." He wasn't asking, and he started cracking eggs before she could respond.

"No," she said. "Thank you."

"Was Jed speakin' true?" He didn't look at her now but turned to pour the eggs into a pan. "Are you thinkin' about getting a new job?"

Cherry's first instinct was to lie. Or at least put him off. She sighed as she tried to find the right thing to say. "I don't know, Daddy. Maybe? I..." She looked around the farmhouse, almost expecting to find it dilapidated and falling down. It wasn't.

The Coopers still came here and cooked meals five days a week. Everyone helped Mama—except her.

"I think I want to," she said. "I just don't know what I'd do here."

"Lee has far more work in that office than he can keep up with," Daddy said, his bright green eyes harboring hope now. "You could work here."

Cherry didn't want to snipe at him, but they'd had this conversation before. Many times. "It's still not a good fit, Daddy," she said slowly.

"The boys are older," he said, as if her brothers were the reason Cherry had left Sweet Water Falls twelve years ago. "Married or about to be. Their wives..." He chuckled and shook his head. "They tamed those boys, Cherry. It won't be bad."

She stood and joined him in the kitchen. At his side, she looked up and gave him a small smile. "It's not them," she said. "It's *me*. This isn't...this isn't for me."

Resignation bloomed in his eyes, and he nodded. "I know."

"I'm sorry." She leaned her head against his bicep and looped her arm through his though he stirred the eggs. "Are you disappointed?"

"In you? Never," he said.

Several beats of silence echoed through the house, and she stepped away from Daddy as he poured his eggs onto a plate. "What time does Mama get up?" she asked.

"Usually 'bout eight," he said, not even looking toward the arched doorway that led into the foyer and then down the hallway. "Will or Lee come by to help her. She has a hard time first thing in the morning, and I can't do as much as I used to."

Alarm blipped through Cherry. Of course she knew her brothers had been stopping by to help Mama—and Daddy—in the morning. She'd just never lived it, seen it, had to breathe it in and accept it for what it was.

Reality.

"I can help her today," she said, wondering if she

could push her breakfast date to lunch. "Help her with her wig and sit with her during breakfast."

Daddy smiled and shook his head. "Nah. Go on your date. Mama is best later in the day, and she'll want to talk to you."

Cherry didn't want to only experience her mother when she was at her best, but she didn't know how to argue this. She'd be here tomorrow morning too, and she'd simply tell Lee or Will or whoever usually came that she'd handle helping their mother then.

"Okay," she said. "I'm going to town to get those breakfast burritos from Hanna's. Jed likes those with the spicy chorizo."

"So do I," Daddy said, his face lit up again. "Get me one for later, would you?"

She laughed and swept a kiss across her father's forehead. "Sure, Daddy." She turned to leave the kitchen, but she paused in the doorway and looked back to her daddy. He sat at the table alone, and it was far too big for him despite his impressive size.

I'm sorry, she thought, her mouth moving through the words. *Disappointed in you? Never.*

He wouldn't say that if he knew the truth about what she'd done. She hurried out of the kitchen and down the hall to her computer. She had about ten minutes before she had to absolutely leave to get the burritos and then get back to Jed's farm in time for breakfast.

And she needed a new job closer to this farm, so Lee

and Will didn't have to shoulder their mother's care alone anymore.

A tiny part of her mind whispered about how close she'd be to Jed too, and she definitely counted him as a reason that it was time for her to come home. Finally.

6

Jed took the steps to his cabin two at a time, the scent of cherry perfume riding the air. Or maybe his excitement to see Cherry had conjured up the idea of cherry-scented everything. The stables he'd cleaned out and refreshed before dawn hadn't even bothered him, not with this breakfast date on the horizon.

He nearly rammed the door, as it didn't quite unlatch in time. He managed to get it open, and he burst into his house, where he'd told Cherry to go ahead and enter. Running late, as usual, Jed's heart pounded when the gorgeous woman spun from the back of the house, where the kitchen counter ran along the wall there.

"Horses alive," she said, her dark eyes wide. "Jed, you scared me."

"Sorry." He jogged around his simple furniture and took her squealing into his arms. "I hate being late." He leaned down to kiss her, as he hadn't really been able to say goodbye properly last night. The movement between them stayed slow and easy, and wow, Jed could not get enough of this woman.

She broke the kiss first, her eyes latching onto his for a moment before she dropped them to his collar. Her perfume held no cherries, but something bright and citrusy, which mingled with the more savory smell of whatever she'd brought for breakfast.

They swayed together, and while Jed's stomach tightened with hunger, he didn't release her. "What's with all the secret talk?" he whispered, keeping his face close to hers.

She drew in a deep breath, her slight shoulders lifting as she did. "I don't know."

"How was sleepin' at your mama's?"

"Okay." She tipped her face back again, and Jed touched his mouth to hers again. Heat and explosions moved between them, and he sure hoped she could feel them as strongly as he did.

He pulled away first this time. "How long are you staying?" He brought her closer, and she laid her cheek against his chest. Jed could hold her like this forever, but he pushed on the brakes in his head. He couldn't get too far ahead of himself. After all, he'd just asked her when she was leaving town to return to her job in San Antonio.

The farm was moving into calving season, and they had a branding day coming up. Their second and final market day was the weekend after Thanksgiving, and if anything, Jed's life was busier in the winter than any other time.

Holidays, family obligations, work, and none of that took into account the commercial things they did at Forrester Farms. The corn maze would be transformed into a Christmas Corn Craze for the month of December, and that had to be done between Thanksgiving and the following Monday as well.

A sense of pure exhaustion moved through him just thinking about the next couple of months, especially when Cherry didn't answer and simply held him in return.

She did straighten after another few seconds and she pushed her hair out of her face. She hadn't braided or tied it back that day, and just like last night, Jed loved the way it flowed over her shoulders like cool, slow-moving lava.

"I went to Hanna's," she said. "I got you that chorizo tornado burrito you like." She lifted the silver foiled package with the green stripe around it."

Jed grinned at her and took it. "Thanks, sweetheart."

"I'm going to stay until next Sunday," she said, giving him a glance.

Surprise burst through him. "Really? You took off the whole week?"

"The whole week."

"Well, I'll be." He unwrapped his burrito and added, "I might not have run if I'd known that."

She giggled, but he moved around the island and sat at the bar. "Seriously, I'm out of shape."

"Yeah, your huge muscles could really use some extra time in the gym." She rolled her eyes and turned back to the assortment of items she'd brought. She lifted a whole handful of them and put them on the island. "I got too much food."

"You usually do." He bit into his burrito and moaned, the salty, spicy flavor of chorizo one of his favorite things in the world.

"Hey," she protested, but she didn't really have a leg to stand on. Cherry liked to be the perfect hostess. He'd seen her bustle around at two weddings now, making sure everyone had what they needed. He'd been to the Cooper's farm for the Fourth of July barbecue and fireworks show. She'd barely looked at him once her brother had come storming over, choosing instead to put out more cookies and refill lemonade cups.

She sat beside him and unwrapped her own burrito, hers with an orange stripe.

"The ham and cheese?" he asked.

"Yes." She sounded defensive, but Jed didn't know why. "I don't like the spice."

"You don't have to," he said, then took another bite of his. He ate, trying to figure out why she had to defend what she ate. He had poked some fun at some of the things she ate—the pho place they'd eaten at last night a good example of that. "It's good, but you don't have to like what I like."

Their eyes met, and Cherry wore mild surprise in her expression. "Thank you," she said quietly, and Jed didn't know what to make of this version of her. He knew the fiery one. The passionate one. The headstrong one. Even the quiet one.

This contemplative, almost soft side of her? She hadn't shown that to him very often, and Jed's world tilted off-balance a little. "What are you going to do today?" he asked. "What's tonight like? When will Rissa bring her baby home?"

"That's a lot of questions," she said.

Cherry hated questions, but Jed couldn't help himself. He took another bite—this one far bigger than necessary —to give himself time to calm the heck down. He didn't need to burst out of the gate like an overeager bull, trying to prove something. All he'd do is get whipped after he fell flat on his face.

Praise the heavens above, his phone chimed, and it was the sound Jed had assigned to Easton. His older brother didn't like waiting for a response, and Jed chewed while he read his brother's text.

Mandatory meeting at two o'clock, he'd said. *Confirm that you'll be in the office on time.*

No *please*. No *thank you*. No explanation. Easton wasn't gruff, per se, but he certainly didn't mince words. He didn't say more than necessary, and he also didn't like questions.

Jed had a tractor to check that day, as well as a pigpen to repair, but he could be at the office where Easton managed a lot of the administrative tasks for Forrester Farms at two. He took another bite, glad he hadn't had to explain himself to Cherry quite yet, and tapped out a single word.

Confirmed.

You'll be late, Easton texted just as Chris also confirmed, with the exact same message.

Jed saw an opportunity here, and he hurried to type. *Who will?* he sent. *Me or Chris?*

I won't be late, Chris said, and Jed started to chuckle. *Besides, Easton, no one will die if I am.*

Seriously, Jed said, piling on Easton now. *You don't even know what I'm doing today. I might have a meeting in town at two.*

You will, Easton said, as he wasn't the fastest texter in the world. He wasn't even close, and Jed laughed out loud that he'd gotten off full sentences while Easton typed seven letters.

"What's so funny?" Cherry asked, peering at his phone. He didn't care if she saw it, and he pushed it closer to her.

You have a meeting in town? Chris asked, and Jed shook his head and took another big bite of breakfast.

He doesn't have a meeting in town, Easton said. *He's being cheeky.*

Jed pulled his phone back and sent, *You said I'd be late. That's rude.*

"You are late a lot," Cherry said.

"I'm busy," he clarified. "It's not like I was out in the barn going, 'oh, I think I'll make Cherry wait for me while I eat this ice cream.'" He shook his head, because he knew he ran late. He didn't need Easton—or Cherry—pointing it out.

It's not rude if it's true, Easton said.

Yes, it is, Jed sent, and only half a second later, Chris said the exact same words. That made Jed smile too, and he tucked his phone away, done with the conversation with his brothers. If he had to put up with them at two o'clock, they weren't getting another moment of his time this morning. Especially not with Cherry here.

Cherry slid him a look out of the corner of her eye. "What flavor do you have out there?"

"What?" Jed searched her face. "Out where? Flavor?"

The corners of her mouth quirked up, a knowing glint in her eyes. "Jed Forrester, you love ice cream with your whole soul. So I'll ask you just once more—what flavor or flavors do you have out in the barn?"

Caught, Jed didn't know how to answer that wouldn't get him in trouble. "First," he said. "I don't eat ice cream before noon. It's a personal rule of mine."

Cherry started to giggle, and that sound drove right

into Jed's heart. He could picture this woman in his life so easily, and he wondered what she saw in her future when it came to him.

Too far ahead, he told himself, and he re-centered on the moment at hand.

"Secondly," he said. "There's no freezer in the barn. Only a fridge. So technically, there are no flavors of ice cream in the barn."

"Technicalities," she said.

"No," he said. "Details. *Important* details."

She half-rolled her eyes as she shook her head, and he caught a glimmer of that deep emerald he'd only seen once. His pulse picked up speed, and he slid his hand along her thigh to her knee.

"Third," he said, moving his mouth closer to her ear and speaking in a lower voice. "There's double chocolate peanut butter and coconut chocolate delight in the *stable*. The freezer down on the end by the wash stall, not the one by the main entrance."

His two favorite flavors paired with chocolate—coconut and peanut butter—and Jed may rotate in other flavors—the banana cream pie was divine—but he always had those two. "And I know exactly how much of each, so don't be takin' your pretty self out there to sneak a bite."

Cherry laughed then, the magical sound of it filling the cabin with joy. He hoped his walls could catch it all and hold it for a long time. Perhaps they could replay it for him that evening, when he lay in bed and tried to fall asleep, Cherry on his mind.

"You're still going to Mandel's," she said, no question mark in sight.

"Is there a better place to get ice cream?" He straightened and removed his hand from her leg.

"Not for you." She gave him a smile and added, "Rissa won't come home until tomorrow afternoon, most likely. I'm headed back to Mama's after this to help her with a few things. Tonight...tonight is open."

"Open," Jed repeated. "I like the sound of that."

"It's actually Saturday night," she said. "Travis and Shay are cooking dinner at the farmhouse, and my nosy brother has already asked me if I'll be there. At all or with a plus-one." She balled up her foil package without looking at him.

Jed's heart banged against his ribs, as if he'd locked it behind bars and it wanted out. He cleared his throat. "I might be able to make that work."

"Yeah?" She turned toward him then, her eyebrows up and hope filling her gaze. "I'm not sure I can endure the big family dinner alone." He heard the words she didn't say—*not when I'm the only single one.*

Except she wasn't single now. She was with him. "If you're gonna be here for eight more days, I'm surprised your family hasn't assigned you a night to cook."

"Oh, they have," she said dryly, lifting up onto her feet

to snag a slim package with no colored band. "Want a churro?"

"Is that a real question?"

She grinned and passed him two, then settled onto her barstool again. "Rissa usually cooks on Tuesdays, and I'm taking her spot this week." She cocked her right eyebrow and added, "You'll come, right?"

"I will clear all of Tuesday *and* Wednesday," Jed said with a wide grin, and Cherry laughed again. He liked that he could get such a response from her, and he reached over and threaded his fingers through hers.

Words piled into his mouth, but he didn't say them. The gesture alone was enough for her to know that he'd hold onto her no matter what she chose to do. This time, he wouldn't give up on them because of distance. He'd stand by her side, and be there when she needed him, and hopefully, they could rescue one another from their lonely lives in separate houses.

Maybe, he cautioned himself. *Again, don't go too fast.*

And for Jed, pressing on the brake was really hard. But in this case, also really necessary.

————

JED WALKED INTO THE OFFICE IN THE MOBILE HOME—THAT operated as their home base—at precisely two o'clock. He still had to move through the front of the trailer, where Amanda, their office administrator, worked. She'd already set up a Christmas tree, and she could be counted on to have any number of holiday signs with cute sayings on them.

Today, she didn't sit at her desk, and Jed walked past it, past the tree, past the sign that read GATHER above the kitchenette at the back of the room, and down the hall to the left. Easton's office took up the front two-thirds of the building, with supplies for their various activities in the commercial corn field in the back part of it.

"Howdy," he said as he walked in. Chris had already sat down, leaving the chair on the right for Jed. He took it as Easton fiddled with something on his computer. The clock ticked, and Jed raised his eyebrows and looked at Chris.

His younger brother rolled his eyes, which made Jed smile. Easton definitely had more arrogance than both him and Chris.

"How was breakfast?" Chris asked.

"Great," Jed said. "Yours?"

"Deb made chocolate chip pancakes," he said with a smile. "So also great."

"Your shirt looks really clean," Jed said, sliding his eyes down his brother's blue-plaid-clad chest and torso. He grinned, because he'd just said that Chris hadn't been out working yet that day.

"Yours is really dirty." Chris grinned on back at him. "How's the sty coming?"

"It's giving me fits," Jed said, his smile sliding back into a straight face. "It never was square, and I think I'm going to rip the whole thing down and start from the ground up."

"Wow," Chris said at the same time Easton said, "Don't do that. I need you to finish it this week so we can get you over to the hay loft before the winter rains come."

Jed turned his gaze on his older brother, everything in the room cooling while they looked at one another. Easton had left Sweet Water Falls for a time, thinking he'd like to do something besides run and manage the family farm. He'd come back after only a few years, and their daddy had welcomed him like he was the Prodigal Son.

Jed didn't have hard feelings, not really. Sometimes he got annoyed by Easton's superiority complex, and now was one of those times. "If I don't build it right, it'll just collapse again," he said. "The hay loft is fine for another couple of weeks."

"He can probably do both," Chris said.

"Not if I have to be out in the fields for calving," Jed said. Someone had to check them every hour. While Forrester Farms wasn't large enough to be termed a cattle ranch, they did have a fair few head on their land. Enough to keep three men busy—and they employed four others, as well as the part-time staff to work the corn maze.

Easton held up his hand, not that Chris or Jed had anything more to say. "We've got problems," he said.

"We do?" Chris asked, leaning forward. "What kind of problems?"

Jed leaned backward and steepled his fingers, listening and watching. Easton gave away so much just in his body language, and Jed knew someone had quit—someone who carried a huge weight around the farm—before Easton sighed.

"Amanda gave her two weeks' notice today," he said, his eyes now glued to something on his desk.

Jed gasped, though that might have been a bit overdramatic. It was better than Chris's shout of, "What?"

A legit shout, and Jed startled, his eyes flying to Chris's and then back to Easton. He wore a look of disapproval now, as if he had any right to be upset about Chris's reaction.

"Her daughter is leaving for school in January," he said. "She's relocating to be near her."

Jed frowned, though he knew Amanda's daughter had some special needs. She'd raised her alone for the past ten years or so, and she'd graduated in the spring. She hadn't started college right away, but she was now, apparently.

He couldn't help thinking that yet another blasted college had thrown a wrench into his life. Still, he cleared his throat and said, "Well, that's good for her, but bad for us."

"We need a new office administrator," Easton said with another overdramatic, overemphasized sigh. He finally looked up from the nonsense on his desk. "Do you guys have any idea of who we could hire?"

"How would we know?" Chris asked. "This is something you advertise for, East."

"I don't want to do that." His brother went back to studying folders, and Jed exchanged a glance with Chris. Chris nodded toward the desk, like Jed should say something.

His big mouth always got him in trouble, and he gave an almost imperceptible shake of his head. He didn't know what to say here.

Easton had fallen in love with their last office administrator—the one before Amanda. Then Bethany had skipped town with a man Forrester Farms had employed for three weeks, and the last Jed had heard, they were married with three or four kids.

His older brother had never really recovered. He dated here and there. He'd gone back to Jenni-Lynn Dennis a couple of times now, the most recent time only a few months ago at the Fourth of July picnic next door. But there was something between the two of them Jed didn't know about, and they'd never really gotten very serious.

"Jed," Chris muttered, and Jed took a deep breath. He had a very real feeling he was about to set off a bomb with himself still in the room.

"Cherry Cooper," he blurted out. "She might be lookin' for a new job, and she'd be real great here, East."

His brother looked at him, his hands frozen over something non-important. "Cherry Cooper?" he repeated, the words coated in disbelief. When he started laughing, embarrassment crept up Jed's spine and settled in his face in the form of heat.

"Don't be ridiculous," Easton said. "We're not hiring your out-of-town girlfriend." He looked at Chris, that conversation obviously over. "Who else?"

7

C herry opened Rissa's front door for her, saying, "Okay, got it," as her sister and Spencer came up the steps to the porch behind her. Sunday afternoon sunshine lit the whole world, and with baby Bronson in the carrier, everything in the whole state of Texas was right.

The whole world, actually, and Cherry hadn't experienced a glow like this in a long, long time.

Jed had had to cancel dinner with her last night, but she'd still gone. Everyone had been on their best behavior for some reason, and Cherry had escaped without having to answer too many questions. She'd texted Will and Lee about Jed anyway, and her oldest brother had come by the house while Cherry had been helping Mama wash and set her wigs.

She'd cleaned up the back porch and covered all the

furniture, put down the shades in the sun porch, and completed that task and other minor ones for Mama and Daddy. Jed had been silent most of the night, and when she'd finally asked him why, he'd said his two o'clock meeting had bled into the whole afternoon, evening, and night.

He'd tell her more today, if she could swing by the farm later.

As Rissa walked into her charming country home with her perfect husband, who carried their darling baby boy, Cherry wasn't sure if she could get away. She wanted to hold Bronson for a good long while so her sister could shower.

She'd make dinner too and do anything else Rissa and Spence needed. "I'll take him," she said, reaching for the carrier the moment Spencer entered the house. "I'll feed him and get dinner going. You guys go take a nap."

They both looked a little shell-shocked and one-hundred percent exhausted. Rissa sighed, her eyes filled with appreciative tears when she faced Cherry. "Thank you," she said. "I would like to shower."

"I'll nap while you do that," Spencer said to his wife. He turned back to Cherry from the mouth of the hallway as Rissa disappeared down it. "You sure you're okay?"

"Totally okay," Cherry said, almost anxious to be alone with the baby. Then, perhaps she could pretend that he was hers. Having a child of her own was one of the things

Cherry had given up six or seven years ago. Maybe even before that.

Now, though, she lifted the tiny, eight-pound human from his protective carrier and settled him into her arms. He grunted and groaned as if she'd disturbed him mightily, stretching one skinny arm above his head, and she cooed at him, smiling all the while.

Bronson settled quickly, and Cherry sank into the rocking chair Will and Travis had made for Rissa. They'd brought it over this morning, and Cherry began to hum as she toed herself and the baby back and forth softly.

Her eyes drifted closed, and such contentment filled her. Only the rhythmic sound of the chair on the hard wood floor sounded in the house, along with her breathing. Warmth from the baby seeped into her, and Cherry swore she heard choirs of angels singing.

Through all of that, keen understanding that the past was in the past filled her. Cherry sighed, the fight with herself finally over. She still had some hard conversations to have, but in that moment, with such a beautiful baby in her arms, she felt like she could say anything.

A light knock sounded on the door, and her eyes flew open. Lee entered, followed by Rosalie. "Hey," he whispered, his face filled with the same light Cherry felt inside her. "We just brought dinner."

Cherry nodded and said, "They went to nap and shower." She smiled at Rosalie, the perfect complement to Lee's gruffer personality. "Where's Ford?"

"We left him and Autumn at Will's," she said, perching on the edge of the couch nearest the rocking chair. "Thought they might be too noisy."

"Do you want to hold him?"

Rosalie definitely looked like she wanted to hold the baby, but she looked up at Lee as he came back into the living room. "No, you look so comfortable with him."

"You can feed him," Cherry said, though she did want to be the best auntie to this little boy. If she didn't live here, she had no idea how that would be possible. Rosalie would live right down the road. Gretchen and Shay too, and Cherry suddenly felt far more left out than she knew possible.

For so long, she'd chosen to be the black sheep. The sister who didn't live here, who didn't *want* to live here, who liked her freedom and independence in the city.

Her throat closed, and she stood and carefully passed baby Bronson to Rosalie. "I'll get his bottle." She met Lee's eyes, and they'd always been able to talk without saying a word. He followed her into the kitchen, where she set about the task of making a bottle.

As she had no children, she had to read the instructions on the side of the formula can, but she got the job done. "Here you go," she said, handing the bottle to Rose. She smiled at Cherry, not really seeing her, because the baby had blinded her.

Cherry knew how she felt.

"C'mon," Lee said under his breath. "Come talk to me out back."

Cherry went with him, her pulse shooting through her body at the speed of light. On the tiny back porch, she and Lee looked over the fields, now recently planted with their red winter wheat.

"You've got a snake in your belly," he said.

"I have to tell you something," she said. "Everyone." She swallowed. "But maybe I'll start with you, and then you can tell me what to do."

"I'm terrible at knowing what to do," Lee grumbled, but he looked at her, and his gaze held acceptance and love, and Cherry knew he'd do whatever he could to help her.

She linked her arm through his and said, "Don't look at me."

"My word," he growled, but he trained his eyes out on the fields. "Happy now?"

She wasn't, but it would be easier to talk if he didn't have his eyes boring into her. "Remember how I said there was more to me leaving Sweet Water Falls than Charlie?" Just mentioning her once-boyfriend made her skin grow cold.

"Yeah," Lee said. "I know you and Daddy sometimes don't—"

"It's not Daddy," Cherry said, cutting him off. She had no idea how to push these words out of her mouth. "I was upset one night," she said, wishing she hadn't. "It doesn't matter. I left when I found out I was pregnant."

Lee held very still. His breath hissed out of his mouth, no shape or syllable to it. "What?" he finally said.

Exactly, she thought. She'd never been married. Her parents would've been so disappointed in her. In her mid-thirties, she should know better, right? She knew how babies were made.

"I didn't want anyone to know," she said, familiar self-loathing creeping up her throat. "So I left. I was almost done with my master's degree, and I just thought...no one will have to know. Everything will be fine."

Lee looked at her, but Cherry leaned her cheek against his bicep so she wouldn't have to bear the weight of his gaze. "Cherry," he whispered. "You could've told me."

Those four words made her whole world better, and she smiled as tears rolled down her face. "I didn't want you to think badly of me."

"I don't," he said. "I wouldn't have."

"I was scared," she said, her voice too high and not even her own.

"I'll bet." He tightened his arm against his side, and in the next moment, turned and drew her into a hug. "No one else knows?"

"You're the first person I've told," she said.

"Even Mama?" he whispered.

"Even Mama." She couldn't even *imagine* telling her mother about her misdeeds.

"Where's the baby now?" Lee asked.

"I lost it," Cherry said. "Only a few weeks after I moved to San Antonio."

Lee exhaled again and held her right where she wanted to be. Safe within his arms. Safe with her brother. Safe and loved, no matter what.

There was a lot more to the story, but Lee didn't ask for the details. Cherry didn't want to talk about them. "Seeing that little baby just made everything...churn up, I guess." She stepped back and wiped her face. She blew out her breath as she faced the fields again. "Thank you, Lee."

"For what?"

"For saying I could've told you." She finally dared to look at him, and Lee wore compassion and worry on his face. "I want to come home."

He graced her with a warm smile. "Then come home."

"I need a job first."

"No, you don't. Just go pack up and come back. You'll find something."

Cherry moved into his side again, and it sure was nice having a tall, strong cowboy for a brother. Especially one as kind and wise as Lee. "You won't tell anyone, will you?"

"Not a soul," he said.

"Not even Rose," Cherry said.

"Not even Rose." He wouldn't either, Cherry knew that. Lee was a man of his word, and he was extraordinarily gifted at keeping secrets.

"All right," she said, breathing out a sigh. "Who's cooking tonight?"

"You're not?"

She looked at him, sure he was joking. "You're kidding," she said.

He chuckled and shook his head. "I thought you were. Rissa and Mama usually do, but…"

"I'll go get pizza," she said, an idea forming in her mind. "Can you guys stay and help with Bronson so Spence and Rissa can rest?"

"Yeah, sure," Lee said.

"Great." Cherry stretched up and kissed his cheek. "Love you, brother."

"I love you too, Cher."

She left him standing on the back porch, and she called in her order for pizza, salad, and breadsticks the moment she got behind the wheel of her car. She texted everyone in the family that she'd have dinner on the farmhouse table in a little over an hour, and then she texted Jed about joining her.

He called, which said Jed to her more than anything else he did. "I want to," he said instead of howdy. "But we're clearing the corn maze tonight to start to get it ready for our Christmas thing."

"All right," she said, a hint of frustration creeping through her. "How about I bring you some dinner, then?"

"You already brought breakfast yesterday."

"Yeah, and I haven't seen you since," she said, starting to feel some attitude. "Maybe you don't want to see me."

"Cherry, don't say that," he said with a sigh.

"What were you going to eat for dinner?"

"I don't know. Frozen pizza?"

"This'll be better than that," she said. "Just say no if you don't want me to come."

He didn't say anything, and Cherry smiled to herself. "All right, cowboy," she said. "I'll see you in a couple of hours."

"Cherry," he said, almost like he was afraid she might hang up on him. "Hurry."

"Yes, sir," she said, clearly flirting with him, and then she ended the call. She was starting to see a future for herself again. A future with a woman who had hopes and dreams, after a few years where she'd stopped allowing herself to think or imagine or hope for anything in her life beyond what she currently had.

But Sweet Water Falls, her family, the farm, that baby, and Jed... Yes, Cherry was ready to start dreaming again, and instead of running from the hometown she'd thought she hated, she wanted to return to it.

———

"PIZZA?" JED SAID WITH A LAUGH A FEW HOURS LATER. HE jogged the remaining distance between the two of them, took the two boxes of pizza she'd brought, and put them on the roof of her car.

He swept her into his arms, twirling her around. "You want me to fall in love with you, don't you?" he teased.

Cherry held onto those glorious shoulders and grinned at him. "Is that what it takes? A couple of pizzas?"

"It doesn't hurt," Jed said, smiling as he lowered his mouth to hers. He kissed her like he hadn't seen her in a month, not just over twenty-four hours. "Mm, you taste like chocolate."

"Guilty," she murmured against his lips. "Mama made her cookie pie."

"Tell me you brought that, and I'll ask you to marry me tonight." He searched her face, but Cherry laughed and shook her head.

"You'd have to fight off my brothers for leftover cookie pie," she said.

"Dang," Jed said good-naturedly. "I guess the proposal will have to wait." He reached for the boxes and led her toward his truck. He helped her up onto the tailgate, then flipped open a box of pizza, and pulled out a slice.

He ate it in silence, and Cherry just enjoyed being outside, in his presence, the scent of cheese and marinara floating on the air.

"I have to tell you somethin'," he said, real serious-like.

She looked at him, nerves pouncing through her chest. "Oh yeah?"

"Yeah." He wiped his mouth with a napkin from the

box. He couldn't look at her, and tension descended on the two of them. "I guess I'll just blurt it out."

"You're pretty good at doing that," she said, teasing him as she reached for his hand.

He squeezed her fingers tightly. "Forrester Farms needs a new office administrator, and I think you'd be perfect for it."

Cherry opened her mouth to respond, but she hadn't been expecting him to say anything like that. "Oh."

"Yeah." He sighed and reached for another piece of pizza.

"I thought you might be telling me one of your secrets."

Jed looked at her, and Cherry smiled. No, she wasn't just going to accept the job outright without thinking things through first. He was her boyfriend. This was his farm. He'd be her boss. All of that knotted and tangled inside her, and no. She wasn't going to accept the job right now. He hadn't even offered it to her.

He'd *told* her about it.

He chuckled and shook his head. "That wasn't a secret." He frowned. "Or maybe it was. I don't know. Easton said I shouldn't tell you, but Chris has been needling me since yesterday afternoon to offer you the job."

"So that's why you were distant last night," she said.

"I wasn't distant," he said. "I was arguing with Easton."

"Ah."

He finished his pizza and said, "We can swap secrets later if you want."

"Later? As opposed to just sitting here and doing it?"

"Yeah." He took out a third piece of pizza and hopped down from the tailgate. "Right now, I want to show you something." He offered her his free hand, and Cherry looked from it to his face. He wore a mischievous smile that went so well with his dark brown cowboy hat, that navy blue shirt, and those jeans. He was cowboy perfection, and he had to know it.

The thing with Jed was, he didn't.

So, wanting to go on an adventure with him, she put her hand in his and said, "All right, cowboy. Show me something."

8

Jed could've eaten three more pieces of pizza, but he'd felt awkward chowing down while Cherry sat there, her legs dangling from the tailgate of his truck. He felt fifteen again, ducking around the corner of the barn so no one would see him sneak a kiss with her.

She wore jeans that tapered to her ankle and a pair of shoes that couldn't go far on the farm. Her pink blouse slipped through his fingers, and she giggled against his mouth. "Is this what you wanted to show me? The side of the barn?"

"No," he said, gaining control of his hormones. "But it was nice, right?"

"Mm." Cherry looked up at him, happiness dancing in her eyes.

"You seem...different," he said, cocking his head

slightly to see her better. She ducked her head, which he could've predicted, and Jed backed up. "Come on." He took her hand and led her along the side of the barn. "So this is something I've been thinking about for a while."

"Is this one of your secrets?" She stumbled slightly behind him, but Jed didn't try to catch her. He'd already said something to push her away, and he wasn't going to act the knight now. It had only made her angry in the past.

He'd spoken true. She *was* different, but he couldn't put his finger on why or how. He did want to whisk her away from her life in San Antonio, but only if she wanted to come to Sweet Water Falls of her own volition.

"Yeah," he said. "It is." He paused suddenly and gripped her hand. "You can't tell anyone."

"I won't," she said, her breath coming in a couple of quick spurts. "Do we have to run there?"

He grinned at her. "You're never happy." He started walking again, slower this time.

"I am too," she argued back.

"You don't want to kiss me by the barn. I'm walking too fast," he said. "It's fine. I know I'm a pedal-to-the-metal guy, and you're not."

"Well, I hope not," Cherry said. "I'm not a guy at all."

"You know what I mean." He'd been teasing, but the conversation turned sober. "I like to go fast, and you're... more cautious."

"Only in some things," she said, refusing to give in to

him. He half-liked that and half-wanted her to just let him be right for once.

"You're doing it again," he said, keeping his eyes forward. He suddenly wasn't sure he wanted to show her his secret.

"Doing what?"

"Arguing with me about how the sky isn't blue."

Cherry said nothing, and a slip of vindication moved through Jed. The fact that she didn't argue meant he'd been right—about her moving slower than him and that she'd been arguing with him on purpose. She didn't mean to, he knew, and guilt seeped into him for feeling victorious that he'd called her out.

"You're not wearing the right shoes," he said, coming to a slower stop once more. "We can see it from here." He gazed past all the fields and cattle in front of him, his focus on the horizon.

Cherry, in the kind part of her heart, looked and waited. Looked some more, even going so far as to shield her eyes from the sinking sun in the south sky. "What am I lookin' at, Jed?"

He swallowed, the lump of fear really hard to get down far enough that he could speak. "I've been talkin' to Lady Jones for the past couple of years." His voice stuck in his throat, and he cleared it out. "Betty Jones?"

"I know the name," Cherry said, her grip firm against his.

"She owns all the land you can see way out there on the horizon."

"Back behind yours," she said, not asking.

"Yeah," he said. "Her husband died five or six years ago, and she's been doin' the best she can. I started helpin' her with some of her bigger tasks one day when I was out on the ATV checking the herd."

"Of course you did," Cherry said.

Jed filed that for now, but he wanted to ask her what she meant by that. Should he not help a neighbor who needed it? A widow, with grown children who'd left their ranch and not returned, even after their daddy's death? Betty had hired help, but it was never enough, a feeling Jed knew well.

"She's getting ready to sell, and she asked me if I wanted to buy her place."

Cherry pulled in a breath, but she didn't ask him if he was going to do it. The question sat there between them anyway.

"My secret is that I want to," he said quietly into the fading light. "I haven't talked to anyone about it yet—besides Betty. And now you."

"You should do it," Cherry said, and that got Jed's eyes off the dark line on the horizon. He focused on Cherry, his smile curving his lips.

"Yeah?" he challenged. "Why should I?"

"Because you'd be a great farm owner," she said.

"It's a ranch," he said. "And not cattle." He looked back out across the land he loved so much.

"What kind of ranch?"

"A rescue ranch," he said. "Right now, she takes in horses, cattle, ducks, pigs, anything really. Any animal that needs help, and she nurses it back to health. She just got a couple of llamas, and she's been over here, trying to figure out how to help them."

"You gave her Petals, didn't you?" Cherry asked, her tone as quiet and reverent as his.

He chuckled and ducked his head. "I'm that transparent, aren't I?"

She leaned her head against his arm and wrapped her other hand around the two of theirs already laced together. "Only to me," she said.

"My daddy has always said that I want to help creatures in need," Jed said, laying his head atop hers. "He's right. It's just this need in my soul."

"You should buy it, then," she said. "And not because you'd manage it well, but because those animals need you."

"Easton will be livid," Jed whispered. "And I have no one to work it with me. I'd have to hire a ton of people, and I don't know how to do that. *He* does that." Jed liked to think about the rescue ranch south of Forrester Farms, but that was all he could do: think about it.

"They need me here," he said.

"They'll make do without you," Cherry said firmly.

He stepped in front of her and turned his back on the land. "How do you know?"

"Because," she said, lifting one shoulder. He took her other hand in his, wishing they could fly away together up into the sky. "That's how the world works. We like to think we're indispensable, but we're not. You could leave this farm, and it might be hard for your brothers for a little bit, but they'd find someone else to do what you do, and then..." She shrugged again. "My job is the same. I like to think I'm good at my job—"

"You *are* good at your job," he said.

"Yeah," she said. "But that doesn't mean someone else can't be good at it too."

He tilted his head again, trying to catch the dying sunlight in her eyes. "Are you saying you're going to quit?"

She gave him a sly smile. "Jed," she said, plenty of flirtatiousness in her tone. "That's a secret."

"Oh, come on," he said, partly frustrated and partly enjoying this game. "I told you one of mine."

Her eyes blazed as they searched his face. She reached up and cradled his jaw in one hand, then the other. He let her hold him there, and the sweetest feeling of adoration moved through him. He felt it coming from her, for him, and as much as that thrilled him, it also surprised him.

This softer side of Cherry held many surprises, and he leaned down and kissed her. That, he knew, and that, she responded to in a predictable way. Jed didn't like the unpredictable, which was why he'd not mentioned Lady Jones's land to anyone.

He'd told her he'd talk to his daddy, and he would. Just not today.

Jed pulled away and leaned his forehead against Cherry's. "Did you mean I have a big heart when you said of course I helped Lady Jones?"

"Yes," she whispered.

Satisfied, he rejoined her at her side, the two of them silent and studying the horizon.

"I have a secret," she finally said, right when Jed's foot had started to fall asleep. He shifted it, and then turned the movement into a step. He turned around, and he and Cherry started making their way back to the parking lot where his truck, her car, and the pizza waited for them.

"Do tell," he said.

"I did a little job searching here in Sweet Water Falls yesterday. And today, while everyone was at church."

Jed kept his eyes trained on the ground, a smile blooming on his face. "That's great," he said.

"There's not much," she admitted. "But Mama needs me here, and I don't know how to be the best aunt in the world from San Antonio."

Jed chuckled. "That baby has you wrapped around his finger already."

"Yes," Cherry whispered. "But that's another secret, Jed. You don't get two in one day."

"Apparently, I do," he whispered back.

They neared the barn, and Cherry slowed. "Jed," she said, serious again.

He paused and looked at her as she tugged her hand away from his. "I'm forty-six, Jed. I can't have babies."

Jed blinked, nowhere near experienced enough with women to know how to respond to that. "All right," he said easily.

"All right?" She turned the fire on in her eyes, and Jed leaned closer, ready to get burned.

"Yeah," he said only inches from her face. "All right."

"You don't want kids?"

"I mean, I don't know. I've never really thought that much about it."

"Who'll inherit your rescue ranch?" she asked.

"Havin' kids doesn't guarantee you an heir," Jed said. "Look at Lady Jones. She has four kids, and none of 'em want that place."

The fight went out of Cherry, but a very important conversation had just happened. Jed slid his hands in his pockets, ready to explore this further. They started along the side of the barn again, and as they approached the corner he'd ducked around earlier to kiss her, he said, "You realize you just asked me if I'm okay not having any kids with you, right?"

"I—"

"Like we'll be together," Jed said. "In the future. Married. But you can't have kids, so we won't be able to have any." He refused to look at her. "And you wanted to know if I'm okay with that, right?"

She said nothing, which was irritated-Cherry-speak for *yes*.

"So I just want you to know I'm okay with that," he said. "And if you wanted a baby, I'd do whatever I could to get you one."

"How would you do that, Jed?" she asked, a slice of acid in the question.

"Adoption," he said simply. They made it past the barn and continued down the road. The parking lot beside the corn maze—which Chris was still plowing under—had street lamps that cast down pools of light.

"Thank you for the pizza, ma'am," he said when they reached her car. "Did you want to take the extra home with you?"

"No," she said quietly.

Jed touched her face, which brought it up, and he tucked her hair behind her ear. "Why are you sad?"

"Why do you ask such hard questions?" she fired back at him.

When Jed was afraid of losing her, shutting her down, or making her go silent, he'd laugh and duck his head. Now, though, he gazed back at her and waited.

"I don't deserve you," she said.

"Funny," he said. "I was just thinkin' the same thing about you." He pulled her flush against him and whispered, "Please don't be sad. I hate it when you're sad."

"You can't fix me, Jed," she said back, something she'd told him previously. Several times.

"I know that," he said. "I'm not trying to fix you, Cherry. I just want to know why me sayin' I want to be with you, whether we can have kids in the future or not, makes you sad."

"It doesn't," she said. "It makes me happy."

"You don't look happy."

She stepped back, her smile soft and silky, and Jed wanted to taste it and hold it against his heart. "I am," she said. "I'm just working through some things."

"You can stay in cabin four any time you need to," he said. "The offer is open, as is the cabin."

She nodded and looked past him to the nearly mown down corn field. "It's not that."

"Then what?" He slipped his fingers through the belt loops on her jeans and brought her against him again. "Tell me how to help you."

Cherry looked up at him and said, "Keep being you, Jed. That's all I need from you."

He nodded, sure that wasn't true. *He* was the lucky one in this relationship, and *he* was the one who didn't deserve her. "Will you think about the job here?" he asked in one final feat of bravery.

"I already am," she said. "Will you send me Easton's number?"

"Oh, I didn't do that yet?" Jed whipped out his phone

and sent her his brother's number, wondering what hive of bees he'd just knocked out of the tree.

Her phone chimed, the sound mingling with her giggle. "Good night, cowboy." She opened her door, but Jed stepped in front of her so she couldn't get in.

"You can't go until I know when I'll see you again," he said.

Their eyes met, the moment powerful, and Cherry said, "I'm helping Mama in the morning. What does lunchtime look like for you tomorrow?"

"Lunchtime looks like kissin' behind the barn," he said with a grin.

Cherry shook her head, though delight danced in her eyes. "You're impossible."

"You know, we don't have to always have a meal to see each other."

"I know," she said. "But Daddy's grilling steak tomorrow night too, and I'm sure he'd love to see you."

Jed snorted, the sound morphing into a laugh. "Yeah, I'm sure that's what he's thinking."

"If you can come," she said. "We eat about five-thirty."

Jed moved out of the way so she could get in her car, which she did. They didn't make plans for who'd cook or bring lunch. Cherry would, and they both knew it. She'd come to his place, and Jed would only need to show up.

He waved to her as she left the parking lot and headed down the road and around the corner out of sight.

Half an hour later, he'd just walked into Chris and

Deb's when his phone rang. His stomach sank to his boots, but he managed to get the extra pizza box onto their kitchen counter while the twins shouted his arrival.

"Just a sec, guys," he said to them, laughing. "I have to answer Uncle Easton." He swiped on the call and escaped out the back door of the house amidst whining and crying from Dylan and Drake. "Howdy, East."

"Did you give Cherry Cooper my number?" his brother demanded, and Jed caged his sigh. He didn't have to bow to his brother; he wasn't king.

"Yep," he said with plenty of pop on the P. "She'd be perfect for this job, Easton, and we need her."

His brother sighed and said, "Fine. She's interviewing on Thursday, and you better be there."

"Fine," Jed said, not willing to apologize for this. At the same time, his stomach jolted and flipped, because while he wanted Cherry back in Sweet Water Falls, he couldn't help wondering if working right there at Forrester Farms was a little too...close.

9

Clarissa Rust woke when she heard Bronson fussing. She slid from underneath the comforter, Spencer's breathing staying even and strong. He'd gone back to work on the farm where they lived that morning, and she didn't want him to have to be exhausted when he left again in a few hours.

Across the hall, she scooped the baby boy into her arms, shushing him quietly. She began to hum as she tucked him against her chest. A certain smell told her he needed to be changed, and she quickly darted across the hall to close her bedroom door, and then Bronson's. He didn't like being changed, as he had a bit of diaper rash already, but she couldn't leave him as he was.

She switched on the small lamp beside the rocking chair and laid him on the changing table. It had been hers, and Mama had stored it in one of the sheds for all these years, finally pulling it out over the summer when she'd learned of Clarissa's pregnancy.

So much love filled the room, and Clarissa worked quickly to get Bronson changed, clean, with ointment on, and re-diapered. He screamed through it, of course, and she hastened to wrap him back into a tight bundle.

"Need help?" Spencer asked behind her, and she turned toward him.

"No," she whispered. "Sorry. I tried to do it fast so you wouldn't wake up."

He approached her, his hand sliding along her lower back, as she lifted Bronson back into her arms. The boy settled now, his eyes wide open as he sought his daddy's voice.

"Hey, bud," Spencer said softly, reaching with his free hand to stroke the boy's flimsy hair on top of his head.

"He was just messy, and now he needs to eat." Clarissa leaned into the strength of her husband. "You can't do that, so just go back to bed."

"All right," he said, but he didn't move. "I can feed him before I go out in the morning. Then you can sleep in."

"Okay," she agreed. They'd been doing a mix of breast and bottle feeding, as Clarissa still had things to do around the shoppe here at Sweet Water Falls Farm. She hadn't done much the past couple of weeks, and the hours slipped through her fingers like smoke since she'd brought her baby home only a few days ago.

Spencer left the room, and Clarissa sank into the

padded rocking chair in the corner of the nursery. Her brothers had made one for the living room, and she sat there in the afternoons and napped while Bronson did the same thing in her arms.

Tonight, after she got him eating, she closed her eyes and rocked gently. She loved this quiet time in the middle of the night between her and her son. She let her mind go wherever it wanted, but as she couldn't get up and *do* anything, it had become a time of reflection for her.

Right now, she thought of Cherry. Her sister slept down the road and around a couple of corners at the farmhouse where they'd grown up together. Cherry hadn't done that in so long, and Clarissa felt some measure of peace when she pictured Cherry at home now.

Bless her, she thought. *With clarity and purpose.* Her sister wanted to do the right thing, Clarissa knew. She just didn't always know what that was. Clarissa didn't either, which was why she relied on others to help her. Spencer, Mama, Daddy, and the Lord.

Cherry had told her she had a job interview that day, but she'd refused to say where. She came over every day, usually about mid-morning, with Mama. They helped Clarissa with her house, with meals, and with Bronson, and then Cherry took Mama home about lunchtime. Their mother couldn't do much more than that, and Daddy had said she'd been napping most of the afternoon each day this week.

Clarissa had told Cherry last night not to bring her.

She needed to rest, and they'd have a quiet house all day since the family didn't gather for dinner on Thursday nights. Cherry had agreed, and she'd then told Clarissa about the job interview.

Cherry never made big family announcements, so Clarissa wasn't sure how many people knew her sister wanted to return to Sweet Water Falls. Lee probably did, as he and Cherry had always been close. Will might too, as Cherry spoke with him about her career a lot. Travis... Clarissa wasn't sure about him.

She was the last Cooper child, with Travis just older than her, so she was close to him. But Cherry and Travis had always had some rift between them Clarissa didn't understand. They were the more competitive Coopers, and she suspected that was it. That, and Travis didn't go out of his way to maintain friendships—at least not with Cherry.

Once Bronson had finished eating, she laid him in her lap and told him what a good baby he was. His pupils were so large in the dim light—they were anyway—and she couldn't wait to watch her newborn become a baby, and then a toddler.

She pressed a kiss to his face and placed him back in the crib. He gurgled and grunted at her, but she left him there to go back to sleep. Tomorrow, he'd be a full week old, and Clarissa's life had changed drastically in such a short amount of time.

She climbed back into bed, and Spencer rolled over,

obviously not asleep. He gathered her into his arms, and she breathed in the male, musky scent of his skin. "Okay?" he asked.

"Yes," she whispered, her eyes closed again. "You're warm."

"Mm."

Clarissa counted him as her greatest blessing, and she fell asleep in the safety of her husband's arms. When she woke, the sunlight streamed through the window to her left, and the scent of coffee hung in the air.

She didn't hear a baby crying, which made her smile. She got up, brushed her teeth, and put on a pair of sweats with a matching sweatshirt. She found Spencer in the kitchen, their baby strapped to his chest, as he fried eggs.

"Then you just flip 'em," he said to Bronson, whose head looked bent at a ninety-degree angle and who faced Spencer's chest, not the stove. He flipped the eggs while she watched, her smile growing.

He put the eggs on a plate and turned, catching sight of her. "Hey, sweetheart." He smiled at her, and she didn't move from where she leaned against the corner of the wall in the hall. "Did you want breakfast?"

"Not fried eggs," she said, pushing away from the wall. "I'll just take coffee."

"You have to eat more than coffee in the mornings now."

She knew that, and she set a couple of pieces of wheat toast just for him. Her appetite in the morning was almost nothing, but she forced herself to eat enough to satisfy Spencer, then she took Bronson from him, kissed him, and waved to him from the front porch as he swung into his old white truck to go to work.

Inside, she bathed Bronson, who liked the warm water and her singing and smiling at him—until the ointment had to go on his diaper rash. "I know, buddy," she said, pure agony pulling through her. Parenthood had brought a whole new range of emotions, and she wished she could take the pain from her son. She'd have done it gladly.

She'd just returned from a walk when Cherry's dark sedan pulled up. Her sister jumped from the car saying, "I've got him, Riss. Have you showered today?"

Clarissa straightened from the stroller, where she'd been bent over to unclip Bronson. "Not yet," she said. "We just went on a walk." Cherry wore a beautiful blouse in black, with white, cream, and gray circles swirling around. Her professional black slacks went well with it and the pair of heels on her feet.

Clarissa had always been jealous of Cherry's clothes, as her sister had such great fashion sense—and the money to buy the clothes she wore to work.

"Did you go to the interview already?" Clarissa asked as her sister lifted Bronson from the stroller. "Because he's going to puke everywhere and ruin that blouse."

Cherry grinned like she couldn't wait for that to happen and put the baby over her shoulder. "I'm finished, yes."

"And?" Clarissa started up the steps after Cherry, leaving the stroller out front. She usually folded it and leaned it against the house, but her interest had focused somewhere else already.

"It went great," Cherry said, her tone cheerful. "I don't know if I'll get it, but I felt good about it."

Inside the house, Clarissa closed the door as Cherry sank into the wooden rocking chair their brothers had made. "Are you going to tell me where it was?"

Cherry grinned at Bronson, then switched her joy to Clarissa. She hadn't seen her sister like this in years. Over a decade. Even when Clarissa had gone to San Antonio and stayed with Cherry while she looked for a chef job, she hadn't seen her sister like this.

She'd never beamed this level of happiness, even before she'd left town. When she'd dated Charlie, she'd clearly been pretending to be happy.

Clarissa couldn't help smiling back at her, and she sat down on the couch and crossed her legs. "You seem so happy, Cherry."

Her smile slipped a little, and she looked back at the baby. "I am," she said.

"So where was the job interview?"

Cherry looked up again, this time looking out the window next to the front door. "Forrester Farms."

Clarissa sucked in a breath. "What? You're going to work a farm? Cherry, you can do that here."

"Not work their farm," she said, switching her gaze

back to Clarissa. "Their office administrator is quitting. The job interview was for that."

Clarissa searched her sister's face. "I don't understand," she said slowly. "You could also do that here. Lee would probably be so grateful for the help, and everyone knows how organized and detail-oriented you are."

"I already talked to Lee about it," Cherry said. "I know I could work here. I know he'd be happy about it. The fact is, I don't want to work here."

"Why not?" Clarissa asked. "It's not that bad." It wasn't bad at all. Clarissa loved what she did on the family farm, as it brought things to people's lives they needed. Sure, just ice cream and spreadable cheese, but that was enough for her.

"I might have a mental roadblock about it," Cherry said. "I can admit that. I do want to come home, but it feels...cheap? for me to just step into a job here just so I can do that."

Clarissa didn't understand, but then again, she'd never really understood Cherry's reasons for why she did what she did. "What about Jed?" she asked.

"What about him?" Cherry stroked her fingertips lovingly along Bronson's head. "He was in the interview. He told me about the job."

"He wants you to come back."

"Of course he does."

Clarissa smiled at her sister, who refused to look at her. "He's in love with you."

Cherry burst out laughing, which surprised Bronson, who started crying. "Oh, baby," she cooed at him, bouncing him in her arms while she giggled in a quieter manner. "I'm sorry to scare you. Hush now."

He quieted down, but Cherry's eyes still danced with merriment. "He's not in love with me."

"Yet," Clarissa said, folding her arms. "So. Will you take that job?"

"If they offer it to me, yeah, I'd take it." Cherry's smile waned. "Why wouldn't I?"

"Mixing business with pleasure," she said. "It's not always smart."

"Jed says he hardly goes into the office there. It's Easton I have to deal with." Cherry rolled her eyes then. "And he's no picnic, let me tell you."

"None of those Forresters are," Clarissa said, grinning again. "Chris is the nicest one, which is why he's married when his two older brothers aren't."

"I like Jed," Cherry said.

"Sure, I know," Clarissa said. "Because he's saltier than you, and you need someone like that to put up with your sass."

Cherry rolled her eyes again. "I'm here holding your baby so you can shower. Go do that instead of insulting me."

"I wasn't insulting you," Clarissa said, giggling as she got to her feet. "You *are* kind of sassy." She stepped over to Cherry and kissed the top of her head. "It's what I love most about you." She leaned down and looked right into her sister's eyes. "And he should too. He's not making you into someone different, is he?"

"No," Cherry said, the word simply falling from her mouth. She looked a little shell-shocked for a moment. She blinked, and the life roared back into her face. "I get to be as sassy as I want with Jed, and he puts up with it."

"Good," Clarissa said, turning to go shower. "I'll be back in a few minutes."

"All right," Cherry said, and Clarissa paused the moment she was out of sight down the hallway. She heard Cherry say, "I'm not too sassy for Jed, baby Bronson."

She smiled to herself, because she'd stumbled upon Cherry telling her baby boy secrets several times over the past few days.

"He's probably *too* nice to me," Cherry mused. "I'll have to talk to him about that."

Of course, Clarissa thought. Even when the man was clearly trying to tame his inner beast to be with Cherry, she wasn't satisfied.

"Now, don't you tell anyone," Cherry said next, and since Bronson couldn't talk, he wouldn't. Clarissa leaned forward so she could see her sister. She gazed down at the sleeping infant, pure joy in the part of her face Clarissa could see. "But I'm going to put in my two weeks' notice on Monday, whether I have a job here or not. I have to be the best aunt in the world, and I can't do that from San Antonio."

Happiness galloped through Clarissa, and she headed down the hall to take that shower. Cherry would make the move without a job, but that didn't mean she'd like it. "If she can get a job first," she said to her reflection, as if she had any control over that. "That would be ideal. Help her to get a job first."

After all, Clarissa just wanted what was best for her sister, and that was clearly to be here with her family. Maybe it had taken a baby to bring her home, but Clarissa didn't care. Stranger things had happened than a baby bringing a family back together, and she just wanted her sister to be happy.

So if that meant she got to tend to Bronson every day, or if she got the job at the farm next door, or she married the handsome Jed Forrester, Clarissa didn't care. As long as Cherry was happy.

10

C herry made the turn onto the lane that led to the corn maze, the same way she had over a week ago. No cars sat in the parking lot today, and in fact, all of the corn had been plowed under. She went past all of that and turned left down another dirt road that had cabins lining both sides of it.

She glanced at cabin four, where she'd stayed previously. This time, she'd slept all nine nights here in Sweet Water Falls at the farmhouse. She'd left Mama and Daddy on the front porch, both of them weeping and sniffling, with promises that she'd call when she got home to San Antonio and that she'd be back real soon.

"Real soon," she murmured now, Jed's cabin growing larger as she approached. He came out onto the porch as she came to a stop, a smile on his face that said he didn't want to have this conversation.

Well, she didn't want to either.

She still got out of the car and went up the steps. "Hey," she said.

"On your way?" He nodded the brim of that sexy cowboy hat toward her car.

"Yeah," she said. Easton had not called about the job yet. She'd not interviewed for anything else. She was due at work tomorrow morning, and she didn't know how to not show up. She had to go back to San Antonio and pack up her house. Get her cats. Cancel utilities and memberships at a gym. All kinds of things.

She couldn't just stay here, though she wanted to.

She stepped into Jed's arms, glad when he sighed and held her against his chest. "I miss you already," she whispered.

"I hate it when you say stuff like that," he said, no softness in his tone.

"Why?" She pulled away. "Most people like knowing they're going to be missed."

His jaw worked as his dark eyes searched hers. "I don't know. I just...hate goodbye."

"I'll be back in two weeks for Thanksgiving."

"Yeah." He looked past her now, out onto his farm. "I know."

She didn't like the boiling in her stomach any more than he did. She had no idea how he actually felt, but from the way he was acting this morning, it wasn't good.

"Have you talked to Easton?" She cleared her throat, hating the question the moment it got voiced.

"He said he's got another couple of interviews." Jed clipped the words out, which indicated his anger. Cherry had thought about telling him one of her secrets this morning—a small one. Nothing too big or heavy.

Now, she just wanted to leave. Instead of giving into that, however, Cherry put her hands on Jed's waist and then ran them up his chest. He looked at her, mild surprise in his eyes. "If I don't get the job here, it's okay," she said. She hitched a smile to the end of the statement. "Want to know why?"

He swiped her hair back off her face, letting the cooler air have a shot at her neck. He dropped his eyes there, softening like a brick of butter in the microwave. "Why?"

"It's a secret," she said, lowering her voice to a whisper.

Jed leaned closer, his other hand moving along her back and bringing her closer to him. "I like secrets."

Cherry smiled to herself, too close to Jed for him to see it. She didn't want to leave with this tension between them. She wanted no regrets when she finally got behind the wheel of her car and waved to this handsome cowboy.

"I already texted my boss, and we have a meeting set for tomorrow morning." Her mouth touched his earlobe as she whispered her secret, and he shivered. Oh, Cherry liked having that power over him, as much as she tried not to think of it like that.

"Are you quittin'?" he whispered back.

"Oh, now that would be two secrets in less than a minute," she said, falling back and gripping the collar of his denim jacket in both of her hands. She grinned up at him. "You have to tell me one of yours before I spill another one."

He smiled at her, and the heavens opened with rays of beautiful light. Before he could say anything, she stretched up and kissed him. The soft hair of his beard tickled her face, and he kissed her back with plenty of energy and enthusiasm, unlike their first kiss when she'd arrived several days ago.

"I don't want you to go," he said, his voice soft and low.

"That's not a secret," she said.

"Sure it was," he said. "I don't like sayin' stuff like that out loud, because then you close off. So I've been keepin' it a secret."

Cherry giggled and watched her hands as she slid them down his chest and back up. No shivers that time, but she sure did like touching him. She looked up as she sobered, and Jed's smile slipped away too. "I don't mean to close off," she said. "This...letting people in—a man." She blew out her breath. "Letting in a man is hard for me. Keeping them out is easy. It's my default. I'm trying."

"I know you are," he said simply. A moment later, another grin kicked up the corners of his mouth. "Was that the second secret?"

She smiled too, but some of her melancholy had eased back into her heart. "No," she said. She exhaled again as she stepped out of his arms. "I think I've said enough for today."

"Oh, come on." He grabbed onto her hand as she pulled it back. "You don't have to go yet." He brought her back into the circle of his arms easily, because she wanted to be there. "Once, when I was a little boy, I wanted to ride horses, but my daddy said no. I snuck away from my chores and saddled up anyway."

"You devil," she said, and he chuckled. "What happened?"

"Nothing happened," he said. "I did my ride, and I put the horse back in the stable. I finished my chores. No one ever said anything to me about it."

"Hmm," she said. "Usually when we disobey like that, something bad happens. You know, the horse breaks his leg or something."

"Yeah," Jed said. "Not this time." He shrugged and blinked his way out of his memory. "That's a secret, I guess."

"Kind of a lame one," she teased, just to get him to smile again, which he did.

"Tell me another of yours then."

"All right," she said, fiddling with his collar now. "Even though I moved to San Antonio twelve years ago." She swallowed and kept going. "And I've been dating like professors and counselors and whatnot, I've never seen myself with someone like that."

"No? Who do you see yourself with then?"

"A cowboy," she said, flicking her eyes up to his and back to his perfectly flat collar. "I'm not even sure I've admitted it out loud to myself."

"Well, you just did, sweetheart." He put one finger under her chin and lifted it so he could kiss her. She sank into his touch and matched his movement, desperate to tell him so much more but not having the courage or the words right now. He pulled away and asked, "Why do you want a cowboy?"

"I don't know," she said, trying to catch her breath. "I guess I believe that a cowboy will always be there for me when I need him. He'll let me be strong when I'm strong, and he'll rescue me when I'm not."

She offered him a small smile, and Jed lifted her hand and kissed the back of it. His eyes never left hers, and she fell a little bit more in love with him. Standing right there, on his farm, in the country silence, she fell and fell.

"I should go," she said, hoping those words would catch her.

"Cherry," he said, and she paused at the seriousness in that deep, gorgeous voice. "I can't imagine a time when you'll need saving, but if one does come, I'd be honored to ride up on my trusty steed and rescue you."

She grinned at him, but he didn't return it. Maybe Clarissa was right, and this man was already in love with her. She pushed against the thought, because she couldn't deal with it right now. "Like you're a prince? And I'm a princess?"

"Yeah," he said real serious. "Just like that."

She kissed him again, because he was morphing into a prince to her, and she wanted to see if he'd taste any differently. He didn't, and she eased out of his arms and behind the wheel. She buckled her belt, waved goodbye, and drove away while he stood on his porch.

When she hit the Interstate, she finally allowed herself to say, "He's your cowboy prince, Cherry. Don't drive him away." She'd done that before, and she didn't want to repeat her mistakes.

———

"CHERRY," DR. FREEMAN SAID AS HE ENTERED HIS OFFICE. "What are you doing here?"

"We have a meeting this morning," she said, rising to her feet. She was back in her cutest, most professional clothes—a green wrap-around skirt with big buttons down the front of it and a butter-colored blouse with tiny black dots. The heels on her feet felt foreign after over a week of sneakers and sandals, but she still knew how to stand and walk in them. "Remember I texted you on Friday morning?"

"Right," he said, though he'd clearly forgotten. He sat behind his desk with a sigh. "Well, what can I do for you?"

Cherry had pictured the meeting going differently. She'd tell him her idea for leaving SATC and all the veterinary students she counseled here, and he'd beg her to stay. He'd never looked at her with any romantic interest whatsoever, despite her multiple attempts over the years to catch his eye.

He wasn't married; no children. He simply wasn't interested in her. Jed was.

Her ideas to probe him and see if she could get a raise or a better office went right out the window. She didn't retake her seat, but instead stood in front of his desk. "I hate to say this," she said, her voice shaking slightly at what she was about to do and say. Dr. Freeman didn't even look away from his computer, and his mouse kept going *click, click, click.*

"But my last day needs to be that Tuesday before Thanksgiving."

That got him to stop checking his email or whatever occupied his attention on the screen. "What? You're quitting?"

"This is my two weeks' notice," she said. "My mama isn't well, and I'm needed in Sweet Water Falls." She nodded like that was that, because it kind of was. She'd have to start stopping by the grocery store on her way home from work and getting boxes. She'd have to pack everything she owned. Put her house up for sale. Figure out where she'd live in Sweet Water Falls that would allow three cats—none of whom were outdoor felines. Mister Whiskers would freak out, and Cherry would probably have to take him to the vet to get some sort of travel sedative for cats.

Her to-do list suddenly doubled, then tripled, and her boss hadn't even said anything yet.

"I—" Dr. Freeman stood too, his dark eyes confused. "Do you not like the job?"

"I like it fine," she said. "My mother has been ill for a very long time." She certainly wasn't going to get into all the complicated reasons she'd stayed away for the past seven years of Mama's illness. "This has nothing to do with the job here, other than it's over two hours to my folks', and I need to be closer."

Dr. Freeman's mouth opened and closed. "All right," he finally said. "I hate to lose you, Cherry. You're so amazing here."

"Well, thank you, Doctor Freeman," she said. "I will have to look for something in Sweet Water Falls. Could I get a letter of recommendation from you?"

"Of course," he said. "Are there any colleges there?"

"No, sir," she said. "A high school. Maybe I can work for the city or a Boys and Girls Club." She had been thinking about her employment options for several days now, but again, Dr. Freeman didn't need that information.

"We'll miss you greatly here." He looked and sounded sincere, and Cherry appreciated that.

She told him as much, and then said she'd find the paperwork she needed to file and get that done with the college. Then she walked out of her boss's office, her step lighter and her heart happier than they'd been in a very long time.

That evening, after she'd finished cleaning up after her meal of take-out Chinese food—she'd hardly eaten out in Sweet Water Falls as the farm sat so far from town—and she'd sprayed the citrus linen air freshener to get rid of the soy sauce smell, she sank onto her couch.

She wore sweats with a leopard print on them, and she remembered a strange, out-of-the-blue question Jed had asked her at Travis's wedding.

Do you own any sweat pants?

She grinned and texted him. *Guess what I'm wearing?*

This sounds dirty, he sent back. Her phone rang, and she answered his call instantly. He was already laughing, and he said, "I don't think a man should ever answer that when a woman asks it."

"Get your mind out of the gutter," she teased. "I have on sweats. Remember when you asked me if I owned any?"

"Did I?"

"You did," she said. "At Trav's wedding. You wanted to know if I was normal or not."

"Wow, and you still went out with me?" He chuckled, and Cherry wished she could be in the same physical space as him.

"I can send you a picture if you'd like."

"Cherry," he said, his laughter fading. He didn't say anything else, and Cherry took a deep breath. "All right," she said, blowing most of it out. "You're the first to know, because you're bullying it out of me. I was going to tell Mama and Daddy first, but—"

"I'm not bullying anything out of you," he said, and she couldn't tell if he was upset or not, because she couldn't see his eyes.

"I quit my job today."

Several beats of silence marched by, and Cherry couldn't stop smiling.

"You quit your job today," Jed repeated.

"That's right," she said, getting up as Feathers swiped her paw against the bell hanging from the back door. "My last day is the Tuesday before Thanksgiving. Then I'm going to move to Sweet Water Falls soon after that."

"I—wow."

Cherry paused at the back door while Feathers ran out. She liked to torment the chickens next door, and sure enough, she stalked straight toward the coop that butted up against the fence between Cherry's yard and her neighbor's. "You don't sound as happy about this as I anticipated you being."

"I *am* happy about it," he said.

"But..." She waited, because there was a great big "but" between them.

"But nothing," he said, a forced lightness to his voice now. "I'm thrilled. Maybe in shock a little. I'm sorry, baby. Of course I'm happy about this." He laughed, and it sounded partly nervous and partly joyful.

Cherry didn't know what to do now, because she'd

thought he'd "Yeehaw!" over the phone, which would've made her laugh, and then they could plan how the prince and the princess could sail off into happily-ever-after.

She really needed to get out of her fantasies sooner. They only made living real life more disappointing.

"Okay," she said, not wanting to talk to him anymore. "I'm going to call my parents."

"Cherry," Jed said.

"I'll talk to you later, okay?"

"Okay," he said, and Cherry hung up a microsecond later. Her chest stung, but she dialed Daddy's number anyway.

"Hey, Cherry-blossom," he said. "You make it back okay?"

"Yes, sir," she said, her voice quivering in a way she hated. She pulled back on her emotions. "Is Mama awake?"

"We just sat down to dinner," he said. "Everyone's here. Want to say hello?"

She didn't, but Daddy didn't understand that. He'd never been one to step out of the spotlight the way Cherry did. "You're on speaker," he said. "Say hi to everyone."

"Heya, Cherry," several voices chorused, and she picked out Lee's, of course. Shay too, and she'd always had a special connection with Travis's wife.

Tears pricked her eyes, and another fantasy played at the front of her mind. "Hi everyone," she said when their greeting had died down. "I guess I have some news for y'all." She drew in a deep breath and heard a tiny cry from a tiny human.

Bronson. She loved that baby so much, and a brand-new reason for quitting and moving home filled her vision.

"I quit at SATC today," she said, making her voice loud and clear. "When I come home for Thanksgiving, I'm going to look for somewhere to live and a new job."

Only a single second of silence stood on the other end of the line, and then rowdy cheering blasted into her ear. Someone whistled, and they surely all had to be clapping, and Cherry let her tears fall down her face as her family—the very people she'd run from twelve years ago—cheered at the news of her return.

Then Lee's voice came into her ear. "I took you off speaker," he yelled, because there was still plenty of chatter and laughter and applauding going on behind him. "Cherry, I'm so glad you're doing this."

"It's time," she said, not caring that her voice cracked. Not with Lee.

"Love you, sis," he said.

"Love you too, little brother."

She ended the call, and her house suddenly felt too quiet and too still. "Why didn't Jed react that way?" she wondered, and then her attention got snatched by her neighbor yelling at Feathers to leave his chickens alone.

She yanked open the back door and called her cat. The feline came streaking toward her, and Cherry lifted her hand in apology to the man next door. He waved back to her too—*no harm, no foul*—and she went back inside, sealing Feathers in the house with her.

Jed called, but Cherry silenced her phone. He couldn't take back his lackluster reaction. He didn't get a do-over. The real question was why wasn't he more excited to have her in Sweet Water Falls permanently?

"Maybe it's all been a show," she murmured as she reached for one of the boxes she'd gotten at the grocery store that day. "He likes the idea of this forbidden, long-distance relationship."

And if she came home, that element of their relationship wouldn't exist anymore.

11

J ed paced the length of his porch, his frustration inching higher and higher with every breath he took. "Pick up the phone, Cherry," he muttered as his fingers typed the same words. He'd called three times now, and she'd obviously silenced her phone. So she wouldn't get his text either.

I was just surprised, he said. *I didn't realize you were really going to quit. I thought you'd want a job here first, that's all.*

Easton had made it very clear that he didn't want to hire Cherry. Jed had stopped by his brother's office that afternoon, and Easton had said those exact words—*I don't want to hire her.*

They'd argued, of course. Cherry was the perfect candidate for the job, but her relationship with Jed made things too complicated.

Easton thinks it would be unwise to hire you here. I'm so sorry. I'm upset with him, and Peanuts hurt his hoof, and Fish ran off, and today's been a terrible day, and I just didn't react well.

Jed collapsed into a chair on his front porch, feeling it wobble a little. That wasn't good. Needed to be fixed. He was so tired, though, and he couldn't see past his phone. He reached out and patted Fish, his black lab, but he didn't look away from Cherry's text string. She just had to answer.

Finally, after several long minutes, a message popped up. *Did Fish come back?*

Relief sprang up inside Jed, and he hurried to say, *Yeah, he's right here. The devil.*

Will Peanuts be okay?

Doc Mortimer is coming tomorrow, he sent to her.

I talked to Easton just now, she said. *It's fine. I can find something else.*

I'm sorry.

His phone rang, and Jed dang near dropped it in his haste to swipe on Cherry's call. "Hey," he said. "I'm so sorry. I'm so happy you're moving here. Where are you going to live? You can have cabin four."

She laughed, and Jed relaxed into the seat back behind him. Laughing was good when it came to Cherry.

"I'm not going to live in cabin four," she said. "Can you imagine? Your brother didn't even think it would be a good idea for us to work on the same property together.

He'll blow a fuse if he finds out I'm living half a block from you."

Jed sighed, because she was probably right. He hated that his brother could influence his life so much. But right now, Easton could. "So where?"

"I don't know," she said. "I'm thinking closer to town. I can drive out to Mama's easily. I'll probably get a job in town."

"Yeah." He sighed. "Cherry, I'm thrilled—*thrilled*—you're going to be here."

"I know you are, cowboy."

"You do?"

"I mean, I figured," she teased. "Are you thrilled to help me move in December?"

"Oh, yeah," he said in a deadpan. "Can't wait for that."

She laughed again, and a smile finally formed on Jed's face. Today really had been a horrible day and talking to her made it better. "You're not...disappointed our relationship won't be secret or forbidden?"

"No," he said quickly, frowning. He reached up and removed his cowboy hat to scrub his hair. "We can still sneak around the barn to kiss if you want."

"I think that's for you," she said.

He chuckled. "Yeah, probably." He let out a sigh and rubbed Fish as the dog pressed into him. His chair gave against the extra weight, but he balanced it. "Anything I can do for you here in town?"

"I'm not sure yet."

Jed's feet came off the ground as Fish pushed into him further, and then he couldn't keep his balance. He yelped as the ear-splitting sound of cracking wood filled the sky, and then he landed hard on his backside on the porch.

"Jed?" Cherry called, but her voice wasn't at his ear anymore. He'd thrown his phone somewhere. "Jed!"

He groaned, not sure he could get his voice to work. "I'll call you back," he yelled and not a moment later, Fish licked his face. "Fish, back *up*." He pushed against the dog's chest, and he moved only to come right back into Jed's personal space.

The canine wore such a look of anxiety that Jed took a moment and said, "All right, bud. I'm all right. You're all right. We're both all right." He scrubbed his fingers along the dog's ears, hoping to erase his turmoil. It worked, and Jed got to his feet gingerly. His tailbone ached, and when he picked up his phone, a crack ran from one end to the other.

"Great," he griped. "Just great." He looked down at Fish as the dog sat on his cowboy boots. "You shouldn't run away." He lectured the dog some more, because if Fish hadn't run away, he wouldn't be so needy now. And if he wasn't so needy now, Jed would still be on the phone with Cherry, in a chair that hadn't broken.

He eyed the damaged furniture, but instead of cleaning it up the way he normally would have, he simply went back inside. Today was an ice-cream-for-dinner day, and he figured he better eat to get sweetened up before he called Cherry again.

———

LEE COOPER DASHED TOWARD THE STEPS, HIS BACK MIGHTILY protesting the weight he carried in his arms. But Autumn would get blown away in wind like this. He reached the porch first and reached back to help Rose. "Go inside, baby," he called to Autumn as he set her on her feet. "Give me the pan, Rose."

She did, and in the next few seconds, they all burst into the farmhouse. He shut the door behind them and took a big breath. "Whew," Lee said loudly as Ford dusted himself off. Behind them, the wind rattled the doorframe, angry they'd escaped so quickly.

"Bring that in here," Rissa said from the arched doorway. "Hello, Rose." Her face softened as she stepped into Lee's fiancée and kissed both of her cheeks. "You kids come with me." She extended one hand to Ford and one to Autumn. "Mama got all the stuff for cookie turkeys."

Autumn cheered and pranced into the kitchen without taking Rissa's hand, and she giggled as she took Ford's and followed the little girl. Lee went into the kitchen, where he slid the pan of stuffing—which had apples baked into it—onto the counter top. "This isn't too hot," he said. Rose had made it at her house, and he'd picked her up a half-hour ago.

"Great," Travis said. "Leave it there." He wore a black apron that went all the way up around his neck, and he whisked a huge glass measuring cup which held cream and butter. Lee didn't need to crowd the kitchen, and he stood at the end of the island and looked down the long table.

At the end of it, Mama sat with all the grandkids—a total of three right now. She held Bronson in the crook of one arm while she showed Autumn how to put gumdrops on a striped cookie to make a turkey fantail.

"Help me set the table," Will said as he approached. "I've only got the silverware out."

"Cherry's not here yet?" he asked. He picked up a stack of Mama's Thanksgiving plates and followed Will as his brother moved around the table with matching bowls.

"Not yet," Will said. "She went to Jed's for their family lunch, and they're not back."

"Must be gettin' serious," Lee said casually. "Two Thanksgiving dinners?"

"I have no idea," Will said. "I'm trying to help her find a job, not asking her about Jed Forrester." He shot Lee a look over his shoulder. "That's more your realm of expertise."

Lee nodded, but he said nothing. He didn't want to betray Cherry's confidence about anything they'd been talking about. She hadn't said much about Jed in the past few weeks since Rissa's baby had been born, but Lee knew they'd rekindled whatever had been going on between them over the summer about then.

"How's the job hunt coming?"

"She's got some good things lined up," Will said. "I'll be shocked if she doesn't get the Emergency Services Coordinator."

"Talkin' about me, boys?" Cherry asked, and Lee twisted to see her entering the kitchen. She only glanced over to Travis before taking Will into a hug.

"Yeah," Will said. "Just a little. About the jobs."

Cherry closed her eyes, her smile about as genuine as Lee had ever seen it. She hugged him next, and Lee held her tightly, watching Jed watch them both from the safety of the arched doorway. Lee nodded to him, and Jed smiled in that big ole cowboy way he had. He certainly seemed to like Cherry, and Lee didn't care who she was with, as long as he treated her right.

"How was your first dinner?"

"Uh, good," Cherry said, stepping back. She cast a look to Jed, who came to her side.

"Howdy, Lee," he said, reaching to shake Lee's hand. "Will."

"Howdy, Jed," they said together.

As Jed shook Will's hand, he said, "The turkey was way overcooked. My mama...well, she tries hard with poultry, but it's always a bit of a mess."

"There was a lot of gravy, though," Cherry said quickly.

"Yeah, because Deb knows how my mama is." He flashed her a smile, and she linked her arm through his.

"You don't cook?" Travis asked, joining the party, and Cherry and Jed backed up to make room for him. Tension rode in his shoulders, and his question almost felt like an attack. Lee tensed, and he wasn't even sure why. Travis wasn't going to start swinging or anything. He hoped.

"A little," Jed said as diplomatically as possible. "I can put together simple stuff. Mostly I eat from the freezer or boxes." He chuckled. "We don't have family dinners at my mama's every night of the week like y'all."

"It's not every night of the week," Travis said, rolling his eyes. He left the group, and Lee exchanged a glance with Will.

"What was that?" Will challenged, following Travis.

Lee simply sighed and pointed down to the end of the table. "I'd go down there if I were you two."

"What's with Travis?" Jed asked under his breath as Lee headed for the kitchen too. Will stood only a couple of feet from Travis, the two of them in a staring contest.

"Stop it," Lee hissed as he joined them. "It's Thanksgiving, and Cherry obviously really likes that man."

"She likes everyone," Travis said, his voice tainted with bitterness.

"What is with you?" Lee asked. "You and Cherry have some fight or something?"

"No," Travis said darkly, his eyes tracking their oldest sister.

"Then what?" Will asked. "Don't make me regret telling Gretchen this would be a good meal. No fighting, I promised her."

"I'm not sure why you'd do that," Lee said, blinking at Will.

"Because we're not fourteen anymore?" Will rolled his eyes. "Travis, *please*. Her daddy and aunt are gonna be here any minute."

Travis dragged his gaze back to Will and Lee. "Fine," he said. "But whoever is doing place cards might not want to put her by me."

"Why not?" Lee wanted this settled. He didn't need this cloud of negativity hanging over the house, and he certainly didn't want to have to jump in between Cherry and Trav at a moment's notice.

But Travis had already turned back to the boiling pots on the stove. Lee looked at Will again and nodded toward Travis. Will shook his head, and Lee shrugged one shoulder as if to say, *your funeral, brother.*

Will drew in a deep breath and tilted his head toward the ceiling. "Lord, give me strength," he muttered. Then he stepped over to Travis and took the wooden spoon from him. He spoke in a low, quiet voice that didn't form meaning in Lee's ears.

He exited the kitchen again, spying the glasses still on the counter. He got busy setting those around the table, smiling at Mama and the children as he went by. Rose, Shay, Gretchen, and Rissa sat on the sun porch with Daddy, and Lee noted that Cherry didn't go join them.

He raised his eyebrows at her, but she simply shook her head and stayed at Jed's side, smiling at Ford when he turned to her and said, "Look, Aunt Cherry. My turkey has two tails."

Aunt Cherry. She wanted to be a good aunt, and Lee couldn't fault her for that. She had come home a lot when Ford was a baby and a little boy, but he hadn't been enough to draw her back for good.

Lee didn't dwell on it. Cherry had changed a lot just in the past year, and he wouldn't fault her for taking the time she needed to heal. He'd not asked her any questions about her pregnancy, which was why they had a great relationship, but Lee would be lying if he said he hadn't lain awake at night, thinking about what had happened and who she'd been with.

"Lee?" Rissa asked, and he turned toward her. "How long until dinner? Daddy wants to know."

"I'll check," he said, and he turned back toward the kitchen.

Travis gestured with one long arm, and Lee counted it as a miracle that he couldn't hear his brother's voice down here. He strode toward them, making his face as stern as possible.

"Can you guys knock it off?" he hissed as he leaned his palms into the island counter.

"You're the one who told me to talk to him," Will said back.

"I don't need to be talked to," Travis said. "Like I'm some little boy who won't share his toys." He shook his head and untied his apron. "Dinner is ready. I'm not going to cause a big scene, and I'm not eating cold mashed potatoes."

The three of them stood there and glowered at each other, and Lee didn't know how to diffuse this situation. He never did with his brothers, and he looked at Will for help.

———

WILLIAM COOPER HAD LEARNED HOW TO COOL HIS TEMPER quite a bit over the past several months, but he wasn't sure why Travis had chosen tonight of all nights to get riled up.

"Travis," he said, wishing he could step in front of Lee. His brother had tamed his surly attitude a lot recently too, and he wanted tonight to be perfect for Rose and Autumn. *And Mama*, Will thought. He wanted the holidays to be perfect for Mama, and surely Travis wanted that too.

"Can you shelve this for now?" Will asked. "For Mama? For Rissa? It's her baby's first Thanksgiving, and she doesn't want a big brawl over the turkey and gravy."

"I don't want that either," Travis said. "Can we just not do this now? I was fine, getting all my frustration out in the cooking."

"You're really fine?" Lee asked.

"Yes," Travis said, rolling his eyes. "I just don't want to talk to Cherry right now."

"Why?" Will asked.

"That's between me and her," Travis said darkly. He stepped away from the huddle and whistled through his teeth. "Time to eat, everyone." He went down the length of the table and helped Mama and the children clean up their turkeys.

The women and Daddy came in from outside, and Will smiled at his wife. Travis softened for Shay too, and Will prayed that he'd be on his best behavior for her, at the very least.

"All right," Trav said. "Will and Lee are going to bring everything over to the table." He nodded to the two of them, and Lee jumped into action. Will did the same, using hot pads if Trav had laid them over the ends of the casserole dishes.

Turkey, stuffing, bowls of mashed potatoes, roasted asparagus with balsamic glaze, creamed corn, freshly baked rolls, honey butter, raspberry butter, brown gravy and white gravy, the dishes went on and on.

Travis named them all as Lee and Will set the dishes down in the middle of the table. "We've got pies later too," he said, his grin wide. "So don't eat too much now."

"I think that's impossible," Daddy said, rubbing his hands together. He grinned from his spot in the middle of the table. "Mama, will you say grace?"

Will put the last stack of napkins on the table and slid into his seat beside his wife, flashing her a smile as Mama nodded at Daddy. She waited for Lee to take his seat too, quiet Ford, and then she smiled up and down the table.

"We are so blessed to have you all here with us," she said, her voice soft yet powerful. Will took Gretchen's hand in his and squeezed. She did the same back to him, and he reminded himself that even if he argued with his siblings, he always had her to comfort him. He tried to do the same for her, especially on days when she had to deal with her daddy's stubbornness. Sometimes Will would take him to his appointments and sit with him while he told the same stories he'd heard before, just to get him to take his medication.

He'd do it everyday, gladly, for Gretchen, because he loved her with all he had.

"Dear Lord," Mama said, and Will bowed his head. His mama didn't allow cowboy hats in the house, and his hung on a hook by the front door. "We thank Thee for family. We're grateful for all the men and women and little boys and girls who've joined our fold." She paused, and Will wasn't sure if it was from emotion or exhaustion.

"Bless us to be thankful for each other," Mama said. "Sometimes we struggle with that, and if there are any here who need to forgive, allow them to do so. If any need to be forgiven, bless them with that as well."

Another pause, and Will glanced up to watch his mama. She'd taught him so much over the years, and he hated watching her struggle to walk, to get out of bed, to cook, to find the right thing to say.

"Bless the food," she said. "Amen."

"Amen," they chorused, and Will added his voice to the rest of the family. Time suspended for a moment, where no one moved. Then Travis reached for the huge platter of turkey, and said, "White meat, Mama?"

Lee helped his son and his soon to be stepdaughter with the creamed corn and rolls, which sat in front of him. The food went around, and Will took too much of everything that came his way.

"How are you going to eat all of that?" Gretchen asked, looking at his plate.

"It's a tough job," he said. "I think I'm up to the challenge."

"Thanksgiving dinner isn't a challenge," Gretchen said. "And remember, I brought those crispy mint squares for dessert." She craned her neck to look over to the island. "I don't see them...but I brought them."

Shayla leaned halfway across the table and picked up the basket of bread. "Trav hid those," she whispered loud enough for everyone to hear. Maybe not the people down at the end of the table where Cherry sat with Jed and Spencer, but definitely her husband. "He loves them, and he's afraid he won't have enough to eat today."

"Hey," Trav said, and Will wanted to tell Shay not to poke the bear. He looked at Trav, but he wasn't about to blow. "You're the one who said we should hide a few so you had breakfast for the next couple of days."

Shay giggled and sat back down. "Did I say that?" She gave Gretchen a knowing look, and Will smiled too. Dinner continued without incident, and Will kept eating far past his comfort level.

"All right," Daddy said as he took a couple of plates into the kitchen. "I want to hear what everyone is grateful for."

A couple of people groaned, one of them Cherry. Will fully expected her to bolt but do it in a Cherry-like fashion that made it seem like she was just stepping out for a moment. Then she wouldn't come back. Will had seen her do it loads of times, and he watched her as she leaned closer to Jed and said something he had to bend closer to hear.

Will hated whispering in a crowd, and he very nearly rolled his eyes. They were both older than him, and they should know better. Cherry was acting like she was sixteen with her first boyfriend, and Jed simply had stars in his eyes.

Cherry wore her hair slicked back into an elegant ponytail that rested at the base of her neck, and her brown and white striped sweater felt festive for turkey day. She'd always been sophisticated and classy, and with Jed at her side, those qualities were only enunciated.

He wasn't a slob or anything, but he wore black plaid with jeans and his hair had clearly been under a cowboy hat for a while today. Will had always liked Jed Forrester just fine, and he glanced over to Travis.

His brother had gotten to his feet, and Will got up to help clear the table too. He snagged another roll before he sat back down, and Daddy stood behind his chair. "All right. Who wants to go first?"

"I will, Daddy," Rissa said, and Will tore off a piece of bread. He could've predicted Rissa's next sentence—anyone at the table could have. "I'm grateful for my husband and baby."

"That's a cop-out," Travis said.

"She can be grateful for whatever she wants," Mama said. "Trav, you're next."

He looked like he might argue but the tension in his jaw disappeared in the next moment. "I'm grateful that it hasn't rained much yet."

"Rain?" Rissa challenged.

"The lack of rain," Trav said back, throwing her a look that traveled the length of the table.

"He can be grateful for whatever he wants," Mama said. Will honestly wasn't sure what had crawled into Trav's breakfast that morning, but he was seriously annoyed by almost everyone here.

"I'll go, Mama," Will said, hoping to diffuse both Rissa and Trav. All eyes turned to him, and Will wished he'd been more prepared for what he'd say. "I'm grateful that we have this farm, where we can all have a place to live, in our own houses, but close to one another."

Silence followed, and Will glanced at Gretchen. "Baby?"

"I'm not going after that," she said.

"Yeah, thanks a lot, Will," Lee said. "Daddy, can we pause this?"

"No," Daddy said, grinning around. "Cherry?"

"Pass," she said.

"I'm grateful for video games," Lee said.

"That's a good one, Daddy," Ford said. "I'm grateful for hacky sacks."

Will grinned at his nephew. "Have you shown Grandma and Grandpa how you can play hacky sack?"

"Not yet," Ford said, his face lighting up.

"You should."

Ford looked at his father. "Dad, can we go get my hacky sack?"

"Not right now," Lee said, shooting a glare at Will.

"What? It's a good distraction," Will said.

"I'm grateful for big families," Rosalie said, leaning toward her daughter.

"I'm grateful for baby cows," Autumn said, and Daddy chuckled.

"Can't follow that," Spencer said, also laughing. "I guess I'm grateful for dairy cows."

"Dairy cows?" Jed asked, a loud laugh following. "I'm grateful for corn."

"Corn?" Cherry asked, grinning at him.

"Your mama said I could be grateful for anything, and I'm grateful for corn."

"Why's that?" Lee asked, though no one had to say why they'd chosen what they'd said. Lee didn't even play video games; his fiancée owned a gaming company, for crying out loud.

"Because Cherry wandered into the maze at my farm, got lost, and I got to help her out of the corn."

Cherry positively beamed at Jed, and Will would give him points for saying the exact right thing.

"I'm grateful for my grandchildren," Daddy said.

"That was mine," Mama said, swatting his arm.

"You can have it too," he said. He surveyed the family at the table. "Who hasn't gone?"

"Cherry," Travis said, and Will threw him a sharp look.

"Your wife hasn't said anything either," Lee said.

Shay smiled at Lee, and then Mama and Daddy. "I'm grateful for good examples in my life."

Will lifted his arm and put it around Gretchen. "Your turn," he murmured, as he was fairly certain Cherry was going to pass again.

"I'm grateful for modern medicine," Gretchen said, and that kept the atmosphere solemn and somber.

Everyone looked at Cherry, and she squirmed. For being the oldest—and a Cooper—she sure didn't like being in the spotlight.

"Cherry-blossom?" Daddy prompted. "Are you going to pass again?"

"No," she said, and she cleared her throat. "I'm grateful for family."

––––––––

TRAVIS WANTED TO LEAVE THE DINNER TABLE. NOW. IT WAS too soon for pie, but he got to his feet and picked up a couple of dishes left in the middle of the table. He could start the dishes, so then he didn't have to listen to everyone fawn over Cherry and how *wonderful* it was that she was back in Sweet Water Falls.

He didn't like the poisonous thoughts eating through him, but he didn't know how to get rid of them. He hated with everything inside him that he'd run into Brandon Alcott a couple of weeks ago. He'd give anything to go back in time and make Will go to the hardware store.

Apparently, Brandon had heard through the small-town rumor mill that Cherry would soon be returning to town. That wasn't hard to believe, as Will had been talking to everyone and their mule about a job for Cherry.

He'd said some terrible things that Travis hadn't wanted to believe. He hadn't told anyone else about them, not even Shay. Everyone could see that he was slowly going rotten on the inside. He had little control over his temper, and he'd been trying to stick to the Berthas since running into stupid Brandon Alcott.

The water ran hot in the sink, and he started rinsing the dishes and loading them into the dishwasher.

Someone came up beside him, and Travis nearly threw the plate and ran.

"Hey," Cherry said.

"Hey." Travis couldn't do this here, but the words choked him.

"Are you okay?" Cherry asked.

He checked over his shoulder, and he caught both Will and Lee watching them. He shook his head and looked back at his sister. "Not really," he said, loading another plate into the dishwasher.

"You've been kind of distant with me," she said.

"Did you ever...date Brandon Alcott?" Travis ignored the water and plates and silverware.

"No," Cherry said, something shuttering over her face.

"He says you did," Travis said, his voice barely louder than the running water.

"It wasn't a relationship," Cherry said, her voice breaking. She turned fully toward him. "What did he tell you?"

Travis faced her too, something storming inside his chest. "He said he slept with you, Cherry. I didn't believe him, and there may have been...a scuffle in the hardware store."

Tears filled her eyes. "It was a long time ago," she whispered. "I've only told Lee. Mama and Daddy don't even know."

"So he wasn't lying."

"I don't know what he said," Cherry said, reaching to

wipe her eyes. She blinked rapidly. "It's the main reason I left town to begin with."

"Everything okay?" Lee asked.

Travis handed him the sponge. "I need to talk to Cherry." He took his sister's hand and led her into the garage.

"Travis," she said.

"I hate feeling this way about you," he said, running his hands through his hair. "I knew you weren't happy here, but I didn't know...this."

"I was in a very bad place," Cherry said. "I'd just realized Charlie was never going to marry me. I was stupid. Brandon was there." She shook her head.

"He was one of my friends," Travis said.

"I can't believe it took him this long to tell you."

"He wanted to know if you were still single."

"We had a one-night stand." Cherry drew in a deep breath. "I got pregnant."

Travis's mouth dropped open. "You did?"

"I ran," she said. "It's taken me twelve long years to come to terms with myself, and I'm sorry." She looked absolutely miserable, and Travis didn't want that for her.

He took her into a hug, and her entire frame shook as she cried. "I'm sorry, Cherry," he whispered. Guilt tugged and pulled and yanked through him. "I've been thinking the worst about you, and it's been eating me up inside. And really, I should've been helping you."

"No one can help me," she whispered. "I'm the only one who can do that." She stepped back. "And before you ask, I lost the baby. There is no child out there. Just my pure humiliation and shame."

Travis searched for the right thing to say. He wasn't entirely sure, but what came out of his mouth was, "Did you hear us when you announced you were coming home?"

"Don't," she said.

"We all want you here. We've wanted you here for a long time."

She said nothing, and Travis gathered her into another hug. "Will you forgive me for being mad at you?"

"Nothing to forgive."

"Nothing for me to forgive either," he said. "Okay?"

"I don't know how to tell Mama," she said.

"Who says you have to tell her?" Travis asked.

"I do," Cherry said. "I have to clear everything, or I'll never stay here."

"And you want to stay." Travis tried a smile, and while Cherry didn't return it, her eyes weren't made of glass anymore either. "Jed wants you to stay."

"If I'm going to be with him, I have to tell him too," she said.

"Everyone has a past," Travis said. "Absolutely every-one. No one's perfect, Cherry."

The door behind him opened, and both Lee and Will stood there. Rissa crowded in behind them. "Travis," she barked. "What are you doin' to her?"

"Nothing," Travis and Cherry said together. He faced

the rest of his siblings and gestured for them to come out into the garage too. They did, and he spread his arms and tried to hold them all at the same time. He could only get his arms around Cherry, patting Will's shoulder, and then Lee.

"I lied in there," he said. "I'm not grateful it hasn't rained yet. Well." He shrugged as much as he was able. "I am, but what I'm really grateful for is you guys. My brothers and sisters."

No one said anything, and Travis simply basked in the fact that he didn't have a demon inside him anymore, threatening to burst out and ruin Thanksgiving for everyone.

"I'm grateful for you too," Cherry said. "For you, Trav, and for all of you."

"Me too," Rissa murmured at the same time as Lee and Will.

Travis met Cherry's eye, and she simply gave him a smile. "All right," he said. "If we're all out here, who's doing the dishes?"

"The better question is who's stopping Daddy from eating the pie straight out of the fridge?" Lee asked.

They all laughed, and Travis hung back as everyone went back inside the farmhouse. He took a deep breath once he was alone, and he looked up toward the heavens. A sigh moved through him, and he finally felt centered again.

"What are you doin' out here?"

He jumped at the strange, almost robotic-cowboy voice, and then laughed when he found his wife standing there, grinning at him. "You have a terrible male voice," he said.

"Admit it," she said. "You thought I was Lee for at least a second." Shay laughed, and Travis joined her.

"Not even a particle of a second," he said, taking her into his arms.

"Are you okay?" she asked, reaching up to run her hand down the side of his face. She loved him openly, and Travis appreciated that so much.

"I am now," he said.

"Cherry looked like she'd been crying."

"Yeah," Travis said. "Healing hurts sometimes, but I think she'll be okay." He opened the door, and they went back inside.

"You know what's not okay?" Shay asked. "Gretchen found where we hid the crispy chocolate squares, and everyone's going nuts over them."

Travis stood still and watched his favorite treat get devoured by no less than three of his siblings—and Gretchen herself. She nodded quietly to a plate on the back counter, where several more sat, and Travis touched his fist to his heart in a silent *thank you*.

"Come on, baby," he said. "Let's go join my loud, crazy family." And they did just that.

12

Jed held the gray mare steady, staring straight into her eyes. *Mares*, he thought. They could kick up and buck at any time, for any reason. *Unpredictable* was the best way to describe them, and Jed couldn't help applying the same word to the woman currently swinging her leg over Bluebell's back.

Cherry landed in the saddle with an "Oof," and a smile. Jed looked away from the mare—who hadn't moved a muscle—and caught the end of her grin.

"Okay?" he asked, looping the reins over Bluebell's head and handing them to Cherry.

"Yeah," she said. "I haven't ridden in a long time."

"Bluebell's retired," he said, swinging up into his saddle. His horse—also a pretty mare who he'd named Stormy—barely twitched her tail.

"She was still a cow horse," Cherry said. "They have a drive."

"That they do." Jed smiled at her while he got comfortable in the saddle. "But she hasn't done that work for about a year now. She's not going to bolt on you." He hoped. Bluebell had been a phenomenal cow horse, and Stormy still was. Easton worked hard with their horses, and in return, they worked hard for the farm.

"We're not going far, are we?"

"Just out to the fence and back," he said. "Then you can see Lady Jones's farm." His chest stormed, but he wanted her to see it up-close and personal. He still hadn't answered the widow about possibly buying her farm, and the task weighed on his mind.

They set off, the morning sky turning lighter by the minute. "No shopping for you on Black Friday?" he asked.

"Not in person," she said. "I did a little bit online this morning already."

"Yeah? It's barely seven."

"They opened their sales at five," she said. "Some at midnight, but I already have so many pairs of shoes that I don't wear..." She laughed lightly, and Jed chuckled with her.

"Are you moving them all here?" he asked. He still couldn't believe Cherry Cooper was moving back to Sweet Water Falls. Especially so soon. When he'd seen her in the corn maze only three weeks ago, the distance between them had been the thing putting all the distance between them.

So much had changed, and he thought, *Unpredictable* again.

He didn't need predictable. In fact, the volatility in his relationship with Cherry was what made it exciting for him. That, and the woman herself. But that could've been because of how unpredictable she was.

He put a stop to the circular thoughts and took a long breath in. Then out. Over and over again.

"Are you meditating?" she asked.

"Just tryin' to be in the moment," he said, cutting her a look out of the corner of his eye. "I don't have a lot of slow moments on the farm, and when I do, I try to just stay inside them."

She nodded, her voice staying quiet. They plodded along slowly, and Bluebell and Stormy minded their manners just fine.

About halfway to the fence line, Cherry said, "I have a secret for you."

Happiness filled him, and he let it shine through in his smile. "Let's hear it."

She adjusted her grip on the reins, and as it tightened, he realized she was nervous about the secret. That sent a shockwave of nerves through him too, and he swallowed.

"Okay," she said. "I hope you won't be mad."

"I hope I won't be either," he said as good-naturedly as

he could. He tacked a smile onto the end of the sentence, but Cherry didn't relax. Which meant he couldn't either.

"I talked to Easton," she said, then cleared her throat. In that two seconds of time, Jed's imagination went wild. What had she talked to him about? The job here? What had his brother said? Had he been rude to Cherry? Had she said something to him to upset him?

Jed spun out of control, and he barely heard Cherry when she said, "And he said the farm could survive without you for a few days."

He blinked, went over the sentence again, and asked, "What?"

"The secret is that I got you a few days off to come to San Antonio and help me pack and get ready to move."

Jed blinked, not sure if this was a good surprise or not. He looked at Cherry, whose face fell. "You don't want to."

"I do," he said quickly. "But I think you and I need to have a talk about what a cowboy should do on his days off."

Cherry sighed and looked away. "Yeah, no one wants to help someone pack. Don't worry about it. It was a dumb idea."

"No," he blurted. "It wasn't. Of course I want to come help you." He nudged Stormy closer to Bluebell, and neither mare threw a fit about the proximity. Reaching out, he took one of Cherry's hands. "You don't have to strangle those," he said gently. "You don't have to hold them at all. She'll just keep walkin'."

He lifted her hand to his lips. "Sorry for my poor reaction. I was surprised."

"Secrets are usually surprising," she murmured.

"That they are." He looked toward the horizon again and released her hand. She went right back to holding the reins too tight, but he didn't correct her again. "When is this vacation?"

She scoffed and he caught her rolling her eyes. "You know what? You're uninvited."

"I'll call Easton." He dug into his front pocket, lifting slightly up in his stirrups, to get his phone out.

"No," Cherry said, the force behind the word enough to make him pause.

Jed looked at her. "No?"

"Monday," she said. "I was going to go back on Monday, finish all the packing, and cleaning, and be ready for when my brothers are coming next weekend." She blinked those heavenly eyelashes at him. "I got you the whole week off, Jed."

His heartbeat started to tap dance in his chest. "I suppose packing and cleaning isn't a twenty-four hour a day job," he mused. "We might have to go to lunch or dinner or even breakfast together. In the city."

"I suppose," she said airily, as if no such thing would be happening.

"You might have to go back to your office because you forgot something, and I'll just have to go with you to meet all your friends."

She made a horrified sound now, and that set Jed into full laughter. When he quieted, he asked, "Where might your boyfriend be staying in the city?"

Cherry swallowed so hard, he heard it above the clomping of the horses' hooves. "I have a three-bedroom house," she said. "Two bathrooms. You'll have your own of everything."

His throat forgot how to swallow. Having her stay in cabin four a few months ago had caused him to lie awake at night, thinking about how close she was to his cabin, and now she wanted him to sleep in the room across the hall from her? In a house she'd lived in for over a decade?

The whole thing would scream Cherry, from the scent to the sight to the bedding. He pictured it in bold patterns and shapes, maybe stripes or polka dots, because while she had always been standoffish and brusque with him, she had a side of her that loved decorating, good fashion, and bright colors.

"All right," he said, barely getting the words out.

"You don't have to strangle yourself," she teased, and Jed whipped his attention back to her. She grinned and laughed, the sound of it soared up into the sky, where it would make the birds happy too.

"This is a big thing for us," he said. "Don't you think?"

"Perhaps," she said.

"Lord," he bellowed into the sky. "This woman never just says yes to me. I'm still waitin' on that, okay?"

Cherry laughed again, and she reached over and

swatted his arm. He took her hand in his, his smile real and wide and genuine as he looked into her eyes. "I really am waiting for that yes," he said.

"I know I've told you yes before," she said.

"Perhaps," he repeated back to her, which made him laugh and her simply smile and shake her head. He sobered and added, "But not with big things, Cher."

"You don't think so?"

"No," he said almost instantly. "You do if it's something like, 'do you want to grab pizza and meet me in the parking lot?' Then you say yes. But if I want to talk about how me going to San Antonio for five days, where I'm going to stay in a bedroom literal feet from you, you won't admit that it's anything more than this horseback ride."

She fell silent, but she didn't pull her hand away. Jed counted that as a victory, since he took all he could get when it came to Cherry. She started to shut down—he watched the blinders go over her expression—and then she pulled back. She came back to him, fire blazing in those deep dark depths, highlighting some of that emerald he'd seen once or twice.

"Maybe I do that," she said.

"Maybe you do."

"Maybe this horseback ride isn't simple for me," she said.

"I know it's not." He also knew they weren't talking about horseback riding either. Talking and admitting how she felt wasn't easy for Cherry. Discussing hard things—

like the future and what their relationship meant or where it could go—wasn't easy for her.

"Maybe I need someone to push me." She started to pull her hand away, and for the first time, Jed wouldn't let her. He held fast to her fingers and when their eyes met, he wasn't sure if he was about to get a smile or a tongue lashing.

The excitement of the unknown did make his desire for this woman swoop and flow through his whole body.

"Maybe you need someone to *fight* with you about some things," he shot back at her. "Maybe you need someone to fight *for* you, who won't let you run away when things get hard, or there's things you don't want to do or talk about."

He raised his eyebrows in a challenge, almost daring her to tell him she didn't need that. Any of it. That she didn't need him.

"May I remind you that *you're* the one who broke up with *me*?"

"May *I* remind *you* that you're the one who said she was going to try to let me in this time? That she wasn't embarrassed of me, and that we didn't have to hide from anyone—even each other?" He looked away then, relaxing his fingers so she could pull away if she wanted to.

To his surprise, she didn't. She kept holding his hand, and after a couple of seconds, it felt nice and normal. His shoulders went down, and he sighed.

"I'm sorry," they said together, and Jed ducked his

head, the top of his cowboy hat facing the sun, and chuckled quietly to himself.

"I *am* trying," Cherry said.

"Mm."

"You coming to San Antonio *is* a big thing for us," she said. "For me." She wouldn't look at him, but Jed didn't need her to.

"Thank you," he said. They reached the fence, and Jed let go of her hand and jumped down. He threw the reins over the top rung and turned to help Cherry down. She slid into his arms, and Jed didn't back up to give her room.

Out here, under the morning sun, with Bluebell staying put and boxing Cherry into his arms, he gazed down at her. "I'm real serious about you, Cherry," he said. "I just want to know if you're serious about me."

She slid her hands down his chest and then back up, watching them instead of looking at him. When she finally raised her eyes to his, Jed didn't need glasses to see her true feelings. "I am," she said. "Why else would I arrange for you to have a week off so we could spend time together in the city?"

In that moment, Jed realized Cherry was a do-er. She might not *say* exactly how she felt. She might never tell him *yes* to a big, hard question for her.

She'd *show* him.

She'd *done* something huge so he could be with her next week.

She'd already said yes—he just hadn't realized it.

"All right," he said, glad for the rays of light that had been beamed into his mind. He leaned down and kissed her, and once again, he got the *yes* in the way she kissed him back. In fact, he wasn't sure how he'd been missing it all this time.

He pulled away and faced the land on the other side of the fence. "All right," he said, exhaling. "This would be the new farm." He really wanted her to like it, because if they did end up together, they'd live on this land with one another.

"It looks great," she said.

He drew her closer to him, a soft golden feeling moving through him. "It looks the same as where we're standing."

"It's great here too." She leaned into him, and Jed took a deep breath of her perfume. He really wanted to be in her life, and he ducked his head closer to her ear. "I'm excited for a city adventure with you."

"You are?"

"For sure," he whispered. "Me, in the city? I'm not even going to know how to walk."

She giggled and turned into him. "It'll be a fun week, I promise."

"You can show me everything you've told me about," he said, thinking he'd probably see and experience a lot of things he never had before in the next seven days of his life. And he wanted that so badly, because Cherry would be the one showing him.

"Holy stomping mares," Jed said only a couple of days later. "Look at that." He pointed to a huge cathedral, and Cherry practically leapt into his arms.

"That's the Cathedral of San Fernando," she said, twisting to look at it again. The stunning white structure took Jed's breath away, though it wasn't the only thing to do so.

"It's incredible," he said. "This whole downtown area is something I've never even imagined."

"You've seen movies," she said, shaking her head. "Quit acting like you've never seen a building over four stories tall."

"Well, there is the hospital in Sweet Water Falls," he said, and Cherry grinned at him.

"Come on." She tugged on his hand. "There's the greatest little bistro up ahead, and I'm starving."

"Yeah?" he asked. "The two hours in the car really worked up an appetite?" He'd fed her at his cabin just before they'd left too. She couldn't be *that* hungry.

As Cherry gave him a sour look, Jed got another big-city, Cherry-specific lesson in his life. This wasn't about the food. This was about Cherry sharing her city-life with him.

"Because I am," he practically bellowed into the city streets. "Practically *starving*."

"All right," she said dryly, and Jed laughed as he pulled

her to him, spinning her into his chest. There weren't a zillion people on the streets, as it was after the start of the work day and super windy right now.

So he had no problem kissing her right there on the streets of San Antonio.

C herry moved around her bedroom, doing nothing. She finally forced herself to sit in the small chair she kept in front of a bookcase. She loved to sit here over the weekend and read and re-read her favorites.

Tonight, she hadn't plucked a tome from the shelf, and she didn't part the curtains. It was dark anyway, and she didn't particularly like having open blinds and curtains when people could see in and she couldn't see them.

Tonight, her mind ran in figure-eights because of the man across the hall. Today had been the very best day of her forty-six years. With Jed in the city with her...Cherry couldn't imagine anything better.

Because while he was country through and through, it had literally been the absolute best experience they'd had together. An early lunch at her favorite bistro with fantastic food. Jed had ordered beef everywhere they'd gone, for lunch and dinner and even for their mid-afternoon snack.

She'd teased him about it tonight while she'd made her grandmother's caramel popcorn. He'd said he'd put some beef bouillon powder on it and love it. They'd laughed and laughed, but Cherry thought there was a kernel of truth to what he'd said. He seemed to have the need for red meat in his blood.

She sighed, finally settled, and got up to change into her pajamas. Once she'd done that, she checked her phone, only to find several texts from Jed.

It's not as dark here as it should be, he'd said. She giggled softly to herself. He'd already told her his worries and fears about sleeping in the city. She'd told him she couldn't stand all the country silence. The way the coyotes could howl, or the sound of a car could send her into a frenzy.

Here, the noise of the city was like ambient sound. She didn't even hear it.

I can hear people driving by, he'd said next.

The bed sure is comfortable though.

My mama told me to bring my eye mask to block out the light. She's a genius.

Cherry shook her head as she started to respond. *You close your eyes, cowboy. That's how you block out the light.*

She hadn't quite finished typing when another text came in. *You must be asleep already. Yeah?*

She quickly finished and sent him the message. She climbed into bed, something inside her life opening right up. It had a Jed-shaped form, and she knew if she let him, he could walk right inside and *be* in her life. Truly be in it.

Close your eyes? he said. *I did that, and there was still all this orange light.*

That's for the cats, she said, a sudden jolt of panic filling her. Then she remembered she'd removed the pet nightlights. *But I took those out and put them in their bedroom.*

I think it's hilarious you have a bedroom for cats.

Here we go again, she said, but she couldn't straighten her mouth. *Me having cats isn't an issue for you, is it?*

They're not as good as dogs, he said. *But no, not an issue.*

Not as good as dogs? Cherry scoffed, her fingers flying now. So engrossed in telling him all the finer points of felines was she that she didn't hear anything happening in her house until he knocked on her door. Loudly.

"Cherry?" he said, plenty of teasing in his voice.

She looked up, her heart beat like striking lightning in her chest and throat.

"I didn't mean it about cats," he said through the door. "You're not mad, are you?"

Cherry looked down at her perfect argument. She'd stopped in the middle of the sentence, and she decided to go with that. She sent the text, then threw her comforter off and got up. His phone dinged loudly in the hallway, and Cherry stifled her smile as she crossed her room and pulled open the door.

"Better than cats," she said, adding a lot of bite to her words.

He looked up from his phone, but Cherry's eyes had started to drift down his frame. The man...she hadn't seen him without the jeans, the cowboy hat, the plaid shirt, and the belt buckle for a while. If ever.

Right now, he wore a pair of dark gray sweat pants, a T-shirt that was clearly for a child with the way it strained across his chest and shoulders, and nothing else. No hat. No belt. No cowboy boots.

She had no idea what to do with that picture of him. The person standing in front of her almost didn't seem like Jed Forrester.

"You're staring," he said, and Cherry yanked her gaze back to his.

"You're not wearing your cowboy hat."

"No, ma'am," he said, rocking back onto his heels. He stumbled, as he wasn't wearing those boots either, and he burst out laughing as he caught himself against the wall behind her. "I don't sleep in my cowboy hat, Cherry."

"Or your boots."

"Or any of it," he said, cocking his head. "Did you think I did?"

"Of course not," she said, recovering fully. Heat filled her face. "I just haven't seen you like this."

He grinned at her. "Like what?"

"Like...normal."

He shook his head, but he wasn't laughing. "Remember when I asked you if you owned sweat pants?"

He had, at Travis's wedding. She only nodded, sure she knew where he was going with this.

"Guess what, sweetheart? I do too. I'm not always in cowboy boots and jeans. Just while I'm working." He folded his arms, and Cherry reached for the doorframe to keep herself from swooning at the sight of all those muscles. "And I'm not working this week."

"You wore jeans today. And a cowboy hat and boots."

He shrugged. "I like them."

"Did you bring anything else?" she challenged, feeling the tide turn in her favor. She reminded herself she didn't need to win anything, least of all a *conversation* with Jed.

"Just this stuff," he said. Their eyes hooked and met, and Cherry had the inexplicable need to throw herself into his arms and kiss him. Such an act would be dangerous, and Cherry didn't want to walk that line tonight.

"I'm not mad about the cats comment."

"Okay," he said quietly. "What time are we getting up in the morning? I was going to ask you that next."

"Whenever," she said. "I know you'll be up early. Make coffee. Go for a walk. I don't care."

"I thought you wanted to show me where you used to go for morning tea," he said.

Cherry smiled at him, because while he kept it hidden, his heart was made of gold. He listened to her, and he wanted to do what made her happy. "They closed a while ago," she said, waving dismissively. She stepped into the hallway, and Jed received her into his arms. "Will you cook for us tomorrow? Then we can do the Riverwalk and get lunch there."

"Absolutely," he murmured.

"I don't have any food," she murmured back, her eyes on his mouth.

"I'll be up before you and go to the store." He leaned down and kissed her, and Cherry could certainly get used to that. Right there in her own home, with Jed kissing her goodnight. The only thing that made this less than a fairy tale was the fact that she then retreated to her bed alone, and Jed did the same.

Once her pulse had quieted, as had her phone, Cherry snapped off the lamp and slid down into her blankets. She stared up at the ceiling, seeing the orange streetlamp glow Jed had referenced. The moment she closed her eyes, it disappeared.

Contentment stole through her, but like a thief in the night, the anxiety prowled right behind it. *You have to tell him about why you left Sweet Water Falls*, she told herself.

She simply didn't want to do it. Not tonight. Not tomorrow. Not any time this week.

Not ever.

Travis knew now, and with Brandon out there talking about it, Cherry figured the sooner she told her parents and Jed, the better. Rissa should probably hear it from her too, but Cherry simply didn't know how to open the door as widely as it needed to be opened.

She also hated that her past indiscretions had to be aired for the whole family to see and know about.

On the nightstand, her phone buzzed, and she rolled toward it. She looked at Jed's message, and everything disquiet inside her went silent.

I'm falling in love with you, Cherry. I know that freaks you out, and I'm freaked out too, but I feel it and I wanted you to know it.

Another message popped up while she tried to figure out if she should answer or not.

Feathers wanted to sleep with me, he said, a picture following. With both of their eyes reflecting the flash on his phone, they looked like aliens—one human and one feline. She burst out laughing as he sent, *Hope that's okay. She likes me.*

Feathers liked everyone, but Cherry didn't tell him that. She had hid while Clarissa was here last year, so maybe the cat didn't like everyone.

It's okay, she sent, and she was speaking to everything he'd sent, including that he was falling in love with her. After all, she was falling in love with him too. While she hadn't pictured her prince actually riding up on a horse, she should've known a country cowboy would be the one to rescue her from her city life.

Perhaps it was time to stop fighting with herself and admit that she wanted a quaint farmhouse, a handsome husband who came home in dirty jeans and boots, and a family in the wilds of Texas.

But if she did, Cherry couldn't quite get past the feeling that she'd waited too long to have anything in the new fantasy blooming through her mind.

———

"THIS IS IT," SHE SAID.

"This is it?" Jed asked, peering across the street.

"There's more to it than there looks," she said, but she was only telling half the truth.

"I thought the Alamo was going to be this huge thing," he said.

"It's what it represents that's so big, Jed," she drawled. "Come on. Let's get one of those audio guides." He wouldn't like that either, and sure enough, the salty cowboy grumbled about having to wear earbuds someone else had already worn.

They went inside the fort, which had been large for its day. Cherry had been here countless times over the past dozen years, but Jed acted like he'd never seen a brick before.

"I think you have a secret to tell me," she said.

He swiped his headphones off and asked, "What?"

"A secret," she said, grinning. She only wore one earbud, because she didn't need to get immersed in the sights and sounds of the Texas Revolution.

"And what would that be?" He cocked his hip and nearly took out a child. She laughed and dragged him out of the way so others could get by him. Schools brought students to the Alamo on a daily basis, and this Thursday was no exception.

"You love history," she said, almost like it was an accusation.

Jed opened his mouth to say something, but his eyes simply searched her face. He snapped his mouth closed.

"You do," she insisted.

"Maybe I do," he said.

"Oh, that's irritating," she said, sticking her second earbud in her ear.

"Now you know exactly how I feel," he said, grinning from ear to ear.

She mimed that she couldn't hear him, and he tipped his head back and laughed. She could one-hundred percent hear that, and so could everyone else within a mile radius. She rolled her eyes and put some distance between them.

Jed followed her, and they continued their self-guided tour with the audiotape. She'd heard it all before, and she couldn't help thinking how Jed not coming right out and saying he liked history had annoyed her.

He'd felt like that often with her, she knew. She just hadn't known how it really felt until now. Something with tiny teeth sliced through her lungs, shredding them more and more until they finally finished at the Alamo and went back out onto the streets of San Antonio.

"Jed," she said, and since she didn't say his name a whole lot, he looked at her with some measure of seriousness. "I'm really sorry for not just telling you stuff." She thought of all the things she still had to divulge, and her mouth turned dry.

"Like what?"

She couldn't even think of an example now. Then one sprang into her mind. "Well, like when you were trying to talk about how you coming to stay with me in the city was a big deal, and I couldn't admit it."

"Is this about the history thing?" He took her hand in his. "Yeah, I like history. I always have. My mama has these old photo albums with all this genealogy in them. I loved looking at those when I was a boy. I still do."

"Why is that?" she asked.

"I don't know," he said. "I think a person's history makes them who they are, you know? Where they come from, and who they come from. It's interesting to me."

A person's history, Cherry thought, suddenly more keen than ever not to tell him about hers. "Did you ever have the chance to get married?" she asked. They hadn't talked much about their previous relationships, and perhaps she could ease into telling him about her past.

He laughed as they crossed the street to the parking lot. "Heavens, no," he said. "I think ours is the longest relationship I've ever had. You might find this hard to believe, but I'm kind of a jerk sometimes."

"I had no idea," she said dryly.

"I think it works for us," he said. "Because you're not Miss Sunshine either."

"I'm not sure if that's a compliment or not," she said.

"I just mean," he said, but then he didn't say what he'd just meant. Cherry glanced at him to find an expression on his face that told her he was thinking hard.

"What do you 'just mean'?" she prompted.

"Nothing," he said.

"It's something."

"I'm already digging my own grave," he said with a smile. "Holdin' the shovel and everything." He shook his head. "No, it's nothing. I didn't mean anything by it." They reached her car, and he opened her door for her. She'd been driving them around the city, because she knew it well and he didn't.

Cherry didn't get behind the wheel. She looked up at Jed, and said, "I know I'm not like other women. I look like them, but I'm not rainbows and sunshine all the time. I know that."

"I don't mind it," he said. "At all." He held something passionate and earnest in his eyes that called to Cherry. "I just think...me and you, maybe it's okay that you're helping me be nicer and I'm helping you be sunnier. That's all."

"You're not a beast who needs to be tamed," she said.

"But if I was, you'd be the princess to do it." He smiled at her, a gesture so warm and wonderful that Cherry could only bask in the beauty of it. "All right?"

She nodded, because she couldn't speak. He leaned down and kissed her, a chaste, quick kiss that ended almost as soon as it began. He left her to get in the car as he went around, and she managed to do that before he did.

They'd planned to go to dinner after their afternoon at the Alamo, and Cherry made the turns to get them to one of her favorite restaurants in the city—The Shack—without having to dedicate too many brain cells to the activity.

She'd never really believed that there was just one person for her. For anyone. But as Jed looked at her in the parking lot, a hint of worry in those gorgeous eyes, she couldn't help buying into that fairy tale a little bit.

Maybe he was her beast, and she was his princess, and they'd both been waiting for the other for a long time.

"Tell me what you're thinking," Jed said.

Cherry couldn't put it into words. She wanted to, but she didn't say stuff the way Jed did. She could quip, sure. She had a quick mind and wit, yes.

But with real feelings of the heart, she'd much rather kiss Jed to tell him what she was thinking. She leaned toward him, and he did the same to her. Right before their lips touched, she whispered, "I'm thinking that maybe I'm falling in love with you too."

The kiss that followed generated enough heat for the astronauts from space to see it on their fancy machines, if such a thing existed.

Jed kissed her and kissed her, keeping them solidly within their own seats and the realm of control Cherry appreciated. He pulled away after a few minutes and asked, "Was that a secret, Cherry Cooper?"

"Yes," she said simply. "Now, don't make me regret telling you."

"No, ma'am," he said, replacing his cowboy hat. "We don't want to miss our reservation. I think you had to call in a favor to even get this one."

"You're right," she said, centering herself after such an amazing kiss. "Let's go." As they walked into the restaurant, Cherry had a feeling she was glimpsing her happily-ever-after.

14

J ed lifted one end of Cherry's couch while Lee hefted the other. "Got it?"

"Yep," her brother said. He glanced over his shoulder as Will and Travis came inside, and they got out of the way quick.

"I'll guide you down the steps," Will said, and Jed moved at Lee's pace. The last thing he wanted was to hurt himself or anyone else. He and Lee were the same age, and Jed knew what forty-four felt like. It ached, that was how it felt.

He'd had one of the best weeks of his life here in San Antonio with Cherry. They'd eaten at some great restaurants. She'd introduced him to her neighbors and friends. They'd seen some historical sites. He'd kissed her every chance he got.

She'd definitely opened the door a little wider for him,

and Jed was trying hard not to shove it all the way open and leap inside. He'd confessed some big things to her on his first night here, but she hadn't shut down, freaked out, or gone into some part of herself he hadn't met yet.

"Gretchen," someone said, and Lee slowed while she moved.

"Sorry," she said. "I wasn't paying attention."

"It's fine," Jed said.

"For him," Lee puffed. "I'm the one walkin' backward."

Jed grinned at him, and Lee went up the ramp and into the moving truck. He'd helped Cherry pack plenty of boxes this week too, and he had some serious doubts about this truck holding all of her possessions.

He'd told her he should've brought his truck, and she'd said, "Yeah, I guess. But then who would've driven it home?" She'd batted those eyelashes at him, and he realized she'd set him up to drive her moving truck for her. She had her sedan, of course, and *someone* had to drive the truck, she'd said.

In reality, Jed was happy to do it. He liked it when Cherry leaned on him or asked him to do something for her.

He and Lee put down the couch, and he'd barely straightened before Travis said, "Get out, guys."

"We just got in," Jed said, but Travis and Will were already coming up the ramp with the love seat.

"I'm trapped in the corner," Lee said.

Travis and Will kept on coming, and Jed barely got out

of the way. "Let's turn it over," Travis said, and he and Will flipped the loveseat and stacked it on the couch.

"I'm back here," Lee said, his voice disgruntled. "Don't put that there. I need to move it to get out. Then we have to slide it back."

"Why didn't y'all do that already?" Will asked.

"Because you came in right on top of us," Jed said, not really sure why he'd joined this brotherly spat.

Lee's poisoned, "Who told you to come out so dang fast with that?" would've done the job just fine.

Will looked at Jed and then Travis. "Pick it up, I guess."

"You guess?" Lee roared from the back of the truck. Jed wisely decided that was his cue to leave, and he jumped down so he didn't get squashed by a still-bickering Travis and Will. Lee slid the couch forward and got free, then pushed it into place himself. He threw a few more pointed words at his brothers before getting out of the truck too, and he looked at everyone standing in the driveway.

"Don't we have stuff to move?" he barked.

That got everyone scurrying about, including Jed. Cherry met him in the front doorway, wiping her hands on a towel, and she asked, "What is goin' on?"

"Your brothers got into a little tiff," he said.

"Travis and Will are acting like we're tryin' to set some Guinness World Record for moving a three-bedroom house," Lee grumbled, coming up the steps behind Jed. "We just started. We don't need to be on top of each other."

"We didn't realize," Will said.

"Obviously," Lee shot back.

"All right," Cherry said, holding up one hand. "Enough. Do I need to put someone on cleaning?"

"No," they all said together, Jed included. He'd rather figure out how to put all the pieces in the moving truck than clean underneath a couch or behind the washing machine. No, thank you.

"Go on, then," Cherry said, plenty of crossness in her tone. "There's beds and dressers next. Put those muscles to good use."

Her brothers glared her down as they went by, and how she withstood that, Jed would never know. She was far stronger than she seemed, that was for dang sure.

"They're scary," he whispered. She turned those eyes on him, and Cherry possessed a pretty powerful glare of her own. "Yikes. So are you. Where do you want me next, princess?"

She frowned and flipped the towel at him. "Don't call me that. Go help with something big. Lord knows He gave you the shoulders for it."

"Yes, ma'am," he said, and he went to help the Cooper brothers with the bigger items. Meanwhile, Cherry, Rosalie, and Clarissa kept moving out boxes, as did Ford and Autumn—any the kids could carry, at least.

Gretchen and Shay stayed outside and organized things, helped direct traffic, and kept mothering Cherry's cats, which she'd put in carriers before everyone had even arrived that morning. Her parents had come too, but they stayed inside and helped clean and direct people there too.

His brother Easton had come, and Jed caught him helping Wayne and Chrissy more than moving much, but he didn't mind. In fact, it seemed they needed someone to entertain them and chat with them, and Easton did excel at that.

Cherry had sold her house that week, but the new buyers wouldn't be closing until the New Year. She said, "I want to leave it clean, but it doesn't have to be perfect," so when everything was packed—and they totally had to use both Lee's and Will's trucks to get it all—Cherry closed her front door and joined everyone outside.

She wore a look Jed had seen before, only a couple of times. He'd seen it when he'd first climbed the steps to the top of the hay bales in the corn maze only five weeks ago.

She was lost.

Lost, and alone, and afraid. He opened his arms, glad when she stepped into the space there and joined him. He didn't look at Lee or Will or Travis or Wayne. They all knew he and Cherry were dating, and Jed wasn't great at hiding how he felt. They could probably all see his adoration of their sister and daughter, and a slip of humiliation moved through him.

Then he told himself it wasn't embarrassing to want to help someone. *Or to love them*, he thought, and he relaxed.

"All right," she said. "Thank you, everyone." She lifted

her phone. "I'll send you the address of my new place. I think I'll beat the truck." She looked up at Jed, who nodded. "I'm going to call for pizza too, so we'll have lunch in Short Tail."

Everyone nodded, and Jed stayed out of the way as she hugged her parents, then stepped into Lee's arms. Jed watched them for a moment, sensing their powerful bond. Then he switched his gaze to her mama and daddy, both of whom looked utterly exhausted.

He went after them and helped Chrissy into the passenger seat of the minivan they'd driven. "You okay?" he asked her. Her face shone with sweat, and her skin bore the same tone as in the cement on Cherry's sidewalk.

"This just wore me out," she said. She still had enough energy to cover his hand where he rested it on the interior door handle. "You and Cherry sure are sweet together."

Jed's eyebrows went up. He looked past her to the driver's seat as Wayne opened the door. "You think so?"

"Yes," Chrissy said. "She'll try to push you out, Jed. It's what she knows best."

He looked back at her, sure Cherry would be upset her mama was saying these things. "I..."

"Chrissy," Wayne said gently, and his wife's eyes drifted closed.

"Don't you let her," Chrissy mumbled. "Okay, cowboy? Don't you let her."

Jed looked at Wayne, not sure what to do or say. He simply looked at his wife with great concern on his face, and then he nodded to Jed. "Will you lower her seat?" he asked. "She gets so tired so fast, and with the drive, and the unfamiliar bed..." He left his sentence there, though Jed felt certain there was so much more to say.

He gently lowered Chrissy's seat so she could sleep, and Wayne twisted to grab a blanket from the back seat. Jed helped to get it over Cherry's mama, and Wayne gave him a pillow to wedge between the seat and the wall of the van. Jed did, then closed the door.

He waved goodbye to them, and as they backed out, Cherry came to his side. "Thank you," she whispered. Jed held very still, just wanting to be in this moment with her.

"They shouldn't come help unpack," he said. "Your mama was real tired."

"I saw you with her," she said.

Jed kept what her mama had said to himself. *For now,* he thought. Cherry was already doing a stressful thing by moving, and he didn't need to get her riled up for a long drive alone by saying something that didn't need to be said.

"I can't come help unpack," Easton said, and that broke Jed's silence.

He turned toward his brother and embraced him. "This was huge," he said. "Thank you for doing this." Four hours of driving in one day wasn't easy for anyone, and Easton had work still to do back on the farm. Heck, Jed didn't think he'd get out of evening chores either, now that his week off had concluded.

He pounded Easton on the back and let his brother go. Cherry handed him a slip of paper with her neat handwriting on it as Easton walked away. "My new address," she said. He didn't even glance at it.

Almost everyone had loaded up, but only her parents had actually left. They were all waiting for her, and Jed admired the love her siblings had for her. Clarissa would probably stop everywhere Cherry did, just to run in to go to the bathroom with her. The four of them wanted their sister back desperately, and Jed hadn't realized it until this morning.

His curiosity about what had driven Cherry away from her family burned through him hotter than ever. He reached up and tucked her hair behind her ear. "You okay?"

"Just sad," she admitted, turning to look at the house. "I've lived here for a long time."

"A new adventure," he whispered, because Cherry loved adventures. Well, part of her did anyway. Another part of her thrived on routine, and while part of her was sad, another part had to be happy too. Relieved, even.

"You're going home," he said. "Kind of. This is what you wanted."

"I know," she said, slightly irritated with him. "It's still hard." She gave him a crisp look. "Just because it's hard doesn't mean I don't want to do it. And it's okay for it to be hard." She started to walk away from him, and Jed blinked at her.

Classic Cherry. Her mood could change faster than the weather. Even as he thought that, the sky overhead rumbled with thunder, and he looked up. "Lord," he said, his mouth barely moving. He didn't know how to finish his prayer, because there weren't words for what he needed today.

No rain?

A sunny Cherry?

Neither was going to happen, so petitioning the Lord for them wasn't worth it. He looked at Cherry and called, "It's okay for it to be hard, sweetheart."

She turned and looked at him, and he put a smile on his face. "Hey, it could be worse."

"How?" she challenged him, that sexy hip cocking out as she planted her hand on it.

"You could be driving the truck," he said as the first drops of rain fell. "In bad weather." He didn't wait for her to answer. He just ran for the moving truck, barely making it inside before the sky opened, and the rain *really* fell.

JED WISHED MOVING SOMEONE IN WINDY, WHIPPY, December weather was easy. It wasn't. By the time he and Cherry's brothers got everything she owned into her new house and set where she wanted it, the sky foamed with steel-colored clouds. Darkness hadn't quite fallen, but nor was there any sunshine to be seen.

"You can go," she said, her voice filled with exhaustion. Lee, Will, and Travis had all just left, and Jed simply wanted to collapse onto her couch and fall asleep with her nearby.

He looked at her and offered a smile. "I don't know if I can make it back to the farm without falling asleep." Not only that, but she had to take him, as he'd been in San Antonio all week with her and didn't have a vehicle.

"I should've gone with Lee," he said, just now realizing it.

"Oh, you can't go," she said, reaching for her keys. "Come on, I'll take you." The weariness on her face matched that in her voice.

"Are you sure?" he asked.

"Yes," she said, coming toward him. "What's the alternative? You stay here? *My* bed isn't even set up yet."

He'd mapped the distance from his cabin to her new house, and it was a seventeen-minute drive.

"I'm not going to stay here tonight anyway," she said, looking around. "I'll stay with Mama and Daddy, and tackle this in the morning."

"Did you just decide that?"

"Yes," she said, moving closer to him. "And I want it noted for the record that I've said yes to you twice now. Just in this conversation." She smiled up at him, and while she was tired, she was still breathtakingly beautiful.

Jed felt lighter, and he smiled too. "I've noted it in the official record," he said.

"Good," she said. "Now, let's go, because I might fall asleep right where I stand."

"One thing first," he said, taking the keys from her. "I'll drive, okay?"

She nodded, because she'd told him once, back when they'd dated over the summer, that she hated driving everywhere. That she thought one of the greatest pros to being married would be that she didn't always have to drive.

"Okay, two things," he said, and then he turned toward the door. "I've got one more secret to tell you on the way back to the farm."

_____

C herry leaned her head back against the rest as Jed drove through the night toward his farm. She'd done it. She'd left San Antonio and her perfect little house in the perfect neighborhood and returned to Sweet Water Falls.

Kind of. Her new place actually sat just across the border of Short Tail, another sleepy little Texas town with great charm, an amazing diner inside the only store, and a single-pump gas station. She was actually closer to downtown Sweet Water Falls where all the shops, restaurants, and grocery stores were than anyone at the farm.

He didn't say anything about his secret, and Cherry didn't have the mental capacity to ask. He pulled into her mama's driveway before she realized it. "Oh," she said and that was all.

"I'll come get you for breakfast," he said quietly. "We can swap vehicles then."

Her first instinct was to argue. She'd been tired before. She could go another few minutes down the road to drop him off and then come back. At the same time, she just wanted to crawl into bed and go to sleep.

"Okay," she said. "Thanks, Jed." She started to get out, and Jed met her at her door by the time she did.

"I talked to Lady Jones," he said, his voice too loud in all this country silence. He took her into his arms. "She said I could come talk to her about the farm in the New Year."

Cherry smiled up at him. "That's great, Jed."

"I want you to come." He swallowed, the movement catching her eye. "That's the secret. I have this appointment, and I don't want to go alone."

Again, she had to analyze her first instinct, which was to tell him no. Of course she didn't need to go with him to this farm he was thinking of buying. He wanted her to, but it wasn't necessary. They weren't married.

She blinked, realizing that Jed wanted to include her, because he was very serious about their relationship. *I'm falling in love with you.*

"All right," she said, deliberately choosing not to say yes. "I don't even have a job yet. I'm sure I can go."

"You'll get a job," he whispered as he leaned closer. "I'm sure of it." He kissed her goodnight, and Cherry melted into his strong arms and tender touch. He didn't kiss her long, and then he walked her up to the door like he was her high school boyfriend dropping her off after the prom.

He backed up, lifted his hand in a wave, and turned to go down the steps. Cherry watched him go, her back pressed into the wooden door behind her. "He's a good man," she whispered to herself. If he bought that farm, he'd *work* it. Day, night, holidays. He'd help animals— something he loved to do—and build new barns, fences, buildings, maybe even a new house. The cowboy was handy and handsome and everything Cherry wanted.

A real prince, and while not that long ago, he'd told her she was no princess, she certainly felt like one on his arm.

———

A FEW DAYS LATER, CHERRY FINISHED TAKING OUT ALL THE notebooks and pens she'd packed into one box, broke it down, and stashed it with several others she'd unpacked that morning. She put the notebooks—all unused, of course—in a cupboard in her kitchen and dropped the pens into the drawer below it.

She loved stationery with her whole heart. She often bought fun notebooks of all shapes and sizes, never intending to use them. Every once in a while, she'd tear a page out to make a list, as she had earlier that day.

Unpack six boxes got crossed off, and the next few items

on her list were errands. *Grocery shopping. Drop off one application and stop by City Hall to pick up another one.* She actually had a meeting with the County Records Office after lunch, and she checked the time on her microwave to see if her sister was running late yet.

Not yet.

Rissa should be here any minute, though, and Cherry dashed out of the kitchen and into her bedroom to change her shirt. She went with something bright and pink, because she wanted to stand out at the Records Office. She was meeting with the manager there—just to ask about the job that had been listed last week and get an application if she felt like it would be a fit for her—and Cherry knew the value of first impressions.

Rhonda Gappmeyer had to be close to Cherry's age, and she ran her fingers through her dark hair, settled the hem of her shirt just right over her jeans, and turned as Rissa called, "Cher, I'm here."

She met her youngest sibling in the kitchen and immediately took her baby nephew from her. "Hello, Bronson." She gave him a kiss and then leaned into Rissa for a hug. "Howdy, Riss."

Her sister pulled back, and while over a decade sepa- rated them, Cherry experienced a closeness to her she hadn't in a while. "Are you ready for this?"

"I think so." Cherry took a deep breath, held it, and then blew it out. "Let's drop off the application first." She swiped her list into her free hand while holding the six-week-old baby in one arm. He'd pinked up, and his cheeks looked like his mother had stuffed them with socks. "Then we can go to lunch. Then I have that appointment with Rhonda at City Hall. Then groceries."

She looked at her sister. "Can we manage all of that? Do you want to drive separately in case you need to take Bronson home?"

"No," Clarissa said, swiping her son's wispy hair off his forehead and giving him a smile. The infant flailed his arms and made a screeching noise, obviously thrilled to see his mama. "He'll be okay. I might have to feed him, but I have a bottle or I can sit in the car while you talk to Rhonda."

Cherry nodded, a new part of her once again mourning some of the choices she'd made in her life. She'd let Charlie Hooper and Brandon Alcott drive her from her hometown, and she'd closed every door to every man who'd ever come knocking.

Even Jed. He just hadn't given up as easily as some others had. He was loud and brash and opinionated...and Cherry sure did like him.

"Jed asked me to come look at a farm with him," Cherry said once she'd strapped the baby in the backseat, taken her seat, and fastened her seatbelt.

Rissa looked at her, her bright green eyes sparkling with shock. "He did? Where?"

"Just right here," Cherry said, her voice not as loud as Rissa's. "It's Betty Jones's land. Her farm."

Rissa put her SUV in reverse and started to back out of Cherry's driveway. "That's great, Cher. Are you going to go?" The fact that she had to ask that question made Cherry look out her window.

"Yeah," she said to her dry and dormant front yard. "I am."

"So you like Jed."

"Yeah," Cherry said, able to admit it now. "I like him a lot."

"Are you going to marry him?" Rissa asked.

"You sound just like Mama," Cherry said with a smile for her sister.

Rissa giggled and shook her shorter hair back out of her face. "Sorry. I didn't mean to jump to that. When you first started your sentence with 'Jed asked me' I thought you were going to say he'd asked you to marry him."

Cherry studied her, but Rissa kept her eyes on the road. "Why would you think that?"

"Cherry." She flicked a glance in her direction, her tone slightly patronizing. "Everyone can see how much he loves you."

Cherry didn't know what to say. "That's...he hasn't said that. And trust me, the man doesn't hold back from sayin' what's on his mind."

Rissa laughed then, a full-on belly laugh. Cherry found such joy swimming in the sound that she did too. "I bet he doesn't," Rissa said, still chuckling. "But Cherry, that's who you need."

"Is it?" Cherry smoothed her hands down her thighs as Rissa started to near the outskirts of town. She'd picked up an application for an office manager at the big music store in town. They held recitals there for a variety of instruments, had rooms private teachers could rent for lessons, and then all of their retail space where they sold everything from grand pianos to ukuleles.

The office manager for a place like that would have to deal with dozens of moving pieces, which Cherry was very well-suited for.

"Absolutely," Rissa said. "You'll put him in his place; he'll put you in yours."

"He has done that a few times," she said.

"As I'm sure you have for him," Rissa said.

"Maybe," Cherry admitted. "Riss." She didn't know how to say what ran through her mind.

Rissa looked at her, then turned into the parking lot outside the music store. She brought her SUV to a stop and looked at Cherry again. "What?"

"It's mostly me that needs to be put in line," she said. "Jed's...great. Wonderful."

"He's still a little salty," Rissa said. "Like Lee."

Cherry smiled then. "Yes, like Lee."

"And he's been married twice."

"Well, just once, technically."

"Rose sure seems to like him," Rissa said. "And Spence puts up with me. We just...find our person, you know? I think Jed is yours, but it doesn't matter what I think."

Cherry nodded, plucked her application from the folder she'd brought it in, and went inside the music store. The man who did the interviews wasn't there, so she couldn't meet him and make a personal connection, which only soured her mood further.

Lunch went well, and then Rissa stayed in the car to feed Bronson while Cherry went inside City Hall. She took deep breath after deep breath while her purse and cell phone went through the metal detector. They had courtrooms here, and no firearms could go inside.

She bypassed the courtrooms and went to the Records Office tucked back into the corner on the first floor. Another woman stood in line ahead of her, and Cherry shifted her feet, not sure if she even needed to check in here.

The nerves running through her bothered her, but she didn't know how to tame them. Just like she didn't know how to control her tongue sometimes, and she didn't know why she couldn't just tell Jed yes sometimes.

The other woman left, and Cherry stepped to the window. The whole thing had a piece of plexiglass from counter to ceiling, and she'd have to pass anything through a slot in front of her. Surprise filled her at the security of this place, and she wondered if she really wanted a job like this.

With an office manager job—or the one here for a full-time county clerk—would allow her to wear all of her professional clothes from San Antonio. She'd gone through her closet, of course, but she owned a lot of nice things, and she'd gotten rid of very little.

She'd driven thirty minutes around the city to work; she could drive into Sweet Water Falls in less time than that. She had all the skills to do the jobs she'd been applying for. It had been disheartening not to secure one on the first day, with the first application, but she reminded herself today was only Wednesday, and this was only the fourth job she'd inquired about.

"Hello," she said. "My name is Cherry Cooper. I have an appointment with Rhonda Gappmeyer at one-fifteen?"

"Yes," the woman there said. She wore her plain brown hair back in a ponytail, but her eyes looked happy enough. "Her office is down the hall to the left there. I'll let her know you're here."

"All right." Cherry turned to leave, and she glanced left before entering the hall. A couple of men stood in the hallway, both in police uniforms. A flash of unease blitzed through her, because she did not want to run into the Sheriff's Deputy before talking to Rhonda.

In that moment, she realized that she might run into Charlie at any time now that she was back in town. Especially if she got the job here.

But neither of the men a few paces away were Charlie. One did look familiar though. Cherry moved to her right out of the office, which would've been her left when she was facing the other way. This hallway was narrow and the dark brown brick on both walls on either side of her made it dark.

Doors stood here, all of them closed, and Cherry wasn't sure if she was just supposed to linger in the hallway or what.

Thankfully, a door at the corner opened, and Rhonda appeared. She wore a darling dark brown skirt in what looked like leather, with huge buttons down the front of it. Her pale pink blouse looked stunning with the skirt, and with her darker complexion and hair.

"Cherry," she said warmly. "Right in here."

"Thank you," Cherry said, entering the office. She expected it to be dark because of the bricks, but it wasn't. It had no windows, but light poured from the ceiling above, and Rhonda had filled the countertop immediately inside the office with various decorations, pictures, and a trio of lamps which provided more light.

Her desk took up one end of the office, and she sat behind that while she said, "Take a seat," and indicated a couple of comfy-looking armchairs in black leather.

Cherry did, wishing she'd changed out of her dark jeans into a pair of black slacks. She told herself this wasn't an interview, and she smiled at Rhonda. "I really just wanted a little more information about the job before I apply. I didn't mean you had to sit down with me."

"I don't mind," Rhonda said, and she pushed something out of her way on her desk. "It's a big position here. It's not an elected position, but because the county isn't over eight thousand in population, the County Clerk also serves as the District Clerk here."

Cherry swallowed. "I didn't know that."

"It's a lot of court meetings," she said. "Transcribing. Documents. A ton of filing." Rhonda smiled like this was easy, easy work. "You're the custodian for all court records. You'd oversee jury selection if needed. You handle all court fees and document fees."

Cherry nodded and tried to put a smile on her face. "So I work the window."

"No." Rhonda gave a light laugh. "You'd have an office like this, but yours is in the back of the building. It has a window." She leaned into her desk. "You have to take minutes at all public city and county meetings. So there's evening work. Then, there's a lot you just get handed that you have to take care of. Stuff you didn't necessarily touch, but need to document and file, date and send out confirmations. A lot of that."

"Okay," Cherry said. She liked Rhonda's energy and spirit, and she too leaned forward. "I think I want to apply. Do I need any special requirements?"

"There's on-the-job training," Rhonda said, pushing herself back and opening a desk drawer. "In fact, District Clerks are required to have twenty hours of training every year."

She stood and handed Cherry a packet of papers. "You worked at SATC in San Antonio?'

"Yes," Cherry said, standing and studying the front

paper. Average application. Name, date of birth, all the usual suspects.

"So you've lived in Texas for longer than twelve months."

"Yes, ma'am," Cherry said, raising her eyes to Rhonda's. "A lot longer than that."

"Are you registered to vote here in Refugio County?"

"No, ma'am."

"That's a requirement," Rhonda said. "Technically, you're supposed to live here for six months too, but I think I can get that waived if the rest of your application looks stellar."

Cherry's heart bobbed in her chest, sagging to the soles of her feet and then rebounding to the back of her throat. "Okay," she said. "Thank you, Miss Gappmeyer."

Rhonda sat back down, obviously not going to walk Cherry the five steps to the door. "Say hi to Will for me," she said. "He supplies all the milk for Marty's ice cream parlor." She smiled at Cherry, who should've known this woman would know someone in her family. Everyone in Sweet Water Falls did. "And give my regards to your parents. I hope your momma is doin' okay."

"She is," Cherry said, flashing a smile she hoped wouldn't hold too much pain. She left the office, the packet feeling like a load of bricks in her hand. She navigated her way to the exit, and she'd very nearly stepped outside when a man called her name.

She turned back and saw the very last person on the planet she ever wanted to see again: Brandon Alcott.

Jogging toward her, wearing a power suit in dark gray, with a purple and blue tie flapping against his abdomen.

Cherry didn't wait for him. She turned and left the building, as if that would stop Brandon from following her. Her heartbeat zig-zagged through her veins, making everything hurt it moved so fast.

"Cherry," he said again, and as disoriented at seeing him as she was, she didn't even know what Rissa's SUV looked like right now. She'd felt like this before—once before. The night Charlie had laughed at her and told her no, he wasn't going to propose. Not before he became the Chief of Police—and that still hadn't happened.

She'd been lost. So humiliated. So broken. So alone.

She'd run to the first man she could find, and she hadn't even known his name. All she'd wanted was someone to *want* her.

"Hey," he said, and Brandon appeared in front of her. He smiled at her, but it felt greasy and so wrong. "I heard you were back in town."

"I don't want to talk to you." She tried to brush by him, but Brandon dodged in front of her again.

"Why not?" His brow wrinkled like he was truly confused. Could he be? They'd spent less than a couple of hours together, twelve years ago. Of course she didn't want to talk to him.

"Cherry?"

She turned toward her sister's voice, relieved to find Rissa stepping onto the curb, her son in her arms. Cherry reached for him, ignoring all of her sister's unspoken questions. She looked past Cherry to Brandon.

"Hello," she said.

"Brandon Alcott," he said, extending his hand.

"Stop it," Cherry barked at him, letting all the saltiness she'd been trying to tame for Jed come out. Because this wasn't Jed. "You're not introducing yourself to her. This isn't happening." She turned away from Brandon and glared at her sister. "Come on, Riss. We still have things to do today."

Rissa said nothing to Brandon, thankfully, but she did follow Cherry back to the SUV at a slower pace. Of course, Cherry marched like she had to get there in the next two seconds or her feet would grow roots and she'd never get free.

She put Bronson in the back seat and extended her hand toward her sister for the keys. "Can I drive?"

"No," Rissa said, her green eyes firing dangerously now too. "Tell me who that was."

"No one," Cherry said, going around the front of the SUV. Brandon stood on the sidewalk several paces away, and she glared at him too. He stood there, still and silent, and Cherry thanked the heavens above for that. Rissa hadn't gotten in, and she only did after Cherry slammed her door.

"Cherry," she said.

"He's some guy," Cherry said, everything in her chest vibrating and boiling now. "When Charlie broke up with me that last time, I was so...devastated. I'd spent so long with him, and I just wanted him to love me. I wanted *anyone* to love me." She looked at Rissa as tears spilled down her face. "I...I did something I regret doing. I went out with him." She indicated the man beyond the windshield. "It was a one-night thing. But I left town because of Charlie, because of complicated things with Mama and Daddy, and because I'd gotten pregnant."

Rissa's eyes widened, and she reached over to grab Cherry's arm.

"I lost the baby the week I moved," she said, sniffling and wiping her eyes. "I never told anyone." She looked out the windshield again, but Brandon had gone. Left. Just like she had. "Can we go?"

"Yes," Rissa said crisply. "Yes, we can." She got the car moving, backed up, out of the parking lot. She drove down the main highway, and Cherry looked out her window at the beachfront property on her right. It wasn't really beachfront, as the highway stood between the houses and condos and the beach, but she figured it was close enough.

Rissa didn't pull into a grocery store. She seemed to be driving aimlessly, and Cherry felt the same way inside. "I haven't told Jed," she said. "Or Mama and Daddy." She turned and looked at Rissa, who wore her anxiety on her face. "Do you think I need to?"

Her sister swallowed and finally flipped on her blinker. She made a U-turn and went back toward the grocer they'd passed. "I don't know, Cher. I think...I don't think you have to confess to everyone, you know? If you want to, and it's part of your healing, then sure, you should tell them. But if not...and you're good with God... then, no. I don't think they need to know."

Cherry nodded and looked out her window again. "I don't know what I should do."

"How do you feel?"

"I don't know what you mean." Cherry reached up and wiped her eyes again. "I can't believe I cried over this. Everything is just so...mixed up right now."

"You weren't crying over him," she said. "Just probably surprised and scared you ran into him."

"Yeah," Cherry said as her sister parked. "But what if that means I'm not ready to move on? I've felt ready to move on—with Jed." She met her sister's eyes, and Cherry didn't want to hold anything back anymore. Not from herself, and not from her family, and not from Jed. "I'm falling in love with him too. You know? What if he doesn't want me either?"

"Oh, sissy." Rissa leaned across the console and took Cherry into her arms. "That's what you need to get past. Not Charlie. Not this one-night stand. Not if you should tell people about it. But that you're worthy of being loved. That you're a lovable person. That of course Jed loves you, because of *you*, not for any other reason."

Cherry held her and tried to reason through what she'd said. "I sometimes don't feel loved," she admitted.

"Which is crazy," Rissa said, pulling away. "Given how many of us think you're a Rockstar." She smiled at Cherry, her own eyes glassy. "Seriously, Cherry, I've looked up to you for my whole life. You're everything I've ever wanted to be."

She nodded, her emotions settling down. "Thank you, Riss."

"I love you," she said. "Everyone out at the farm does. Everyone you meet does, because you're *so* good at making people feel seen." She unbuckled as Bronson started to fuss. "Now, come on. Our window of good behavior with this baby is running out."

Cherry went inside to get her groceries, her mind revolving around what Rissa had said. All she'd ever wanted was to be seen, and so yes, she worked really hard at making sure those around her knew she saw them, their efforts, and their worth.

Jed sees you, she thought, and that was her answer. She didn't need to tell anyone else about what had happened so long ago...except him. She didn't want there to be anything between them, which meant he got to know all of her secrets.

Every last one.

16

Jed pressed the nail gun to the last of the shingles and it went *pop-pop! Pop-pop!* and the job was done. He stood straight and groaned as his back made the same noise as the nail gun just had. Easton so owed him for this.

He cleaned up, sweeping debris over the lip of the roof and onto the tarp below. He'd be able to gather it all up and dump it in their community dumpster easier that way. He reattached the rain gutters, then finally, finally, folded the ladder and put it in the back of his truck.

Dusk had started to cover Texas, and Jed had been putting in long hours in the past couple of weeks since returning from San Antonio. He had nothing to complain about, however, because he now saw his girlfriend each and every day.

He hadn't run into Cherry yet today, but he figured he'd see her waiting on his front steps. If they didn't have plans, that was usually where he found her. Once or twice, he'd gone out to her new place in Short Tail, but with calving happening, and all the other work he had around the farm, she usually came to him.

She hadn't started a new job yet, and she'd gotten a little glassy-eyed when he'd asked her about it last night. "You've had two interviews with the city," he said. "You'll get the clerk job."

Probably not until after the holidays, which stressed her out, but Jed felt certain she'd get that job. Then, she'd have to work some evenings, and he wouldn't get to see her sitting on his steps. "You can go to her," he said, bending to pick up the tarp with the minor debris from the re-shingling of his brother's cabin.

With all of that cleaned up, Jed headed over to the equipment shed where they kept the ATVs. He was on the field check that evening, and Chris had put double-duty headlamps on one of their machines so they could see in the dark.

He noticed an extra black car parked out front when he pulled in, and he grinned for all he was worth as Cherry straightened from her sleek sedan. She wore her hair back and up, revealing that gorgeous neck and those ears he loved to kiss.

"Hello, beautiful lady," he said, plenty of flirtatiousness in his voice. "What're you doin' here?"

"Chris said you were on the evening field check," she said, coming around the front of her car. She leaned her palms into him and tipped up to kiss him. Jed kissed her back, but he didn't take her into his arms and *kiss her*. He still had work to do today, and if he was lucky, he could get her to come with him.

"I figured sitting on your steps would be a waste of my time tonight." She smiled at him, and Jed regretted the tame kiss.

"It would," he said. "I should've texted you. I figured I'd be out and back in no time." He nodded toward the souped-up ATV. "Do you want to go for a ride?"

"In the dark?" She eyed the machine like it might tip her off the back of it on purpose.

"Sure," Jed said. "Fish comes all the time." In fact, his dog trotted out of the equipment shed in that moment, his brother not far behind.

"Hey, Chris," Jed called. He bent down to scratch the black lab's ears as he said, "Heya, Fishy. Did you find Chris to bother this afternoon while I was on the roof?" The dog just grinned up at him, and he turned to his brother, who was doing the same. They hugged, and then Chris stood next to Cherry and grinned at her.

Jed didn't introduce them, because they'd met loads of times in the past. His heartbeat did thump strangely, and he wasn't sure why.

"Did Jed invite you to our Christmas Eve dinner?" Chris asked.

Oh, right. That was why. Jed's adrenaline spiked, and he blinked past all the whiteness in his vision. Cherry came back into focus, and she'd cocked one sexy hip at him.

"No," she said. "He hasn't mentioned it."

"Yes," he said quickly, shooting his brother a look that Chris absorbed easily. "I did. I said I wanted you to come, but I didn't know all the details."

"Christmas Eve," Chris said. "Five o'clock is when Mama brings out the first appetizer. It's just a parade of food and gifts from there."

Cherry nodded to Chris and looked at Jed. "Seems like he knows the details."

"Mama texted us this morning," he said. "I was knee-deep in the corrals, and then I've been on Easton's roof all afternoon." He gestured to his black lab, who'd laid on his cowboy boots and panted. "Ask Fish."

"Fish did have to come find me this afternoon," Chris said.

"Do I need to bring anything?" Cherry asked.

"Mama won't let you serve it if you do," Jed said, smiling. He couldn't believe he was bringing a woman home for Christmas. Panic struck him like a rattlesnake. "Do you want to meet my mama and daddy before the party?"

"How big will the party be?" she asked.

"Just us," Jed said, stepping in front of Chris and taking Cherry by the shoulders. "Me and you and Fish. Chris and Deb and the twins. And Easton."

"He's not bringing a date?" Cherry looked at Jed openly, and he could see all the way into her very core. She was good, and gorgeous, and genuinely concerned about others.

"I doubt it," Jed said. "He's not seein' anyone."

"He might bring Jenni-Lynn," Chris said from behind him. "I think he was waiting to see if you were bringing Cherry."

Jed twisted to look at Chris, irritated he was still standing there. "Great," he said. "Don't you—?"

"So you should probably text him your plans," Chris said.

Jed blinked and growled. "Thanks, Daddy." He stepped away from Cherry to face his brother. "I've never had to text Easton my plans."

"Things are different now," Chris said. He searched Jed's face, and he must've seen the dangerous glint in his eyes, because he backed up. Finally. "C'mon, Fish. Your daddy's goin' out on the ATV, and the back seat is full."

Fish looked up at Jed, who couldn't stop his smile. "He's right, bud. Cherry's comin' with me tonight."

"I don't want to take his seat," Cherry said, slipping her fingers into Jed's.

He squeezed her hand and barely tilted his head toward her without taking his eyes from the canine's. "He's a dog."

"He's your best friend."

"Not tonight." He looked at her fully. "Do you want to sit here while I take Fish out to check the herd?"

She smiled at him. "No, sir."

"Then why are you arguing with me?"

"I don't know," she said. "It's fun?"

"C'mon, Fish," Chris said, and he sounded dangerously close to laughing. Jed glared at him, and that only made the first chuckle come out of his brother's mouth.

"Go on," he said to the dog, who got hesitantly to his feet. "I'll see you at home. Thanks, Chris."

"Yep." His brother walked away, and Fish followed him, looking back once.

"He's so sad he can't go," Cherry said.

"Again, he's a dog." Jed indicated the ATV. "I'll give him lots of belly rubs tonight, and he'll be fine."

She giggled and waited for him to swing his leg over first. As she balanced her hands on his shoulders and dropped onto the seat behind him, shivers ran down Jed's arms. "Is that what you do?" she asked. "Give belly rubs to make up for things?"

"For Fish," he said.

"What about me?" she asked.

"What about you?"

"If you had to make something up to me, what would you do?"

Jed started up the ATV, the loud engine drowning out all other sound. She leaned closer to him, pressing into his back. "I don't know," he said over his shoulder. "What should I do?" In the past, when Cherry had put him in the doghouse, he'd gone to her and apologized. He'd used the mouth she said she didn't like, and he talked, and then he kissed her. That had worked so far.

"I like flowers," she said into his ear.

He grinned and got the ATV moving. They'd roam through the fields and check for cows in labor. He'd already been praying there wouldn't be any, but he sent up another silent plea.

"What kind of flowers?" he asked as they got beyond the equipment shed. The ATV would cut through the quiet out here, and Jed normally didn't mind it. Tonight, it made talking to Cherry harder.

"I love the amaryllis," she said. "But that's not usually what someone gives to someone else. I loved growing them in pots in San Antonio."

"Roses?" he guessed.

"I guess," she said, which meant *no* in Cherry-speak.

"Not roses," Jed said, scanning both sides of the dirt path he drove down. "Lilies? Daffodils? Tulips?"

"I do like tulips," she said, and she leaned away from him, this conversation clearly over. Jed drove through the fields, didn't see anything alarming, and returned to the equipment shed. His stomach roared at him, but he didn't want to cook tonight.

In a burst of exhaustion and without thinking, he

asked, "Do you want to head over to my mama's, and see if she has anything to eat?"

Cherry looked at him, and under the orange glow from the lights on the outside of the equipment building, she looked stunned by alien light. "Your mama's?"

"I'm starving and don't want to cook." He grinned at her, hoping his boyish innocence would win him some points.

"How do you know she's cooked?"

"She always does," he said.

Something Jed couldn't quite place crossed Cherry's face. She looked away and said, "Must be nice."

He recognized the hurt in those words, and he said, "Cher," gripping her fingers so she couldn't get too far from him. "I'm sorry." He didn't know what else to say, and so he simply said, "I'm trying to come up with something to say to help you feel better about your mama. I know she's a good cook."

When she tugged her hand away, he let her go. She turned and walked away slowly, tucking her hands into her back pockets. "Do you ever just...look at the sky and wonder why life isn't fair?"

"Yes." He followed her, but because he knew Cherry, he didn't try to touch her. "I mean, not every night or anything, but sometimes."

"Yeah," she said. "Sometimes." She faced him again, everything wide open on her face. "I'm not bad in the kitchen, but I'm not great either."

"Yes, you are," he said. "I've tasted the food and desserts you've made."

"Not as good as your mama."

"Who cares?" he asked, finally feeling brave enough to reach out and touch her. "Mama loves you, and we can spend more time together."

"I've met your mother," she said, smiling at him.

"Not since you've really been mine," he said.

Her eyes widened, and she faced him fully. "Is that what I am? Yours?"

Jed swallowed hard, because he wasn't sure if the glint was a weird play of the orange light, danger, or simply interest. He shrugged like he didn't care one way or the other, but he did. Oh, he did.

"I don't own you," he said quietly. "But I'd say, 'Mama, this is the beautiful Cherry Cooper, *my* girlfriend.' Not like, *a* girlfriend or something like that."

"You could say the woman I'm dating."

Annoyance touched Jed's heart. "Yeah," he said, his voice turning hard. "I could. What do you want me to say?"

Cherry took a step back. "I don't care."

"Seems like you do." He folded his arms and glared at her, his hunger multiplying with this wretched conversation.

She blinked, and then she moved right into his personal space. "Don't go all salty on me, Jed," she said, pulling his arms apart and down out of the fold. He could've resisted her if he wanted to, but he didn't. "I was just asking."

"Is it wrong of me to think of you as mine?" he challenged. "Because I do, Cherry. I like you." He cleared his throat and swallowed down the other L-word. She wasn't ready to hear it, and Jed couldn't believe it had popped into his head at all. "I like you a lot. I like seeing you every day, and I like thinking about you, and I sure do like holding your hand and kissing you and riding around the fields in the dark with you. So, I need to know if it's okay if I think of you as mine."

She searched his face, only inches from him. "If I'm yours, can you be mine?" she asked.

"Yes," he said simply.

"Do you *want* me, Jed?" She wasn't teasing him. She didn't cock her head and bat her eyelashes. She'd just asked, and she sure seemed serious.

"Yes," he said again.

She closed the distance between them in a breath of time, and Jed did take her into his arms this time. He kissed her like he meant to kiss her, and he hoped he was interpreting her actions correctly as she kissed him back. Cherry might never tell him the same thing—that she wanted him—but he could feel it in her fingertips as they moved around his ears and into his hair, in the way she kissed him back, and the way she pressed into him, getting as close as she could.

"Come on," he finally said, his voice rough and ragged. "Let's go see what my parents have to eat."

———

CHRISTMAS EVE CAME IN THE BLINK OF AN EYE. JED AND HIS brothers had agreed to skeleton chores around the farm for the next several days, which meant minimal feeding, watering, and checking on the pregnant cows. That was it. So he'd slept late for the first time since being in San Antonio with Cherry, and he only got up when his alarm went off for the fourth time.

Jed tucked in his shirt now, having just showered in anticipation of his family party. It began in about a half-hour, and he needed to leave to pick up Cherry. He slid his belt buckle into place, grabbed his hat from the bathroom counter, and looked into his own eyes.

"You look decent," he told himself, and then he left the cabin. At Cherry's, he didn't even make it to the porch before she opened the door and stepped out. She looked far more than decent.

She looked phenomenal. She wore a dark red dress that went to her elbows and fell to her knees and looked like it could be silk or some colored water for how easily it moved.

"Wow," he said, whistling in the next moment. She turned and posed for him, holding up the bottle of apple cider as if it was a monumental award she'd won. "Don't you look festive?" He slid his hand along her hip and around to her back. "I'm just wearin' jeans."

"I wouldn't expect anything less," she said.

"You decided to bring the apple cider."

"It's the peach kind," she said, dropping her eyes to it. "I don't know how to show up empty-handed."

Jed grinned at her and leaned down to kiss her. She stopped him with, "Don't you dare mess up my makeup, Jed Forrester."

"A little Christmas Eve kiss," he whispered before matching his mouth to hers. He didn't go too fast or too far, and he pulled away with her dark pink lips still perfectly lined and colored. "Not a single smudge," he said, wiping his thumb down the side of her mouth.

She checked in the mirror in his truck anyway, something Jed simply smiled about. So much about Cherry made him smile, and when she crossed her legs and looked at him, he looked right on back. "What?" he asked.

"Do you have any other secrets?" she asked.

"Sure," he said. "You should know I want about a hundred animals. I can't say no if there's a dog who needs help. It's why Daddy banned me from goin' to town when I was seventeen." He chuckled at the memory. "I used to bring home a few dogs every time, because I couldn't not go by the animal shelter, and then I couldn't leave them there."

"Wow," she said, her smile bright and glorious. "So a lot of dogs. You just have Fish right now."

"I rarely go to town," he said. "Even now."

"Even now?"

"Yep."

"Who gets your groceries?"

"I go up in Beeville," he said. "It's almost the same distance, and there's no animal shelter." He flashed her a smile, but Cherry was still blinking her way through what he'd said. He chuckled and as he got back on the road that would take them back to Forrester Farms, he said, "I told you it wouldn't be a problem if we didn't have kids. We'll just have horses, dogs, cats, and ponies."

"Horses and ponies are the same thing," she said.

"Oh-ho, no, they're not," he said, shaking his head.

"At least you included cats," she said.

He chuckled again, and Cherry put her hand in his. When they arrived at his mama and daddy's house, Jed eyed the front door. No one came out on the porch here. "It's just dinner," he said.

Last week, when he'd brought her here to meet his parents as his official girlfriend, they'd eaten alone after the introductions. His parents had been their usual selves —quiet and normal. His mama never pushed him too much. His daddy had retired from the farm, which meant he was much less harsh than he'd been when Jed was growing up.

He happily mowed his lawn now, and put in a big garden in the spring, and he'd entered the pumpkin contest this year with a gourd that weighed five hundred and forty-five pounds. He hadn't won, as Hank Willis down the road even further had taken the prize with a whopping six-hundred-ten-pounder. Daddy was already scheming how to grow a bigger pumpkin next year.

"All right," he said with a sigh, but Cherry's fingers in his tightened.

"Will you come to my house tomorrow?" she asked.

Jed swung his attention back to her. "For Christmas Day?"

"Yeah," she said, smiling. "Tomorrow's Christmas Day, Jed."

He grinned too, his smile spreading slowly across his face. "Your house? Or your mama's house?"

"My mama's," she said. "We're having a big family lunch about noon. It'll be so loud and noisy, with everyone there—my uncle is bringing his family from the Dallas area—but...I want you there."

Everything inside Jed softened when she said those words, and he leaned toward her and touched his lips to hers. "Then I'll be there."

"Thank you."

"I just want it noted for the official record that you invited me to your holiday family party far later than I invited you."

"You barely invited me at all," she said. "Chris mentioned it."

"*I* mentioned it," Jed said, shaking his head. "I can't

help it if you don't listen when I talk." He turned and started getting out of the truck.

"I listen when you talk," she called after him, and she stayed put until he came around and opened her door for her. She twisted her knees to face him, one heeled foot reaching for the runner on his truck. She didn't scoot forward though, and Jed looked up the length of her leg to her face, heat building in him with every inch of her. "I noted it for the official record," she said.

It was a clear concession, and Jed nodded to her in all seriousness. "Thank you," he said.

She slid to the ground then, and Jed put his hand in hers again. They entered the farmhouse together, and it happened to be when everyone in his family burst into laughter about something.

"Oh, Jed's here," Daddy said, and he came to greet them. "Howdy, son. Howdy, Miss Cherry."

"Hey, Daddy." Jed hugged his father and added, "Merry Christmas."

"Yes, Merry Christmas," Daddy said. He hugged Cherry too, while Jed nodded to Easton and Chris. His older brother hadn't brought a date, and for some reason, that made Jed relax a little bit. He wasn't sure why, other than Easton had tried a relationship with Jenni-Lynn Dennis several times and it never worked between them.

He supposed one might be able to say that about him and Cherry, but he dismissed the idea. They'd broken up once, not four times.

After introductions had gone around, Mama said, "All right, all right. Everyone sit somewhere." She ducked behind the temporary curtain she'd hung down the middle of the kitchen, separating the dining room table from the island and appliances.

"She doesn't tell you the menu?" Cherry asked.

"Never," Jed said. "It's a surprise, marched out one dish at a time." He looked at Cherry and raised his eyebrows. "Couch or dining room chair?" he asked as the twins yelled and ran for their booster seats, which Chris or Deb had attached to kitchen chairs.

"I don't want to try to eat from a couch," she said. "I'll spill on my dress." She looked down at herself as if to make sure she wore the dress she'd wanted to.

"Table then," he said, and they joined Chris, Deb, and Daddy at the table.

"Everyone's at the table?" Easton asked, sounding totally put out. "Fine. I'll come sit in there." He heaved himself out of the recliner in the living room like it was a great chore.

"You can sit wherever you'd like, dear," Mama said as she ducked around the curtain, and Jed grinned first at her and then Easton. A less mature version of himself probably would've added, "Yeah," in the past, but tonight, Jed said nothing.

She turned back to the stove, went around the curtain, and added, "I'm almost ready for the first appetizer."

Cherry met his eyes, her eyebrows going up. Jed put

his hand on her knee under the table, and he watched as Mama came into the sectioned dining area, a huge platter in her hands.

"Eggs!" one of the twins yelled, and Jed laughed at his enthusiasm. "Nana, love devil-il-ed-ed eggs," Drake added. He banged his spoon on the table, and Deb plucked it from his hand.

"You don't need a spoon to eat a deviled egg," she said.

"Deviled, bud," Chris said. "Just deviled."

His mother put the platter on the table, and Jed let the twins go first. They clearly wanted the treat more than anyone else. "I'll take one," Cherry said with sophistication, and he let her put one half of one egg on her plate. He took four and passed the platter to Chris.

"Apricot kielbasa," his mom said before the platter had even gone to Deb.

"Oh my goodness," Cherry said. "That looks divine."

"It's pretty divine," Jed agreed. "It's fried sausage with apricot preserves and Dijon mustard. My mama makes the preserves herself."

Cherry took plenty of that, and she moaned at her first bite.

"Christmas tree veggie tray," Mama announced, and she set a big tray of vegetables that she'd arranged into a Christmas tree. Broccoli made most of the tree, with red and yellow peppers as the strings of lights, and bits of cauliflower and cherry tomatoes for bulbs.

"I like these sugar peas," Jed said, snatching a couple

from the branches of the tree. They made it look like the Christmas tree shape, what with their pointed ends, and he took a lot of the ranch dip too. "Mama makes this from scratch too."

"This is so cute," Cherry said. "Jed, put those peas back so I can get a picture for my mama." She reached to take the peas from his plate while he still spooned dip onto it, and he watched as she rearranged them, then stood to snap a picture. She looked at it with adoration on her face, and Chris elbowed him.

"Ow," Jed said, swinging his head toward Chris. "What was that for?"

"You're salivating over her," he said under his breath.

"No, I'm not." He glanced over to Easton, who watched him too. Daddy was too busy with the apricot kielbasa to notice Jed. "She took my sugar snap peas." He reached for them again and told himself not to stare at Cherry anymore.

Easier said than done, but he felt like he did a decent job as Mama kept bringing out food. She brought the main dishes one right after the other until the table groaned with candied ham, mashed potatoes, country gravy, roasted corn pudding, green bean casserole, and his favorite, roasted carrots and Brussel sprouts.

"I didn't know you ate vegetables," Cherry said as he piled his plate high with them.

He scoffed and handed the pan to Chris. "I do if they're good," he said.

"Or someone else makes them for him," Easton said.

"Like you're roasting veggies at your house," Jed said, stabbing a half of a sprout. It was sweet and tangy from the glaze, and he over-exaggerated how much he liked it.

"Now don't fill up on veggies," Mama said. "There's plenty of desserts to come."

Jed grinned at her, because he had room for anything else she might bring out. He checked on Cherry to make sure she had what she needed. She leaned closer, so he did too, and she said, "I'm not sure I've ever heard a mother say not to fill up on veggies."

He chortled, then burst out laughing, which he knew was far too loud for this intimate Christmas meal. "Sorry," he said as Daddy gave him a glare.

"My goodness," Mama said from her spot right next to Cherry. "She must be someone special to get you to laugh like that."

"Ma," Jed said at the same time Cherry said, "I'm sitting right here."

Jed looked from her to his mother, his heart firing at him hard. He swallowed quickly and said, "She is someone special, Mama, and it has nothing to do with making me laugh."

"Sorry," Cherry murmured, her eyes falling to her plate where she pushed her food around with her fork.

"I didn't mean anything," Mama said, blinking at Jed and then focusing on Cherry. "I'm sorry, dear." She covered Cherry's hand with hers, and that got Cherry to look up. Mama offered her a sweet smile, and Cherry gave a soft one in return.

"I'm just not used to being called special, ma'am."

Jed put his hand on her knee again and squeezed, hoping she got the message. She *was* special to him. She absolutely was.

17

William Cooper paused outside his front door and took a deep breath. Way in through his stomach, the way his therapist had taught him. He exhaled, keeping his mouth closed. Again, he breathed, shedding the cares of the day. It didn't matter that four dairy deliveries had gone out late today.

Another breath, and this time he blew the air out through his mouth in a long, controlled exhale. It didn't matter how much work he had to do tomorrow before dawn. He'd get up, and he'd do it. It didn't matter that once that work finished, he then needed to run to his wife's shop and help her get closed up for a couple of days.

He loved working with Gretchen, and then tomorrow night, they'd go collect her daddy from his house in Short

Tail, and along with her aunt, they'd celebrate a new year together with his family at the big white farmhouse.

Lee would be moving in there as soon as Trav's new place was finished. Mama and Daddy would take this cabin Will currently stood in front of. After all the house jumbling, Will and Gretchen would have a bigger place to raise their family.

A smile touched his mouth, then his heart, and finally his soul. He opened the door to the scent of baking chocolate, and Gretchen, his gorgeous, beautiful wife turned from the sink at the back of the house. "There you are," she said. "I was about to send Lee a nasty text." She smiled at him, and Will knew she'd do no such thing. Even if she was frustrated with the amount of work the Cooper brothers did, she'd only ever talk to Will about it.

"Here I am," he said, taking off his cowboy hat and hanging it on the hook beside the door. He ran his hands through his hair as he went through the living room and past the dining room set that had once belonged to Gretchen's mama.

He arrived in the kitchen, and he stepped next to her at the sink where she washed out a big glass bowl. "You made brownies."

"Mm hm." She sniffled too, and Will kept his head down as he slid his arm around her waist. He drew her into him, and Gretchen leaned against his chest, her hands still working the last of the batter off the bowl.

"I love coming home to brownies," he said quietly, so

glad he'd taken his time to leave work behind on the farm, so he could now be Will-the-husband. "But not more than coming home to you."

She smiled, rinsed out the bowl, and he let her get away from him as she put it on the towel next to the sink. Only then did she let out her breath and face him. He said nothing, though plenty of questions flowed between them.

"I'm just emotional," she said. "There's nothing wrong."

"You'd tell me if there was," he said, not phrasing it as a question.

"Of course." She stepped into him and he held her, nothing as sweet as holding his wife in their home.

"Trav's house is lookin' good," he said. "It's going to be done by the end of February. We'll move in March, and that's plenty of time to have everything set up for when the baby comes."

"I'd say so," Gretchen said, her voice quiet too. She moved back and wiped her eyes again. "I almost told Maggie today. I seem to burst into tears at the strangest times." She shook her head, and Will watched the frustration roll across her face.

"We can tell everyone tomorrow night," he said. "Then it's just done."

"Is it too early?" she asked.

"Baby, I don't know stuff like that," Will said with a smile. He knew his wife was pregnant, and she'd told him she was due July twelfth. That was what he knew, and he didn't much care about pregnancy announcement proto- cols. He knew he was beyond thrilled, and he couldn't wait to be a father.

Watching Rissa and Spence the past couple of months as they'd become parents had been fascinating for him, and Trav and Shay would have their little girl in only three more months. As fit as Shay was, and as fast as she ran, even she'd slowed down. She and Will still ran together most mornings, and he'd barely been able to keep up with her pre-pregnancy.

"You just tell me what you want me to do," he said. "And I'll do it."

"We should tell them," she said.

"Great." Will tried to keep his voice even and calm, but he suddenly couldn't stop smiling.

"You've been dying to tell everyone."

"I can't deny that." Will glanced over to the stove, and saw the brownies still had almost an hour before they even came out of the oven. "Am I makin' dinner?"

"It's your specialty," she said. They'd been eating at the farmhouse about half the time these days, because Will really liked more quiet in the evenings, and Gretchen sometimes worked late in her chocolatier shop.

"I don't know about specialty," he said, but Gretchen got out of the way so he could open the fridge to see what they had inside. He didn't want to spend the evening in the kitchen, not when he could lay his head in his wife's lap and let her brush her fingers through his hair while she watched something on the television. Or she'd text with her employees or her daddy while Will ignored his phone completely.

He always paid for that in the morning when he walked into the administration office, but Lee was starting to get the idea that Will didn't want to work all the time. In the past couple of weeks, the texts had slowed in the evening, as Lee and Rose got closer and closer to their wedding day.

"Breakfast?" he asked, and Gretchen said, "I'll make chocolate coffee."

He fried sausage links and scrambled eggs, and together, they put dinner on the table for the two of them. Will liked sitting down at an actual table and eating, and as he reached for Gretchen's hand so they could say grace, she caught him off-guard with, "Do you want a boy or a girl?"

Will recovered nicely and took a handful of sausage links, really focusing on the task so he wouldn't have to look at her. "Honestly?"

"Yes," she said. "Honestly, always, honey."

He smiled when she called him honey, as she usually made his name into a term of endearment.

"I'd prefer a girl," he said. "Then maybe she'll have some of your more personable qualities."

"Oh, she'll have red hair," Gretchen said with a smile as she took a big scoop of scrambled eggs. "And you do realize that you have two sisters and neither of them are all that...personable."

"I think they're trying," Will said in defense of Cherry and Clarissa. "And with more of you in her than me, she'll have a better chance."

Gretchen laughed and covered his hand with hers. "You realize that the baby is fifty percent of both of us whether it's a boy or a girl, right?"

"I took genetics once upon a time," he said dryly.

"And your mama is the sweetest woman in Texas, and that she still got the five of you." She grinned at Will, who decided to breathe out and embrace who he was: a Cooper.

And yes, Coopers had tempers, and they argued, and they shouted at family parties. But the Coopers knew how to forgive too, and they knew how to change, and they knew how to love deep.

"I suppose whether she's a girl or a boy, she'll still be a Cooper," Will said.

"That's right," Gretchen said, grinning. "Now stop hogging the sausage and pass it over here."

"You haven't even given me a drop of the chocolate coffee," he shot back, and they swapped food for drink and continued their meal. As they cleaned up together, Will took a moment to embrace his very normal, mundane life.

"I love you, Gretchen," he said as she loaded the last coffee mug into their dishwasher.

She turned into his arms and looped hers around the back of his neck. "I love you too, Will."

He kissed her, every time like the very first time.

———

SHAYLA COOPER RESTED HER HAND ON HER PREGNANT BELLY and watched the bare branches bend in the breeze beyond the bay window. The farmhouse held plenty of Cooper cowboy noise, but she didn't hear it at all. Not even her husband's voice could penetrate the bubble she'd created for herself.

Someone sat beside her, and Shay did turn when her mother-in-law put her hand on her wrist. She offered Chrissy a smile, but it shook, as it had been for the past several days. Chrissy said nothing, but then again, she'd never had to before.

Despite her own hardships, Chrissy had been over to the small house where Shay and Trav lived several times in the past couple of months, helping to pick out the items they'd order for the nursery. Their new house wasn't finished yet, so Shay hadn't actually ordered anything. But she had it all ready to go once everything finally fell into place.

Trav went by the build every single day, but Shay had stopped doing that. She almost wanted it to be a surprise when Travis finally drove them up to their new house and walked her inside.

"Only a couple more months now," Chrissy finally said.

"Until the house or the baby?" Shay asked.

"The house," Chrissy said. "Three for the baby. Plenty of time to get moved and set up."

Shay nodded and went back to gazing out the window. "Chrissy," she said, turning her hand and sliding it into the older woman's. She never spent any holidays with her own family, for despite finally getting married, the chasm between her and her mother seemed bottomless.

Another wave of emotion overpowered Shay, and she honestly couldn't wait to have this baby so her hormones would go back to normal.

"Yes, dear?" Chrissy asked in that quiet, gentle, yet so powerful way she did.

"Our little girl only has half a heart," she said, the words coming out even and well-practiced. Because she had practiced them. Over and over she'd said them to herself, inside her mind, to her reflection in the mirror, with the doctor, to Trav, over and over and over.

They hadn't told anyone yet, and Shay felt this invisible barrier between her and everyone else—sometimes even Trav—and she hated it.

"You can't keep the sixes," Trav yelled from the table, where he played games with his brothers, their wives or girlfriends, and his sisters and their significant others. Shay hadn't wanted to get involved in that. Not today.

"Yes, I can," Will yelled back. "Get the rules, Lee."

"He's right," Rissa said, which didn't indicate if she meant Trav or Will. Either of them could've been right for all Shay knew.

Outside, the branches bent in the breeze as it blew into a wind, and they couldn't do anything about it. They simply went with it, and Shay felt like she needed to be more like the boughs of the trees.

Bendable. At the very least, she wanted to be flexible enough to allow the Lord to shape her into who she needed to be, so she could learn to be the mother of a baby, then a child, then a teenager, then a woman, who only had half a heart.

"You're having a girl?" Chrissy asked, seemingly not even hearing the part about the health issues of the baby. "Oh, that's wonderful."

Shay turned away from the wintery backyard. She normally didn't mind winter in Texas, because it didn't snow. Everything just turned brown, and because of Travis, she'd learned to find beauty in all the shades of the earth, especially browns.

"Did you hear the part where she only has half of her heart?"

"It's a miracle what modern medicine can do these days," Chrissy said, her smile firm and intact. She squeezed Shay's hand, which admittedly barely felt like much to Shay, and leaned her head against her shoulder while everyone continued to argue around them. "I don't know much, Shay," she said. "But this I do know: God would not have given you a baby with only half a heart if you could not handle it."

"Okay," she said, because she didn't want reassurances. She wasn't sure what she wanted. She and Trav had already argued about this privately, and he hadn't known how to reassure her either. That was when she'd told him she didn't want such things. She knew she was a strong woman. She ran her own company, with plenty of creativity and vision for their monthly subscription boxes, new clothing lines, and continued innovation in the outdoor products she sold.

"I'm sorry this troubles you," Chrissy said.

"Thank you," Shay said quietly. Troubled was a good word for how she felt, as there didn't seem to be a solution to this. She couldn't make the rest of her daughter's heart grow. The doctors had assured her and Trav that babies and children and people in general lived happy, long lives with only half a heart.

They were monitoring everything now, and Shay had a myriad of extra doctor's appointments on the horizon.

"Hey," Trav said, and Shay looked away from the outdoors again. He tore his gaze from his mother to look at her. "Are you okay?"

"Yes," she said, scooting to the edge of the couch so she could stand. Trav extended his hand, and she took it. "Sorry, were you talking to me?"

"Yeah," he said. "But it wasn't anything important." He helped her stand, and his grip on her hand stayed far firmer than his mother's. "Gretchen, Rissa, and Rose are going to put a movie on in the sun porch, and they wondered if you wanted to join them."

Shay looked toward the door that led out to the sun porch, and sure enough, the women had gathered there. Even Cherry had gone, and she alone turned to look at Shay, questions in her eyes. She felt so removed from them for a reason she couldn't name. She hated the feeling, but she couldn't swallow it away despite her efforts.

"I suppose you're going to be talking business," she said, glancing over to Lee, who stood at the table with a bag of chips in his hands. Will sat across from him, a tablet in front of him. But none of the Coopers played games on devices, least of all the men.

Definitely business.

"A little," Trav said. "Daddy's going to show us a few things, and then Will got a new tracking system for his deliveries he wants to show us."

"Dinner will be in about an hour," Chrissy said, and she pushed herself away from the back of the couch too. Trav helped her stand as well, steadying her for much longer than he had Shay.

"I can help in the kitchen," Shay said.

"Everything is ready, sweetheart," Trav said. "We're just waiting for Jed to show up with pizza, and he just left his farm. Thus, an hour."

"There's plenty of appetizers if you're hungry now," Chrissy said.

"Cherry took the fruit tray and dip out to the sun porch."

"Take *me* out to the sun porch," Chrissy said, and Trav obliged, moving slowly with her. Shay went after them, because she didn't need to make a scene on New Year's Eve. This was the complete wrong time to be sad.

Cherry linked her arm through Shay's the moment she arrived on the sun porch, and they sat on the loveseat together. "Why do you look like you'd rather be anywhere but here?"

"Go see your favorite auntie," Rissa said, stepping over to them and handing her fussy baby to her sister. Bronson became the perfect distraction, and it took Cherry several minutes to quiet him.

"I can't wait to meet your baby," Cherry said, giving Shay a smile.

"It's a girl," Shay said, because she and Trav had decided to tell everyone. They just didn't want to make a big announcement.

Cherry's dark eyes blazed with joy. "That's great, Shay." She gazed down at Bronson too. "Did you hear that, baby boy? A girl cousin to play with." Bronson, now two months old, kicked and smiled at her. Of course. Cherry worked charms with the baby, which was why Rissa brought him to her when he wouldn't settle down.

"What are you going to name her?" she asked.

Shay shook her head. "We're not sure. Trav wants

something from the family, but he's looking through your family history right now."

"My grandmother's name was Cherry," she said, smiling at Bronson.

"Don't you want that for your little girl?" Shay asked.

Cherry met her eyes with surprise. She searched her face for too long, and Shay finally looked down at her lap. "How old do you think I am?" Cherry asked.

Foolishness filled Shay. "Right. Sorry." Cherry patted her arm, but Shay continued with, "I think fifty is the new forty, though, Cherry. Lots of women your age are having babies."

Again, Cherry searched her face, this time with an edge of hope there that hadn't been before. "I'm miles from that," Cherry said,

"Really?" Shay asked. "Seems like you and Jed are getting serious. No?"

"I suppose," she said, looking back to the baby. Shay wouldn't get more out of her, she knew, because Cherry wasn't like her brothers. She didn't let every thought she had come out of her mouth.

"Jed's here," someone called a while later, and Rissa immediately paused the movie. None of them had truly been watching it anyway.

"Praise the stars," she said. "I'm starving."

Cherry stood with the sleeping baby in her arms, and she only gave him up for Jed. Shay took him, and she went into the kitchen last. Various snacks lined the table and kitchen island, and Jed had only added several boxes of pizza. Maybe a dozen. With this lot, it took quite a bit to satisfy their hunger.

With most families, food meant there'd be a spell of quiet while they ate, but with the Coopers, it only meant more shouting. Shay usually didn't mind, and tonight was no exception. She never had shoved her way into the fray to get the best piece of pizza—one could lose a limb doing that—and so she stood out of the way and accepted the plate Ford brought to her.

"Thank you, bud," she said, taking the plate and giving the boy a kiss on the top of his head. She looked up and met Lee's eyes, who nodded at her.

So he knew. Trav must've told his brothers about their baby. Her husband looked away before she could attract his gaze, and Shay ducked her head and smiled. He'd always taken such great care of her, and she settled at the table beside Chrissy.

Wayne brought his wife a plate of pizza, a slice of three different kinds, when everyone knew she'd eat a few bites and be full. "Thank you, baby," she said, and Wayne gently clapped his hand to her shoulder before limping back toward the food.

Shay took a bite of her all-meat pizza and watched as Cherry interacted with Jed. They clearly cared about one another, and she remembered the excitement and rush of such new love.

Love.

This farmhouse was filled with it, and Shay let it heal the part of her that had broken when the doctor had said her and Trav's little girl wasn't entirely normal.

"All right," Will bellowed, and he stood at the head of the table. "Gretchen and I have an announcement."

Shay's eyes flew to Gretchen, and she couldn't believe she hadn't seen the glow about her before. She could now.

"We're having a baby," Will said, his grin expanding from ear to ear. "She's due in July."

Chaos, cheers, and congratulations lifted into the air, and Shay rose to her feet to offer them too. After all, a new baby—even one with half a heart—was cause for a huge celebration.

———

CHRISSY COOPER'S BODY CONTINUED TO BETRAY HER. Everything ached, and she wasn't sure how she still had her eyes open. The pizza had been consumed. Will and Gretchen had made their announcement. Shay had cheered considerably. Rissa and Spence had taken their baby home an hour ago, despite the fact that the clock hadn't struck midnight yet.

Wayne, Chrissy's beloved soulmate, had slept on the couch for an hour while their children watched a movie or something on their phones. Chrissy hadn't dared close her eyes, for fear that she'd miss something too important.

Something she desperately wanted to see, breathe in, experience, and remember.

Her heart hurt at the thought of not being here to cradle Will's first baby. Or to see Cherry finally settle into herself and finally accept who she was. Not only that, but she obviously enjoyed being with Jed Forrester more than anyone else, and Chrissy hoped she wouldn't stand in her own way of true happiness. Who'd have thought that Cherry's joy had been living next door to Sweet Water Falls Farm all this time?

Chrissy closed her eyes and thanked the Good Lord above that Cherry had finally come home. She'd been needed and wanted here for a long time, and Chrissy should've known it would've taken a good cowboy, with a pure heart and a loud voice, to rein her in. Rope her heart and give her permission to be herself.

"Mama," Cherry said now, and Chrissy opened her eyes. It took a moment for her oldest child to come into focus, but when she did, Chrissy saw how beautiful her daughter was. "Let's get you to bed."

"I want to see the New Year," Chrissy said. She'd been fighting the cancer raging through her body for a long time, and she was so very tired. No matter how much she slept, she never felt rested, not mentally or emotionally. Physically, perhaps, for a time. She could carry the mental load until it got too great, and then she let Wayne put her in bed so she could sleep. When she was asleep, she didn't have to think or feel or worry about all of the things she might miss after she was gone.

"You're very pale," Cherry said, sitting beside her. She didn't try to take any of the blanket covering Chrissy, who always felt on the outer edge of cold, even under comfy, warm blankets. "I think you should go to bed."

"And I think you should marry that handsome cowboy before I die," Chrissy said, giving Cherry a smile and a light laugh. She hurried to add, "I don't care if you do or not, Cher. I just want you to be happy, and you sure seem happy with him."

Cherry buried her arm under Chrissy's blanket and laced it through hers. "You know what, Mama? I am happy with him."

"I'm glad," Chrissy said. And she was. "How long until midnight?"

"Another half-hour, Mama."

"I'm just going to close my eyes for twenty-nine minutes, okay?" She turned and met Cherry's eyes. "Will you wake me so I can see the New Year?"

"Yes," Cherry whispered, and Chrissy knew she'd keep her promise. She did drift, catching snatches of conversation she wasn't entirely sure were actually happening in this moment. Her memory could play tricks on her sometimes, and she imagined patches of the past seventy-three years, the majority of them which she'd spent with Wayne and their children.

Cherry had always loved a good party, and she'd staged many here at the farmhouse.

Lee had always been so loyal and dutiful, and Chrissy couldn't find a day in her memory where her oldest son hadn't been in this house, taking care of her and Wayne.

Will had always been hardworking and honest, and nothing about him had changed as he'd aged—until he'd met Gretchen. Now, in addition to being the good person he was, he was dedicated to her happiness. He and Lee had helped Chrissy for months or maybe a year, and she was so grateful for them.

Travis had always been witty and smart, and Chrissy sometimes thought he might be her favorite son. He always knew how to cheer her up, and she couldn't wait to watch him become a father.

Clarissa had always been opinionated and somewhat desperate to have her voice heard. For her to get married first and spur the others into finding love in their own lives had been a great blessing in Chrissy's life. Watching her be a mother and wife and chef brought joy to everyone on the family farm.

"Mama," Cherry said, and Chrissy tried to come back from the place where she drifted. It took a few seconds, and Cherry saying her name again, but she managed to do it.

"Cherry."

"Only forty-five seconds, Mama."

She tried to sit up and managed it part-way. Cherry

helped her the rest of the way, and Chrissy had managed to get to her feet in time to count down with her husband, children, and their spouses and significant others until the clock struck midnight.

"Happy New Year!" several of them cried, including Cherry.

Chrissy simply smiled, because a new year was a great thing indeed.

"Happy New Year, Mama," Cherry said, kissing her cheek.

"Happy New Year, dear."

Cherry danced over to Jed, took his face in her hands and kissed him squarely on the mouth, which made Chrissy smile. All of her sons did the same with their wives, and Chrissy turned into Wayne's arms.

"I love you, dearest," he said. "Happy New Year."

She wasn't able to voice the words back to him before he kissed her, and Chrissy decided she could go this year and all would be okay. She didn't necessarily want to leave Wayne and the children here, but she could if the Lord called her home.

She could.

18

J ed pulled up to the Hallmark store, which sat in the same strip mall as several restaurants he'd never eaten at. He'd told Cherry he rarely came to Sweet Water Falls, and he'd told the truth. If one of them didn't cook, Cherry brought something from town to his cabin.

As he got out and jogged up to the sidewalk, he thought he should probably take her to dinner more often. It was just such a long way and took such a big chunk of his time that he hadn't.

Cherry didn't seem upset that he hadn't, but Jed knew she liked getting dressed up and going out. She still didn't have a job, though he was still certain she'd get the City Clerk appointment. Everything in government took forever, he'd told her, but she'd started applying to other places around town.

He wasn't sure how much longer she could go without an income, because they hadn't talked about her finances much. They'd talked about several other things, including what kind of house she'd like, and what he might do with the Jones' farm if he ended up buying it.

In Jed's mind, there was no *if*. He wanted that farm, and he'd come to the Hallmark store today to get a card for Lady Jones. He and Cherry would be visiting her farm over the weekend, and Cherry had said she'd bake her "famous" cherry white chocolate cookies.

He smiled just thinking of those, as she'd been so excited to find the old recipe in her mama's box. She'd been named after her nana, and that recipe had been hers. She'd apparently won the county fair with the cookies, and Jed would never say no to sweets. Or Cherry.

Inside the Hallmark store, he paused. He didn't do a lot of shopping in the first place, and certainly not in a store with breakables and the scent of orangey roses.

"Howdy, sir," a woman said, her smile far too bright. "Can I help you find something?"

"Yes," he said, blinking away from something pink and fluffy he couldn't even identify. "I need a card."

"A greeting card?"

"Yes, ma'am."

"What kind of card?"

"Uh..." Jed suddenly wasn't sure. "Not for a birthday or anything. Or an anniversary." He reached up and ran his hand through his hair and reseated his cowboy hat. "I just want to like, say hello. Or something."

The woman smiled at him. "Our 'or something' section is over here." She led the way, and Jed gladly moved away from the crystalline figures and other things his big cowboy hands could ruin.

She left him to browse the greeting cards, and Jed blinked at the vast assortment of them. The door dinged a few times, but no one ever came into his circle of concentration. He finally selected a card with a landscape of horses on it, which felt fitting, and the words, "Hay, I think you're neeeight."

Cheesy, sure, but Jed wasn't trying to be anything but that. He finally clued back into the world around him, the light coming in from the storefront's windows making him blink. Others talked in the store, and Jed expected female voices but got male.

"Can you imagine?" one of them asked. "No way. I'd never give this card to my girlfriend."

Jed went around the end of the row and peered down the next aisle. Two men stood there, laughing at the variety of cards in front of them. He didn't know them, but they couldn't be that much younger than him. They wore business suits, and Jed had heard through the grapevine that a couple of new corporations had come to Sweet Water Falls.

They probably worked for those companies. They weren't like him. They weren't cowboys working their family land. They weren't men who hadn't left Texas in decades, not because they couldn't, but because they didn't want to.

For some reason, Jed went down the aisle a single step and looked at the birthday cards there. The two men looked at cards on the other side of the aisle, which were clearly for significant others.

"Look at this one," one of them said. "You needed this years ago."

Jed ducked his head just as the card got passed from one to the other. "When you met that woman in the bar, and then she left because you couldn't make her stay."

"Whatever, dude," the second man said. "She left because she was with me when she wasn't even broken up with Charlie, and she was embarrassed."

The name *Charlie* tickled Jed's eardrums, but he wished it didn't. His stomach felt like he'd swallowed stones. He had to get out of this store, right now.

"And he was my friend, as was her brother."

"Those Coopers sure are getting married left and right," the first man said, and Jed couldn't walk away now.

In fact, he turned fully toward the two men and walked toward them. "Hey," he said. "Do you know the Coopers?"

Both men faced him, and Jed still didn't know them. The smiles slipped from their faces, though, and Jed felt some level of vindication.

"He does," the first man said. "He dated the oldest daughter once."

"No," the other man said quickly, swallowing afterward. All of his bluster and tough guy façade had fled. "We didn't date. It was one night."

Jed wasn't sure if that was better or not. "What's your name?"

"Brandon Alcott," he said. "You're Jed Forrester. You're seeing her now."

"Yes," Jed said. "And the Coopers are good people, so y'all might want to censor what you're sayin' where others can overhear."

"We didn't say anything bad," the first man said, his chin going up. Jed wanted to tell him that only made it a better target.

His fingers curled into fists, but he wouldn't swing. *For Cherry*, he told himself. She wouldn't condone fighting, certainly not with a couple of clowns like this.

"You made it sound like they were doing something wrong by getting married *right and left*."

"Maybe they are," he said.

"All right," Jed said with a smile. "I'm going to go. Nice meetin' y'all."

He turned and headed for the end of the aisle, and he'd very nearly reached it when the first man who hadn't given his name said, "Cherry's not who you think she is."

Jed gritted his teeth, clenched his fists, and kept on walking.

———

HE PULLED UP TO CHERRY'S HOUSE ALMOST AN HOUR LATER, and he had to work hard not to bang on the door and demand an explanation. He deserved one, didn't he?

Do you? he asked himself.

He hadn't known her a decade ago when she'd left Sweet Water Falls. He did know she'd once dated the Sheriff's Deputy for a long, long time, and that he'd broken her heart. Brandon and his sidekick sure had made it sound like Cherry had then had a one-night stand with Brandon before she'd put her hometown in her rearview mirror.

They'd talked about their past relationships, or so Jed had thought.

He knocked on the door as calmly as he could, and he heard Cherry yell, "Coming!" from inside. It took her several long seconds to come, and when she did, she wiped her hands on a kitchen towel.

"Oh, hello, cowboy," she said, leaning one delicious hip into the doorway. "I didn't know you were stopping by this afternoon."

Jed didn't know what to say now. *Does this matter?* he questioned himself once more. If he had to go around town and hear people talk about her, he wanted to know the truth.

"Tell me about when you left Sweet Water Falls," he said. He delivered the sentence with such a calm, venomous tone that Cherry's smile and flirtatious vibe dried up before the sound of his voice had truly finished filling the space between them.

"What happened?" she asked.

"Nothing," he said. "I just want to know about why you left."

"I told you about Charlie."

Yeah, she had. And he'd believed her. Looking at her now, the two of them squaring off on her front porch, and Jed didn't want to do this. Something inside him drove him forward. The truth. He had to know the truth if there was any hope of a future between him and Cherry.

"Is there anything else?"

She folded her arms, her throat working as she swallowed.

"There is," he said. "I've seen this look on your face before." He sighed and shook his head. "I thought we weren't keeping secrets."

"I just haven't told all of mine yet," she said, her voice tinny. "Have you?"

"All the big ones," he said, bringing his gaze back to hers. "Yes, all the *important* ones."

"I'm just a little bit behind you," she said. "That's all." She took a step toward him and put one hand on his chest. He backed up, because he didn't want her taking comfort from him while she told him this secret. He'd allowed that in the past, but right now? She had to do this on her own.

Her hand fell back to her side as shock flowed through her expression. It only stayed for a second, and then she covered over it with the perfect way she shuttered everyone and everything off. Including him.

"I made a lot of mistakes at that time in my life," she said, falling back to the doorway. "I've made a lot since. It seems every man I date turns out to be a mistake." Her words struck him right in the throat, and he sucked in a breath.

Was he a mistake?

Just another one of Cherry's mistakes, he thought.

She rubbed her forehead, not aware of what she'd done to him. Not aware that she'd shot chemicals into his blood that would eat him from the inside out.

"Do you know Brandon Alcott?" he asked, somewhat surprised his voice still worked.

She gasped then, and her eyes searched his face. "I know him," she whispered.

"He said for a night," Jed said, lifting his chin, fully aware it made him a better target. He felt like his whole body—his heart, his mind, his very soul—had been target practice for this woman. And she'd shot him through the heart, hooked it, and yanked it out.

He couldn't stand here, and the same urge he'd had in the Hallmark store to leave overcame him again. "I have to go," he said, turning and practically jumping down the steps.

"Jed," she called after him. He turned at the bottom of

the steps and ducked his head, sort of turning back to her. "I can explain."

"Bring dinner," he said. "I have work to do." With that, he walked away, got behind the wheel, and drove away from Cherry's house without looking back. He didn't need to be made the fool of anymore for her, but he'd still left the door open should she want to nudge it and then walk inside.

But that was up to her, and Jed seriously doubted that she'd do it. He'd been the one kicking at her doors for months now, and any ground he'd gained was because she *allowed* it, not because she wanted it.

Not because she *wanted him.*

19

Cherry's stomach rioted all afternoon and well into the evening. The scent of the pizza she picked up about seven-thirty actually made her gag. She put a smile on her face, thanked the girl behind the counter, and took the three boxes to her car.

With them getting a ride in the backseat, she made the forty-five minute drive to Forrester Farms by going west and then north, around the long way.

So it really took her over an hour, and she was able to go past Betty Jones's farm along the way.

Jed's cabin had a light shining out of every window, which told her he was inside, waiting for her. "Not just waiting," Cherry said, a metallic taste in her mouth. "He's expecting you."

That thought gave her hope and courage, and she got out of her car, slammed the door hard, and turned to get the pizza. She fully expected to see Jed standing on his porch when she faced the cabin again, and he did not disappoint her.

This is good, she told herself. *He wants to listen to you. He didn't break-up with you. Don't blow this.*

Cherry wielded the pizza like a shield, something she'd never had to do before, and approached the bottom of the steps. Jed Forrester made her do a lot of things she'd never done before.

He didn't speak, but Cherry knew this was about her. "Evenin'," she drawled, putting her foot on the bottom step. Committed now, she went all the way to the top.

Jed leaned against the pillar there, his face shadowed from his cowboy hat. She'd noticed that he wore his indoors, something her mama would never allow. At the farmhouse, he did take it off and hang it on the rack with her brothers'. So he respected her mama's rules.

He respected her.

Panic plunged through her. Would he respect her after this confession?

"Inside?" she asked.

He turned and went inside, leaving the door open for her. She followed him, and in his kitchen, he took the pizza boxes, and said, "Thanks for coming."

"You didn't think I was going to." Cherry tucked her hands into her pockets and looked around his kitchen. He'd cleaned it, probably while he was waiting, and she didn't see any evidence of his dinner.

"I had a bowl of cereal about forty minutes ago," he said.

"I drove the long way," she said. "By the Jones farm."

His eyes came to hers. "You did?"

She nodded, every cell in her body trembling. "Jed, I'm so embarrassed."

"Why?"

She took a deep breath and told herself to just begin. Begin, and keep going. "I dated Charlie Hooper for a long time. Eight years. Maybe nine. He promised me over and over that as soon as he got this promotion, we'd get married. Then it was that position. Then he needed to do the K9 training, then he thought he might go to Chicago and do the FBI training."

She swallowed, but this was important backstory. "I loved him so much, I couldn't see the lies. I couldn't see that he didn't really love me. He loved the *idea* of me. He didn't want to be alone."

Just like her. Cherry didn't want to be alone. But now...

"I figured out after a while that being alone was better than being with someone who didn't love me. Who didn't want me."

Jed nodded, his attention still on her as he flipped open each pizza box. She'd gotten Texas barbecue chicken, because he loved that. And then a white ham and pineapple—also one of his favorites—and then all-meat with mushrooms, because she'd heard him order that before.

How the man could eat mushrooms, she didn't know. But she knew he loved them, and she needed something to win him back. Food might work, but with Jed, she never knew.

"I stayed with him, even after I knew I shouldn't. No one in my family liked him. Anyway, one night we went to dinner at Carver's. You know, the really nice steakhouse? Couples get engaged there. I thought maybe he'd changed his mind. I was all dressed up. Perfect. Ready."

She slumped onto one of Jed's barstools while he got down plates. He picked up two pieces of the ham and pineapple and served it to her first. His eyes met hers, and tears filled her whole body.

"Thank you," she murmured.

He joined her with a plate full of pizza before she picked up her first slice. Even then, she didn't take a bite. Not yet. He didn't either.

"I made so many mistakes with Charlie," she said. "When he broke up with me at Carver's, he laughed. He said he needed to be Chief before he could even *think* about getting married, and even then, he'd have to be really careful about who that person was."

She shook her head and bit off the pointy end of her pizza. The Alfredo and ham made so much creamy saltiness in her mouth that she found the strength to go on.

"I left, blubbering. So angry. And instead of going home and figuring out my life, I made another bad decision."

Jed finally took a bite of pizza, and eating had to mean he wasn't too mad, right?

"I went to some bar a few miles down the road. The Burro or something. There was a guy there. I didn't care. I went home with him instead, because I just..." She blew out her breath and stared across the island, the pizza, the sink, and out the back window. Darkness had already covered Texas, and Cherry had felt it infect her life previously too.

"I just wanted someone to love me." She knew intimacy was more than physical, but that night, she'd been so distraught. So upset. "I felt like the past ten years of my life had been a huge waste."

"I'm sorry," Jed whispered.

Cherry put down her pizza, the worst still not out yet. "I didn't know Brandon Alcott. I figured out he was friends with Trav and Charlie, and that was awful enough. A few weeks later, I discovered I was pregnant. I left town."

Jed's head jerked toward hers, but Cherry turned away from him. "That's why you left?"

"Yes."

"So you have a child."

When she didn't answer immediately, he said, "That's a *huge* secret, Cherry."

She swallowed the lump in her throat. "I don't have a child. I lost the baby only a couple of weeks later."

"Oh."

They sat there, only the hum of his refrigerator for

sound, neither of them eating despite the astronomical amount of food she'd brought.

"So Charlie was a huge mistake," Cherry said. "Brandon was. Every relationship in San Antonio—real or the ones I imagined between me and my stupid boss—they were all mistakes. Every man I get mixed up with turns out to be a mistake."

Jed drew in a breath, but Cherry didn't dare look at him yet. Her neck started to ache on the left side from how she kept it ducked from him, but she didn't care.

She'd known this would be hard, and it was. Harder than she'd even imagined.

She took one more bite of pizza and then pushed her plate away. "It's late. I should go." She slid from the barstool, sure Jed would come after her. Tell her not to go. She didn't need to do that, because it was barely eight-thirty.

She walked through his house, and only Fish got up to say goodbye. She paused and bent down to pat the dog. "I'm sorry, Fish," she said, hopefully loud enough for Jed to hear too. "Maybe he'll feed you my uneaten pizza."

She twisted the doorknob and left the cabin. Jed would feed Fish a lot of pizza, because while he was forever telling Cherry that he was just a dog, Jed wanted him to be happy too. And pizza made everyone happy.

Except Cherry.

She drove home, the light coming from her house more subdued and definitely not as welcoming. Just inside the door, she stopped and surveyed the space. She'd been here almost a month, and she'd done a lot to make this place hers.

She'd sewn curtains with Shay and put them up. She and Rissa had gone shopping at the holiday fair and purchased a couple of pillows in Cherry's style. They rested on the couch, smiling at her in pinks, blues, and yellows.

She didn't cook much, but she'd already done her dishes that day—right when Jed had stopped by, actually.

Feathers appeared at the mouth of the hall, and Cherry gazed at the cat. "Mrow," she said, and that got Cherry to move away from the closed front door.

"Yeah," she said to the feline. "That's how I feel too." She collected a pint of ice cream from the freezer and went down the hall to her bedroom. This house only had two of them, without a master suite.

A big bathroom sat between the two bedrooms, and each one had a door leading into it. If she kept the door closed in the spare bedroom, Cherry could pretend she had a master retreat, with a complete en suite, when she didn't.

She'd been pretending for so much of her life, and she was so tired of that.

She pulled out her phone and sent a quick text to Jed. *I didn't mean to keep it from you. I was planning on telling you. I don't want to pretend it's nothing, but it was twelve years ago. I don't want us to be nothing either.*

She would reveal so much if she sent that, but she didn't know how to not let him know. She *wanted* him to know.

"You do," she said, and with that, she hit send.

Jed answered about a minute later, but Cherry had plugged her phone in and dug into the ice cream by then. It took her an extra moment to get to her phone, and she read quickly.

We're not nothing, sweetheart. I'll talk to you tomorrow.

Relief flooded her, and Cherry laid back against her pillows. She'd been fighting the urge to cry since Jed had banged on her front door and said the name Brandon Alcott.

She didn't fight anymore, and she let the tears roll down her face. "Thank you," she said, because the cleansing force of forgiveness was very real to her in that moment. Not only from the Lord, but from the people here on earth she didn't want to think badly of her.

20

J ed couldn't stop thinking about Cherry, and not always in the best way. He worried that he hadn't reacted right with her. He had moments of anger and then more moments of regret that he'd been angry at her for something that had happened a long time ago.

He didn't want to judge her, as he wasn't perfect himself. His mama and daddy had taken him to church growing up, and Jed believed most people really were good. Even if he hadn't attended a sermon in a while, he still knew he could pray, and he still believed God could and would forgive him.

And not just him. Anyone who honestly tried to do better. Cherry was one of those.

And yet, he found himself judging her. Then he felt guilty about that.

Jed definitely existed in a state of turmoil, and that, combined with his workload now that the farm was operating back on a normal schedule, kept him from making the drive to Short Tail.

His busyness kept him from texting, and he'd never really called Cherry during the day all that often.

Distance grew between them, and Jed hated it. He could repair pigsties, barns, fences, and goat pens. But he didn't know how to build a bridge between him and the woman he'd started to fall in love with.

The day for him and Cherry to go visit Betty Jones's farm came, and he texted her that morning that he wasn't feeling well. He canceled with Betty as well, rescheduled for the next week, and went to Mama's for breakfast.

"Hello, son," she said, rising to get him a mug. "Do you want coffee?"

He sighed as he sat at the dining room table, where only a couple of weeks ago, he'd shared a glorious Christmas Eve meal with his family—and Cherry.

"Yes, please," he said at the same time Daddy said, "That sigh doesn't sound good."

The back door opened about then, and Chris asked, "Jed's sighin' again?"

"I'm not," Jed said, pushing his cowboy hat forward to hide his face.

"You did," Daddy said.

Mama set a mug of hot coffee in front of Jed, and he

reached for the sugar bowl. He spooned in one, two, three scoops while Chris said he wanted coffee too, please.

"Three huge spoons," he said next. "Something's going on."

"Nothin's going on," Jed said.

"I heard him sighing out in the stables a couple of days ago," Chris said. "He goes out there to talk to the horses when he's upset."

"I'm not upset," Jed said, though he was starting to feel upset.

"What are you upset about?" Mama asked, placing Chris's coffee on the table and retaking her seat.

"It's not Stonehenge, is it?" Daddy asked. "I know you can get him to settle into a good cow horse."

"Stonehenge is comin' along," Jed said. The horse did have a stubborn streak, but most mares did, and she'd actually need it when trying to get back the stubborn cows that wandered from the herd. "Once I get her going, Easton's gonna train her for the NRCHA."

"That's great," Daddy said. He'd entered several National Reined Cow Horse Association events over the years, and he had registered sires in the group. Easton rode really well, and he was especially gifted in the herd work segment of the three-part competition. He counted on Jed to get the horses up to speed with their reining, and then he took over for cutting and cow working.

"It's Cherry," Chris said, calmly lifting his mug to his lips.

Jed threw him a death glare and took an overzealous gulp of his coffee. Big mistake, as it was hot, and it scorched his throat. He choked and coughed, and Chris calmly set his mug down and smiled.

"It's Cherry." He said it without room to argue, and Jed found he couldn't anyway.

With everyone looking at him, he stirred his coffee, the storms inside him increasing. "I...don't know. I learned something about her, and I'm...off-kilter. That's all."

"You'll get back to yourself," Daddy said.

"You better," Mama said, her voice more severe than Jed was expecting. He looked at her and raised his eyebrows. "Oh, come on, son. She's the best woman you've ever dated. I've never seen you light up the way she lights you up. Ever."

Jed didn't want to argue, but he didn't have to agree either. He took a delicate sip of his coffee now, his mind running away from him again.

"Remember when Deb rejected my first proposal?" Chris asked, and Jed jerked his attention across the table to his brother. He wore a small smile, but his eyes told Jed he was somewhere in the past. "I was devastated. I thought, well, that's that, and I tried to move on."

"You did not," Mama said, swatting Chris's hand. "You moped around here for an afternoon, and then you said, 'I have to get her back, Mama. How do I do it?'"

Chris gave her a smile. "Sounds about right." He

looked back at Jed, his eyes turning more marbled. "How'd I do it?"

Jed opened his mouth to speak, but it was too dry. He swallowed and tried again. "You came to me. I said you get over there and you talk to her. You tell her she's the one for you, and you love her, and you'll do whatever you have to do to make her happy."

"Mm." Chris took another sip of his coffee.

"Cherry and I didn't break up." Jed omitted the part where he hadn't told her anything he'd advised Chris to do. "I didn't actually think you'd do it. I haven't had a girlfriend for longer than two months, ever."

"Well, it worked."

"You're better at talking than me."

"That's hogwash."

Jed looked away, because he'd never had a problem telling Cherry what he thought. But what he felt? Yeah, he'd maybe led in that arena too, but this felt more delicate. Like whatever he said would decide their fate.

"She said I was a mistake," he whispered.

No one said anything, and the pain that had been sitting quietly in Jed's chest stung him, and it stung hard. It radiated out with every passing second of silence until he couldn't breathe.

"Yeah." He drained the last of his coffee, almost smashed the mug back to the table, and stood. "I have to get to work."

"Jed," Mama said after him, but Jed strode away.

He hated that Cherry had used that word—*mistake*—and he hated that he'd been mentioned in proximity to it. He never wanted to feel like that, but he couldn't ignore it either.

He didn't know what to do. In the movies, princes weren't told they were a mistake, and so he strapped on his tool belt, checked his truck for the lumber and supplies he needed, and he whistled for Fish to come from wherever the dog had gone.

With him loaded in the passenger seat, Jed looked at the black lab and said, "We've got to get the outer calving sheds shored up, all right, boy?" He peered up and out the windshield at the stormy sky. It matched his mood. "There's gonna be some wind this weekend, and it's better to fix things before they collapse."

If only he knew how to do that with Cherry, because it certainly felt like they were on the brink of a break-up.

———

LATER THAT NIGHT, JED PULLED UP TO CHERRY'S HOUSE. She sat on the front porch with a gray cat in her lap, and the smile on her face told him how much he'd missed her.

"You're a stupid, stupid cowboy," he muttered as he put his truck in park. He got out, because there wasn't anything to prolong, and he took her steps two at a time, which meant he leapt them in two strides.

"Wow," she said, squinting as she looked up at him.

"What was that?" She laughed, and Jed lowered himself to the steps beside her.

"I don't know," he said, chuckling. He reached over and took her hand, erasing the distance between them. It felt good. "I've missed you."

He lifted her hand to his lips and kissed the inside of her wrist. She sighed and leaned her head against his bicep. Neither of them spoke, and Jed let the silence stitch together the things that had unraveled between them.

He knew that would only last for so long, and they did have some serious talking to do. He simply didn't want to start.

It seemed Cherry didn't either, and she was probably waiting for him to start. He *had* just let her walk out on him a few nights ago. He hadn't known what to say.

Every man I date turns out to be a mistake had pierced his lungs, and he was just now learning how to breathe again.

"Thank you for the pizza the other night," he said, taking the first baby step into the conversation. "You didn't have to leave all of it."

"Is there any left?" she asked.

"No," he admitted. "It's easy to heat up for breakfast, lunch, and dinner." He tried to smile at her, but it felt broken on his face. "Cherry, I'm sorry I let you walk out the other night. I'm sure that's not what you wanted from me." He ducked his head and studied the worn paint on the step at his feet.

"It's okay," she said. "I imagine it was a lot to take in."

"Yes and no," he said.

"What does that mean?"

"I don't care about what happened twelve years ago." He took a breath, and something twinged in his chest. "I really don't. Then sometimes I do, and I get mad. But not about what happened. But that you think all of your relationships are mistakes."

"Charlie was a mistake, and Brandon sure as heck was."

"That's two men," Jed said quietly.

Cherry tugged her hand out of his and clasped it with her own, studying the front of his truck like it would tell her what to say. The gray cat had fled, and Jed didn't know where.

"Would the baby have been a mistake?" he asked.

"I don't know," she said. "I didn't have a baby."

"But would you have viewed it that way?"

Cherry heaved a sigh. A legit heave, like she'd rather be anywhere else, doing anything else, with anyone else, than with him, having this talk. "I suppose not," she finally admitted.

"Because I thought you wanted kids," he said. "That's all."

"We already talked about that, Jed."

"Yeah." They had. It wasn't that he cared all that much, but he'd like Cherry to just be *real*. "Can you just tell me the truth for five minutes?"

"I am," she said. "I don't lie to you. Not now. Not ever."

"You fight me," he said. "On things. Sometimes."

"Not much anymore," she said, doing exactly what he'd said she did. Fight him on some things.

"You want kids, right?" he asked, his tone somewhat of a bark. Maybe if he just got through this the way he did a frustrating conversation with Easton, he could be on the other side of it. Better there than here, in his opinion.

"Yes," she said, plenty of exasperation in her voice. "But Jed, I'm forty-six. I know the limits of female reproduction."

"All right," he said. "I'm not saying you'll have them. I just wanted you to admit you'd like a family."

"I would, all right?" She glared at him, but Jed shook his head.

Irritation fired through him. "Maybe this is a mistake." He got to his feet. "You said it the other night, and I didn't want to believe it. But you know what? Maybe you're right." He jogged down the steps as Cherry called, "What? Why would this be a mistake?"

He turned back to her at the bottom of the steps. She'd gotten to her feet too. "That's what you said. You said every relationship you have is a mistake. And I didn't like that. It made me feel like I'm a mistake. Just your next relationship mistake, and once you figure it out, that'll be it."

"That's not what I meant." She folded her arms and stood her ground at the top of the porch.

"But maybe you're right," he said again, pure misery lacing through him now. "We've never really gotten along. I'm salty, and you have to put me in my place. I push you to say and do things you don't want to say or do. It's *work*, Cherry, and it should be easy."

"Who told you that?"

No one had told him that. He'd seen the way Chris and Deb could communicate without words. One look from his wife, and Chris knew what she needed. He *knew*.

Mama and Daddy weren't perfect, but they did so much for one another. They'd raised their family in sync, without much argument about things. They laughed and joked, and they'd always sat next to one another at church. Always across from each other at dinner. Always beside each other on the couch when they watched movies together.

Jed could see—*anyone* could see—that they loved one another and felt most comfortable *together*.

"No one," he said, his voice quieter. He'd seen her parents too, and their love and devotion to one another was obvious. Heck, even her loud, sometimes obnoxious, brothers had relationships that cooled them down with a simple look from their wives.

When Cherry looked at him, she actually added to the storm.

"It's just something I can see," he said. "And feel. And I love you. I hate saying it like this, but I do. I can't *not* say it, but just because I love you doesn't mean we're good together."

He shook his head, because he knew how much nonsense was coming from his mouth. He didn't understand it in his brain, but his heart knew.

"I'm sorry," he said. "I hope you can learn from me—from this mistake—and go on to find the man who doesn't make your blood boil, and who doesn't push all the wrong buttons inside you. I honestly never meant to do any of that."

He held up both hands in surrender, not encouraged to stay much longer by the dark, loathsome glare on Cherry's face. He backed up, wondering when he could turn and walk away.

Shouldn't she say something first?

He waited.

Anything?

"Come *on*, Cherry," he said, beyond done with this conversation.

"Come on, what?" she asked.

"You don't have anything to say?" he asked. "I'm standing here, telling you I love you, but we can't be together. You must *feel something*."

She reached up and wiped her right eye. Just the flick of her hand. There, then back into the fold. "If you don't think it's right, then go. I'm not going to try to convince you it is."

"But how do *you* feel?" he asked. "Do *you* think we're good together? Honestly."

She'd told him that she just wanted to be loved when she'd run to Brandon. He'd just told her he loved her.

Yeah, and she didn't say it back, he thought.

"I'll leave it up to you," he said. "I don't think there's anything else for me to say, and you know where to find me."

He did turn and walk away then, and when he got behind the wheel and faced the house again, Cherry had come down the steps after him.

"Jed," she said, and he rolled down his window. He leaned his elbow on the door and looked at her. Waited.

She finally said, "Don't go."

Jed didn't want to go. He opened his door and dropped to the ground. He closed the distance between them and took her into his arms. "I think you need time to figure out if I'm not a mistake."

"I didn't mean that. Not the way you're taking it."

"You also didn't say you loved me," he said. He stepped back, his own emotions swirling and rising and pricking his eyes. "I'm always at the farm. And I'm going to see Betty's on Wednesday next week. You're still welcome to come, and no one at Forrester Farms will ever turn you away." He reached up and wiped the tears from under her eyes. "I love you. I want you. But only if *you* think we can be real with each other, all the time. Not just when it's easy. And only if *you* think I'm not just your next mistake."

His voice hitched, and he really needed to leave. "And only if *you* think we can make this work. Because I'll do everything I can to make it work. Because it'll take both of us."

She nodded, and Jed did too. He hated leaving her here like this, but it wouldn't be fair to either of them if he stayed.

So he didn't.

21

Cherry didn't get out of bed until the sun had greeted the Texas day, yawned halfway over the land, and started its descent in the west. Her stomach growled at her, and the pitiful meowing of Mister Whiskers finally got her out of bed and off her phone.

She'd ignored Rissa's texts, as well as Lee's, because once her fingers started flying, she knew she'd tell them that she'd once again messed up. Made a big mistake. This time, it wasn't in who she'd chosen to date. It was how she'd treated Jed.

She hadn't meant he was a mistake, though she could see why he'd think that. She had told him that every man she dated turned out to be a mistake. Something Daddy used to tell her ran through her mind.

When the same thing keeps happening, darlin, it might be time to look at the common factor.

They'd been talking about her grades, of course. As the oldest, she'd often taken the brunt of her parents' displeasure. They loosened up with every child, and with Will, they'd had to learn to let go completely. He was smart, but he was completely disinterested in book learning. He sometimes hadn't turned something in sheerly out of spite, because he thought the assignment was dumb or had no merit.

Back then, *she'd* been the common factor every time she got in trouble in art class. *She* couldn't keep her mouth shut.

Now, *she* was the common factor for all of her relationships being huge mistakes. And honestly, that was a huge burden that weighed her down and made her sad from the inside out.

She fed her cats and shuffled back into her bedroom. She hadn't gotten dressed that day, because why should she? She didn't have a job to get to. The second week of January didn't require her to do yard work. No one in her family needed her to show up and help them.

She'd just sunk back into bed and pulled the comforter over her cold feet when her doorbell rang. Cherry closed her eyes and sighed. She did not move.

It was probably Mrs. Bowen, the woman down the lane who'd been stopping by and dropping hints about her son, a man who lived with her and baked the most excellent breads and rolls. She'd brought some of those by every time she came, and Cherry suddenly threw off her blanket and got to her feet.

Some freshly baked bread, even if done by a man she had no interest in, should help some of her sadness. She'd run out of ice cream and had no drive to get to Mandel's to get more.

Her stomach rumbled as she walked, and she hadn't gained the corner yet when the doorbell rang again. "Coming!" she called, and she hurried to open the door.

Sure enough, Mrs. Bowen stood there, but this time, so did her son. Cherry looked from the older woman with graying blonde hair to the tall man next to her. No way they were related. Mrs. Bowen maybe weighed one hundred pounds soaking wet and stood five feet tall. The giant next to her easily weighed three times that and towered a good foot over her.

"Cherry," she said brightly, thrusting forward the loaf of bread she held. "Shane made this for you. It's pumpkin rye bread."

"Oh," she said, forced to take the bread. Warmth seeped through the bottom of the brown paper bag. She did love pumpkin-flavored things, and the Texan in her wouldn't allow her to be rude. "Thank you."

Shane hadn't shaved that day—or any day in the previous month or two. Or six. She smiled at him anyway, but she did not want to invite them in.

"It's really good with honey butter," he said, his voice low and rumbly.

"Okay," Cherry said. "Thank you."

"Shane had a question for you," his mother prompted, looking up at her son with slitted eyes.

Before he embarrassed all three of them currently standing on the porch, Cherry said, "My boyfriend is coming by later, and I'll tell him to bring some of his mother's honey butter. She always has some on-hand."

Mrs. Bowen's gaze whipped back to Cherry's, her eyes wide now.

"I told you, Mother," Shane said. He held up one hand in Cherry's direction, almost like a peace offering. "I do hope you enjoy the bread, Cherry. I'm starting an online delivery service if you're interested."

"I am," Cherry said, brightening. "That sounds fantastic, Shane."

"Yeah, I'm just looking for someone to help me organize the details."

Cherry actually took a step outside. "I'm looking for a job."

Shane stalled his retreat. "You are?"

She waved the hand not holding the pumpkin bread. "I mean, kind of? I have a third interview with the city on Monday, and I might get that job, but it's taking forever, and I could help you…" She cleared her throat. "I used to work for San Antonio Technical College," she said. "I'm good at details."

"What job at the city?" Mrs. Bowen asked.

Cherry looked at her and smiled though the woman's gaze had turned a tad severe. She didn't know these people, because she'd always been rushing here or there whenever Mrs. Bowen had brought bread by. Once, she'd left the entire whole wheat loaf at her sister's, and Spencer had texted her that he loved it and wanted more of it.

"The County Clerk, ma'am," Cherry said.

"Rhonda is a friend of mine," Mrs. Bowen said like her influence alone would win Cherry the job.

"That's fantastic," Cherry said, playing up her kindness. She switched her gaze back to Shane. "If you want me to look over some things, I'm more than happy to do it."

"I don't really have much," he said, taking a step closer to her. "I've been using social media and taking orders that way."

"No website?"

He shook his head and said, "They're expensive."

"People do them themselves these days," she said. "I was the web admin for the veterinary program one year. It's not too hard."

"You can build a website?"

She smiled at him. "Some of them are drag-and-drop, honestly. It's not too terrible." She backed up and toed Feathers out of the way. Her other two cats were probably cowering under her bed. "Do you have a couple of minutes right now? I could show you a website builder you could literally do tonight."

"Sure," Shane said, stepping forward. "Thanks, Cherry."

"Sure," she said. She let him go by her by pressing herself as far as she could into the door, and she gave Mrs. Bowen a smile. "Thanks so much, Mrs. Bowen. I won't keep him for too long." Then she closed the door, hopefully not in a horribly rude manner. But she also didn't want to invite her in.

"Thanks," Shane said, sighing as he turned around. "I've been trying to move out of my mom's place and start this business, but she keeps finding a reason why I need to stay."

Cherry went into the kitchen ahead of him. "Why do you need to stay?"

"Her back," he said. "Her hip. She can't drive herself to this doctor's appointment." He shook his head. "I love my mother." He smiled at her. "I had a big corporate job in Dallas, but it burned me out. I want to have a bakery, but I only want to make bread."

"Okay," Cherry said, nodding. "Then do that."

"Most bakeries have everything," he said. "Desserts, brownies, tarts. I don't want to do any of that."

"Then don't," Cherry said, not seeing the problem. "Your shop will stand out *because* it's not like every other." She moved over to the small dining room table, only then realizing that she still wore her pajama pants

—a pair of fuzzy pink things covered in bright rainbows.

Shane hadn't commented on them yet, and she wondered what he'd say if they worked for a couple of hours and her boyfriend didn't show up. She set her worries out of her mind and flipped open her laptop. "Okay, so we used Create-Site at the college," she said. "But there are a ton of really easy website builders you can use. People do it all the time, no web design necessary."

While Shane looked at the site she pulled up, she cut a slice of bread for both of them and set an alarm for forty-five minutes. She'd tell him she had to shower and get ready at that time, and he'd leave. Easy.

In fact, it was that easy, and Shane waved to her as he trundled away forty-five minutes later. Cherry receded into her house, no plans to shower and get ready to go anywhere. Her heart still beat with happiness, because she'd helped someone that day. It felt good, the same way she'd felt by going over to Rissa's and helping her sister with Bronson. Or the way she felt when Mama needed help, and Cherry could provide it.

She wanted to help Jed see that he was the best thing that had ever happened to her.

I love you.

I can't not say it.

I love you. I want you.

Cherry ran her hands down her face, and then back up and through her hair. She'd eaten only pumpkin rye bread that day, and she didn't care about that. She cared that she'd cut herself off from the people who cared about her.

Her parents. Her brothers and sisters.

Today was a Wednesday, and that meant Lee would be cooking at the farmhouse. She picked up her phone and navigated to his texts.

Are you coming to dinner tonight at Mama's? I need your help with a macaroni salad if so.

Tears pricked her eyes. He needed her.

Rissa's text had said, *What are you doing this morning? Bronson is teething and being the biggest bear and I'm supposed to get my hair cut.*

Then several minutes later, when Cherry hadn't answered: *Never mind. I asked Shay to do it. She's out today and said she would.*

Then, a couple of hours later: *My new haircut!*

Where are you? Why aren't you answering? Are you coming to dinner at the farmhouse tonight?

Until five minutes ago, Cherry had no intention of going to her parents' house for dinner. Now, she jumped to her feet and hustled down the hall to get ready. She needed their help.

She needed to get Jed back for good.

He'd left everything up to her, which semi-annoyed her for a reason she couldn't name. But perhaps Will or Lee could help with that. Perhaps Rissa could come up with the right thing to say to him so he'd know *he* was not a mistake. Perhaps Gretchen would know how to deal with a grumpy cowboy—or Shay or Rose.

She knew they'd all be there, and she knew she better be too. Otherwise, she might lose Jed Forrester for good this time, and that was completely unacceptable.

An hour later, Cherry pulled up to the white farmhouse. Three trucks sat out front, and she pulled alongside Will's. In just six short months, everyone in her family would have a baby except for her.

She sat with the thought for a moment, expecting it to ache, drive deep into her heart and pinch, or make her eyes burn with unshed tears.

It didn't.

This time, the idea that her brothers and sister were having kids only opened a door of opportunity for her to truly be the best aunt in the world. She could babysit—if she'd look at her texts. She could take them when their parents needed a relaxing weekend. She could spoil them on their birthdays.

She could mother without actually having children of her own.

The realization felt so huge and so wide open and so amazing that she wanted to text Jed and tell him about it. Fear held her back from doing so, and instead, she got out of her car and went inside the farmhouse.

"...not how you do it," Will said. "It's only a quarter cup of mayo and a whole cup of sour cream."

"I don't think so," Lee argued back. "Just let me text

Cherry."

She stepped into the kitchen and paused, taking in the two of them. "I'm right here."

"Finally," Lee said, his dark eyes boring into hers. "Why'd you go off-grid today?"

"I didn't," she said, though she totally had. "I just didn't respond to you within two seconds of getting your text."

"You didn't respond at all." He glared for another moment and then gestured her forward. His expression softened as she walked toward him, and she knew this was going to be the night she exposed her true self to everyone, him included. "I'm making the chicken pasta salad, and I don't have the recipe."

"Why not?" Cherry asked, picking up the rubber spatula and starting to stir the dressing-less salad.

"Autumn, uh, used it for something," he said.

"Rabbit bedding," Cherry and Will said together. They laughed, and Lee rolled his eyes.

"You're going to have to discipline her at some point," Cherry teased.

"No, I'm not," Lee shot back. "She's not my biological daughter, and Rose and I are figuring things out."

At that moment, Rose walked in, and she'd obviously come straight from work. She held her daughter's hand, and she wore the type of sophisticated clothes Cherry once had. She'd changed into a pair of jeans and a plaid

V-neck, so no one had to know she'd spent the day in her fuzzy pajamas.

"What are we figuring out?" Rose asked.

"Nothing," Lee said, abandoning the meal prep completely. He went over to Rose and kissed her hello, lifted a squealing Autumn into his arms, and faced Cherry and Will again.

Cherry sighed at how wonderful and amazing her brother was, and how perfectly he and Rose looked together. She stilled that image in her mind, knowing not everything for Lee and Rose had always been well, quite so rosy.

"Will," she said. "Did you and Gretchen always get along so well?"

He snorted and laughed. "No." He sobered quickly. "Wait. Why?"

She shook her head too and said, "It's a cup of mayo and half a cup of sour cream."

"I told you," Lee said, setting Autumn on her feet and adding, "Gramma's on the sun porch, baby." The little girl skipped in that direction, and they all watched her go outside with Mama, Daddy, and Queenie, the golden retriever who never got too far from Mama.

"You weren't right either," Will quipped. "It's half a cup of sour cream, not a quarter."

"Better than no mayo at all." Lee picked up the jar and started scooping it into the bowl with the pasta, shredded chicken, peas, and cheese chunks. "Now, why do you smell like you just showered twenty minutes ago?" He raised his eyebrows at Cherry. "And you totally went dark today, just admit it."

Those last three words sounded like something Jed would've said, and Cherry drew in a deep, steeling breath. "All right," she said, glancing over to the table, which was empty. Travis's truck was here, but neither he nor Shay were in the room. Cherry didn't want to tell the story more than once, but she had a feeling she'd be doing exactly that. After all, Rissa wasn't here yet either. Neither was Gretchen.

"Jed and I broke up," she said, and Will made a noise somewhere between a yelp and a gasp.

Lee sighed and shook his head. "Cherry. Really?"

"You have literally never liked anyone I've dated," she said, her voice stern as she stirred his pasta salad for him. "And this is never going to be cold enough in time for dinner."

"Yeah, well, I like Jed," Lee said, his surly attitude back in place. "And you did too, and I can't believe he broke up with you." He took the rubber spatula from her and turned toward the fridge with the bowl of salad.

"Cherry," Will said as Lee was busy with something else. He hadn't said his piece yet, but he would. "You two were so...good together." She looked at Rose, who nodded, her gaze broadcasting her sympathy.

"Yeah," Lee agreed, spinning back to them. "He promised me—he *promised* me—he wouldn't hurt you."

She wiped her eyes, which made Lee morph into a more supportive brother. "Cherry," he said much softer.

"*I* messed up," she said. "*I* hurt him."

"He's no picnic," Will said. "He probably said *some*thing."

"Break-ups are usually two-sided," Rose said.

"I'm here," Gretchen called. "And I have so many extra spiders today, so I hope y'all are dying for chocolate and butterscotch." She blew into the kitchen like a chocolate-scented wind, and Cherry smiled at her with blurred vision from her tears.

"Oh, I interrupted something," Gretchen said, hurrying to set down her trays. She kissed Will quickly, and all eyes came back to Cherry.

"What is goin' on in here?" Rissa demanded. She stalked closer, and her hair had been cut to her shoulders in a near-bob. It was adorable, and Cherry realized she hadn't responded to her either. She surveyed the huddle of them, her eyes landing on Cherry's too.

"Where's Trav?" she asked.

"Garage," Lee said. "I'll get 'im." He moved away before Cherry could say it was okay. But it wasn't. She needed everyone if she was going to find a way to get Jed back.

Travis and Shay came into the house, Trav wiping his hands on a cloth that already looked dirty. "What?" he asked, coming to a stop at the end of the island. "What-ever happened, I didn't do it."

Will rolled his eyes as he exhaled, and Rissa said, "You are so childish, Trav."

"What?" he shot back. "Do you know how many things Will and I took the blame for when we were kids? You and Cherry were always pinning something on us."

"This isn't something bad," Rissa said.

"Cherry needs our help," Lee said, his voice loud enough to silence the argument. All eyes came back to her. "Right, Cher?"

She nodded, so grateful for each of them. "I messed up with Jed. Yes, he's salty, but I think I might be saltier. So I need some help figuring out the sweetest way in the world to get him back."

"Oh, boy," Shay said, pulling out a barstool. She sat down and so did Rissa.

Spence bounced their baby beside her, ready to listen. "Go on," he said. "And I think the non-Coopers should get to weigh in first."

"What?" Rissa practically screeched, spinning toward her husband and son. "Why?"

"Because," Spence said with a smile. "Rose, Gretchen, Shay, and I know a little something about you Coopers and your...awesomeness."

"We know how to deal with a grumpy cowboy," Gretchen said.

"Or a redheaded, temperamental cowgirl," Spence said. "Who I love with my whole heart."

Cherry exchanged a glance with Lee, then Will, Trav,

and finally Rissa. They all shrugged. They knew who they were, and yes, they'd each gotten someone to tame them, sweeten them, and love them.

Cherry could too.

"All right," Rissa said, speaking for all of them. "Now, start at the beginning, so we have the whole picture."

22

L ee listened to Cherry without interruption. Rissa did plenty of that for the whole family, and even Gretchen shot her a look or two during Cherry's long, somewhat drawn-out recount of the past several months.

Then years. Her whole dating history, going back to age twenty-five, when she'd first met Charlie Hooper.

Oh, how Lee wished he could go back in time and make sure the two of them never met. Charlie had messed Cherry up something fierce.

The overprotective gene inside him fired hard while she spoke, and he exchanged more than one glance with Will and Trav, easily seeing they felt the same way. The Cooper men might have their problems—and take plenty of teasing for them too—but one wasn't that they didn't know how to love.

"That's it," Cherry finally said.

"Well," Lee drawled, as both Will and Trav had looked at him first. Rissa would jump in anytime she wanted, and the in-laws always held back.

At least in Lee's view they did. Perhaps the Cooper genes simply wouldn't allow someone else to have and voice an opinion ahead of them. Rose, Shay, and Gretchen watched him, as did Spence, though he bounced his baby, rocking from left to right as he did.

"Well what, Lee?" Rissa asked, her tone suggesting impatience. Lee recognized it, because the same thing often rose through him.

"I just want to point out that I think we'll have plenty of time for the mac salad to be ready," he said with a smile.

Cherry tilted her head and scoffed, and so Lee wouldn't break down in front of everyone, he grabbed her roughly and drew her into a hug. "Really," he said. "First is that I'm sorry you've been dealing with all of...this for so long."

"Me too," Will said, and he piled into the hug. Then Trav, Shay, and Gretchen. Rissa and Spence and Rose came around the island and did the same thing, enveloping Cherry in a circle of love and adoration Lee could feel pumping through his whole body.

He hoped and prayed Cherry could feel it too. She sniffled, which indicated she could.

"Second," he said. "It's clear you love Jed Forrester."

Lee stepped back, and that caused the huddle to shift. Everyone re-took their places, and since Cherry didn't deny how she felt about Jed, Lee decided to run with it.

"No affirmation," Will said.

"None at all," Spence said.

"No wonder Jed said to come when you're ready," Rose said. "Which, I have to say, is the perfect way to deal with you Coopers."

Lee cast her a hooded look, ducking his head as if he wore his cowboy hat and could partially hide behind the brim. "What does that mean?"

"It means, Mister Cooper, that sometimes you guys need more time to think about things. You need to sit on your front steps and sigh and lament and consider what you *really* want. Then, you act."

"I'm sure that's not *that* true," Lee said.

"It's pretty accurate," Shay said, glancing at Trav. He smiled at her and drew her into his side.

"I do like having more time to think through things," he said. "Then I can come up with a logical, rational response, and not the first thing that comes into my head."

"Rissa likes having more time too," Spence said, and Lee's sister whipped around and gave him a glare.

"I'm right here, and I can speak for myself."

Lee started to chuckle, because her reaction was so Rissa. And so Cooper.

"But Rose is right," Rissa said, almost in a British accent, which made Lee roll his eyes.

"So you have the time, Cher," he said. "What have you thought about?"

"It's only been one day," she said.

"So you're going to torture the man for longer than necessary?" Shay asked, and something passed between her and Cherry. Lee tried to maintain good relationships with all of his siblings, and now his in-laws too. Cherry was likable and fun, and he wasn't surprised at all that she and Shay had become friends.

Because he spent so much time in the admin office for the dairy operation, he sometimes missed some family functions. He sometimes missed all of the gossip in the family—which was fine by him. He sometimes missed who was fighting, and who wasn't, and who had become friends while he managed the million pieces here at Cooper & Company.

"No," Cherry said defensively. "Not longer than necessary." She gave everyone a small smile, her shoulders strong and sure.

All at once, they fell. "Fine. I'm in love with Jed Forrester, all right?"

Lee grinned at her and reached for Rose's hand. He lifted it to his lips and kissed it and looked at Will. He and Cherry had a good relationship too, and sometimes he could say something that Lee had said a million times, and Cherry would hear it differently.

"Why is that so hard for you to say?" Will asked. "Especially to us?"

"Or to him?" Spencer asked. "Because Cherry, that's all he wants. I'm the only brother-in-law, and I can assure you that he's...nervous about being in this family of amazing men. He knows who you have to look to for an example of a good husband and a good father, and the standard is high."

Everyone looked at Spence, because he didn't often say a whole lot. Lee had watched him and Rissa over the past couple of years, and yes, he loved her deeply. But *she* led the conversations for them. *She* spoke to the Coopers for them. *She* made almost all the announcements and invites on behalf of her and Spence.

"He wants you to love him so badly," Spencer said quietly. "If he's said it out loud to you..." He shook his head. "He just wants to hear it back. Shouted, preferably."

"From a rooftop," Lee added, and Cherry's gaze flew back to him.

"Lee, you devil." She swatted at him, and he laughed, breaking the somber mood. "I'm afraid of heights."

Lee dodged her and folded his arms as if she could really hurt him. "Does he know that?"

"That I'm afraid of heights?"

"Yeah."

"Yes," she said.

"So he'll know what it cost you to get up on a roof and shout your love to him."

"If she shows up at his house and whispers it, he'll

know," Gretchen said. "Getting her to say it out loud to us was like watching someone gnaw off their own arm."

"That is not true," Cherry said, planting her hands on her hips now.

"Just to save her life," Rissa added. "It's like she's more willing to die than do the gnawing, and it makes no sense."

"Hey," Lee said, holding up one hand as he witnessed Cherry start to crumble. "It does make sense, you guys. Don't say it doesn't. Cherry just spent twenty hours telling us *why* it makes sense, and we can't devalue that."

"Hours?" Cherry demanded.

"It was al long story," Lee said, grinning, and Cherry rolled her eyes.

"Sorry," Rissa said. "You're right, Lee. Sorry, Cherry." She touched one hand to her heart in a show of sincerity.

"I have a hard time expressing deep feelings," Cherry said. "That doesn't mean I don't have them."

"And how do you express them to Jed?" Travis asked. "Because how you communicate is just as important as what you're trying to say."

"I do things," Cherry said. "At least that's what Jed tells me. I don't tell him I love him, I show him. I don't say I'm happy about whatever, I show that I am."

"I can see that," Lee said.

"How?" Cherry said.

"A good example is where you are right now," he said.

"By my count, you missed four texts from me today, and at least that many from Rissa."

"And she asked you to babysit, and you love that baby," Shay said. "So I knew it was something huge too. I called you, and you didn't pick up."

Cherry pointed her eyes toward the ground, which made Lee's heart hurt. "And yet, here you are. You showed up."

"I needed help," she whispered. "I came out of selfish reasons."

"But who did you go to?" Will asked gently. "Us. Because you know we won't judge you or ridicule you." He cut a look at Trav. "Much."

"Right," Trav said with a smile. "You showed up, because you know your family is important to you."

"So you have to show up for Jed," Rissa said.

"And you can't make him wait forever," Shay added.

"And you *have* to shout to the world how much you love him," Spence said.

Cherry glared around at each of them, and then surveyed the group. "Can I at least take something he likes? That's usually what I do. I show up with food, and we eat, and I apologize and confess, and then we're okay."

"Honey," Gretchen said, smiling and moving next to Cherry. She put her arm around her and gave her a side-hug. "You want more than okay this time. You don't *ever* want him to wonder how you feel."

"She's right," Lee said. "What did I do to get Rose back?"

Cherry looked at Rose, who only nodded. "I can't play the guitar," she said.

"I did something really hard for me," Lee said, swallowing. "I had to swallow my pride, think about Rose and what *she* wanted most, and then I made it happen."

"I'm no good at 'making things happen,'" Cherry complained.

"Cher," Lee said. "Half of my dates with Rose wouldn't have happened without you. You are the queen of making things happen."

"I agree," Rissa said quietly. "The first person I texted when Spencer showed up here was you. You coached me through the whole relationship."

"I thought that was that cowboy on TV," Spence said. They all laughed, and Lee looked at Trav again. He hadn't said a whole lot during this conversation, and it was his turn to drive home the point.

"No more food," Shay said. "Or take food, but it can't be the main thing."

"Jed likes to eat," Cherry said. "More than y'all, though I don't know how that's possible." She looked at Will, Travis, Rissa, and then Lee.

"Tell me what would mean the most to him," Lee said. "Not something verbal, because you'll do that when you get there. A place. A thing. What matters most to Jed right now that you can...I don't know.

Disrupt?" He looked at Rose, who nodded. "That you can interrupt and show him *and* tell him that you love him?"

Cherry pressed one hand over her eyes and took a deep breath. "He wants to buy the Jones farm," she said, her voice holding a touch of awe as she lowered her hand. Hope shone in her eyes. "We were supposed to go look at it together a few days ago, but he canceled and rescheduled for next week."

"That's it," Trav said. "You call Betty Jones right now, and you ask her what time Jed is supposed to be there. Then you show up a few minutes—"

"An hour," Shay interjected.

Trav looked at her with surprise, and she nodded. Trav did too, then said, "All right. An hour early, and you do whatever you have to do to tell him you love him, want him, whatever."

"Not whatever," Shay said, slapping her husband's chest. "Cherry, take the food. Take the banner. Get up on the roof. Do it all. Don't leave anything on the table, and Jed will never leave you again."

His sister swallowed, but she nodded, and Lee found her one of the strongest women he knew. "All right," she said. "But I'm gonna need some help next Wednesday."

"Funny," Lee said, looking at his brothers and grinning. "We just talked about having a minimal work day next week, and it's on..."

"Wednesday," Will, Trav, and Lee said together.

With everyone beaming at Cherry, she looked like she might throw up.

"Okay?" Lee asked, putting his arm around his sister.

She leaned into his strength and said, "Okay."

"What's goin' on in here?" Daddy asked. "Are we eating before midnight, or what?"

"You're just now noticing, Daddy," Rissa said, getting to her feet. "So calm down. I'll get Mama."

"I'll get Autumn," Rose said, going with Rissa.

"I'll set the table," Will said, and Gretchen joined him.

As everyone scurried about to get dinner on the table —albeit forty-five minutes late—Lee could only marvel at the beauty of families.

He and Cherry exchanged a glance as he got the mac salad out of the fridge. "Plan it, sissy," he said. "And we'll be there to help you carry out the details."

"Can you say the words for me?" she grumbled.

"Nope," he said. "You're the only one who can do that."

23

Jed woke on Wednesday morning before his alarm. To be honest, he wasn't sure he'd truly fallen asleep the night before. He dozed, and that was about all, since he'd driven away from Cherry's house in Short Tail over a week ago.

He sighed and swung his legs over the edge of the bed. "I gotta be honest, Lord," he said into the quiet darkness. "I did not think it would take her this long."

Perhaps everything he'd thought she felt wasn't true. Perhaps she kissed every man the way she kissed him. Perhaps Cherry Cooper would never come tell him she loved him.

His heart continued to beat, though every time he thought of Cherry he was certain it would crack and stop. It hadn't yet, and that was almost as disappointing as not seeing the brunette he loved for the past seven days.

His alarm went off, and Jed reached for his phone. After silencing it, he saw no texts from Cherry. No missed calls. Nothing.

Of course, he thought. Why should today be any different from the past several days? He had no reason to think it would be, but today's alarm made his heart bump a couple of extra times.

The note on his alarm said, *Lady Jones Farm Visit*, and this should be one of the most exciting days of his life.

Cherry should be at the farm with him, and Jed exhaled again. His first thought was to cancel the visit for a second time, but almost as quickly as that idea had entered his mind, he dismissed it. He'd done that once before, and he didn't want to do that to the widow again.

He didn't want to do it to himself again.

He wanted to see the farm, as he'd spoken to his family about it over the weekend. Easton had stared into Jed's face, but thankfully, glares couldn't actually produce new holes in one's face. So he'd woken up on Monday morning with just the two eyes, the nose, and the mouth and nothing more.

Easton wasn't happy, because Jed worked like a dog around Forrester Farms. Daddy had been shocked, to put it mildly, but by the end of Jed's explanation of why he wanted the farm and what he hoped to do with it, he'd been smiling as if he'd known all along that Jed would buy a farm, fix it up, and turn it into a rescue facility for animals.

As Jed thought about it, that was exactly what he wanted. He simply wanted Cherry at his side while he did it.

He put his phone down on the nightstand and plugged it back in, then rose, and headed for the shower. If he didn't plug in the phone, he'd take it with him and stew over calling her.

"You can't," he told himself firmly as he brushed his teeth. As he brewed coffee. As he loaded Fish into the passenger seat.

He was going to Betty's first thing this morning, but he'd left in time to stop by his parents' house for a second cup of coffee.

He certainly didn't need the extra stimulant, but he wanted to talk to his daddy one more time. As if Daddy knew Jed would be coming by this morning, he sat in a rocking chair on the front porch, facing East and watching the sun come up. "Mornin'," he said.

"Mornin'," Jed echoed back to him. He accepted the mug of coffee from his father and sank into his mother's chair. He emitted another sigh without meaning to.

"It's a good day," Daddy said. "Sun's gonna be bright. Probably a couple of cows born."

"Yep," Jed said. He loved the simple life. He loved cataloguing a day as good if the sun came out and a baby calf got born. He loved fresh air and using a hammer to put broken things back together.

He didn't mind the long, hot summers in Texas, nor

the wind, nor anything else Mother Nature could throw at him. He didn't mind the long hours, though he thought that might change if he had a wife and family waiting for him at home.

"I think I'm gonna get a new dog," Jed finally said.

Daddy chuckled, and he said, "I think you're gonna get more than that."

"I'm goin' to see Lady Jones today."

"I've got the money for you." Daddy tapped the table between them, and Jed looked at the slip of paper there.

His throat worked against itself, a lump suddenly there. "Thank you," he managed to say, and now that he knew that not everyone could get such words out as easily as he seemed to, he knew how much a simple phrase of gratitude was worth. He knew what it meant.

"I could've bought it myself," he said.

"I know that," Daddy said. "And like we said on Sunday, Mama and I have been puttin' a little something away for you for a long time." He looked across the small table to Jed, who gazed back at him. "We've known you wouldn't stay here forever. Because you took so long to decide, there's more than I thought there'd be." He grinned at Jed, who had no choice but to smile back.

He reached over and covered his father's hand with his. He squeezed and said, "I really appreciate it. I think this is the right move for me."

He'd still be close to his family. He could literally hop the fence and run through the fields to his parents' house, but it would be faster to get in the truck and drive the five minutes down the road and around the corner.

"What about Cherry?" Daddy asked.

"Haven't heard from her," Jed said, the words tasting as sour as his voice sounded. He drained the rest of his coffee in a couple of big swigs and said, "I have to get goin'. I don't want to keep Betty waiting."

He stood and bent down to hug his father. He took the check, turned, and found his mother standing in the doorway. Emotion filled him, and he gathered her into a tight hug.

"I love you, son," she said, and Jed's heartbeat flailed inside his chest. Why couldn't Cherry love him? Was he really that salty?

He'd been over everything they'd said to one another in the past six or eight months. He'd apologized. So had she. She'd made some mistakes. So had he. He'd fallen in love with her.

Why hadn't she fallen in love with him?

He didn't want to try again. He didn't want to start over with someone new. For him, there was no one but Cherry Cooper, and he honestly didn't know how to deal with the fact that she hadn't at least texted. Not once.

He left his parents' house, left the farm, and turned left to go down and around the corner to Lady Jones's farm. He was a couple of minutes early, but she wouldn't mind. She'd told him last week that she got up with the sun, and that had crested the horizon about fifteen minutes ago.

She'd probably have a fresh pot of coffee on for him, and if he was lucky, some of her famous sausage, egg, and cheese blintzes. Jed could really use more than the empty sugar calories of coffee, and his heart beat skipped and settled strangely in his chest.

"Too much caffeine," he muttered to himself, and then he said, "Come on, Fish. Let's go get this done." He got out of the truck, and Fish came across the seats to jump down from his side.

Jed normally wouldn't have let him do that, but today, everything felt a little odd. Something wasn't quite right here at the farm either, but Jed couldn't put his finger on what. A strange, new scent floated on the air, and Jed took a deep breath, trying to place it.

He couldn't.

He could make his way to the porch and up the sagging steps. He could fix these. *I will*, he told himself as he arrived at the brown-painted door.

He'd fix that too. Probably rip it out and replace it with something new. He'd seen the house and several of the outbuildings before, and they all had good bones. Some of them needed a little makeover. Some needed a new exercise regimen to get them in shape. Jed could—and would—do all of it. He was actually looking forward to it.

He enjoyed the work on his family farm too, but there was something about *owning* the farm and working it that he wanted to experience. He didn't want to walk into East-on's office and say, "The hay loft is good to go."

He wanted to walk in his own front door, knowing that he'd worked on and repaired what needed to be worked on and repaired on his own land that day. No accountability necessary.

He knocked on Betty's door, and a dog answered with a couple of short barks. "Right here," he said to Fish, who sat at his feet. He was alert and at attention, but he sat.

"Coming," Betty called, and Jed's nerves tripled. He wasn't even sure why. After his visit today, he planned to make an offer on the farm, and then he needed to get to town to deposit the check his father had given him.

He should be back to his cabin by noon, and the stupid optimist in him wondered if Cherry would be waiting with lunch. She'd never done a peace offering without food. Neither had he, so he wasn't complaining.

She loved going out to eat, and had once told him that she got lunch five days a week with someone from her office. Or a group. Sometimes just herself. But she ate out for lunch every single weekday.

He'd never say no to ice cream, pizza, something with chocolate in it, or any other baked good. Pie, cobbler, bread, rolls, he liked them all. Immensely.

Not as much as Cherry—he didn't like anything as much as her.

The door in front of him opened, and Betty Jones stood there, her white hair wisping out in every direction from her head. Jed swiped his cowboy hat from his head and pressed it over his pulse. "Morning, ma'am," he said. "I hope I'm not too early. You said there was no such thing as too early."

But she still wore her bathrobe, a pair of yellow fuzzy slippers on her feet. "Nope, nope," she said. "Come in, Jed. I've got the coffee going."

He didn't know how to tell her no, and he smiled as he ducked his way inside the house. It smelled like the coffee she'd proclaimed to make, and Jed caught another note too.

Perfume.

He scanned the area, his heart pounding up inside his mouth now. Betty wasn't the one wearing perfume. Someone else had been here.

He went past the love seat and the recliner, past the little black and white dog on the latter, and into the kitchen.

Someone had been here, and they'd brought bread. Loaf after loaf of it sat on the counter, all lined up like soldiers. A round loaf that had an X carved in the top. A dark brown loaf that looked like rye, with whole oatmeal on the top. A white one shaped like a traditional loaf from the grocer.

Seven, eight, nine loaves of bread sat on the counter.

Not only that, but a plate of butter, and three jars of jam rested with them. He pulled in a breath at the sight of the jars.

He reached out and touched the nearest one, which had a piece of fabric covered in cherries spilling between the lid and the metal ring that twisted closed.

He knew these jars of jam. He'd seen them before at the Cooper's, as he'd been there for their Christmas meal.

He spun around, expecting Cherry to be at Betty's side. She wasn't. In fact, Betty herself headed for the hall.

"Help yourself to some bread," she said. "I've got a toaster that makes four slices at a time. I'll get dressed, and we'll go out and feed the animals."

"Okay," Jed said, because he was already talking to her back. She disappeared, and Jed returned his attention to the bread.

He would like some, and he picked up the nearest loaf and turned it over. She had to have gotten it from some-where, and he found a sticker on the bottom of the clear plastic bag the bread had been wrapped in.

It read, *The Bread Boy*, but Jed had never heard of it. It could be a new shop in Sweet Water Falls for all he knew.

The loaf wasn't sliced, but a knife sat on a cutting board, practically inviting him to get the job done. He did —restraining himself to two pieces of the sourdough— and set them in the toaster.

The house didn't move while the appliance did its work. Jed found it oddly quiet, and he wondered if he should make sure Betty was okay.

Then his toast popped up, and her dog made an appearance. He sat right next to Fish, both of them begging for bread and butter. Jed didn't blame them one bit, because a hot, crispy piece of toast with butter and jam was a real treat.

He slathered butter on his bread, then opened the jar of peach preserves. Cherry's mother had made these, and he wondered if Chrissy had come to see Betty. Perhaps she'd brought the bread too.

By seven-thirty in the morning?

He shook his head, answering himself. No way. Cherry had said her mother slept late, and she always needed help in the mornings until the pain worked its way out of her system. If she'd brought this bread, it wasn't this morning.

He'd just finished his breakfast of the gods, fed each dog a couple of tasty bites, and dusted his hands clean of crumbs when Betty returned.

"All right," she said, reaching for her cowgirl hat. "Ready?"

"Yes, ma'am." Jed cast one last look at the jars of jam and followed her and the dogs out the back door. He paused on the deck, searching for...something. Someone. He honestly didn't know what.

"Betty," he said. "Where'd you get that jam?"

"Ham?" she said over her shoulder. "No ham this year. I didn't get a pig at the fair."

"Not ham," he said. "*Jam.*"

She didn't answer, and she went past the barn where he knew she kept the feed. Jed could barely keep up with her, and he jogged a few steps to get to her side. "Aren't we feeding the animals?"

"Yes," she clipped out, her goal singular—and it wasn't to feed the animals. She started straight ahead, and she must go to the mall in the mornings and do some of that elderly mall walking, because she was moving *fast*. "I just need to check on something in the storage shed first."

"What?" Jed asked. "I can do it, Lady Jones. You shouldn't be getting' in that shed. The whole thing needs to be stabilized."

She slowed as they went past the hay barn, and her farm opened up a bit at that point. They'd gone past a couple of paddocks for her horses, the goat pen, and a small pig sty. She'd told him she only ever got one pig at a time, and only to raise and then eat for a big family meal. Since none of her children had gotten married this year, she had no need for one she'd said.

Fields flowed before him, and he stumbled and caught himself quickly when he saw someone standing on top of the storage shed.

"Eagles alive," he said, his eyes taking an extra moment to pick out features and assign an identity to Cherry Cooper. "Get down," he called, waving his hand.

She waved back, and the whole building swayed. She *had* to feel that, and the panic registered on her face as she flung out her other arm to balance herself.

"What is she doing up there?" he asked Betty as he took off at a run. The storage shed stood two stories high, and surely she'd leaned a ladder against it to get to the roof.

Jed was surprised that extra weight on one side hadn't toppled the whole thing. "Cherry," he called. "That shed isn't sturdy. Come on down."

"No," she called, and Jed slowed his run to a walk. "I have to tell you something, and I'm going to do it from right here."

Jed paused, utterly confused. He felt like he had all the pieces in front of him, but he couldn't make them line up into the right puzzle.

A breeze blew, and Cherry steadied herself. Jed couldn't watch her fall off that shed, but he obviously couldn't make her get down either. She spread her arms wide, and Jed dang near closed his eyes as the building moved again.

"I love you, Jed Forrester," Cherry called. More than called. She yelled it into the sky. Bellowed it into the atmosphere. "I love you, and I want you to know it. I need you in my life, and I'm ready to conquer all of my fears as long as you're the one at my side, holding my hand, and whispering to me that I can."

Jed's heart swelled with every word she said. She loved him. Finally, *finally*, Jed heard what he wanted to hear.

And it wasn't a whisper. And it wasn't done with actions. The words echoed in his ears, and his mind, and he could bottle them and hold onto them forever.

In that silence, he seized on another phrase too. *Face all my fears.*

One of Cherry's biggest fears was heights.

"Dear Lord," he whispered under his breath. He got moving again, praying harder than he ever had in his life. Wouldn't it just be cruel to finally find someone he loved only to have them taken from him?

"Come on down," he pleaded. "Please." He dashed around the side of it while Cherry said, "Not until you promise to kiss me when I get to the ground."

"I promise," he yelled, having lost sight of her. The ladder stood propped against the back of the shed, and Jed held it steady while Cherry came up and over the pinnacle of the roof.

"Careful," he said. "I can't believe you did this. And why'd you choose the most rickety building on the property?"

She stumbled and swayed as she caught herself. Jed yelped and started up the ladder. "Cherry," he said, hearing a thud.

He climbed faster than he ever had before and poked his head over the edge of the roof. She sat only a few feet from him—out of arm's reach—with her feet flat, knees up, palms planted against the shingles.

"You're insane," he said, breathless. "And this shed is seriously going to collapse with both of us up here." He reached for her. "Come on. Take my hand, and I'll help you down."

She looked at him, complete trust in her expression. Trust and love. "I love you," she said again.

Jed grinned at her, still straining to get closer to her. "Took you long enough."

She inched toward him, her beauty shining through in her smile. "Did I make you wait too long? I was helping Shane get his bread shop going, so I could bring one of your favorite foods."

"It's been the longest week of my life," Jed admitted, the tips of his fingers finally touching hers. "I got you."

He went down the ladder, rung by rung, Cherry following him. When they both finally stood on solid ground, he faced her. "Don't ever do that again. At least not until I buy this place and fix up every building."

She put her palms against his chest and slid them up, something she did that he adored. It made him feel strong and desirable. "Okay," she said. "Now, I think you promised me a kiss."

24

Cherry gazed up at Jed, who didn't immediately lean down to kiss her. She wasn't sure what he was thinking, so she reached up and brushed his hair along his ear and under his hat. "What are you thinking?"

"You said you loved me."

"I do," she said, the words coming easily now that she'd been up on that shed, in the breeze, and shouted the words, "I love you," as loudly as she could.

She smiled at him. "Is that hard for you to believe?"

"No," he said quickly, the corners of his mouth twitching up. "Seven days, Cherry."

"There was a lot to plan," she said, her ribcage suddenly too tight around her heart. She hadn't imagined he'd be salty about how long it had taken her to plan the perfect declaration of love.

"I wanted it to *mean* something," she said. "So coming here to this farm that you want—that I want to live on with you—was important. And that was today." She shuffled her feet closer to him, really pressing into his chest now. "I'm sorry," she murmured. "Please forgive me for making you wait seven days. Or even seven seconds for me to tell you how I feel."

Jed gazed down at her, that familiar sizzle in the twinkle of his eye now. "Honestly, sweetheart, I'd wait forever for you."

She closed her eyes, her happiness the blissful kind that she'd seen others wear on their wedding days and which resided in Rissa's eyes every time she looked at her beautiful baby.

Jed came closer, and Cherry knew, because she sensed him. He breathed out, the scent of peach jam on his breath, and she tensed. "You ate toast before you came out."

"I adore toast," he whispered. "Especially with your mama's jam."

"That's why I brought all the bread," she said.

"I'd love you even without the food gifts," he said, his lips catching slightly on hers. Fire built within her, burning with anticipation.

"But they make things better, right?" she asked.

"Toast makes everything better." He kissed her then, his lips soft and firm at the same time. An explosion went off in her head, and she wanted to move fast.

But Jed kept things slow, and while he usually told her how he felt with words, today, he showed her with how tenderly and passionately he kissed her.

———

"AND THAT'S IT," JED SAID AN HOUR LATER. THEY'D JUST gone around the farm, and he'd pointed out everything. Literally everything. Cherry knew more about Betty Jones's farm now than she truly cared to. But she wanted to hold Jed's hand and share in his enthusiasm. He clearly had big plans for this property, and he said, "Mama and Daddy gave me a bunch of money."

Cherry looked up at him and found contriteness on his face. "Wow, really?"

"They said they've always known I'd need a place of my own."

"Hmm." Cherry swung their hands in an over-exaggerated way. "What are you going to name it?"

"I don't know," he said. "Do you have any ideas?"

Cherry thought while the farmhouse came back into view. They went past the dual stable and as they passed the goat pen, she said, "It's a rescue ranch."

"I want to do animal rescue, yes," he said. "But I want to work with the State Fair too. I want to employ cowboys who need rescuing too."

Cherry loved that his heart held this quality, and she couldn't wait to see what he did with this land. "What about something simple? Rescue Ranch? Or like, Cowboy Ranch?"

"Cowboy Ranch," he said, trying out each word in his mouth as he spoke slowly. "Seems fairly generic."

"My family's farm is called Sweet Water Falls," she said dryly. "It's literally the same as the town."

"People could bring their animals to us for recovery or rehabilitation," he said. "So maybe it is a ranch where you can get access to great cowboys."

Cherry grinned up at him. "Where are you gonna find these 'great cowboys'?"

Jed shrugged one shoulder, spun her away from him, and pulled her back in. "I have a few friends I can ask." He held her tight and danced her in a slow circle. "You can help if you want. You're a good judge of character."

"Am I?" She laughed, tipping her head back and letting the sound fly, the same way she had when she'd shouted to Jed and Betty and all the animals and the world that she loved Jed Forrester.

She sobered and looked at the cowboy she loved. "If I wanted to work on a farm, I'd have taken over for my daddy."

"So that's a no?" he challenged.

"I want to live here with you," she said. "Support you in whatever you need. If you want to have interviews over dinner, I'm game."

"But?" he prompted, and Cherry liked that he knew there was a but.

"But I met this guy who lives on my lane in Short Tail, and he wants to start a bread bakery. I want to help him. Be the admin behind that effort. He wants to bake. I'll be the bakery manager."

Jed's eyebrows flew up, and he nodded toward the house. "The Bread Boy?"

Cherry nodded, another giggle escaping. "It was good bread, right?"

"Delicious," Jed said.

"I've been working with him for a few days already," she said. "I know a lot of people in town, and I've found him a location and everything."

"So you're already working with him." Jed wore wariness in his expression now. "You should sign something with him, Cherry. How are you getting paid?"

"Don't worry, Mister Forrester," she said. "We're meeting for lunch today to go over the contract I had Gretchen help me with. She owns her own chocolate shop, you know."

"I'm aware," Jed said.

"Can you come?" she asked, realizing her plan to surprise him with her declaration of love had some drawbacks. "I figured you'd be here in the morning, and you could afford an hour for lunch. I want you to meet Shane."

"I can spare some time for lunch with you," he said.

"And Shane," she said.

"And Shane." They started for the house again, and

Jed whistled for Fish to join them. "So are you going to be an investor?"

"Yes," she said. "That's what I'd like to be. He's the genius with yeast. I'm the one with admin experience. It's a win-win."

"And how did you meet this Shane?"

"His momma lives on my lane, and he lives with her. She's been bringing me bread, and last week, she made him come with her. He, uh, was going to ask me out, but I saved us both the trouble. We've been talking and brainstorming since."

Jed chuckled and lifted her hand to his mouth for a kiss. "You're an amazing woman, Cherry."

She smiled a soft smile to herself, the kind that moved past the exterior and embedded itself in her heart. "I love you, Jed."

"And I love you, Cherry."

25

Travis Cooper found himself once again running up his front steps after a frantic text from his wife. The first time, she'd fallen on one of her morning runs with Will, and he'd found her bleeding in the tiny bathroom that sat between the two bedrooms in the microscopic cottage they shared.

This time, she'd told him to *get home quick*, because *she's coming*.

She being their baby.

Which was a real problem, as she wasn't due to be born for three more weeks. Yes, Shay looked like she might pop at any moment. She'd been uncomfortable for a couple of months now. She only went to work when absolutely necessary, and she ran everything else from her computer or phone here at the cabin on the farm, where she could lie in bed or on the couch.

He didn't want to be disappointed on his daughter's birthday. The baby already had some tough times ahead, as she only had half a heart. Everything else had developed exactly right. Just not her most vital organ.

Travis had thought he'd lose his heart the day he and Shay had found out. But he hadn't. If anything, the news that his precious child would need help throughout her life had made his heart stronger.

"Shay," he called as he burst through the door. She wasn't in the living room or kitchen, but she called to him from down the hall.

He sprinted that way, not seeing her in the bathroom, and detoured into their bedroom. She sat on the edge of the bed, pain etched in every line on her face. "I need help," she said.

Travis couldn't take in all the details at once, but something had happened in here. The blankets sat askew, and Shay's baby bag waited half-packed—or half-unpacked—on top of the dresser.

"I'm here," he said. "Tell me what to do." He arrived at her side, anxious and yet strangely calm. She got to her feet, and he held her under each elbow.

"We need to go to the hospital," she said. "My contractions have started."

Travis caught sight of the wet stain on the bed, but he didn't comment on it. "Let's go."

"The bag isn't packed," Shay said, her voice cracking. "We haven't moved." She continued to move toward the door, and Travis switched from being in front of her to following behind.

He kept his hands on her, just in case she stumbled, fell, or started having contractions and needed help standing.

Their new house sat about a mile from this one, and no it wasn't finished yet. Almost, but not quite. With a carpet recall that had delayed them, and then the contractor's father passing away, they were a few weeks behind on finishing up the house.

Combined with the baby coming early, and Shay didn't have the house or nursery she wanted to bring their little girl home to.

"Did you call Rissa?"

Shay groaned and then snapped, "I called you, cowboy."

Travis blinked but said nothing. "I'll call her," he said. Outside on the porch, he looked next door, but Rissa wasn't there. She took Bronson to the shoppe to make cheese and ice cream nearly every day. She wouldn't just be waiting on the front porch for Shay to go into labor.

He helped his wife into the passenger seat and grinned at her. "Hey, it's not the middle of the night."

She smiled back, but hers held a lot of nerves. "I didn't mean to snap at you back there."

"It's fine," he said, choosing not to reveal why he wanted to call his sister. If Rissa and Cherry knew that Shay didn't have her nursery set up, they'd come do it.

So even though Shay might murder him in his sleep if he didn't get them to the hospital soon, he took ten seconds standing outside his door to text the family text.

Then everyone would know.

Shay's gone into labor. We're headed to the hospital. I'll text you when we know more.

He got behind the wheel, tossed his phone into the cupholder, and started toward the hospital.

Shay's phone went off a few times in the few minutes it took to get to the main highway and really pick up speed.

"Thank you, Trav," she said.

"For what?" He reached over and took her hand in his.

She wept quietly and said, "They're going to get the nursery ready."

He smiled at her. "Great."

"I don't know how," she said, sniffling. "The stuff I want isn't in yet."

"You ordered it, right?" he asked.

She nodded, and Travis focused his attention out the windshield. "Then Cherry and Rissa will find a way. They're like a hurricane, Shay. You'll see."

She giggled at his comment, the sound quickly morphing into a gasp. She whimpered, pulled her hand from him, and pressed it against her belly.

Trav pressed harder on the gas pedal, because while he was anxious to meet his daughter, he didn't want it to happen on the side of the road.

Although... "Remember when we first met?" he asked.

Shay looked at him with wide eyes filled with pain. "It was right here along this road," he continued. "I thought you were stunningly gorgeous, of course, even with a small dog."

She breathed, and Travis congratulated himself for doing a great thing. He chuckled and shook his head. "I kicked myself for months for letting my big mouth run away from me. But thankfully, I ran into you at the feed store later."

"Literally," she said, her voice only slightly strained. She hadn't eased up on the tenseness in her body though.

"Hey, you're the one who jumped up on the runner of the dump truck," he said.

"And then you asked me out in the weirdest, vaguest way ever."

"I took you to a *ball*," he said. "Like a *princess*."

Shay sighed, the air hissing out of her mouth, and Travis watched her relax. "It's over."

"Mm," he said, his thoughts back on his dating relationship with Shay. He had taken her to the Fall Ball, but she hadn't wanted that to be their first date. She'd made him *work* for that ball, and Travis had done it happily.

Because he wanted and loved Shay.

The rest of the drive to the hospital passed quickly, with Travis bringing up something funny or nostalgic that had happened to them over the past couple of years, and then he dashed inside to get help for his wife.

———

Hours later, he stood at her shoulder as the first wails of a newborn filled the air. He could barely move, as wonder had rooted his cowboy boots to the floor.

"Oh," he said as the doctor lifted the tiny infant. "There she is, Shay. Look."

She didn't respond, and a nurse took the baby and turned away.

"You can go, Daddy," the doctor said, and Travis quickly stepped over to the incubator where two nurses worked to wipe down his daughter. She cried and screamed like they were torturing her, and they both smiled. One said, "Oh, she's a healthy one," like the carrying on the girl was doing was actually good.

"Healthy lungs," the other said. They didn't handle her with care, and the next thing Trav knew, they'd bundled her and plopped her into his arms.

He gazed down at the now-quiet baby, seeing himself in her physical features. She had the Cooper nose, and every hair on her head shone in tones of dark, deep, red gold. "Hello, baby," he whispered as he lifted his daughter to kiss her.

She wiggled in his arms, and he sure hoped she recognized his voice. He tucked her close and turned back to the bed.

"She's done," the doctor said as he stood. "Good work, Shay. Look, here she is." He grinned at Trav, who moved to Shay's side and carefully slid their daughter into her arms.

"She's so perfect," Shay whispered.

"She is," Trav said.

"We'll have the cardiologist come down when she can," the nurse said. "We'll let her know she was born."

The other nurse stepped up to Shay's other side, a clipboard at the ready. "Do y'all have a name for this little one?"

Shay looked at Trav, and Trav looked at Shay. "I want Christie," she said.

"Okay," he said. "And Louise after your grandmother?" The Christie was a nod to Mama. They'd added a T and made it an IE instead of a Y, but the name was in honor of her.

"Yes," Shay murmured, looking back at Christie Louise Cooper. Trav told the nurse the name and how to spell it, and then someone came to move them into a recovery room.

At that point, Trav got back on the family text. Messages had been flying for hours—this was Shay's first baby, after all. It had taken a while to get her here—and Trav couldn't possibly read them all.

So he simply typed in the name of his new baby and sent that.

Then, *Shay did amazing. She's with the baby now, and we're in a recovery room. I'm not sure where we'll end up, but y'all can come over now if you'd like.*

Cherry was the first to respond: *I'm here. What did the cardiologist say?*

Haven't met with her yet, Trav said, unsurprised that his oldest sister was already at the hospital.

He looked up as a nurse came in, with yet another clipboard in her hand. "Excuse me," he said before she could begin speaking. "What room will we be in?"

"This one," she said. "You'll stay here until she gets discharged." She smiled at Shay, and Trav quickly moved to the door to check the room number.

Room 713, he sent, fully expecting a barrage of family members to start showing up. Exhaustion pulled through him, but he wouldn't have it any other way.

Once the nurse left, he smiled at Shay and she grinned back at him. "Love you, baby," he said.

"I love you too," Shay said. "Do you want to hold her?"

"Yes," he said, and he took his baby into his arms and started to hum to her. She looked at him with dark, dark eyes which wouldn't focus, and all he could do was sigh and think, *Thank you, Lord, for this perfect life and perfect little girl.*

———

SHAY EYED THE MOB OF CARS PARKED IN FRONT OF THE TINY cabin she and Trav had lived in together since their wedding. One in particular stood out to her.

"Trav," she said.

"She wanted to come," he said, pulling up beside her mother's car. "She's been here for the past couple of days helping in the nursery." He put the truck in park and looked over to Shay, his eyes darting into the backseat where their new arrival rode.

Christie snoozed in her carseat, and Shay had never been as charmed by a human being as she was the baby. Maybe Trav. Fine, definitely Trav.

Christie was only two days old, but she'd already manifested her...spicy personality. She could wail like nothing Shay had ever heard a baby do before when she was hungry, but she also gave the best snuggles in the world when she'd been satisfied.

Shay's heartbeat trembled through her veins. Her mother had come. She'd likely brought other family members, and Shay swallowed back her anxiety.

She'd felt like this before, when she'd had to deal with Kylie and Sweetspot. When she'd ventured out on her own as the sole owner of her outdoor outfitters company. When she'd fought with her mother and siblings.

Shay loved them; they were family. But she chose to spend her time with the Coopers, because they didn't criticize her every move, hold the past against her, or keep a grudge for years and years.

"All right," she said as Travis got out of the truck. He went to the back to retrieve their daughter, and that left Shay to get out and face the cabin, nothing else to occupy her.

"Come on, hon," Trav said, coming around the tailgate to her side. "They're not going to bite."

"Sometimes they do," she said. He knew. He'd endured a few tense dinners and parties at her parents' house. "If Daddy's here, it might be okay."

"He's here," Trav said. "They want to meet their grand-daughter badly." He offered her an encouraging, kind smile, and with him at her side, Shay was able to take the first step.

Then several more, and she went all the way into the house. A group of people stood behind the couch in the living room, as well as throughout the kitchen.

"Welcome home!" they shouted, and instant tears came to Shay's eyes. Christie screeched, obviously surprised by the loud noise and not liking it.

Shay let Trav deal with her as women—Shay's mom included—rushed forward to assist. Cherry was there, and Rissa, of course.

Shay loved them both, as they'd been nothing but kind, loving, and supportive to her. Gretchen had brought a zillion chocolates, if the trays on the counter meant anything. She arrived in front of Shay and took her into a hug. "You're home now," she said, and that about summed up everything.

Home.

Shay could always come home and be accepted and feel comfortable in her own skin.

"Baby doll," her daddy said, and Gretchen released

her so Shay could hug him. He held her tight, and somewhere outside of the loving circle of his arms, she heard her mother cooing over Christie.

"Love you, Shayla," Daddy said, and Shay repeated the sentiment back to him. She then turned toward her mother, who held the baby in her arms.

Their eyes met, and Mom wore the biggest, brightest, kindest smile Shay had ever seen. That only kicked down all the defensive walls she'd put up between the two of them, and she stepped over to her mother and daughter.

"We gave her the middle name of Louise," she said, her voice thick as honey. "After your mama." She stroked Christie's pretty, wispy hair back, the soft spot on the top of her head pulsing a bit.

"She's beautiful, Shay," Mom said, and she drew her into a one-armed hug that Christie certainly didn't like. She fussed over being smashed, and Mom half-laughed and half-cried as she stepped back and soothed the tiny girl.

"She's got opinions," she said, beaming at the baby. "That's good, Christie. You're gonna need those."

"Around here, she will," Lee said, and he took Shay into a hug too, holding her close and adding, "Congratulations, Shay. Mama is dying for you to see the nursery, but you take your time."

Shay held onto his broad shoulders too, because Lee could be gruff and surly, but he was really just a big teddy bear with a heart of marshmallow once that outer layer got removed.

"Let's go see it," she said, new anticipation building in her stomach. "We would've been fine. We're moving so soon anyway."

Will had come to Lee's side, and he grinned at Shay. "You say that like Mama would allow a baby to come into this family under 'fine' conditions." He handed her a tall glass of sweet tea, and her love for Trav's brother doubled.

She took a sip, spotted Chrissy near the hallway, standing next to Wayne, and she went that way. "Nursery reveal," she called, and that got almost everyone's attention.

She first hugged Chrissy and Wayne, wanting to say so much to them. To thank them for always including her in their family. For making her feel so comfortable on their farm and in their home. For raising a fine son, even if he acted cross sometimes.

"Come on, dear," Chrissy said, and she took the first shuffle-step down the hall. She went all the way into the nursery, as did Wayne, but Shay paused in the doorway.

The walls had been painted a soft yellow, almost the same color as freshly churned butter. Nearly white, especially with the afternoon sunlight hitting it.

"Oh," fell from her lips. The bright white furniture she'd wanted sat there, all in the proper place, just as she and Cherry had sketched out.

The fully constructed crib waited for her, with bright

pink-and-white striped bumpers and bedding. A white rocking chair sat in the corner, where Shay could look out the window as she rocked Christie back to sleep. A dark forest green pad sat on it, and she teared up again at the sight of her favorite color in the room.

She hadn't wanted a changing table, because the bedroom was so small, and the third item in the room made her excitement shoot off the chart.

"You got the jogging stroller." She stepped into the room to examine it. "How? They were on backorder until June."

"Cherry pulled some strings," Rissa said.

"Just a few," Cherry said, both of them joining her in the room. The stroller was put together too, and all the work of getting this room cleared, painted, furniture put together and in shone in every inch.

She knew the people who'd done this loved her, Trav, and now Christie.

She turned back to Cherry and Rissa and hugged them together. "Thank you."

"Your daddy put together the crib," Cherry whispered, her grip on Shay's shoulders tight. "Your mama painted for hours. Will and Lee worked hard to get that rocking chair perfect, and I even sewed that cushion for you."

"I made so much food," Rissa said with a laugh. "Spence filled your fridge with it." Shay pulled away, unable to speak though she wanted to voice her gratitude.

She figured the tears flowing down her face got the point across.

"Rose got the art," Rissa said, wiping her face. "Gretchen did all the prep work while we were off getting things."

"I supervised. You would not *believe* some of the ideas I had to veto, Shay," Chrissy said from behind Shay, and that caused everyone to laugh.

Shay stepped past Rissa and Cherry to Rose and Gretchen. "Thank you," she said, hugging them. She embraced Will and Lee again, telling them how grateful she was. She hugged her mama and daddy again. Her brother and sister who'd come. She found Trav at the end of the hall, holding their baby, and she took her from him.

"Come see," she said to both of them, and the crowd made way for them to take their daughter into her new nursery, even if they'd only be there for a few weeks.

"Look how loved we are," she said, and Trav slid his arm around her waist.

"Thanks, everyone," he said, his voice the tiniest bit pinched. He could show anger and frustration real easily, but some of his softer emotions got dammed up.

"Yes," Shay said, still weeping and ready to stop. "Thank you."

Christie squirmed and grunted, to which everyone smiled or laughed, and then Shay nodded to Chrissy. "Sit, Nana, and let's get this grandbaby into your arms."

26

"Rose!"

Her shouted name made Rosalie Reynolds turn from the mirror. Her sister had arrived, and that meant her parents too.

She moved away from the dresser in her bedroom, calling, "Back here."

Natasha appeared at the end of the hall. "The USS Thumper got out. I forgot."

"Shoot." Rose jogged forward to hug her younger sister. "It's fine, Nat. He's a rabbit."

"Autumn went after him."

"Then we'll get him back." Rose stepped back and held onto her sister's shoulders. "Are you ready for an amazing beach day?"

"It's too cold, Mama says." Nat frowned and pushed her new bangs out of her eyes. "Is it too cold, Rose?"

Rose hadn't really been paying attention to the weather. The forecast only went out seven days, and she was getting married in eight. "I don't know," she said. "Surely we can at least drive there and walk down to the waves. You can get your feet wet."

Nat turned toward their mother as she came inside. "I can get my feet wet."

Mom sighed, and Rose gave her a look that said, *Let me do it, Mom.*

Her mom nodded, and Rose went to greet her parents. Daddy didn't come in, because he was off with Autumn trying to rescue the demon white rabbit determined to flee the only home he'd ever known. Rose wasn't quite sure how Thumper would survive out on the farm. There were a lot of dogs, horses, and people, and they couldn't put up a gate across the front door of the farmhouse. It was never locked and anyone and everyone who wanted to come in, did.

She had, many times. No knocking required.

Lee and Ford were also moving into the house today. Travis and Shay's house had been finished a couple of weeks ago, and the Coopers had done a marathon weekend of moving them from one cabin to another.

Then Will and Gretchen had moved in with Lee a few days later. It was going...okay. But everyone was anxious to get this last move done.

With Will's cabin empty, Wayne and Chrissy had been moving things from their farmhouse of the past fifty years to the much smaller cabin. All of their children had been helping, if only for a few minutes each day. That was all Lee could manage, but he did it.

Cherry and Rissa had helped their mama clean everything out. Trav drove loads to the Salvation Army for donations. Will and Lee moved boxes and furniture.

The last big move was today. Chrissy and Wayne would be out of the farmhouse in the morning. Lee and Ford in it by dinnertime. Rose had asked her family to come help, because she was moving a few of her things into the farmhouse now too.

She wouldn't make the move permanent until she and Lee were married, and eight days seemed impossibly far away.

"We got 'im," Daddy said, carrying the overweight chonk of a rabbit into the house, both hands clenched around the mammal's middle. That didn't make Thumper happy, and Rose laughed right out loud at the disgruntled look on his bunny face.

Autumn skipped into the house, of course. "He was hidin' under the bushes, Mama."

"How'd you get him out?" Rose asked as Daddy placed Thumper on the couch. The rabbit wiggled his nose like he'd never been on a couch before.

"I took out some kale," she said.

"All right," Rose said, clapping her hands now that the Thumper debacle was fixed. "Lunch? Then a quick trip to the beach? Then we can grab dinner and go out to Lee's."

"Good plan!" Nat yelled, and Rose ducked out of instinct. Her sister stood right behind her, and such a loud noise so close had startled her.

"Get the sunscreen," she said, nodding to Autumn. "If you want to brave the water, you can. Put on your swimming suit."

"Come help me, Aunt Nat," Autumn said, taking Nat's hand. The two of them went down the hall, and Rose faced her parents.

"Thank you," she said. "For coming to help." She stepped into her father's arms. "Has Nat been talking a lot?"

"I don't think she stopped once the whole way." Daddy smiled as he stepped back, but he looked worn around the edges. Mama too.

"Let me take her this afternoon," Rose said. "You guys stay here with Thumper. Once he trusts you, he'll even curl up on your chest and sleep with you." She offered them a smile, and the fact that they didn't protest told her just how tiring the drive had been.

She turned at the sound of giggling from down the hall, and she caught sight of her perfectly clean kitchen. She cleaned when stressed, and her stress revealed itself in strange ways.

A couple of hours later, Rose looked up from her book as Autumn yelled, "Mister Lee is here!"

She sat up straighter and watched her daughter sprint up the beach toward the parking lot. Rose sat huddled in one of the beach chairs she'd hauled from the car while Nat and Autumn had gone to the water's edge. She wore a hooded sweatshirt and she pushed the hood back as she stood and turned in the direction her daughter had gone.

Sure enough, her fiancé came toward them, wearing a pair of colorful swim shorts like he'd be joining the girls in the water. He grinned and bent down as Autumn approached, and he lifted her and tossed her into the air, both of them laughing as he did.

Rose loved watching them, because everything Lee did felt authentic and true to his character. He adored children, and Rose wanted to give him so many. She worried from time to time about what would happen with Curious Kids—her game company that she'd founded, ran, and still designed all the content for—if she started having a lot of babies.

Lee had told her he'd support her any way she wanted, but he ran his family's farm now. He was the boss, and once the move was done, he'd be living in the main farmhouse. He was the perfect person to take over Cooper & Company and Sweet Water Falls, and Rose didn't want to make his burden more than it was.

As Lee set Autumn on the sand and lifted his eyes to hers, Rose had the very distinct feeling that she'd be very happy without Curious Kids. She'd been made to be at Lee's side, and that was exactly where she wanted to be.

He took her into his arms as Autumn went back toward Nat and the waves. "Mm, reading?"

"Yes," she said. "I'm surprised you made the drive."

"It's crazy at the farm," he said, his voice taking on a dark tint. "Trust me, it's better I'm here."

Rose looked up at him, concern spiking through her. "Yeah? Is it going to be intense tomorrow?"

He met her eye, a frown forming between his. "You've met my family, right?" He looked up and gazed out at the ocean again. "We make everything into a big deal. Picking up the wrong lamp causes an all-out war."

Rose grinned at him, because she knew his love for his family ran as deep as his irritation. "Whose lamp did you touch, Lee?"

"*I* didn't touch it," he said. "But Cherry took a lamp that Will had just bought, thinking it went to the farmhouse, and you'd have thought she clubbed him with it and then stole his favorite cowboy boots." He shook his head, no smile or chuckle in sight.

Rose giggled, because that sounded like classic William Cooper behavior. He'd curbed a lot of that in recent months since marrying Gretchen and then finding out they were going to be parents. But sometimes, that redheaded gene came out with a vengeance. It happened to Lee too, and Rose knew she hadn't seen the last of his temper. She simply loved him anyway, because he tried very hard, and he really was made of muscles around marshmallow.

He sank into Nat's chair, and Rose retook hers. She laced her fingers through his, her book forgotten. Lee was here now, and he was the only distraction she ever needed.

————

THE FOLLOWING MORNING, ROSE PULLED UP TO THE farmhouse, several pickup trucks already parked there. The sun had risen already, because April was well into itself, and the afternoons were nearly unbearable already.

She reminded herself that she'd chosen to get married in the afternoon, right here on this farm, and that she needed to call Violet and make sure the misters would be good to go.

Rose went up to the house alone, as her parents, Nat, and Autumn were at least fifteen minutes behind her. She'd told Lee she'd be here at nine a.m. and she didn't want to be late for his moving day.

She didn't knock on the front door, but went right inside the way she usually did. Voices echoed into the lobby from the kitchen, but they didn't sound angry.

So far so good, she thought. She went under the arch and into the kitchen, where someone—probably Rissa—had set up a breakfast bar. Breads and muffins as far as the eye could see sat on the island, along with plates of butter, knives, and jars of Chrissy's homemade jam.

"Rose," Cherry said. "Have you eaten? You can break our tie." She rushed at Rose, which wasn't a good sign.

She almost wanted to throw up her hands to ward off Lee's sister. Or protect her face. Something.

"Break the tie?" Rose asked.

"I brought two new offerings from The Bread Boy," Cherry said. "We're voting on which one Shane should put on the menu next week." Cherry had been working with Shane Bowen and his new, start-up bread-only bakery in Sweet Water Falls for a few months now. They'd been quite the talk of the town in recent weeks, as Shane offered a free slice of his "bread of the week" to specifically-name people. A new name every day. It was a marketing strategy Cherry had come up with to get people into the shop. And it had worked really well.

She and Lee had ordered all the bread for the bruschetta for their wedding from Shane, and when Rose had gone to taste it, she'd had a very hard time choosing which one she wanted.

Of course, she and Lee seemed to like night and day different things, so he'd liked the ones she'd vetoed immediately. He let her pick, claiming he trusted her palette more than his, and Rose had narrowed it down to a sourdough option and a dark rye option. Both would be delicious with the tomato, olive, and mushroom toppings the caterers were doing.

Gretchen was making the wedding cake, of course. Rissa and her ice cream shoppe would supply all the ice cream. The main course was a pizza buffet, as everyone in the Cooper family adored pizza, and it was easy to make for a crowd.

The caterer, a woman named Sage Grady, had designed a menu that was both upscale and farm-friendly, so the cowboys and townspeople would be equally satisfied.

Rose had wanted something chic, but country, and the salami, basil, and honey pizza fit the bill.

"First," Cherry said. "We have an apple loaf." She nodded to Lee, who dutifully handed Rose a chunk of bread.

She put it in her mouth, but there were no apple chunks. It wasn't a doughnut, and the bread merely came with the tang of a green apple.

"It's better toasted," Rissa said right as a toaster popped up a piece of bread. "With the caramel butter." She raised her eyebrows in Rose's direction, and Rose nodded.

"Like a caramel apple."

"In bread form," Gretchen said, her whole face lit up. It was obvious which bread flavor she'd chosen.

Rose accepted the piece of toast, and she took a bite. A moan started in her taste buds and quickly moved down her throat. She got salt from the butter, cream, that hint of caramel and apple, all in a crunchy bite of toast.

"This is amazing," she said, looking around at the others. Lee had voted for this one as well, she could tell. Will too, if his giant grin meant anything. Rissa and

Spence looked indifferent, playing their perfect poker faces.

"What's my other choice?" she asked.

Cherry turned to the counter and picked up another chunk of bread. "This is a Swiss and sage loaf."

Rose generally liked savory things over sweet, but she could smell the bread before she popped the square into her mouth. Too much cheese. The sharp Swiss flavor punched her in the back of the throat, but she managed not to give away too much.

"It's also better toasted," Rissa said. "With a honey butter that tones down the cheese." She doctored up another piece of toast, and Rose took a few bites. She didn't want to finish it, and she held it out to the group, clearly offering it to them.

Half of them groaned and the other half cheered. Cherry grinned the hardest, and she turned to Jed, planting both of her palms against his chest.

"I think I have a hidden superpower I didn't know about."

"Creating bread flavors?" he asked, chuckling. Rose loved watching the two of them interact, and she wondered when Jed was going to propose. She didn't bother Cherry with personal questions like that. Rissa would, or Chrissy, or even Shay. Sometimes Lee, and Rose would just hear about it via text or over a meal with him. He had a very close relationship with his sister, and Rose found that endearing for both of them as well.

"Shane will be thrilled," Cherry said. "Thanks, everyone, for participating in the taste-test." She turned and faced them, her hand falling to Jed's at her side.

"Can I have another piece of that caramel apple toast?" Rose asked.

"We can leave it out," Lee said almost the moment she finished speaking. "Daylight's burning. Let's get started."

Everyone looked from him to her and back. Rose gave him a smile, and Lee sighed. "Fine. One more piece of toast for everyone, and then we've got two families to move, and it's hot already."

Another cheer went up, and Rose kept her eyes glued to Lee as he came to her side and pressed a kiss to her forehead. "Sorry," she murmured.

"It's their funeral," he said. "I just hope they don't complain to me when it's ninety degrees and they're moving my heavy entertainment center."

Rose snuggled into his side and said, "I love you, Lee. One more week."

"One more week," he murmured too, and then he took her hand and took her out of the kitchen.

"No toast?" she asked playfully.

"After," he said as he lowered his head to kiss her. She didn't have to ask after what, because kissing Lee was far better than toast, even an apple-flavored slice with caramel butter.

27

J ed knew how to work hard, and the second weekend of April had him hauling someone else's furniture, boxes, and clothing from one house to another.

He wouldn't be anywhere else on this gorgeous Saturday, and he couldn't stop smiling at everyone he went by.

Spencer Rust, Clarissa's husband. He'd gladly shown up to help Lee and Ford move from their cabin into the big white farmhouse.

Wayne and Chrissy were moving into Will's cabin, as he'd vacated it the previous week. Or two weeks.

Jed had a lot going on, and he couldn't keep track of everything going on at three farms. His family's, Cherry's family's, and his new ranch—Cowboy Ranch in Sweet Water Falls.

The sale had gone through at the end of March, and

Betty's children had come and done the same thing the Cooper siblings were doing now: They'd moved her out of her house.

Off her property.

Jed had gotten the keys to the house, the barns, to every gate and outbuilding, all of it, about a week and a half ago, and he'd simply stared at them.

Sometimes he still did, marveling at how many there were and that they belonged to him.

Him.

He hadn't moved onto the ranch yet, because he wanted to renovate the house before he had to live in it. No one needed his cabin, and the commute from farm to farm took seven minutes.

He'd been working eighteen hours per day since taking possession of those keys, because Betty had left all of her animals. They had to be fed and watered and taken care of, and Jed still had work to do around his family ranch too.

That would end at the end of April, as Easton had found a couple of new cowboys to work at Forrester Farms, the same way he had with the office manager.

Cherry had gotten the job at the County Clerk's office, and she'd turned it down. She'd gone all-in with Shane Bowen and The Bread Boy. She worked there from dawn to mid-afternoon, and then she'd show up on Jed's ranch and putter around with him.

Sometimes she sat on her phone while he ripped down outdated kitchen cabinets. Sometimes she'd pick up a paintbrush and help him update the color of the walls in the living room. Once, she'd changed his wash only to call to him with some measure of panic that the appliance was leaking.

Jed anticipated many moments of brief panic as he discovered all the cracks and issues on his new ranch.

He wouldn't have it any other way, and he didn't want to go through all of those terrible moments alone. His pulse skipped and stumbled as he thought about asking Cherry to be his wife.

They'd talked about marriage plenty of times. Cherry had brought it up; he had too. They'd talked about the horses and dogs they wanted, and he'd consulted with her several times about the décor, paint colors, and other fixtures she might like for the house.

He just hadn't gotten the question asked yet.

The diamond currently sat in his jeans pocket, and after Jed delivered the bookcase to the bedroom where Ford would live in the farmhouse, he patted his leg just to make sure the ring still rode there.

It did, and Jed had a feeling the day was winding down. The breads lined up on the counter in the kitchen had gotten picked over, and as Jed stepped into the hallway, he nearly got decapitated by Travis as he hauled in a full-length mirror.

"Sorry," they said in tandem, and Trav added a grunt,

because the free-standing mirror was heavy and he had to adjust it.

Jed got out of the hallway as Will came through the front door with part of an obviously handmade and hand carved bed frame.

"Don't stop," Lee called. "We're right behind you."

Jed dashed forward to help Will, and together, they maneuvered the frame around the corner, down the hall, and then through the doorway.

They breathed hard and then flattened themselves against the wall as Lee and Spencer came in with the second piece.

They worked together to make the corners square and the bed frame strong and sure.

Rose and Ford came into the room with his twin mattress, and Jed grinned at both of them.

Something about the Coopers exuded magic, and Jed sure did like basking in it.

"How much more?" Lee asked.

"Whatever's in that truck," Rose said, wiping her hair back. "Your cabin is empty now."

"Besides my stuff," Will said.

"Yes, besides Will and Gretchen's things," Rose said, flashing him a quick smile.

"Let's go see, bud," Lee said, giving his son a nudge toward the door. Jed stood crammed back in the corner, so he left the room last.

The line of people went into the kitchen, not back

outside to see what else was in the truck, so Jed followed them.

The whole Cooper family had congregated there, and Rissa and Cherry moved about the kitchen, both of them cooking.

"Tacos in about fifteen minutes," Rissa said, and everyone cheered. It wasn't loud and didn't last long, because it had been quite the day already.

Jed's hand went to his pocket, and while he'd thought a lot about how he'd ask Cherry to marry him, he'd never been in her kitchen while she browned ground beef.

Chatter and laughter filled the room as several people took seats at the long dining room table. Jed stood as a hinge, halfway between the activity in the kitchen and the conversations at the table.

Cherry's parents sat on a couch across from the table, Ford next to Wayne, showing him something in a notebook.

Jed didn't know what came over him, but he didn't mind having eyes on him. He had a loud voice, and as he withdrew the diamond from his pocket, he yelled, "Can I get everyone's attention, please?"

Yes, he could. Easier than he thought too, from his experiences with the Coopers and his stories from Cherry's childhood.

"Cherry," he said, his heartbeat nearly deafening him. "Can you come here for a second?"

"I'm cooking," she said.

"Now is not the time to argue with him," Rissa said, meeting Jed's eyes. Something meaningful passed between them, and she stepped over to Cherry without looking away from Jed. "Go on."

"I'm *cooking*," Cherry said, still not getting it.

"Cherry," Lee said, standing from his spot at the table. He came to stand beside Jed, and they exchanged a glance. Lee gave Jed a smile, and he knew Cherry's brother was on his side.

Will and Travis came to stand with him too, so that by the time Cherry relinquished the wooden spoon to her sister, Jed stood with all of her brothers.

"What?" she asked, and she faced him with some level of irritation on her face. He watched it fall away when she saw him.

He smiled at her. "You're doing that thing where you tell me the sky isn't blue just so I won't be right."

Cherry took a breath, obviously thought about saying something—probably that the sky *wasn't* blue right now, because the sun had started to set. It was *navy*, or orange, or pink. But not blue.

Instead of saying anything, she exhaled. "Okay," she said. "But you're stalling us all from eating."

"It's a risk I'm willing to take," Jed said, his thoughts completely clear now.

"Dangerous," Travis said with a chuckle, and Jed tossed him a smile.

Jed's back and legs ached as he bent and got down on

both knees.

"Jed Forrester," Cherry said, her voice pitching up.

"I'm in love with you," he said. "Cherry Cooper. We've talked about the farm time and time again, and I think we should get married as fast as possible so you can live there with me, and we can work on building all of the things we talk about."

He held up the diamond ring. "I know you like shiny things, and *big* shiny things, and I picked this out for you."

Cherry covered her mouth with her hands, and Jed noticed the tremble in them.

"Will you marry me?" he asked.

The whole farmhouse held its breath, and all the people inside it did too. Jed included.

Jed shook his head, and added, "This is the one time I need you to say yes to me, sweetheart."

"Okay," she said.

"No," Jed said, though his knees hurt and he wanted to stand up. "I'm not accepting 'okay' to a proposal."

"Cherry," Shay hissed.

She grinned at him. "All right, I'll marry you."

"Nope," he said. "I'm standing up now."

"No," Cherry said, rushing forward. She knelt on the floor in front of him, sliding toward him. She looked at the ring, then up at him.

He could see her fear, but also her pure joy and desire for him. "Yes," she whispered.

"Oh, your mama can't hear you. Can you, Chrissy?" he called.

"I didn't hear her," Chrissy said back.

Jed quirked his right eyebrow at Cherry, the playfulness between them off the charts. "In your dilapidated shed voice."

"Her what?" Gretchen asked.

"Yes," Cherry yelled. "Yes, Jed Forrester, I'll marry you!"

The farmhouse erupted into cheers then—at least ten times louder than the reaction to tacos, thank goodness.

She leaned forward and kissed him right there on the floor of the farmhouse where she'd grown up, and he kissed her right on back.

Lee whistled through his teeth, and Will and Travis weren't quiet with the catcalling. Cherry broke the kiss with her laughter, and Jed took Lee's hand so he could get back to his feet.

He groaned, his back very unhappy with him for kneeling for so long. "I'm too old for that," he said, chuckling.

"Jed," Cherry said. "You didn't put the ring on my finger."

He turned back to her as Lee said, "Congrats, Jed."

"Oh, didn't I?" He looked at the diamond in his hand. "Look at that." He made no move to slide it onto her ring finger.

"Jed."

"You wouldn't say yes."

"Don't be salty about that," she said, moving into him and putting both palms against his chest.

"I'm salty," he said, clearly teasing her.

"Fine," she said. "I take back the yes."

"You can't take it back," Will said, and Jed burst out laughing.

He grabbed Cherry's hand as she fell back a step, and he slid the ring onto her finger. "There."

Cherry looked down at her hand and the diamond.

"Happy?" Jed asked.

She looked up at him, stars in her eyes. "Yes," she said again, and to Jed, it was the best "yes" Jed had heard.

He kissed her again, and instead of cheering this time, Travis said, "All right, enough kissing. How long until tacos?"

Jed broke the kiss this time, and he ducked his head, took Cherry's hand, and they left the kitchen. He made it all the way to the front porch before he took her into his arms and kissed her again.

This time, it wasn't a laughing kiss while her family cheered. It was the kiss of a man who loved a woman, and the kiss of a woman who'd finally—*finally*—said yes to her salty cowboy.

28

C herry gathered her skirt so it wouldn't drag in the sand, then stepped out of her sandals and left them on the boardwalk, the way everyone else in the wedding party had done. She wouldn't be walking down the aisle with anyone—not today at least— as Lee and Rose had designed their wedding a tad differently than that of a traditional ceremony.

Just the fact that the Coopers had driven to the beach for this was wildly off-kilter, but Cherry sighed at the sight of the perfectly white chairs with tall, straight backs. Pale pink bows drifted in the breeze, and she joined the swell of guests already under the two big tents that provided some protection from the sun.

At the end of the aisle, an altar made of wood, leather, and petals waited under a flap that kept it shaded but provided a superb view of the ocean beyond. The blue, evening sky with wispy clouds drifting through the deepening colors, the scent of frosting which hung in the air, the way a smile felt like it infused love into her heart—all things Cherry adored about weddings.

This one felt special, of course, because this was Lee. Emotion crowded into her throat, but she took her spot in the front row with Gretchen. Shay and Rissa and Spence stood on the other side, and Cherry turned back toward the entrance to the tent.

Mama and Daddy stood there, and they carefully stepped off the boardwalk and came slowly down the aisle. Speakers secured in the corners of the tent piped in pretty music, and Mama wore a smile that would rival a queen's as she made her slow journey to the front row. Right behind her came Lee, flanked by Will and Travis—almost like they were some sort of cowboy posse that shouldn't be messed with.

A glow emanated from Lee that only accompanied a groom on his wedding day, but he didn't smile. Cherry rolled her eyes at him, and that got the corners of his mouth to lift ever so slightly. Trav and Will seriously walked while they scanned the crowd, as if they expected trouble to jump out at any moment.

"Hey," Jed whispered as he arrived from behind Cherry. So maybe her brothers were right to look for issues. She laughed to herself, because Jed wasn't trouble unless she counted how erratically he made her pulse bounce through her veins.

"There you are," she hissed back to him, threading her fingers through his. "You almost missed it."

"I was helping...someone."

She looked at him, but he zipped his lips and pointed toward her brothers. "Hmm," she said, a clear indication that she didn't enjoy his secret-keeping. But she did turn back to her siblings as they arrived at the altar. Lee took up his position at the front, accepted a hug and kiss from Mama and then Daddy, who moved to sit on the end of the first row where Cherry stood.

Will moved to the left, and Gretchen joined him. Trav went to the right, and Shay joined him. Rissa and Spence fell in line on that side, and Cherry and Jed went to the left with Will and Gretchen.

Their perfectly balanced family, now that she had someone too. The sparkle of the diamond on her left hand caught her eye, and she looked down at it. She nearly got blinded, as the sun seemed to have honed in on the gem, and it threw light around the tent.

Down at the other end of the aisle, Rose's parents and sister stepped off the boardwalk and began the trek to the altar. Cherry opened her free arm for Nat as the woman arrived, and she patted the younger woman's forearm and gave her a smile.

"You look beautiful," she whispered. Nat wore the same pale pink as Cherry, Gretchen, Rissa, and Shay, and because she was dark-haired and skinned too, it was a fabulous color on her.

Movement in front of her took her attention from Nat, and Cherry pulled in a breath at the sight of Rose as she held her full skirt in her hands, positioned herself at the head of the aisle, and smoothed out her dress. It hugged her from the bodice to her waist, and then fell as if draped over an umbrella. She radiated light and joy to the whole tent, and Cherry wasn't the only one who sighed.

Beside her, Nat sniffled, and Cherry kept her tucked close and tight. She knew how confusing and upsetting weddings could be, and her heart wept for Natasha.

Rose didn't move, though her eyes had locked with Lee's. Ford came out from behind the crowd, and he looked like the most handsome nine-year-old on the planet. He wore a tuxedo, same as his father. He wore the same wide-brimmed cowboy hat, and Cherry had helped him color the stitching on his cowboy boots, so they were completely blacked out too.

He offered his arm to Rose, and she curtseyed and took it. No one else in the Cooper family had married anyone with children, so this was all new for them. None of them had gotten married on the beach either, but Rose, Autumn, and Nat loved the beach, and it wasn't that far from the farm.

Autumn came from the left, and she wore the most darling party dress in bright pink to keep with the bridal colors of rose, sage green, and robin's egg blue. She took her mother's hand, and when the three of them were properly joined together, they all faced the altar —and Lee.

He shifted nervously in the sand, but Cherry felt certain only she could tell. He wore no emotions on his face whatsoever, but with every step Rose took toward him, his smile grew a little more. Millimeter by millimeter, his mouth turned upward until his son, his almost-wife, and his nearly-stepdaughter stood in front of him.

He bent down and brushed his lips against Autumn's cheek, said something to her, and then she went to stand beside Rose's mom. Lee hugged his son, and Cherry loved seeing her gruff, rough, handsome brother soften for his child. He'd always been stern but absolutely tender with Ford, and his son moved to stand in front of Cherry.

She gave him a smile, and Ford returned it. Lee took Rose's hand, and they turned toward the altar. The pastor stepped behind the altar, and Cherry adjusted so she was facing the altar too.

"Please be seated," Pastor Olson said, and he waited while the crowd did that. Once everyone settled, he continued with, "Gathering together is always such a blessing. When townspeople, friends, and family get together, the joy and love they have for one another can be felt. I can feel it here, with Leland Cooper and Rosalie Reynolds and their families. Those who've come to celebrate with them have brought a great spirit with them, and pure happiness is here."

Cherry's smile slipped. She wanted the pastor to get to

the meat of the ceremony, and she cut a glance at Lee. He obviously did too.

"I believe you two wrote vows for one another," Pastor Olson said, getting to things now.

"Yes," Lee said, digging into his inside jacket pocket. He pulled out a wrinkled piece of paper, and Rose turned away from Cherry so she couldn't see her face.

She still heard her ask, "You wrote it down?"

He looked up from the paper. "Yes. You didn't?"

She giggled and shook her head, and Lee shifted again. "Well, I had to write it down." He cleared his throat and focused on the paper again. "Rose, Rosalie." He ground his voice against his vocal cords again, and Cherry almost winced for him. The tension around the altar rose, and she sensed movement behind her.

She willed Will to stay where he was, and she shot a look behind Pastor Olson to Trav, who looked like he might go help Lee read his vows too. Rissa caught Cherry's eye, and she wore concern too.

Another second went by, then two. The silence filling the tent was absolute, as the wind had decided now was a great time to die.

"Lee," Rose said, and he looked up. "You don't need the paper." She put her hand over it and gently pushed down, lowering his hand with the paper in it. "Just pretend it's a song you're going to sing to me." She smiled, and Lee stuffed the paper back into his pocket.

"Rose," he said again, his voice clear now, no gruffness

to be heard. "Last year, you caught my eye from across the room, and I haven't been able to see anyone since. I haven't been perfect with how things have gone between us, but every time you tell me what I'm doing wrong, I do my best to fix it. Because I love you. I love your daughter, and I think we'll be able to build an amazing life together."

He swallowed, and while that wasn't quite the version of his vows he'd practiced at the farmhouse last night. Cherry gave him an encouraging smile, but he didn't look her direction. "All right," he drawled. "That's it."

Rose reached up and touched her fingertips to Lee's lapel, right over his heart. "Lee, I noticed you at math night, mostly because of your cowboy staring." A few people laughed, Cherry included. Lee included, which said a lot about how far her brother had come in his transformation.

"I dubbed you Handsome, because you made my nearly dead heart beat in a way it hadn't in a long time. I wondered about you, and while a few of our first interactions didn't go exactly according to the fairy tales, everything else did."

He inched closer to her, his hand sliding along her hip. His smile told Cherry how much her brother loved the woman in front of him, and she leaned back into Jed, hoping he'd look at her like this on their wedding day.

"You've been my Prince Charming Cowboy, and I love you, I love your son, I love your family, and I love your farm. I don't expect things to be perfect, but I do expect that we'll live happily-ever-after, with a little work, a little sacrifice, and a lot of love."

"What beautiful sentiments," Pastor Olson said, beaming at everyone. He moved out from behind the altar and stood in front of Rose and Lee on the other side of it, his back to the crowd. After he'd gone through the traditional question for Rose, she said, "I do," and Pastor Olson turned to Lee.

"Leland Howard Cooper, do you take Rosalie Millicent Reynolds to be your lawfully wedded wife? To love, to cherish, and to cleave unto until you both shall go all the way of this earth?"

"I do," Lee said, and his smile exploded onto his face.

"I now pronounce you husband and wife," Pastor Olson said. Then he sprinted out of the way, and Cherry burst out laughing. He'd apparently officiated weddings for her family before, and he knew the uproar about to happen.

Lee took Rose into his arms fully, bent her back, and kissed her to the enormous noise of over one hundred pairs of hands clapping, a whole choir of cowboys hooting and hollering, and plenty of whistling.

Cherry's voice wouldn't sound, because she was weeping. She applauded as loud as she could while Jed whistled behind her. Lee lifted Rose out of the dip, and they faced their adoring crowd. He lifted their joined hands, and Cherry yelled to Nat. "Come on," she said. "Let's go give them a hug."

She didn't beat Mama or Daddy, but Cherry was very next in line to hug her brother, and he gripped her with the power of a python while she did the same back to him. After a few long moments, he stepped back and looked into her eyes. "You're next."

"I'm last," she said, reaching up to wipe her eyes. She'd likely ruined her makeup, but she didn't care. It would be dark soon, and with the flickering tiki torches that would light their dinner service, no one would know.

"Perhaps last is the best of all," he said. Then Will swept him away. Cherry turned, suddenly lost, and Jed took her hand.

Then she wasn't lost at all. She melted into his side, where she always wanted to be, and he leaned down among all the chaos, and said, "So are you sure we have to wait until the end of August? We could get married right now."

She turned and looked up at him. "What?"

"Your parents are here and dressed, as are mine. All of your siblings..." He left the words there, and Cherry shook her head.

"No," she said, and he grinned good-naturedly. Things changed in her head, though, but she held back from saying anything until she could sort through her feelings. Right now, she wanted to bask in the rightness of this wedding, and when it was time to move over to the tables for dinner and dancing, she did that.

———

A COUPLE OF HOURS LATER, WITH THE FIRELIGHT DANCING along the edges of the dance floor, Cherry stood with Rissa, Spence, and Jed. She held baby Bronson in her arms, though he was a chunky six-month-old now. Lee carefully cut a piece of cake and then turned toward his new bride.

Rose wore a wild look on her face, but Lee fed her the chocolate cake delicately so none spilled or dripped onto her dress. She took a chunk and looked like she would do the same for him.

Instead, she mashed it into his face, and he jerked backward. Laughter filled the sky, and Cherry joined hers to it. Everyone cheered, and the crowd who'd stayed through dinner surged forward to get dessert.

"Mama wants Bronson," Rissa said, taking her boy from Cherry. "And I think your cowboy wants to dance with you." She sparkled like the stars in the sky as she looked at Cherry, and she and Spencer left to go give Bronson to Mama, who sat next to Daddy on a wicker couch along the edge of the dance floor.

Cherry sighed and turned back to Jed. "I'm ready to get out of this dress," she said, tugging along the fabric under her arm. "It's starting to itch."

He looked at her with a glow in his eyes. "You look like a princess." He ran his fingers along her bare shoulder. "I do want to dance with you."

She sagged into his arms, glad he could hold her up and smile at the same time. "Do you dance, cowboy?"

"Don't all princes?" he teased.

"Yes," she said, cataloguing her use of the word. "They do." She let him lead her onto the dance floor, where they blended in with the other couples who'd opted to do that over taking a piece of chocolate cake back to their table.

She never wanted to be in anyone else's arms except for Jed's, and she rested her cheek against his chest, perfectly content. "Jed," she said after a few moments. "I've been thinking."

"All right," he said cautiously. "Is this a good kind of thinking or a bad kind of thinking?"

"What if we got married in July?"

"July?" he said, really drawing out the word into three syllables. "Outside, Cherry? Do you know what the weather's like in July?"

"About the same as August," she said lightly. "It's mid-April now. I need a couple of months." She peered up at him, willing him to understand.

"A couple of months is June," he said. "And Deb's due in July. June really would be better." He raised his eyebrows, clearly asking a serious question.

"June?" she mimicked, lowering her voice and adding plenty of disbelief to it. "Do you know what the weather is like in June, Jed?" She backed out of his arms. "Maybe we should wait until December."

"No, no," Jed said, grabbing her wrist and bringing her back into his arms. He held her against his body as they swayed, and Cherry tipped her head back to look at him. "June," he murmured. "July. August. I don't care, as long as it's sooner and not later."

"You won't even have the house where you want it by then."

"It's where I want it right now," he said. "Because if you're there, then it doesn't matter if it's a cave."

Cherry couldn't help smiling at him, because he did know exactly what to say to make her feel loved and cherished. "A cave? I'm not living in a cave."

"Why not?" he challenged. "Some princesses lived in stone castles, and that's basically a cave."

"They had towers," she said. "And servants."

Jed ducked his head and ran the tip of his nose down the side of her face, his breath washing over her neck and making her shiver. "I'll be your servant," he whispered just before he kissed her.

Cherry kissed him back, this glorious man she loved. She loved that she could argue with him, and that she could tease him, and that she could be herself with him—salty or sweet. He got to do the same with her. He broke the kiss, as they were dancing in public at a family wedding, and looked into her eyes.

"All right," she said, not using the word yes this time.

"End of May?" She swallowed, because that only gave her six weeks. Six weeks to put together a whole wedding. She hadn't really started yet, though she'd sat down with Mama and gone over a couple of things after the proposal last weekend.

Jed chuckled and brushed his knuckles down the side of her face. "End of May it is, my princess." He kissed her again, barely pulling his lips from hers to murmur, "I love you, Cherry Cooper."

He tried to kiss her again, but Cherry wanted to speak first. She kept distance between them, her neck aching and a headache forming along her forehead. "I love you too, Jed," she said. Then she kissed him so he'd know what she'd said was absolutely true.

———

Aw, I love Cherry and Jed so very much! If you're interested in a few more chapters for the "series epilogue," keep reading!

SERIES EPILOGUE

1

"Come on baby," Clarissa said as she opened the door. Spring sunshine and a blast of warm air flowed into the cabin. "Let's go see Daddy."

Bronson perked up at that, as the boy loved his father.

Rissa did too, and she scooped her seven-month-old into her arms and took him outside to the porch. On the sidewalk in front of the cabin, she'd packed a red wagon with blankets to help Bronson sit up and stay inside, and she placed him in the center of them. "You've got your toys there." She handed him a plastic ring of colorful beads that went straight into his mouth.

With him teething right now, almost everything did.

She thought about her sister as she made the walk from her house to the shoppe, where Spencer should be closing out the day. He worked a lot around the farm, and since he was once going to be her replacement at the ice cream shoppe which also sold spreadable cheeses, flavored milks, and other assorted dairy products, he'd been helping out there a lot since Bronson had been born.

You'll need to be in the kitchen tomorrow, Rissa told herself. And she would. Cherry's wedding was only one more week away, and they still hadn't finalized the last ice cream flavor. She'd wanted something fruity, but all of the concoctions Rissa had come up with hadn't satisfied her.

She hadn't done much with peaches yet, and Rissa felt sure that tomorrow's peach pie ice cream recipe would win over her sister. And Jed. He'd been a hard nut to crack too, and Rissa had made four different chocolate bases before he'd declared one "perfect." She suspected that he'd done that on purpose just to get more free ice cream, but the thought only made her smile.

Jed was perfect for Cherry, and Rissa liked being around the two of them, even when they argued. Their passion for life, for each other, and for the farm they were building together was palpable, and it reminded Rissa that life was good. Life was meant to be lived loudly. Life could be fun, and sad, and good, and bad all at the same time.

The shoppe came into view, and a moment later, Spence stepped outside. He turned back to lock the door, and Rissa smiled though she and Bronson lingered too far away for her to call out to him. "Look, buddy," she said to their son. "There's Daddy."

Bronson babbled and tossed his ring, the same as he usually did. Spence looked her way, and Rissa waved her free hand. Her husband's smile lit up the landscape, though the sun still shone in the sky. It was on its way down, and by the time they returned to their cabin, it would be fully dark. Rissa had learned that whenever they made the quick drive to Hope Eternal Ranch, they'd be there for a while.

She didn't mind, because she liked all of Spencer's friends over there. More importantly, he needed them, and Rissa never wanted to take something from him that fed his soul.

He came toward her, his smile huge too, and when she could, she called, "All done?"

"Yep." He broke into a jog and reached them quickly. "Good sales today too. Almost everything is gone."

"Leading into summer barbecues," she said, enjoying the slow advance of his hand along her waist. Spencer never rushed anything, and Rissa had learned the value of that from him. Their marriage over the past few years hadn't been perfect, but it had been perfect for her. She'd learned a lot about herself, about him, and about sacrifice, compromise, and love too.

She smiled up at him, and he lowered his head to kiss her. "How was your day?" he murmured just before touching his lips to hers. She kissed him slowly, her hands sliding along his waist too. His cowboy hat fell off, but he didn't make a move to retrieve it. Behind them in the wagon, Bronson continued to talk to himself in his baby language. He'd only been saying a few words for a couple of months now, mostly "da-da-da" and "ba-ba-ba." He did love his father, and he loved to eat. Anything else he was unhappy about, he just cried.

Spence pulled away, the moment between them still and glorious. "Good," Rissa said as she opened her eyes. "I perfected the peach pie ice cream recipe, and I'm going to come try it after church tomorrow."

He bent to pick up his hat. "Sounds fun."

"You can nap with Bronson and then come try it?" She lifted her eyebrows as a punctuation mark to her suggestion, and Spence nodded as he took the handle to the wagon. They walked toward the parking lot, where he'd parked his truck.

"We don't have to bring anything?" she asked.

"Oh, shoot." Spencer passed the handle to her and jogged toward the shoppe. "I said I'd bring the cheese for the hamburgers."

She knew that, of course. That was why she'd asked. She loaded the baby into his car seat while Spence ran back inside the shoppe to get the promised cheese. He came out with a huge loaf of sliced cheese, got behind the wheel, and with everyone buckled and ready, started the drive to Hope Eternal Ranch.

They pulled up to the main house there, only to be greeted by several canines. "Ted's here," Spencer said, his smile already slipping into place. He sometimes came over to Hope Eternal to work out with his friends, and when he did, Rissa knew he had something heavy weighing on his mind. Sometimes he wanted to work through some things before he talked to her about it, and she'd learned not to get too worked up over it.

He still confided in her. He still loved her. But the men here had a special relationship with him, and she grinned too as the tall, burly, bushy, black-haired form of Ted Burrows came to the top of the porch steps. Spence launched himself out of the truck, and Ted came jogging down the steps.

The two of them collided about the middle of the lawn, and tears pressed into Rissa's eyes. Having good people in Spence's life meant a great deal to her. She had all of her siblings, their spouses, and her parents. It was okay for Spence to have his cowboys here at this ranch.

By the time she got Bronson out of the backseat, Ted had clapped one of his huge hands on Spencer's shoulder, both of them beaming from ear to ear. "Look at your baby," Ted drawled. He reached for Bronson, and the boy went right to him. "He's huge."

"Seven months," Spencer said, obvious pride in his voice. "Where's your crew?"

"Oh, Emma's still got cookies in the oven back at our place," Ted said, smiling down at Bronson now. He might be one of the biggest men Rissa had ever met, and he had a heart to match. He and Emma had four children now, plus all the dogs, as well as a teacup piglet that sometimes caused more trouble than Rissa would personally put up with. "Look at you, baby," he cooed at Bronson, who reached up to touch his beard.

"It's too hot out here," another cowboy drawled, and Spencer turned that way.

"Nate," he said, and he left Rissa with Ted.

"Evenin', ma'am," Ted said, nodding at her.

"You're asking for trouble." Rissa planted her hands on her hips. Ted laughed and she stepped into his arms for a hug. She kissed both of his cheeks and added, "He likes you, so you can keep him all night if you'd like."

"I'll keep him as long as I can," Ted promised, the two of them walking toward the house now. "Emma has this idea in her head that we need another baby, so I doubt I'll get him for the whole night."

"You don't want another baby?"

"I'd be fine," Ted said. "But Susie's only nine months old; barely older than yours. Do you want another baby right now?" He tossed her a look that told her of his exhaustion. "One baby is one thing," he said. "Two and you're outnumbered. This third one? I don't even know if I'm coming or going." He chuckled and went up the steps, Rissa in his wake.

Nate pounded Spence on the back, and he stepped away to hug Rissa too. He was the glue that held this ranch together, at least according to Spencer. Rissa thought his auburn-haired wife was the true stickiness,

and the moment they all went inside, Ginger Mulbury looked their way.

She put down the rubber spatula she'd been using, said something to Jess, another cowboy's wife, and came toward Spence, Rissa, and Bronson. "I want the baby," she said from several paces away.

"She said I could have him all night," Ted said, swinging Bronson over his other hip and further from Ginger.

She gave him a smile that said, *Nice try, cowboy*, and hugged Spencer and then Rissa. "How are you?" she murmured. "You look rested for having a seven-month-old." How she could remember the age of children that weren't hers, Rissa didn't know. Ginger was always so even, and so calm, and Rissa wondered how her red-headed genes hadn't impacted her the way the ones in the Cooper family had obviously infected every one of her siblings—and herself.

"Good." Rissa sank into Ginger's arms, because hugging her was like hugging Mama. She sometimes came to Hope Eternal for iced tea in the afternoons, but she hadn't since Bronson had been born. "We need to get together more often."

"Now that it's summer, we will," Ginger promised. She stepped back and smiled warmly at Rissa. "In fact, we'll be at Cherry's wedding next weekend."

"I mean for desserts and teas," Rissa said. "Or lunch." She hadn't put on a luncheon in such a long time. "I bet

Lee would let me have the farmhouse, and we can have a huge luncheon for anyone who can come." She smiled, the plans already forming in her mind.

"Tell me when, and I'll be there."

"Me too," Jill said as she came inside behind Rissa and Spence. She held the hand of a little girl who had to be turning six soon. "Say hi, Savvy."

"Hello," the girl said, her blonde hair just about the cutest thing Rissa had seen in a while. No one in her family would have much blonde, as they all had dark hair and eyes like the Coopers, with the exception of Gretchen. Their one hope, and whose first baby would be here in only seven more weeks. Rissa could hardly wait to meet her new nephew.

"Howdy," Spence said, reaching for the girl's hand. "Your daddy says you have a new horse to show me."

Savannah's face lit up, and she looked from her mom to Spencer as she moved toward him. "Can I, Mama?"

"Yes," Jill said with a smile. The girl took Spencer back out the front door, and Rissa realized she had a complete second family over here to interact with. She hugged Jill hello, and they joined everyone in the kitchen. Ginger put a big bowl of pasta salad in the fridge, and Rissa looked around at the chaos and mess that remained.

"I'm glad I don't live here," Ginger said with a laugh. "Let's go see how things are going outside. I think they needed chairs and shades set up."

"Dallas and Luke are doing the shades now," Nate

said, putting his arm around his wife. They had a four-teen-year-old boy named Connor who'd been Nate's brother's son. He'd been with Nate since the death of his father, and they'd added two more kids to their family over the years. Ward, named after Nate's brother was seven, and MaryJane was four. Ginger was currently pregnant and due about the same time as Gretchen, and Rissa liked how spaced-out their family was. She didn't want to have baby after baby the way Emma seemed to, and she wasn't surprised the brunette wanted another baby though Susie was only nine months old.

"Cookies," Emma said in that moment, and Rissa turned to go help her. Emma was a phenomenal cook, and the idea that she should plan the luncheon with Emma struck Rissa so strongly that she couldn't keep it to herself.

"These look amazing," she said of the large cookies on the tray she took from Emma.

"Rissa," she said with a pleasant edge in her voice. "You're here." They both set down their trays of cookies, where cowboy hands reached for them instantly, and then Rissa drew Emma into a hug.

"I want to do a summer luncheon," she said. "Will you help me plan it?"

Emma pulled back, her dark eyes wide. "A summer luncheon."

"Yes," Rissa said. "My family does the huge Fourth of July thing—which y'all are invited to, remember?" She looked around the kitchen, where at least one member of the five families she and Spencer spent so much time with, stood, snacked, or smiled. They nodded, and satisfied that they'd come to Sweet Water Falls Farm for the holiday, she turned back to Emma.

"But I want to do a luncheon. A ladies luncheon at the farm. Our farmhands will probably have to be invited. My siblings and their families. But they can eat the leftovers."

"I just told Hannah that I wanted to do a luncheon," Emma said, turning as her daughter came up behind her. "And Missy needs to do a big project for her culinary class." She put her arm around her daughter's shoulders, and Rissa marveled at how quickly children could grow up.

"You're doing a culinary class?" she asked, so many of her cells lighting up.

"Rissa went to culinary school," Emma said.

Missy brightened, and while she'd always been kind, she'd also been a teenager, and that meant she couldn't like what adults did. "You did?"

"Yep," Rissa said. "What's your big project?"

"I'm doing an online extension class," she said. "From SATC? I have to do a big meal before the end of August."

Rissa looked at Emma, who gazed back at her. "This will be perfect then. The three of us will plan it, and you can cook most of it. Whatever you have to do to earn the credit."

"Really?" Missy lunged at Rissa and hugged her. "That would be perfect, Miss Rissa. Thank you."

They giggled together, and as Rissa pulled back, she asked, "Who do you have for the class at SATC? My sister was a counselor there for a long time, you know."

"I didn't know that," Missy said. "Chance Laramal? He's French."

"Ooh, French," Rissa said, and Missy smiled. They both picked up cookies, and she noticed Emma edging over to her husband, where she promptly took Bronson from him. Rissa smiled to herself, gave Ted a shoulder-shrug, and bit into her dark chocolate cookie.

Pure happiness flowed through her, because Emma was a master baker, and the cookie was crisp on the edges, soft in the middle, and contained all the chocolate one required for the perfect dessert.

The back door opened again, and someone called, "All right, chairs and shades are up. Let's move the party outside."

She went with the crowd, taking the tray of cookies with her. Everyone brought something with them, and the food got set up on a couple of long tables in the shade provided by a row of pine trees. Several feet away, multiple shades provided more areas of respite from the sun, and they surrounded the fire pit, where Slate and Dallas now worked to get the flames dancing.

Spencer's laughter floated on the air, and Rissa went around the cabin where Ginger and Nate lived to find her husband standing in the middle of the road as Savannah paraded her horse away from him.

"Wow," Rissa said, noting the beauty of the horse. "What a pretty gray mare."

"She's gonna be something big one day," Spencer said, taking Rissa's hand in his. He lifted it to his lips and kissed her. "I love you. Thanks for coming here with me."

"I love it here," she said truthfully. Their eyes met, and Spence leaned down and kissed her again.

"I did too," he said. "Once. It's so nice to come back and feel like I still belong."

She leaned into his side as Savannah swung her horse around. She really was a great handler. "Rodeo?" Rissa asked.

"Something," Spencer said. "It's like she speaks their language."

"Slate's calm," Rissa said, referencing the child's father.

"So you're saying there's some chance our kids won't go from zero to sixty in one second," Spencer joked.

Rissa nudged him with her hip. "You've already mellowed me, cowboy." Bronson wasn't nearly as spicy as Trav's daughter, Christie. Hoo boy, he and Shay had their work cut out for them with her.

"Time to put Goldie away," Jill called, and Savannah started to argue with her. "They've got the fire going, and now's the best time for marshmallows."

"I can have dessert first?" Savannah turned her horse around and urged him into a trot. Jill rolled her eyes, gave Rissa a look, and went back toward the fire pit.

"Can I?" Spencer whispered, and Rissa giggled with him.

"Yes," she said. "I've already eaten a cookie, so we can definitely have dessert first."

"You know what's great on Emma's cookies?" They started back around the cabin. "Roasted marshmallows." He grinned at her, and Rissa once again felt the heavens open up and angels singing from above.

So much love existed on this ranch, which was a lot like hers. The people here showed it in different ways than her brothers did at Sweet Water Falls Farm. But she belonged here, and she belonged there, and she belonged with Spencer Rust.

"I love you," she said as they reached the corner of the cabin and the festivities came into view. Spencer looked at her, and Rissa gave him a smile. "Just in case you didn't know."

"I know," he said. "I've always known." He smiled at her, and that soft, sexiness she'd always been attracted to sparked inside her. She tipped up to kiss him, and she only stopped when a baby started laughing.

She sucked in a breath and immediately found Bronson with Connor and Missy. "He's laughing," she said. Her baby had smiled, of course. But the gut laughing coming from him while the teens laughed with him? She'd never heard that before.

She and Spence went over to their child, both of them laughing as Connor held up a piece of lettuce, "hiding" behind it. Bronson thought that was the funniest thing ever, and when Connor burst out from behind it and said, "Boo!" Bronson burst into another round of giggles.

Rissa and Spence did too, and she was once again reminded of how good and simple life could be.

2

Jed reached for his cowboy hat, wondering if Cherry would notice it was exactly like the one he always wore, just brand new. He fitted it onto his head, adjusting it because the hatband was still a bit too tight.

He'd donned the tuxedo against his wishes, because Cherry wanted it. At least the air conditioning blew down his collar and across his face. The sun had been brutal in Texas this week, and while he suspected his bride-to-be would've preferred an outdoor wedding, that had been his one stipulation.

She didn't want to be outside in this heat, he knew. She'd told him last night as they'd looked at the weather and finalized their flight out of San Antonio.

Jed thanked his lucky stars that Cherry wanted a mid-day wedding. They'd be on a plane by five o'clock that night, on their way to the cooler mountain temperatures in the Montana Rockies. They'd get to hike, river raft, and spend time together. She'd handled all of the arrangements for their honeymoon, their wedding, the luncheon following, and everything.

Jed had bent to her will in all things, and she never had brought up the venue after they'd first seen The Rose Wing. Housed in a corner of the biggest, nicest hotel and convention center in downtown Sweet Water Falls, this venue could accommodate their small service, which they'd only invited immediate family members to, and then their bigger luncheon. That was the event Jed had let his parents invite anyone around town they wanted, and Cherry had done the same for her mama and daddy.

Knocking sounded on the door, and Jed turned toward it. Easton entered, and he wore a dark suit too. Chris came after him, as did Daddy. They all wore the same suit, right down to the matte black cowboy boots. Jed grinned at them, love overflowing in his heart. "Hey," he said, and he took Easton into a hug.

"Lookin' good," Easton said, though something in his voice pinched. Jed had talked to him a dozen times about leaving Forrester Farms, and he'd thought Easton was okay with it. Perhaps he wasn't super keen on being the only single Forrester left, and Jed had to admit he was glad he wasn't in Easton's boots.

He released his older brother and stepped into the arms of his younger one. "You smell nice," Chris said, and they both burst out laughing. He'd given Jed this cologne specifically for his wedding day, and the bond between them had only strengthened.

"You ready for this?" Chris asked.

"More than ready," Jed said. He adjusted his bowtie and faced his father. "Daddy." He couldn't say much more, and thankfully, his dad wrapped him in a hug.

"Your mother wants to come in."

"She can," Jed said. "Go get her." He wanted to hug his mother too, and then he wanted to get this show on the road. He went with his dad, who opened the door, and Jed saw Mama standing in the hall.

"Mama," he said, suddenly embarrassed that she'd been waiting out there alone.

"Oh, my boy," she said, already weeping. She flew into Jed's arms, and he held her tightly.

"Mama," he said thickly. "I'm not a boy."

She didn't say he'd always be her little boy the way she normally did, but Jed heard it anyway. She stepped back and said, "Everyone is ready."

"Yeah?" Jed looked down the hall, but he couldn't see the wedding hall from his position. "Well, let's do this, then." He'd wanted to be Cherry Cooper's husband for months now, and he still couldn't believe she'd agreed to an earlier wedding date.

They'd been working around their new farm and in the house, and Jed felt like he'd gotten it to the point where she could move in and be comfortable enough.

There were still several projects he wanted to complete, but she'd said he could build bookshelves, install the lockers for dirty boots by the back door, and redo the guest bathroom any old time.

He'd agreed with her, kissed her until the sun had set, and agreed to be dressed and ready by eleven o'clock this morning. He glanced at his watch, a piece of jewelry his grandfather had given to his father, and that Chris had worn on his wedding day too. Jed would give it back to his daddy after today, and hopefully one day, Easton would wear it. Then another Forrester—one of Chris's kids most likely.

He still had four minutes to spare before the wedding began, but that put him one minute behind Cherry's schedule. No wedding planner would take on their event, because they needed more than six weeks to put everything together. He was supposed to be standing at the altar with five minutes to go, so everyone could get in position except for Cherry and her father.

"Let's go, guys," he said, and he led the way down the hall and across the gold-tinted lobby. It ran in veins along the marble floor, and the room where his wedding would take place had been marked with large towers of flowers. Brightly colored ones in red, orange, and yellow. Some tulips, which Jed had labored to plant along the front of the house on their new farm.

She also loved the amaryllis, and Jed expected to see those in the centerpieces on the tables for their luncheon.

He bypassed the big ballroom where they'd feed everyone and went into the wedding hall instead.

Only a few rows of chairs had been set up, but they had pale pink ribbons tied to the tops of them. They didn't wave in the breeze, because there wasn't one. A stack of hay bales waited at the front of the room, and someone had stuck all kinds of blooms into the top one. In the second one, a brightly blitzed J sat slightly higher than the C, and they made Jed smile widely.

He nodded his wide-brim hat to the family members who'd come, including Lee and Will, their wives, Travis and his, and Chrissy Cooper. His family followed him, save for an uncle, who sat in the third row and beamed at Jed, who smiled back. The pastor stood off to the side, and Jed gave him a nod too before taking his spot in front of the altar.

The breath in his lungs felt like it had been there for far too long, and he forced himself to release it. His shoulders went down, and some of the tension he'd been harboring there bled out. He watched the doorway, expecting Cherry to appear at any moment. She didn't, and Jed felt sure that more than four minutes had gone by.

Wispy piano music came through the speakers, and Jed wished it would change to the wedding march. Except Cherry had refused to use the wedding march. She'd called it "campy" and "cheesy," and though her family owned a dairy farm, she didn't want anything cheesy.

He refused to look at his watch, though it had to be past eleven by now. A pit opened up in his stomach, and he shot a glance to Chris. He'd really shouted, *Go find out what's going on!* without saying a word. His brother shook his head and indicated he should calm down by pressing his palm toward the floor.

Jed couldn't calm down. Cherry was late to her own wedding.

He shifted his feet, and he bent his head closer to the pastor as he neared. But Pastor Olson said nothing. What was there to say?

He'd taken one step forward when the music switched, and Jed hurried to retake his position. He couldn't wait to see Cherry, because then he'd know what was going on. Music with a beat, less piano, and more country funk filled the room, and Jed began to tap his toe.

Cherry stepped into the double-doorway, her gown something only she could pull off. It looked like it had been painted onto her body, and the skirt didn't flare until her knees. She put one elegant hand on her hip and pushed the other one out, her smile sultry and flirty at the same time.

Her dark hair had been pulled up and knotted on top of her head, and her makeup looked flawless even from here. White, glinting jewels hung from her earlobes and rested along her collarbone, and wow, Jed couldn't even think. Her beauty had always stunned him into silence, and today was no exception.

Her daddy entered the doorway from the other side, offered her his arm, and Cherry took it. She gave him a smile, and together, they faced Jed. She matched their steps to the beat, and before he knew it, she stood at his side.

Her daddy kissed her cheek, then shook Jed's hand. He moved to stand beside his wife, and everyone in the audience sat down. Jed looked at Cherry, but she didn't give a single thing away. Nothing.

"Okay?" he murmured.

She nodded, her façade fluttering for the briefest of moments. She faced the altar and the pastor behind it, and Jed hastened to follow her lead. He had a feeling he'd be doing that a lot moving forward, and he didn't mind one little bit.

"Welcome," Pastor Olson said. "I feel like I've done a lot of weddings for the Coopers lately." A spattering of laughter moved through the family. "Cherry has found herself one of the better cowboys in Sweet Water Falls, and I was told not to go on too long before getting the marriage done."

More laughter, including some from Cherry herself. Jed's lungs still vibrated in a strange way, his nerves making full breaths somewhat difficult. He glanced at her, and she seemed relaxed. She wasn't.

"Jed also grabbed me and said he had a few things to say."

"He did?" Cherry asked, swinging her attention to him. "You did?"

"Just a couple of things," Jed said, swallowing. He didn't pull out a card or a paper the way Lee had. He'd written everything down a couple of times, and he'd gone over it and over it.

"I thought we weren't writing vows," Cherry hissed, glancing out to the crowd like she had someone to impress.

"I found yours," Jed said, cocking his eyebrow at her. "So unless you tell me that we *are* going to exchange vows, I just have a couple of things to say."

Cherry's jaw worked, and Jed grinned at her. "Cherry," he said, reaching down deep for his courage. "I've always been better than you at saying what I think and feel. Sort of." He waggled his head like what he'd said wasn't quite true. "You certainly don't hold back on telling me when I'm wrong."

Several people laughed, but Jed didn't want to stir up Cherry's ire. "I love that about you," he said earnestly. "I love that you're willing to be yourself with me. I love who that woman is. I can't wait to spend my life with her, and I hope that you'll always tell me what I'm doing wrong...and what I'm doing right."

Her eyes shone, and he squeezed her hand. "So I vow to be the best man I can for you. To say what needs to be said, and do what needs to be done. To take care of you, cherish you, provide for you, and be there when you need me."

"And not be there when I don't need you," she said.

He chuckled and ducked his head. "Yeah," he said. "That too." He looked right into her eyes. "I love you, Cherry Cooper. I have for a long time, and I'm thrilled to be standing here, about to be your husband."

She sniffled and wiped the corner of her eye.

"Your turn," he prompted, grinning at her though his emotions stormed through his body like a hurricane about to hit land.

"Jed." She shook her head. "I can't believe you ruined my surprise."

"You shouldn't leave your notes out for everyone to see," he teased.

She smiled and reached up to cradle his face. "I love you," she said. "For loving me, as imperfect as I am. I love that you're sweet with me. I love that you're tender in quiet moments. But I love that you'll climb a ladder to help me down, and tell me exactly what you think, even if I won't like it." She put her other hand on the other side of his face, and he took her into his arms.

"You're my salty cowboy, and I can't wait to build our life together at Cowboy Ranch." She touched her lips to his, and Jed shouldn't have expected anything but non-traditional from Cherry.

"Since you've already pledged yourself to each other," Pastor Olson said. "By the power vested in me by the great state of Texas, I now pronounce you man and wife. You can officially kiss your bride, and you can officially kiss your groom." He grinned at Cherry, and Jed didn't waste another moment.

He slid his hand up Cherry's back and along the length of her slender neck as he lowered his head toward hers. He took off his hat and put it between the two of them and the audience, which had started to clap politely. He and Cherry looked at one another in the intimate space, and he whispered, "I love you."

"I love you too," she whispered back, and then Jed pressed his brand-new cowboy hat to her back and kissed her.

His new wife.

That brought the room to erupting, with Cherry's brothers seemingly having a contest with his to see who could be the loudest. Jed didn't care. Everything he'd ever wanted stood in his arms, and he wanted to kiss Cherry forever.

3

W ill opened the door to the farmhouse and called, "We're here," into the depths of it. Now that Lee and Rose lived here, Will did try to announce himself whenever he came over. They still hosted family dinners nearly every night, and the front door was never locked. Not much had changed, other than Will only had to go next door to help Mama in the mornings, and he'd once walked in on Lee and Rose making out in the kitchen.

Thus, he announced himself whenever he came over. Today it didn't matter, because everyone had been invited to the farmhouse for the annual Cooper family fireworks party. An evening picnic, entertainment in the form of a radio playing patriotic music from various places around the country, and then a personal fireworks show out over the cornfield that ran behind the house.

"In here," Trav said, poking his head out of the kitchen. "Lee's not back from the office yet, but he said to get everything laid out."

The activity in the kitchen suggested that his siblings had taken Lee's orders to heart. Cherry currently set a tray of sliced hoagie sandwiches on the end of the food table near the big windows at the back of the house. Next to her, Rissa lined up bags of chips, and Shay, who had her baby strapped to her body, was setting out cans of soda next to a metal bucket of ice.

Will went toward the table too, the platter of fruit he carried getting really heavy. He set it down next to the covered bowl of potato salad—Mama's family recipe— and Gretchen followed with the mint brownies she'd spent all morning baking.

They added their food to the table just as Daddy yelled from the back deck. "Hot dogs and burgers are ready. Saddle up!"

"I told you we'd miss the prayer," Gretchen said at his side.

"Sorry, sweetheart." He took her hand and squeezed. She hadn't been moving very fast lately, and truth be told, Will liked sleeping in these days. Shay ran with Christie in the jogging stroller, but as Gretchen's due date approached, Will had been staying home to help her get out to the chocolate shop on time.

Will got out of the way as Rose said, "Coming through

with fixin's." She put a massive tray down with leaf lettuce, sliced tomatoes, avocados, and onions, crispy bacon slices, caramelized onions for those who didn't like them raw, pickles, and several fried eggs.

Mama came right behind her with a couple of bags of buns, and Will reached to take those from her. "Mama," he said. "Go sit down. I'll bring you some food."

She didn't have time to argue before Lee arrived and said, "Come on, Mama. I've got your lemonade and sweet tea out here." He smiled at Will. "You made it."

"Yep," Will said. "Are you getting her food?"

"You can," Lee said.

"Burger with potato salad, Mama?" Will asked, reaching for a paper plate at the end of the table.

"Yes, please," she said, her voice only slightly raspy. Travis had gone over that morning to help Mama out of bed and into the shower, and Will's guilt for staying behind closed doors with his very pregnant wife needled him. As he grabbed Mama's favorite kind of chips—sour cream and onion—and then doctored up her bun with mustard, mayo, and lettuce, he told himself that everyone on the farm helped out. Everyone had good days and bad, and he didn't have to be the one doing everything all the time.

He and Gretchen had just had this conversation, as the day neared when their baby would be born. She wouldn't be able to go, go, go all the time at her shop, and Will wanted her to know it was okay to be tired. It was okay to sleep. It was okay to take care of herself.

She'd thrown that back at him, which admittedly, he deserved. Out of the two of them, he slept the least, and he worked the most. He always wanted to be available for his family—especially Mama—and as he put a giant scoop of potato salad on her top bun, he reminded himself that he was okay to let his brothers and sisters help.

They all lived here, within ten minutes of Mama. She didn't want for anything, and Will took his turn.

He went out to the deck, accepted a smile and a burger from Daddy, and then took the food toward Mama.

"My goodness," she said, just the way he'd predicted she would. "This is huge."

"Eat half," he said, knowing she wouldn't even do that.

"Sit with me for a minute," she said, her mother's eyes holding something in them that Will didn't like. He hated that she could see past his perfectly showered exterior. That she knew what troubled him before he even spoke.

Still, he did love sitting with her, and he couldn't think of a time in the past few years where he'd left after a talk with Mama that hadn't soothed him and helped him take the next step in his life. He sighed as he sat, and he wiped his hand back through his long hair and reseated his hat on his head.

Tables had been set up along the perimeter of the deck, as well as out in the grass beyond the steps.

Cowboys started filling those, and Will's siblings and their spouses took the tables in the sun porch or on the deck. He didn't know where Gretchen had got to, but he could probably find her with Shay and Rose, Cherry and Rissa, once he finished here.

"Just a few more days until your baby will be here." Mama placed a chip in her mouth and looked at him. "You don't have to be the perfect father the minute he's born."

Will looked at her, everything laid out between them and he hadn't even said anything yet. "How did you know what to do?"

"You learn," she said, plucking another chip from her pile. He should probably make her eat her protein first, but Will wasn't about to do that. "And you have some killer instincts already. You'll know what to do."

He glanced over to Shay, who laughed as she patted her baby's back. She certainly seemed to know what to do. Will had watched Travis with his daughter too, and everything had seemed so natural. Lee and Rose had merged their families, and while Will knew some of the inner workings of that, and that not everything was pretty and as tidy as it seemed from a distance, Lee still always knew exactly what to do.

Will didn't. He never had. He knew how to work hard, and he knew how to run. "I'm a little nervous," he said.

"I know." Mama smashed her top bun laden with potato salad onto her burger and looked at him. "I'd be worried if you weren't." She gave him a smile and looked at her picnic dinner. "Now, the real worry should be on whether I can fit my mouth around this burger or not." She grinned at him and bent her head low to bite into the burger.

The sight of her made Will laugh, because while Mama had a lot going on in her life in terms of pain and poor health, she was still a vibrant, loving woman. She got a big bite and beamed at him with sloppy potato salad on her face.

"What's happenin' over here?" Daddy asked, putting down his plate. Will couldn't see a spare centimeter of paper, and he had no doubt Daddy would eat everything he'd taken.

"Nothing." Will got to his feet. "Mama's just tellin' me that to be a good dad, all I have to do is take really big bites of my food." He bent down and gave Mama a hug, then stepped into his father's arms. He'd softened so much in the past year, and Will appreciated him as a man more than he ever had.

"I love you, Daddy."

"I know you do." Daddy held him tightly and added, "You'll love that little boy you're about to have, and if you let that love guide you, you won't do wrong by him." He pulled back and looked at Will, bright fire in his dark green eyes. He nodded once, like that was that, and then he sat down next to Mama. He sighed and said, "I'm gonna let Lee grill from now on. My feet hurt."

They laughed together, the sound musical, and Will walked away from them. He found Gretchen with an empty seat next to her in the bright sunshine, and Will asked her, "Do you need something to drink, love?"

"I got two cans of soda," she said, indicating them. Her blue eyes searched his face, and he didn't try to hide the conversation with his parents from her. "Are you okay?"

"Yeah." He looked toward the food tables, satisfied that nothing had run out yet. "Did you happen to save any of those brownies for later?" They always hid some treats in the shed behind the house so they could have a late-night sweet snack while the fireworks went off.

Her face relaxed into a beautiful smile, and she giggled. "Yes," she said in a conspiratorial whisper. "Now go get your food before you get me in trouble."

"I knew you'd held back some of your brownies," Cherry said, and that was Will's cue to get out of there.

"There's plenty," Gretchen said, her voice a forced kind of casual that made Will fall in love with her even as he walked away from her. "I'm not going to stop you from bagging some up and hiding them for you and Jed."

"They'll melt," Cherry said.

"You're forty-six years old," Lee drawled. "You can't figure out where to put brownies so they won't melt?"

Will went inside then, blocking out the argument of his siblings. He turned back and looked at them, catching Cherry as she tossed a potato chip at Lee. An uproar started, and all he could do was stand there and chuckle, the love he had for his family filling him from top to bottom.

"Hello," someone called, and Will turned at the familiar voice.

"Reggie," he said, moving toward Gretchen's daddy. "You made it."

"Cory was late," the old man griped, his oxygen machine hissing as he exhaled. "But yes, we made it."

Will shook his hand, then Gretchen's older brother's, and finally he stepped into her aunt Patty and gave her a kiss on the cheek. "I'm glad. Come eat. There's plenty."

"I told you we wouldn't miss out on the food," Cory said, turning back to help his wife with one of their kids. He and Missy had three, and the youngest looked like he'd grown a foot since Will had seen him last.

He smiled around at all of them and said, "I don't think we ever run out of food here." He indicated they should all go in front of him, and he scanned the tables for where they could all sit. Gretchen seemed to sense that he should've been back with his food by now, and when she saw her family, she jumped to her feet.

Well, she couldn't really do that with her big baby belly, but Will knew she'd moved as quickly as she could. Watching her carry their son had been a unique experience for Will. She'd been in pain he could do nothing about. Her feet had swollen, and none of Mama's home remedies had worked. Every day, every hour, every slight of discomfort she'd endured, Will loved and appreciated.

He loved her so very much, and he couldn't help sliding his hand along her belly and then her hip as she came into the house. "Love you," he whispered, and she looked at him with surprise.

His feelings rarely showed themselves in proper situations, but Gretchen had learned to take the moment when he vocalized his emotions. "I love you too," she said back. "Howdy, Daddy." She moved toward her father, who barked at Cory as to what he wanted on his plate. With his oxygen tank and cane, he couldn't hold a plate and dish food.

"Baby," he said, softening the moment he laid eyes on Gretchen. He hugged her and kissed her. "Still a boy?" He looked down at his daughter's belly. "I was so hoping it would be a girl, and you'd get to name her after your mama."

"I know, Daddy," Gretchen said, just as she had the other times her father had said as much. "But as far as we know, he's still a boy."

"Still thinking Elijah?" her daddy asked.

"Yes," she said. "Or something like that." She tossed a look to Will, but he said nothing. Out of all of his brothers, he'd learned that skill the best since becoming married. "Now, come on and let's find you a spot or you won't have a good view of the fireworks."

———

GRETCHEN COOPER STIRRED THE CRISPY RICE CEREAL INTO melted marshmallows, a song stuck in the back of her throat. She loved working in the kitchen early in the morning, before anyone else came in. Just because it was her home kitchen didn't make the silence and the first golden rays of light coming through the slats in the blinds any less magnificent.

She finished combining everything and poured the treat into a nine by thirteen-inch pan. She buttered her fingers and pressed down the cereal until it was good and compact. She'd melt dipping chocolate just before dinner, cut the treats into squares, skewer them, and make half of them covered in chocolate.

She and Will made dinner for the family every Friday night. They'd been serving it at the farmhouse where the main family meals had been for ages, but tonight, Will had texted everyone to say dinner would be here at their cabin. With her baby due tomorrow, Gretchen hadn't gone into Sweet Water Taffy today, nor would she for the next few weeks. She could do business from her phone, and she had a very capable chef and manager in Charlise.

A hint of stress entered her shoulders, and Gretchen took a deep breath to push it away. She never got that far, because a slice of pain went through her chest and down into her abdomen. Or maybe it had come from her abdomen. She wasn't sure.

What she knew was that she suddenly couldn't breathe properly. It felt like someone had thrown her into an ice-cold swimming pool and her head had just broken the surface. She gasped, sucking at air she couldn't find.

Another wave of white-hot pain moved through her, this time from hip to shoulder, across her body. Her lower back ached something fierce, and she braced herself against the countertop with both palms pressing into it.

She'd never gone into labor before, but a voice in her head screamed at her that this was what it felt like. Tears sprang to her eyes, partly from the pain, but also because it was finally time to meet her boy.

Her phone had been on the counter a moment ago, but Gretchen took long seconds to find it now. When she did, she fumbled to get to Will's text, where she finally gained control of herself enough to tap the phone icon, then the speakerphone button.

"Heya, baby," he drawled after only one ring. "I just left to go help Jed move his horses. We'll be back by lunchtime."

"Will," she panted. "Are you driving?"

"I'm with Lee," he said. "What's wrong?"

"I think I'm going into labor," she said, though only the echo of pain remained in her body. Had she imagined the slicing, hot motions of only a few moments ago? Everything with her pregnancy had felt long and short at the same time. She almost couldn't remember a time when she hadn't been pregnant, though she'd spent the first thirty-nine years of her life that way.

"We'll head back," Will said, his tone suddenly sharp and tight. "Lee, turn around right now."

"Why?" he asked.

"Do it," Will snapped. "Gretchen's going to have the baby." To her, he said, "Hon, we'll be right there, okay? I'm maybe ten minutes away."

"Okay." Sudden foolishness cut through her now. What if she'd made a mistake? She'd had a tiny bit of pain. She didn't even know if it had been a contraction or not. The call ended, and Gretchen continued to war with herself.

"The hospital is thirty minutes away," she said. "You could easily need to be there by then."

She moved into the living room and sat down, then put her legs up on the couch too so she was partially reclining against the armrest. "Better to be safe than sorry, right?" Looking up at the ceiling, she began to pray. "Please let him come today." Her eyes filled with tears. "I'm ready for him to come, and I don't want to inconvenience Will."

She prayed for another contraction, but none came. Tears streaked from her eyes, and Gretchen lifted her phone to call Will again. How stupid would *false alarm, sorry,* feel as it came out of her mouth?

Really stupid.

In the next moment, an agonizing blast of hurt hit her, and she dropped her phone. A yell tore from her mouth, and she clutched her stomach where all of the trauma was happening. She rolled onto her side and brought her knees up, anything to try to soothe the pain pouring through her.

The contraction seemed to go on for a long time, but again, Gretchen's sense of time was warped. She did stay in the fetal position as much as possible after the pain subsided, trying to catch her breath and think of where her phone had gone.

She'd just regained most of her senses when everything turned tight in her body again. "Will," she moaned as another contraction started.

Then he said, "I'm here, sweetheart." He ran down the length of the couch and called, "Where are you?"

"Here," she said, and he spun toward her. "I can't... move." She panted too, because while she'd once broken her leg and she'd suffered through the emotional trauma of her chocolate shop catching fire, she'd never experienced anything like this before.

"Okay." Will dropped to his knees in front of her, his hands hovering over her. Pure helplessness and anxiety flowed from him. "Tell me what to do."

She loved how he took care of her, and she reached for his face. "Get me to the hospital, cowboy." She drew in as deep of a breath as she could, and added, "As soon as this contraction ends, I should be able to stand."

He took her hand and kissed it. "It's going to be okay."

"I've got the truck running," Lee said, coming into the house. "What else do you need?"

"There's a bag in the closet," Gretchen said.

"Got it," Lee said.

The pain started to ebb, and she squeezed Will's hand. "Now," she said.

"Now?" he asked.

"Now."

4

Rose entered the hospital with her heels clicking against the tile. Lee had called earlier that day to say Gretchen had gone into labor. He'd just watched his brother drive off the ranch toward the hospital, and Will would keep them all up-to-date.

He had too, and since Rose had a meeting with one of her cardboard suppliers in New Jersey that afternoon, she'd stayed at the office to work. Autumn and Ford spent their days with Lee, his mother, Rissa, or Shay, as there wasn't any school to occupy them. Lee made Ford work, and he'd even bought Autumn a pair of cowgirl boots and a hat so she could start doing some age-appropriate things around Sweet Water Falls Farm.

Any fears Rose had had about being Lee's wife had dried up within the first twenty-four hours of their marriage. Yes, people came and went from the farmhouse day and night. She'd simply learned to expect it. Yes, they still ate dinner at her dining room table almost every night. She simply didn't have to cook. Yes, she'd had to learn to juggle things with her ex-husband in California so he could still be involved in their daughter's life. She'd simply started sending him videos and pictures every few days. Easy.

Her life at the farm *was* easy, and Rose loved it.

"Maternity?" she asked the woman sitting at the information desk. She'd been here before—she'd delivered Autumn in this very hospital—but her mind didn't seem to be firing on all cylinders for some reason.

She knew the reason, but no one else did. Not even Lee. She fought against the tears threatening to make an appearance and nodded as the woman said maternity was on the third floor.

The moment the elevator doors opened, she knew she'd found the right place. Wayne's laughter reached her ears, and she smiled. She reined in her tears and smiled as she stepped out of the car and turned to her left. Autumn danced down at the end of the hall, and she was the source of the laughing and clapping taking place in this hospital.

"What in the world?" she asked herself as she strode closer. Her five-year-old galloped around like a horse, then did a high-kick and fell into the splits. Cowboy whooping and hollering filled the air, and Rose found herself joining her applause to that of the family she'd married into.

Lee spotted her first, and he got to his feet and came toward her. "Hey, sweetheart." He pulled her into a hug and held on tight. "How was work?"

"Good," she said, her voice catching on itself. She couldn't hide it even if she tried.

Lee pulled back and looked at her, surprised. "Not good?"

She shook her head, her emotions all over the place. They'd been married for two months now, and no one would be surprised when they started their family. Lee was quite a few years older than her, and he hadn't been shy in saying he wanted more children.

"Will just came out to say he'd been born." Lee watched her with concern in his eyes. "They named him Eli Reginald Cooper, after her daddy."

"That's so sweet," Rose said. She put her hand on Lee's chest. "What would you name our baby?"

His eyes zipped between hers. "I don't know," he said slowly. He was so handsome and so good to her, and Rose let her smile slip into place. He didn't return it, because while Lee loved her—Rose could see it and feel it every moment they were together, and all day long when he texted her or sent her something he thought she'd find funny—he wasn't fake. He didn't smile over hard things. He thought about them, and talked to her, and they made plans.

They'd been working through how he should parent Autumn, as her biological father wasn't in Texas at all, and Lee loved the little girl with a fierceness only rivaled by her dad. He wanted to treat her as his own, but there had been a few snags, as she wasn't a nine-year-old boy, and she wasn't used to living on a dairy farm.

"What's goin' on?" He glanced over his shoulder and edged them away from his parents and kids. No one else waited in the little lobby, and a measure of gratitude for that moved through Rose.

She took a breath and leaned into his strength. His hand slipped along her waist, and she fiddled with the collar on his plaid shirt. "I'm pregnant, Handsome." Her throat closed, and she half-choked, half-sobbed.

Lee's arms went fully around her, holding her in place. "You are?"

She nodded, the beginnings of reality starting to settle into her heart. She dared to glance up at him, nearly getting blinded by his smile now. "That's great." His big, boisterous laugh followed, and Rose couldn't help but bask in the beauty of it. This man knew how to love deep and hard, and she didn't know what she'd done to attract his attention and be worthy of that love; she was only glad she had.

He wiped her tears and asked, "Are you happy?"

She sniffled and nodded. "Yes," she whispered.

"When did you find out?"

"About lunchtime." She stretched up and kissed him

quickly. "Someone canceled on me, so I ran to the grocery store to get a test and a sandwich."

"You didn't even tell me you were late."

Rose shrugged one shoulder. "I didn't want to get any hopes up."

Lee bent down and kissed her properly this time, and Rose loved kissing her husband. She pulled away when the elevator behind her dinged and Travis said, "This is it." Keeping her face buried in Lee's chest, Rose could pretend the rest of the world didn't exist. She didn't have to think about what would happen with her gaming company, or how Nat would take the news, or how long they should wait to tell their families about her pregnancy.

It was just her and Lee, and he'd handle anything hard she didn't want to.

"Howdy," Lee said, and Travis returned the greeting and went over to the couches. "I assume we're not telling anyone," he said in a much quieter voice.

"No," Rose whispered, looking up and into his eyes again. "I love you Lee Cooper."

He beamed at her again. "I love you too, Rose."

"Do you want a boy or a girl?"

"Seein' as how we already have one of each, I don't think it matters much."

"So a boy," she said, grinning as she teased him.

"I know how to deal with boys," he admitted. His smile didn't slip an inch.

"You do a great job with Autumn," she whispered, pushing her fingers up and into his hair. "She adores you. I adore you."

"And Curious Kids?"

She shook her head. "I think I'll sell it."

His eyebrows flew toward the ceiling. "Really?"

"I can see myself in that white farmhouse," she said. "I love it there. I love being your wife, and I love being a mom."

He tracked his fingertips down the side of her face. "You're a good mom," he said. "The best."

"Mm." She let her eyes drift closed so she could focus on the heat and roughness from Lee's touch.

"So you want a girl," he murmured.

She grinned and accepted his kiss. If they kept this up for too long, they'd be making the announcement without meaning to. So Rose pulled away and gazed at him again, realizing they'd started to sway again. "I know what to do with girls," she said.

He chuckled and shook his head. "I sure do love you, Rose."

"I love you too, Lee."

He led her back to his family then, and Rose enjoyed how easily she fit into them. Rissa and her family arrived, and then Cherry and Jed showed up with boxes of pizza. Rose wasn't sure the waiting area outside of maternity was meant for a Cooper family party, but no one came out to shush them.

Will finally returned, this time carrying a bundle wrapped in blue. Rose got to her feet, because she loved babies too. But she let Cherry and Rissa and Chrissy have baby Eli first, and when it was finally her turn, she could only gaze down at the tiny boy with pure love streaming through her.

The Coopers may be loud, with some fiery tempers and quick wit. But they knew how to love. They knew how to be kind to everyone. They knew how to apologize, and sacrifice, and make the most beautiful babies in the world.

Eli had wispy blonde hair that Rose could barely see, and she pressed a kiss to his fair forehead. "You look just like your momma," she whispered.

"Thank goodness," Trav joked. "Can you imagine if he took after Will?"

"Hey," Will said, and the two brothers laughed.

"It is interesting that he's blonde," Rose said, looking up. "He'll stand out from the rest of you."

Will looked at his son with wonder, and Rose handed the baby back to him. "He's beautiful, Will. How's Gretchen?"

"Doing well," he said. "She's probably cursing me that I'm out here and she's not." He stood and smiled around at everyone. "See y'all back at the farm. I'll let you know when we're comin' home."

"Yep," Lee said, already standing too. He extended his hand to Rose, who took it. They collected their kids and started saying good-byes. Rose let Lee take the lead of getting the children where they needed to go while she thought about what Will had said.

See y'all back at the farm.

Sweet Water Falls Farm was such a special place, and Rose closed her eyes and thought, *Thank you for allowing me to find a place to belong on that farm.*

Everyone who came there belonged, and she hoped she could carry on that feeling and that tradition for many years to come.

———

Please leave a review for Cherry, Jed, Rissa and Spence (and Bronson!), Travis and Shay, Will and Gretchen, and Lee and Rose! I hope you've enjoyed your time with the Cooper family as much as I have - and I hope to see you again inside one of the "families" where we can all find a place to belong together. <3

Keep reading for a sneak peek at the next book set in Sweet Water Falls - **THE LOVE LIST**. It's part Texas, part Southern charm on Hilton Head Island. It's part sweet romance and part women's friendship fiction.

It's all amazing, and it's coming May 17. *You can preorder it now on any retailer.*

SNEAK PEEK! THE LOVE LIST
CHAPTER ONE:

Beatrice Callahan's steps sent vibrations up her legs and through her core. The mailman had just arrived, and she may or may not have been standing at the window for the past several days, watching for a particular piece of mail.

She'd seen it, and the large, official letter had triggered something inside her. What, she didn't know. She simply felt different now than she had before she'd seen that envelope. Then she'd grabbed her keys and purse and gone into the garage.

"Afternoon," the man called from down at the end of her drive, and Bea lifted her hand in a wave. After all, he wasn't the one who'd taken his sweet time signing the divorce papers. He wasn't the one who'd insisted that Bea could have either alimony or her car, but not both. He wasn't the one who'd wanted to go through their assets one by one and make sure everything came out fair.

Fair. She scoffed as she got behind the wheel of her SUV—the same one she'd had for the past three years, thank you very much. Norton, her now-ex-husband, if that envelope meant what Bea thought it did—had filed for divorce fourteen months ago. He'd moved out the day before that. He'd been fighting with her over ticky-tack things every day since.

There was no *fair* after twenty-five years of marriage. Not in Bea's book—and thankfully, not in the State of Texas either. She had plenty of friends around the Sweet Water Falls area in Texas, and one of them happened to be a fantastic divorce attorney.

Vera had gotten the alimony *and* the SUV, and before Bea had seen her brilliance in front of a judge, she hadn't understood why Nort wanted to "settle things on their own."

Oh, she knew now, and it had nothing to do with him being fair to Bea.

She went down the dirt lane and past the mail truck, where the mustached man who came every afternoon still stuffed flyers and other useless mail in her box. She didn't wave this time, her memories of when her oldest son, Ted, had built the red-brick pillar for the mailbox. He'd been fifteen and trying to earn his Eagle Scout award. He'd called friends and neighbors to come help; he'd gone to the local hardware store and talked to the owner to get the supplies donated; he'd built not only their mailbox tower, but five others along the highway north of Sweet Water Falls—one for everyone who hadn't yet been able to fund their own construction.

Tears pricked her eyes at her sweet Teddy Bear. He wasn't so young anymore, and he'd listen to her tell him the news that the divorce was final later that day. He wouldn't like it, but he'd listen.

Then he'd ask her what she was going to do next.

Bea wondered that herself, her eyes drying up before any real tears fell. Thankfully. She couldn't show up at the salon with red-rimmed eyes and a crazy demand for the hairstyle she'd been planning for the day when the divorce papers arrived.

"You don't need to wonder," she told herself. "You made a list."

And she had. The list of things Bea had put together hung on her refrigerator, and she hadn't grabbed it in her haste to leave the house. She'd stuffed her feet into the first pair of shoes she could find, grabbed her purse, and strode out of the house.

She'd get the mail later. Get the proof that the nightmare she'd been enduring for over a year was really done.

Then, she'd get her life back.

———

"ALL OF IT," SHE SAID A HALF-HOUR LATER. HER SLATE-BLUE eyes met the hazel-green ones of her stylist, Mae.

Mae's expression showed shock, and she released Bea's as she kept running her fingers through her hair. "It is starting to go gray in some spots."

"I don't want to color it anymore," Bea said. Her part-sandy, part-golden blonde had been coming from a bottle for decades. She'd done it mostly to keep up appearances at church, be the arm-candy Nort required for his ritzy financial firm, and to keep the other women in her Thursday Night Supper Club from guessing her true age.

All idiotic reasons, in Bea's opinion. And seeing as how Bea was now single, and all three of her children were out of the house, living their lives at various colleges and in towns across Texas, she didn't have to dye her hair anymore.

"And yes," she said, smoothing her hands down her thighs under the drape that would become very important once Mae started cutting. "I want it all gone. I want that." She nodded to her phone, where she'd brought up a cute, classy, and sophisticated cut. One she'd seen on older actresses as they aged.

At forty-five, Bea wasn't heading into a retirement home, but she was the second-oldest in her Supper Club. They'd all been guessing her age for years, and when they got together later this week... Well, Cass would be thrilled to know she was younger than Bea by five months.

"We can do a pixie," Mae said, looking up into the

mirror again. She kept smoothing her hands through Bea's hair. "You have beautiful hair. It's not too thick, so it won't poke out strangely."

"That sounds like a plus," Bea said with a small smile. At this point in her life, she'd take all the positives she could get.

"Bangs?" Mae asked. "I think you have a great face-shape for short hair. But I think we should go easy on chopping off too much up here. We can always take more off. I can't put it back on."

"Okay," Bea said, admiring the shape of her jawline. She did have a nicely shaped face, with jawbones that tapered into a soft point at her chin. She usually wore makeup to accentuate her cheekbones, but today wasn't one of those days.

"You can do an up style, or down," Mae said, holding her longer hair closer to the scalp. "I'll show you how to style it both ways."

"That would be fantastic," Bea said, and Mae got to work. Without having to color her hair first, Bea simply watched as Mae sprayed it down with a water bottle and started cutting. Ten inches hit the floor, and then Mae got out the clippers.

Bea swallowed hard. There really was no going back from this. *Like so much else in your life right now*, she thought.

She took a steeling breath, because she didn't want to go back to the life she'd had with Norton. She didn't want to go back to the woman she'd been before the divorce papers. The woman who always dressed right, who always had dinner on the table at six-thirty, who had literally never cut her hair shorter than her shoulders, even when she'd had children and it had turned dry and brittle and should've probably been shorter to preserve the health of it.

Norton liked showing her off in her clothes. He liked eating right when he returned home, so he could spend evenings in his office. He liked her long hair.

Mae switched on the clippers, and the buzzing, rumbling noise of them suddenly represented a brand-new day for Beatrice Callahan.

The hair on the back of her head fell away and though she couldn't quite see it, Bea could definitely feel it.

And it felt amazing.

When she returned home a couple of hours later, she stopped by the mailbox first. After gathering all the mail —which seemed like an unusually large load, though she supposed they had just come out of a holiday weekend— she sat behind the wheel again, the air conditioning blowing softly and the radio volume low.

She put everything else aside, keeping the legal-sized envelope in her hands. It couldn't be more than a centimeter thick, and most of that was probably the cardboard envelope. The seal for the State of Texas sat on it, and Bea took a deep breath.

"It has to be the finalized divorce," she said to herself.

Norton hadn't contacted her for some weeks now, and neither had his lawyer. Her lawyer hadn't either, and when Bea had inquired about it, Vera had said he'd most likely agreed to their terms—finally—and would be signing soon.

"Watch your mail," she'd said, and that had started the afternoon vigils in Bea's beautiful farmhouse. She lived out in the middle of nowhere, her closest neighbors one-point-nine miles away. Everyone out here had a farm or a ranch, even Bea, though she didn't use her land the way the other families did.

Norton had wanted to "move to the country" once he'd gotten more well-known in the area. He had always existed on the wrong side of paranoid, and since Bea loved the more wild parts of Texas, she hadn't protested. She could get to town easily, and sometimes the drive actually soothed her.

She found the courage to open the envelope, and sure enough, the front page on the packet of papers she pulled out told her that her divorce from Norton Bailey Callahan was now final.

Bea sighed as she sagged into the seat behind her. "Finally," she said, more relief and...happiness than she'd expected flowing through her. She pressed her eyes closed and thanked the Good Lord above for releasing her from this burden, and then she pressed the papers back into the envelope and tossed it over to the passenger seat along with the rest of the junk mail.

After trundling down the dirt lane to the house, she parked in the garage, gathered all the mail, and went inside. She stepped through the mudroom, saying, "Wouldn't it be nice if I had a little dog to greet me when I got home?" and deposited the mail on her kitchen counter.

Without another glance at it, she turned to the fridge and got down her list.

It wasn't a to-do list. Not really.

"It's a bucket list," she said, her eyes catching on the top item.

Finalize divorce.

She didn't know anyone in their right mind who would actually add that to a bucket list, so she amended her thoughts.

"No," she said, hating how loud her voice sounded in her quiet, empty house. She and Nort had raised three children, all of them having lived in this house for at least a decade before they'd grown up, graduated from high school, and gone on their own adventures.

"It's not a to-do list." She opened the drawer on the end of the bank of cabinets and pulled out a pen. Lord knew she had plenty of to-do lists—the fridge did too, as it practically groaned under the weight of the many and varied lists she kept there.

She needed one for the front yard, one for the back-yard, one for the schedule of when the town services came out into the county to collect recycling and trash.

She needed a list of what she had in the fridge that would expire soon, and items she needed at the grocery store that she was currently out of.

A list for Monday, one for Tuesday, and one for what she needed to take to church that week so she could talk to the pastor's wife about their upcoming Summer Faire.

So she had a lot of lists. Over the years, her husband and children had teased her about them, but no one minded when Bea had every single thing they needed when the family took trips to the beach. She even remembered the ice packs and the aloe vera for her youngest son, who always thought he didn't need to wear sunscreen.

"Not a to-do list," she mused. "Not a bucket list."

She crossed off the top item, another dose of comfort, of satisfaction, of pure respite making her feel warm and sleepy. She'd done it. She'd endured, and she'd won. Maybe not everything she'd wanted to keep, but she hadn't been beaten, and that alone felt like a victory.

She scanned the items on the list. *Go for a walk and get lost.*

Visit the beach and listen to the ocean.

Fly a kite you don't think you can control.

Visit ten National Parks.

Cut your hair short.

She crossed that last one off too, a new measure of happiness stealing through her. Mae had styled her bangs up, and Bea felt like a Rockstar. A middle-aged rockstar, but a celebrity nonetheless.

Her heartbeat picked up speed as she picked up the pen. She scrawled, *Get a puppy* onto her list, grinning at the new item with renewed vigor.

Her refrigerator hummed, adding some ambient noise to the house. As she poured herself some sweet tea, continued to ignore the mail, and instead looked over her list again, she knew what it was.

"It's a love list." She laughed. "A list of all the things I'd love to do in my life, now that I'm...well, now that I'm in this new stage of my life."

With that, she returned the list to the fridge, bypassed the mail once again, and headed for her back porch. After all, a day or two ago, she'd put, *Spend more time in your porch swing* to her newly named love list, and she needed to do exactly that.

SNEAK PEEK! THE LOVE LIST CHAPTER TWO:

"Stewart, can you hang the piñata?" Bea said a couple of days later. Her daughter and oldest child, Meredith, turned from the dining room table, where she'd been laying out the gaudy plastic silverware.

"Mom, you got a piñata?"

"It's in the garage," she said, her pulse increasing slightly as her eyes skidded across the time on the microwave. "They'll be here in literally minutes."

"I can hang a piñata," Stewart said, sliding his hand along Meredith's forearm as he passed her. Bea didn't stare long, because she didn't need to call any more attention to herself. Stewart and Meredith had gotten engaged recently, and Bea was absolutely over the moon for them. She was. One-hundred percent thrilled.

Their wedding date sat months away, and to her

knowledge, Meredith hadn't done much more than circle the date on the calendar. She was practicing a lot for her final performance piece, which would be in two weeks' time, and then she'd be finished with her semester at UT-Austin.

She'd be finished with her dual-major in English and piano performance as well. She'd been planning for her graduation, and Bea had promised that she'd then come to Austin to help her daughter start planning the wedding after that. *One event at a time*, she'd thought then, as she did now.

Stewart Spalding was a good man. Three years older than Meredith, he didn't have to deal with college finals, dates, or deadlines. He owned a music store in Austin where Meredith went to play quite often, and they'd met and fallen in love through music, dancing, and their shared love of unique doughnuts.

He retrieved the piñata from the garage and took the rope from the counter, freeing up the space there that Bea needed, and slid open the glass door that took him outside to the shaded patio.

"Will your Supper Club ladies even want to hit a piñata?" Meredith asked, and Bea averted her eyes. The Supper Club sounded so proper. So Southern socialite. That was why she'd always banned her family from the house on the third Thursday of the month, once every six months when she had to host at her house.

Nort had taken the kids to movies, over to his parents,

or who knew where. Bea didn't ask too many questions, because then she didn't have to answer any herself.

Not that she and her friends got raging drunk and went rowdy. But the laughter could be a bit...cackly sometimes, especially if Lauren had some steam to blow off. She worked a high-stress job at a marketing firm, and she had two cats at home to vent to if she needed it.

And then her ladies in the Thursday Night Supper Club.

She had no husband and no children, and it was always Joy who tacked on the word, "Yet," whenever Lauren would lament that she really had become her neighborhood's "cat lady" despite her power suits, high heels, and flawless performances for big-name clients like Nike and Coca-Cola.

"I think they'll enjoy it," Bea said airily. "Thank you for coming to help." That was code for, *You've never stayed for Supper Club. The moment Stewart's done with the piñata, you should go.*

"Of course," Meredith said, stepping in front of Bea so she couldn't take the enormous bowl of homemade salsa over to the table. "Mama."

Bea stopped and looked at her daughter. Meredith stood a couple of inches taller than her, courtesy of her father's genes, and she had the most wonderfully long, powerful fingers. She'd been playing the piano since age four, and Bea had taught her herself until she'd realized how talented her daughter was.

Meredith definitely inhabited a special place in Bea's heart, and she put down the bowl of salsa to hug her daughter. "Are you sure you're okay?" Meredith asked.

"Yes," Bea whispered, sinking into the embrace and holding her daughter tightly. Oh, how she'd wanted to hold onto her at age thirteen and never let her grow all the way up. Children changed so much in their teen years, and not everything had been pleasant. But Bea loved her children fiercely, and she'd cried the day each of her children had moved out.

She knew it was good for them. She was happy for them. She simply wanted to hold on for just a little longer. Right there, in that moment. *Hold tight. Don't change. Stay with me; stay the same.*

Meredith moved and pulled back, and Bea forced herself to release her. She took a moment to cage her emotions back where they belonged so they wouldn't sound in her voice. "I've waited for those papers for months, Mere. I'm good."

She picked up the bowl of salsa and had just placed it on the table when Stewart poked his head into the house. "All set, Bea."

"Thank you, Stewart." She embraced him too, and he fished his keys out of the taco party favors Bea had strewn all over the desk. She had more in the living room on the coffee table, and her kitchen looked like it had spat out streamers in bright red, orange, yellow, and green.

Her daughter and future son-in-law went out the front

door, and Bea followed them onto the porch though the timer on the pork enchiladas beeped behind her in the kitchen. As Meredith and Stewart got in their car, another one turned down the driveway in the distance.

Giddiness pranced through Bea at the sight of that stark white, oversized SUV.

Cassandra had been named the designated driver, and she'd have everyone in that ten-passenger vehicle easing to the side of the road so Stewart could get off the property.

Bea grinned and grinned, turning just as Cass started inching forward again. She hurried to grab the oven mitts and get the main dish out. She stopped the timer, caught a glimpse of the piñata as she set a pitcher of margaritas on the table, and turned just as the side door that led into the garage opened.

"Aye yai yai!" Lauren said, leading the other ladies into the house. She wore a feather boa in pink and purple, which clashed terribly with the other Mexican décor Bea had labored to put up that afternoon.

She laughed anyway and started toward her friends. Lauren stopped beside the refrigerator, the hand waving her boa falling to her side. Behind her, the other women piled up until Cass said, "Why are we stopping here? I'm not even out of the mudroom yet."

Lauren stumbled forward as Cass pushed her way through, and then she halted too. "Oh."

"What?" Bea asked, though she knew exactly what.

Lauren's dark eyes hadn't settled on Bea's at all, flitting all over around her face and hair as they did. Cass reached up with one perfectly manicured hand and actually ran her fingers through her own hair.

Joy, who'd cut her hair short a couple of years ago, grinned like she'd just seen a leprechaun and would surely follow the fellow to his stash of gold. Her blue eyes twinkled like stars in the heavens, and she started laughing first.

Bea grinned at her, and then flicked a glance at Sage, the oldest woman in their group. She still wore her hair long, though she vowed she'd never dyed it to keep it the rich, earthy brown color it was.

"Is there something on my face?" Bea asked, switching her gaze to Bessie, the singular redhead in their group. She actually had gorgeous waves of blonde hair, with just a hint of strawberry in it. Bea had always been in awe of her hair, and that hadn't changed despite her new cut.

"I have been sampling those chips with the hint of lime." She made an over-exaggerated swipe of her hand across her mouth, though she already knew she had nothing there. "They're really good."

"Your hair," Cass said.

"It's gorgeous," Joy said, stepping past the still-staring Lauren and embracing Bea. "You're beautiful."

"Thanks," Bea said, letting her eyes drift closed so she didn't have to look into the shell-shocked faces of her best friends. She supposed she could've sent a text, but then she wouldn't have been able to surprise them with her new haircut and see their reactions.

"When did you do this?" Lauren asked, taking Joy's place in front of Bea as the other woman stepped back. "I do like it." She ran her fingertips along Bea's hairline and over her ear, as if she had to touch Bea's hair to convince herself of her statement. "It's very...sophisticated."

"Tuesday," Bea said.

"So the divorce papers came." Cass circled Bea like she'd have a party in the back and needed to make sure the remoteness of her house hadn't finally worn her down enough to go with a mullet.

"Yes," Bea said without any lift in her chin. She didn't need to defend herself to her friends. Not these ones, anyway. Perhaps some of the women at church, but not her Supper Club ladies.

"She's added *get a puppy* to her list," Sage said, taking the bright blue paper from the fridge. Bea's chest tightened, but she said nothing. Sage held up the paper. "And she's labeled it a love list."

"A love list?" no less than three women chorused together. Bessie tried to grab for the paper, but Sage lifted it out of her reach. Bessie had been divorced for about five years now, and Bea had texted her on Tuesday, so the news of the finalized divorce wasn't novel for everyone. Apparently, this list was, though she couldn't see how. All of her friends knew she made lists obsessively.

Bea laughed and rolled her eyes, pressing through the

women in the kitchen to Sage. "Come on, it's not that big of a deal." She took the list with a mock glare at Sage, who only grinned at her, and refastened it to the fridge. Out of all of them, only Sage stood shorter than Bea—and was older—and they had a special bond.

"Don't rip my list." She turned back to everyone, who'd crowded into the kitchen with her.

"A puppy?" Lauren asked, wrinkling her nose.

"I like dogs," Bea said. "They're good friends."

"You do know a dog is different than a puppy, right?" Cass asked. "I told Conrad that, and he didn't get it until he was up three times in the night to potty train Beryl."

Joy plucked a chip from the bowl and crunched it, and Sage couldn't seem to stop smiling.

"I'm aware," Bea said, opening a drawer and taking out a serving spoon. "And who loves Beryl now? Hmm?" She pointed the oversized utensil at Cass, her eyebrows cocked. The other women laughed, and Cass didn't argue, which meant that yes, of course, *she* was Beryl-the-golden-retriever's mother.

"Now, come on," Bea said. "It's a fiesta! We're not going to talk about my divorce, or my crazy ideas on my list tonight." She picked up the remote for the CD player and hit play. Loud, obnoxious music with plenty of maracas, guitars, and a fiddle filled the house. When the first trumpets entered the fray, Bea threw her arms up and started a cha-cha line.

"Come on," she yelled over the music. "The food is hot

and ready, and there's plenty to drink over here." She danced the way around the end of the peninsula to the table, all six of them laughing already.

The dance line broke up, and pure joy filled her at the sight of her friends grabbing cheap plastic plates the color of tomatoes and turning to the counter behind them, chatter breaking out among pairs or trios. She took an extra moment to soak in their goodness, the ready way they loved her and accepted her, and how much she appreciated their friendship and who they were.

Then Cass turned, her left eyebrow cocked, and Bea hastened to grab the last plate from the table and join her best friend. "You're okay?" Cass asked. "For real?"

"For real, for real," Bea said, her heart feeling like she really might be for the first time since everything had started months ago.

Cass put her arm around Bea and squeezed her tight. "Okay. You know I'm here if you're not, for even a moment."

"There will be good days and bad days," Lauren called down the line. "At least that's how I am."

Bea said nothing as she exchanged a silent glance with Bessie, because she didn't know what life would be like as a single, never-married woman. She'd been married. Now she wasn't. There was a difference, but she believed Lauren. Today had been a good day, but she'd been busy cooking, cleaning, and decorating. Her daughter had come to visit. She hadn't had time to lament about her newly single status or what tomorrow might look like.

They each moved through the line, and Bea took plenty of enchiladas, pico de gallo, and cilantro lime rice. She covered the latter in black beans and returned to the table. "I got you all your own taco maracas," she said, turning to the desk to get the party favors.

She passed them out, each woman who got theirs immediately shaking it to the beat of the music still blasting through the house. Bea grinned as she grabbed one of the last remaining plastic margarita glasses and poured herself a drink, and she lifted her cup and said, "To taco night!"

"To taco night!" everyone yelled.

Sage hurried to pour herself a drink, and she lifted her cup a little late, giggling all the while.

Bea set her cup down and took a heaping handful of the lime-flavored chips and put them on a second, smaller plate. She had just reached for the salsa when Sage said, "To Bea's love list!"

"To Bea's love list!" everyone cried.

Sage hadn't sat yet, and she twisted to get the remote control. The music muted in the next moment, and she held the blue paper with Bea's list on it. "I think," she said while Bea's heartbeat ricocheted through her whole body. "We should get to pick the next thing Bea does." When she looked up, her dark brown eyes sparkled with mischief, and Bea started shaking her head.

"Great idea," Bessie said, snatching the list in such a way that the paper crunched more than Bea liked. "Let's pass it around during dinner, and then we'll vote."

"You guys," Bea said.

"Oh, come on, Bea," Sage said, hitting a button on the remote again. The music blared back to life. "Lighten up. It's a fiesta!"

She couldn't hold them back now, and after she stress-ate her way through a plate of chips and salsa while Lauren and Joy consulted over her list, she decided she didn't care. Every single thing she'd put on that list was something that would bring joy and yes, love, to her life.

So let them pick, she thought, her mood lightening. *It might even be fun.*

———

THE LOVE LIST is coming in May 2022, and you can preorder it on any ebook retailer now.

BOOKS IN THE SWEET WATER FALLS FARM ROMANCE SERIES

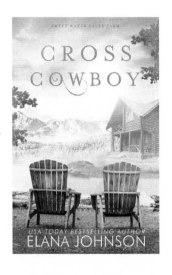

Cross Cowboy, Book 1: He's been accused of being far too blunt. Like that time he accused her of stealing her company from her best friend... Can Travis and Shayla overcome their differences and find a happily-ever-after together?

GRUMPY COWBOY

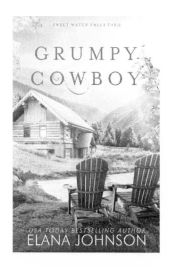

Grumpy Cowboy, Book 2: He can find the negative in any situation. Like that time he got upset with the woman who brought him a free chocolate-and-caramel-covered apple because it had melted in his truck... Can William and Gretchen start over and make a healthy relationship after it's started to wilt?

SURLY COWBOY

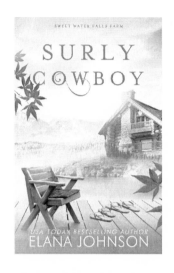

Surly Cowboy, Book 3: He's got a reputation to uphold and he's not all that amused the way regular people are. Like that time he stood there straight-faced and silent while every-one else in the audience cheered and clapped for that educational demo... Can Lee and Rosalie let bygones be bygones and make a family filled with joy?

SALTY COWBOY

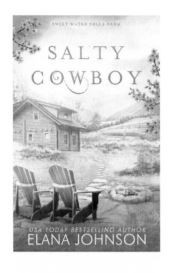

Salty Cowboy, Book 4: The last Cooper sibling is looking for love...she just wishes it wouldn't be in her hometown, or with the saltiest cowboy on the planet. But something about Jed Forrester has Cherry all a-flutter, and he'll be darned if he's going to let her get away. But Jed may have met his match when it comes to his quick tongue and salty attitude...

BOOKS IN THE HOPE ETERNAL RANCH ROMANCE SERIES

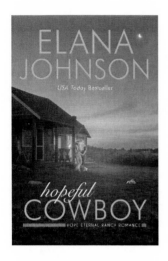

Hopeful Cowboy, Book 1: Can Ginger and Nate find their happily-ever-after, keep up their duties on the ranch, and build a family? Or will the risk be too great for them both?

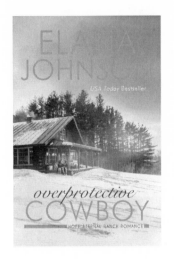

Overprotective Cowboy, Book 2: Can Ted and Emma face their pasts so they can truly be ready to step into the future together? Or will everything between them fall apart once the truth comes out?

Rugged Cowboy, Book 3: He's a cowboy mechanic with two kids and an ex-wife on the run. She connects better to horses than humans. Can Dallas and Jess find their way to each other at Hope Eternal Ranch?

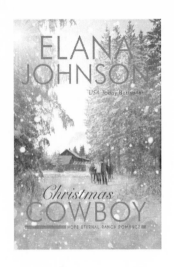

Christmas Cowboy, Book 4: He needs to start a new story for his life. She's dealing with a lot of family issues. This Christmas, can Slate and Jill find solace in each other at Hope Eternal Ranch?

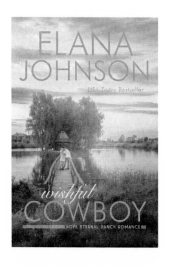

Wishful Cowboy, Book 5: He needs somewhere to belong. She has a heart as wide as the Texas sky. Can Luke and Hannah find their one true love in each other?

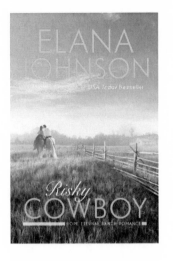

Risky Cowboy, Book 6: She's tired of making cheese and ice cream on her family's dairy farm, but when the cowboy hired to replace her turns out to be an ex-boyfriend, Clarissa suddenly isn't so sure about leaving town... Will Spencer risk it all to convince Clarissa to stay and give him a second chance?

BOOKS IN THE HAWTHORNE HARBOR ROMANCE SERIES

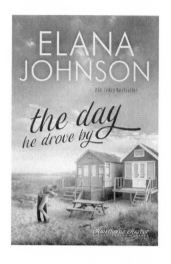

The Day He Drove By (Hawthorne Harbor Second Chance Romance, Book 1): A widowed florist, her ten-year-old daughter, and the paramedic who delivered the girl a decade earlier...

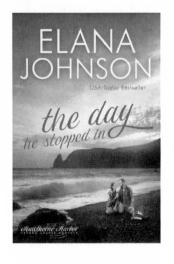

The Day He Stopped In (Hawthorne Harbor Second Chance Romance, Book 2): Janey Germaine is tired of entertaining tourists in Olympic National Park all day and trying to keep her twelve-year-old son occupied at night. When longtime friend and the Chief of Police, Adam Herrin, offers to take the boy on a ride-along one fall evening, Janey starts to see him in a different light. Do they have the courage to take their relationship out of the friend zone?

The Day He Said Hello (Hawthorne Harbor Second Chance Romance, Book 3): Bennett Patterson is content with his boring firefighting job and his big great dane...until he comes face-to-face with his high school girlfriend, Jennie Zimmerman, who swore she'd never return to Hawthorne Harbor. Can they rekindle their old flame? Or will their opposite personalities keep them apart?

The Day He Let Go (Hawthorne Harbor Second Chance Romance, Book 4): Trent Baker is ready for another relationship, and he's hopeful he can find someone who wants him and to be a mother to his son. Lauren Michaels runs her own general contract company, and she's never thought she has a maternal bone in her body. But when she gets a second chance with the handsome K9 cop who blew her off when she first came to town, she can't say no... Can Trent and Lauren make their differences into strengths and build a family?

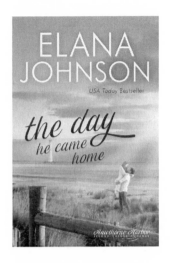

The Day He Came Home (Hawthorne Harbor Second Chance Romance, Book 5): A wounded Marine returns to Hawthorne Harbor years after the woman he was married to for exactly one week before she got an annulment...and then a baby nine months later. Can Hunter and Alice make a family out of past heartache?

The Day He Asked Again (Hawthorne Harbor Second Chance Romance, Book 6): A Coast Guard captain would rather spend his time on the sea...unless he's with the woman he's been crushing on for months. Can Brooklynn and Dave make their second chance stick?

ABOUT ELANA

Elana Johnson is the USA Today bestselling and Kindle All-Star author of dozens of clean and wholesome contemporary romance novels. She lives in Utah, where she mothers two fur babies, works with her husband full-time, and eats a lot of veggies while writing. Find her on her website at elanajohnson.com.

Made in United States
North Haven, CT
29 June 2022

20768695R00283